MIDNIGHT ROOMS

MIDNIGHT ROOMS

a novel

DONYAE COLES

AMISTAD

An Imprint of HarperCollinsPublishers

MIDNIGHT ROOMS. Copyright © 2024 by Donyae Coles. All rights reserved. Printed in the United States of America. No part of this book may be used or reproduced in any manner whatsoever without written permission except in the case of brief quotations embodied in critical articles and reviews. For information, address HarperCollins Publishers, 195 Broadway, New York, NY 10007.

HarperCollins books may be purchased for educational, business, or sales promotional use. For information, please email the Special Markets Department at SPsales@harpercollins.com.

FIRST EDITION

Designed by Yvonne Chan

Circular window on page iii © t0m15/stock.adobe.com
Illustration details on page iii adapted from image by Perfect PNG/stock.adobe.com
Other windows on chapter-opening pages © Chorna_L/stock.adobe.com

Library of Congress Cataloging-in-Publication Data has been applied for.

ISBN 978-0-06-322809-2

24 25 26 27 28 LBC 5 4 3 2 1

To my beloveds, Fats and Forte

Chapter One

Orabella stood at the threshold of the parlor, uninvited but determined to be present, for the matter of this strange man's visit concerned her and only her.

The room was the same as it always was, nothing had been done to make it fancier. No fresh flowers or even any beverages. No indication that this meeting was significant or special, and perhaps, Orabella reasoned in that moment, to her uncle it was not. It was, after all, not a decision that would greatly alter his life.

The same two couches that had always been there sat facing each other, their arms on one side towards the doorway she waited in, the others towards a single chair where her uncle, Worrell Mumthrope, sat as if on a throne. This was the perfect place for her to meet the man, to see him clearly. The light was good, the room respectable, but, she thought, she hadn't been meant to see him at all so it didn't matter where this meeting happened. It was not for her benefit. If she were bolder, she would have taken the seat across from the stranger, but she was not. The intrusion was already unlike her.

The stranger noticed her before her uncle did and for a moment they regarded each other, but there was no magic in it, time did not stop. Her heart beat rabbit-quick in her, the rhythm her nerves played to, but the man seemed calm for the handful of seconds that their notice of each other went unseen by her uncle. Only enough time to make note of his appearance.

Dark pants and work boots rested under a plain shirt and jacket. There was no finery in this man's clothing or his face. There wasn't much to see of it, his face. A brush of unsightly beard matched the shaggy hair from his head that covered his features. Fine or as dull as the rest of him, she couldn't tell. Except she could see a crooked nose and pale eyes that peeked from the thicket. His eyebrow raised just so, lips parted to say something, and she wondered what he thought of her now that he had seen her.

Now that he knew, for sure, that she was Black.

The brown dress did nothing to flatter her. The cut and fit of it were well enough, the full skirts and bodice lying correctly on her frame, but the color blended with her skin and made her seem drab, a little finch, seen briefly and forgotten just as quickly. Orabella had worn it more for its lack of grace. The impression she wanted to make was *forgettable*. A woman not worth his time, or anyone's. No color on her full lips or high cheeks. Above her rounded nose her eyes were deep brown, near to the black of her hair, which she'd left loose. Pinned back only with a weak clasp to keep it from her face and fingers that would tug on the curls that floated lightly about her head and shoulders. Even then the shorter flyaway curls escaped their confines and shot out at odd angles from her.

I am an unkempt thing, unsuitable for a wife, she had wanted to say, but the man was also unkempt, and in her efforts to prove a poor match, she had matched him. He did not look of society; Orabella could not imagine him in the salons of Bristol with his thick beard and shaggy hair. He looked out of place even in the parlor surrounded by rose-colored cushions. As did she.

Her uncle was a businessman, the family had earned their wealth in textiles. It followed—it was her assumption—that this stranger must also be of similar standing, but she could not imagine what sort of business he would have with their family dressed and presenting as he was.

Orabella had no room, she knew, to think so poorly of him. She was her own curiosity, so much so that even the status of her family, darling in Bristol, was not enough to force any suitable men to look past her quirks and shyness. The wealth of the Mumthropes would not flow through her to them through marriage. Her own father had died penniless when she was nine, and her mother long before that. She had been dead so long that Orabella couldn't tell whether she remembered her face, when she had cause to think of it, or if the woman in her memories was only an abstraction of her own face, the only thing of note her mother had left her. Her memory for such things had never been strong.

And her father had left her his family. Her family now.

He's lied to him, she decided, holding the smile on her face and herself still, keeping the rabbit pace of her heart from the rest of her. *Told him there was a reward for me.*

Finally her uncle noticed that the man's attentions were no longer with him and he turned to her, disapproval on his face. "Orabella." Her name curt, a curse on his tongue.

The sounds of the morning, muffled by the glass, pushed back against their collective silence. Horses on cobbles, laundry women shouting greetings to day workers. A very normal morning except it was not.

Midmorning and she should be out with her aunt, attending to errands and society meetings. Orabella had feigned ill to meet this man, to shoo him away with the reality of her being. A little chain of gossip carried between the maids to her ears. It was they who had overheard the Mister and the Missus discussing a caller. A gentleman caller. In the hall, just before a door cracked open, her door, they spoke freely. Enough for her to hear that there was a man coming, that gentlemen came for only one thing. The plan was haphazard, foolish, and weak but still she had stayed home, dressed carelessly, and come to the threshold to see him and to be seen.

The man moved first, standing to greet her. Efficient, graceless, and utilitarian like the rest of him. Confident.

Twenty-six, and this man was her first true suitor. He was not the first man she had ever encountered; she had been in society before, but he was the first to come to her uncle's parlor.

The attention of society was only curiosity about the Mumthropes' strange niece. A few polite questions about her childhood, clumsy attempts to sniff out overlooked details that would prove she didn't really belong there, with them. A scandal to entertain and then, finding nothing, the game was quickly forgotten. But the other women, scorned in their minds, did not care that the attention meant nothing. Aching for company, Orabella found that she did not care either. But no one really doubted that she was the daughter of Peter Mumthrope, even if she did not share anything of his complexion and flaxen hair. If she were not, why else would she be there? If not for the debt of family.

Orabella was never sure if her father's family, her family, disdained the union because of who she was or simply because her father had not married the woman they chose for him. It no longer mattered. Her father was dead and all that was left of him, left of either of her parents, was Orabella. And now her uncle hoped she would pass that lingering debt to another the only way she could.

Through marriage. She would become another's family and finally, finally, the Mumthropes would be free of her.

The man bowed slightly. "Good morning, miss," he said in a voice that was softer than what she expected.

Polite, she would match him. "Good morning, sir," she replied.

"Orabella," her uncle repeated, his face turning red from the neck. He looked like a crane: he was thin in all ways—his body, his lips, his nose, even his graying hair. Her uncle kept her and everyone at arm's length except in his anger. "You were to be resting this morning."

The words she had prepared for this moment spilled easily from her lips as she gestured to the glass door that led out of the room and into the garden.

"I am sorry to be a bother. I thought you were conducting business in the office and only wished to walk in the garden. I thought some fresh air would help."

Her uncle rubbed his forehead, as if the motion would hold back his temper. "Please find something else to occupy yourself until we've finished here. My apologies, Mr. Blakersby. I assure you, she is generally far more acquiescent." At this last word he glared at her, meaning clear.

Orabella's cheeks ached, but even turned to the garden door she kept the mask, pushing back against her uncle more, making a liar of him. He would yell later, curse her, threaten to throw her in the street. Empty threats: He couldn't let others see him abandon his poor niece, what would people say?

"I am sure, sir," the bearded man said without turning to her uncle, his words curt but hinting at an education, a history, not openly reflected in his appearance. "May I escort you on your walk, Miss Mumthrope?"

He had asked her. Not her uncle. The strange man's focus

rested on her, Worrell forgotten. If she were bolder she would have laughed then. *I can manage my backyard on my own,* she would have quipped and sent that efficient, shabby man on his way. But she was not. All she had was her smile, her manners.

"Anything that you wish to know of her, I am happy to speak to you about," her uncle said. An abrupt shake of his head, the jut of chin, all of it meaning *go away*. But the man, Mr. Blakersby, had directed his query at *her* and did not react to Worrell's silent communications. The answer he waited for was hers.

"Yes, of course." She hadn't known she would accept and now, wrapped in the nervous thrill of it, she suppressed the bubble of laughter. She clasped her hands in front of her and stepped forward.

"Fine. I will wait for your return here." Defeated, her uncle turned away.

The smell of spring and the hint of a far river on the March air blew into the room. Still cold but changing, warming under the pale sun. She opened the door herself, her hands cold and jittery with nerves, but he, following her, did not remark on the breach of manners. That he should hold the door for her and that she had rushed through it, no thought for him. A thoughtless woman. Unsuitable.

He shut the door. And they, outside, were alone.

The garden was not a large thing. Between the perfectly square plots there was room only to kneel for planting. The only place to walk was the one path that led down the middle and to a bench at its center. In the spring and summer, the bushes and trees would burst into life, creating the illusion of distance from the glass doors, but in March, winter still kissing the air, the branches were bare.

She expected him to take her arm, but he did not touch her.

He kept an arm's length between their bodies. They walked along the garden path in silence, yet she could feel his eyes on her as they passed the empty plots that waited for flowers. A head and a half taller, he matched his pace with hers. Polite. She would be the same. His closeness became a weight, heavier than his eyes had been now that they were alone.

"There's a bench in the center where we can sit if you like. You can see that yourself. But still, I thought . . . Oh." She ended with a laugh, a nervous chuckle, to stop more useless words. Words, any words, would break up the strange feeling in her gut, stop the heat rising to her cheeks as she fought to keep herself from falling into anxious, pointless babble.

He grunted, a wordless agreement. She clasped her hands to keep them from hair, sleeve, skirt. Focused on the bench. A simple affair, a slab of stone on two pillars, Romanesque, to match further statues her aunt had explained would come but had, in all the years Orabella had been in the home, never quite arrived.

"Will you join me?" she asked, at a loss for what to say next. She expected him to speak on himself, but he remained silent. His desires and motives were something she could only guess at, and she had no good map to navigate with—the ones she had learned so well already did not seem to apply. His eyes were strange seas. Mr. Blakersby motioned for her to sit, as if it were his garden and she the guest in it.

He took his seat next to her, the distance between them closing, the bench smaller than the path had been. Before her were the glass door and the room she would normally be sitting in, working on her knitting, awaiting the delivery of the society papers for the day. She expected to see her uncle staring back at her, angry and watching. Something familiar to settle her growing discomfort. The window was empty.

"I would assume you know why I have come here this morning," Mr. Blakersby spoke, pulling her attention back to him.

The sound of his voice startled her, low but it carried. Like waves. Like his eyes. Closer now, she could see their color, a shade trapped between blue and gray. His face, too, startling, close. The skin that peeked through all the hair surrounding it held the color close to an unripe peach, near white. There were no lines around his eyes; she couldn't place his age although, she thought, he must know hers. "Yes," she answered slowly. "You came to speak of marriage."

"And are you agreeable to this?" Solemn, serious, he awaited her answer as he had awaited it before.

Orabella laughed. There was no stopping it: nerves. She covered her mouth with her hand to stifle the snorting sound. It was a joke, surely. Her uncle had lied. Mr. Blakersby was polite. She would be honest. "Sir, I do not know you or what grand stories my uncle has led you to believe, but there is no worth in marrying me. My uncle and aunt's care for me is considered little more than charity. My dowry is a token and not worth being saddled with my person for the rest of your life." A short, impersonal summary, a repetition of what had been said of her, to her, before.

This, the truth, impossibly, pleased him. Wave batting shells and glass against the shore, a chuckle, more controlled than her own laugh had been. His manners were better than his clothing. "You have no prospects, you are nearing twenty-six years of age, and it is no secret that your uncle is becoming tired of spending so much charity, as you put it, upon you. So, if you do not agree, which is perfectly fine, then what will you do?"

Slippery, wet, live things twisted through the mud-filled space that Orabella's belly had become. Worms and a hole instead of stomach and guts. No plan, all her thoughts dripped from her fingers mingled with the worms of her insides. She had expected nothing but to disrupt, hoping that only the true view of herself would be enough to force his withdrawal; but then he had asked to join her, and if not, then what? "I don't know. No one has ever asked me."

His fingers slid along the back of her hand, over the bony curve of her knuckle to her pinkie. The touch turned the worms to butterflies, wings brushing the inside of her belly, fluttering, mad, hungry for freedom. The touch ended but the pressure tingled over her skin. A memory, a ghost.

"The worth is in you, there are merits to your person that a man in my position finds advantageous. I don't care about your dowry; you may keep it for yourself, if you'd like. What I need is a wife and I believe you will make a fine one. If it is all the same to you, are you agreeable?"

"Can I wait to give you your answer?" Orabella asked, expecting his denial, and was surprised again.

"Let me tell you a story, then, to give you some time." His fingers took up the path of her hand they had so recently abandoned, traced the bones and veins of it. His thumb slipped under her sleeve to find the pulse at her wrist.

Was it attraction? The question turned over in Orabella's mind as his fingers moved over hers, not more than a whisper, featherlight. Lighter than his beard and work clothes would assume. She looked down at the stone where their fingers met. Hers finch-brown and his peach-white, smoothing over them. This man was unknown. Her hand stayed still.

"You attended a gathering at the Percys' two summers past. One of the very last you went to. I presume your uncle stopped paying for new dresses once your cousin married and no longer needed an escort. And your aunt wouldn't let you attend in last season's clothing for fear it would look poorly on them."

Orabella's fingers twitched. The party, she didn't recall, but the story rang true. Yes, she had gone with her cousin. Yes, there were no more dresses when her cousin was married and away. Who was this man?

"A pity." Mr. Blakersby's hand shifted, found further intrusion in the opening of her sleeve. The cold air bit at the newly exposed skin swallowed by the heat of his touch.

"I think I would have remembered someone who looked like you at the Percys'," she replied, but her memory, a flickering, untrustworthy thing, could not be relied on. Had she seen him? Would she have noticed?

"You wouldn't remember me, but I was there. I saw you. I was just leaving the card game that night when you passed on your way to dance. You wore a green dress and had a smile that wasn't quite a smile. And I thought I would like to see your real smile."

"If that's all . . ." She turned to him, faced him fully, and smiled. Simple, no great task, the ghost of the aching in her checks pinching at them again now. It was the same smile she used in parlors and at parties alike, wide eyes, lips stretched just so, no teeth, polite, controlled. "Now, there, you've seen it. There's no reason to continue."

"No, that's not your real smile, I've seen that one before. I'm sure it's not the best of you." His fingers slipped further, wide palm a paw on her wrist, her arm captured in his long fingers. "I don't think anyone's seen your real smile but I aim to. I aim to bring it out of you. I need a wife, Orabella, beautiful Orabella. It is in my favor that the men of Bristol are fools."

Goose bumps rose all along her arms and she released a shuddering breath. It had all gone too far. This wasn't proper. She tore herself away from him and wrapped her hand around her own wrist to stamp out the touch of his. "You are too close, sir," she scolded, but he was still close, the bench was small, and every shift of his body brushed against hers. Close.

"Forgive me, you must think me strange. I am just overcome. I have waited a very long time to sit next to you and ask you this. I can care for you. I can give you a life beyond this place."

"If you were so taken with me, then why have you waited two summers? Have you only just come into money or is my uncle so desperate to be rid of me he hired a day worker to propose?" She tried to sound flippant by imitating the debutantes, mimicking their jaunty head toss, their high tone. It sounded mad and forced but she hoped it was enough to fool him. To push him away, give her space to breathe, to think. A breath and it became clear, the pieces falling into place. The strange man in the parlor suddenly not so strange. "Wait, you've come about my uncle's debts. Is that it? Am I meant to clear whatever he owed you from the card table?"

"I was not fit to take you as a wife two years ago." Whisper soft. "I could not care for you then, now I can. Buying your uncle's debt, canceling it, is what gained me this time with you, yes, but it's up to you if you come with me."

"You could have lied; wouldn't it have been better if you lied?" she asked, but the answer didn't matter. The stranger had already paid, and if she said no, her uncle would try again for a profit. She thought she should feel something but there was only resignation.

"If I lied about that, then you wouldn't believe me about anything else. But it's the truth, Orabella: I am thirty-one years old and I find myself in the position of needing a wife. You are quiet, well-mannered, healthy. I will never trade you to settle a card game and will care for you without complaint. If you cannot believe that I am taken with you, then is this, that I will treat you better than you have been, not enough?"

Orabella looked at him again. His plain clothing, his beard and messy hair, and she thought that his age seemed right. There were no grays on his head, no wrinkles around his eyes, and besides, she looked no better. Her stomach turned, her head felt like it would float away if not for the stone in her throat. She swallowed but it refused to move.

"I would have your answer now. I wish to leave the city tomorrow. I have matters to attend to at my family estate."

By his tone it was all he would say. There was no more time, he had told her everything there was to tell. She looked again at the empty window and read a threat in it. That *no* would lead to another man, a worse man. "Yes," she answered. "Yes."

His lips brushed her cheek, the barest pressure. Orabella put her fingers over the space they had passed. The skin tingled and danced and the stone in her throat finally sank, rolled into her middle. She could feel her face was not what it should be, that it was not poised and pulled into place, that it was as out of sorts as her hair.

A hand, his hand, hovered in front of her. How long? She wasn't sure. *Take it, stand, smile, say "thank you."* Order from the confusion, no answers needed, a pattern to follow. This time he offered his arm and she took it. Orderly he walked them both back to the door in silence. There was nothing more to discuss.

"We will be married in the morning, Orabella."

"What?" This was not how things were expected. Was it a test? Orabella wasn't sure; he wasn't like anyone else, with his society manners and his dockworker look.

"Don't pull yourself back now, my dear. You've been so bold already." His voice dripped with laughter.

A joke, then, Orabella reasoned, and she put the smile, the smile he called false, back to her face. It was what was expected but his own lips twitched downward before he matched it.

"It's all right, dear," he hummed, and the stone in her turned to butterflies.

She stopped the *what* from leaving her lips. He would think her dull and she did not want him to think her dull.

He opened the door for her, led her inside. "How rude to leave us like this," he said in the same low voice. He kept her arm tucked into his and she didn't know what to make of it all, so she made nothing of it.

"I'll get my uncle," she said, moving to pull away, but his hand moved around hers, held her still.

"No, he'll come. Worrell!" he called like he'd call a servant.

A moment and then Orabella's uncle appeared, huffing, red-faced, eyes darting between them.

Mr. Blakersby spoke first and quickly. "I will be back in the morning with the Registrar, and we will be married. We will leave directly following the ceremony."

"Impossible. It takes weeks to attain a license that way. Why not go about things in a more suitable manner?" Worrell smiled, pleased and pleasing, crossing the room to sit; there was more to discuss between them, but Mr. Blakersby stood still.

She looked at her newly betrothed, sure now that he must be something other than he appeared. Blakersby. She turned the name over in her mind, tried to place it. Wondered whether he was someone of note. Realized that if he was, society would be interested in him, then. Interested in her.

"We will be married in the morning before the Registrar."

Her uncle silenced, the man, her fiancé, turned his eyes on her. "Pack lightly, bring only what you cannot replace. I will provide everything you need and anything else you desire. Wear clothing suitable for travel."

"That's a broad statement; there's almost nothing that can't be replaced." Bold because she couldn't follow the whirlwind of change. There was no etiquette for her position and the words escaped before she could stop them, thoughtless. Nothing left to be but bold. And he smiled.

"Then bring nothing but your person. I will see you in the morning. Good day." He released her. Orabella's arm slipped from his grasp, and she cradled it, the pressure of his hold still there but fading.

"Wait," she called. Shouted too loud—he was only at the threshold—but she had made a mistake, an embarrassing oversight.

He turned his shaggy head towards her. "Yes, Orabella?"

"I don't know your name, sir."

"Elias."

"Elias," she repeated. "Orabella. Of course, you know that, how silly of me."

"It has been a pleasure to meet you, Orabella." He passed into the hall, the sound of the front door shutting heralding his exit. Orabella turned back expecting to be met with anger; he had been disrespected by Elias, but the uncle who met her was all smiles and uncharacteristic warmth. *This morning has been . . . very unexpected*, she thought.

"You won't do better than a Blakersby. Old money, they are, some distant relation to our people through marriage, I believe. They've been in Oxbury for years. An odd sort, I hear, but you'll be all right. Stay quiet, keep yourself well. This is your chance to be something more than, well . . . This is the best we can do for you, out of respect for your father."

She nodded. "Thank you, Uncle."

"You had better go pack while there's time. You've tea, I believe, with your aunt this afternoon."

"Thank you for reminding me. I had forgotten," she mumbled.

He grunted. It was like her to forget. The day was like any other, only it wasn't.

In the hall she leaned into a corner, her face hot, her hands cold. She took deep shuddering breaths to calm herself. *Was that the right choice?* Everything had been so fast, so overwhelming. She had agreed and he had kissed her. Elias wasn't the first gentleman to touch her cheek, but he felt different. A queasy feeling started in her belly, spreading lower. Elias had kissed her and she had agreed to marry him. *It's done, there's nothing else.* Orabella composed herself and made her way up the stairs.

She stayed on the third floor. Too hot in the summer, too cold in the winter, but she liked it anyway because it was hers. Simple, it had not changed at all from when she had first come to the house. A mirror hung on the wall with a table under it for her combs. Small wardrobe for her clothing. The same creaky bed covered with the same quilt. She ran her fingers over the piece. *Should I bring it?* There was no need, there would be blankets, but it had been hers for so long. She toyed with the fraying edge, avoided everything else.

When she finally looked up, the sun had moved and she knew she couldn't put it all off any longer. There was a trunk waiting, the same trunk that she had come with as a child. She was never meant to stay, not really. She pulled it out.

Orabella gathered her combs and stationery; they seemed easy choices. An old book of fairy stories from her father gave her pause. It had been years since she read it. She opened it to an illustrated page of a monster in a castle. She put it in the trunk, moved on to her closet.

It would be time for tea soon, and after that, morning. Orabella began folding her dresses and tried not to think at all about why she was doing so.

Chapter Two

L ate afternoon, the sun had already started to set. March had been mild thus far, slow to turn to spring, but the sun was there. The days were longer than they had been weeks before but still night came quickly. Orabella walked alone down a street busy with the rush of the last of the day, the threat of twilight, and wished she had been able to come through earlier. Her afternoon had been taken up by the visits to her aunt's friends. When her aunt told them that Orabella was leaving suddenly to be a governess, she nodded and smiled, agreeing. The story her aunt told didn't matter, the ending was the same either way.

There had been time to think: she lost herself in windows while her aunt chatted. Four houses, an hour at each, a seed planted in four pots. Orabella was going to be a governess. Orabella was going away. Orabella was finally making something of herself. And then the gardening was over and she was free to go. Down a familiar street for the last time.

To go to church. To see Jane.

Her body knew the path. She could make it to the church by

memory, a quarter of an hour's walk, maybe a bit more from the Hanovers', the last stop on her aunt's tour. St. Martha's sat nestled among the residential buildings. Her feet carried her forward, while Orabella's mind raced along other paths.

Her own desires didn't seem to matter under the urgency of her situation. She couldn't see the future, only the options presented. There was only Elias or the unknown, which may not have been worse. It likely wouldn't have been better, she didn't think. There would always be more card games, more debts, and fewer people willing to pay them. What she wanted from her situation was secondary to the fact that it was her situation. It hurt to think of, so she tried to focus on other aspects. She hadn't left Bristol in years.

The sun held up, bright, but the weather was cold. Orabella wrapped her shawl tighter around herself as she walked. Women were visiting with each other in doorways, enjoying the last of the sun, their laughter mingling with the other sounds of the city turning over from day to night. The last of the day's deliveries were being made by men in mule-drawn carts and boys on foot. The day workers, those not needed for dinner and bed service, were leaving, chatting back and forth about whatever gossip they had gleaned between their chores. It happened all around her as she passed the town houses, crossing familiar streets. Work was ending. The day was ending. Winter was ending. Everything around Orabella was ending.

Will there be anywhere to walk there? Is it another little city? A town? Or just . . . his home? There hadn't been any time to ask, to get any idea, and he hadn't said. She looked up in time to see the faces of a group of young men as she ran into them. "I'm so sorry, excuse me! I was lost in my thoughts," she said, stepping aside. They grunted in lieu of an apology, their faces pulled down in annoyance as they kept walking, brushing off her touch. Orabella watched them as she fixed her skirts and resettled her shawl. *Maybe I'll do better somewhere not so crowded.*

She looked back at the sun. The light wouldn't hold forever. She continued her walk, her pace quicker, her mind on her steps.

St. Martha's wasn't much to look at but its worn-down charm comforted Orabella where the priest's words, when she listened, often failed. St. Martha's didn't tower over the homes around it so much as scrape the sky just past their roofs. It would have been lost if not for its modest sprawl outward, the small space given to the house of God. The very tips of the steeple caught the light of the sun and it trickled down the slate shingles to the stone walls before falling into shadows. The stained glass of the windows wasn't placed correctly to catch the light so they remained muted no matter the time of day. The golden halo of its namesake, St. Martha, appeared brown, her red cloak wine-dark, the emerald green of the hills a dull, deep color. Instead of a beautiful field, the saint stood on a rolling ocean, held up by divinity.

"Ah! Orabella! I wasn't expecting to see you today!"

Orabella held out her hands for Sister Jennine Ignatius. Jane to everyone who knew her. Her face was slim with deep-set eyes. Her hair was always hidden by her habit, but her brows were bright red. She would have seemed severe if not for her ever-present smile. They were close in age, Jane a little older. Orabella had asked long ago what had driven Jane to the Church; she said only that she had felt called. No dark secret, no scandalous story.

Jane came down the steps to meet Orabella and they exchanged a quick embrace before Orabella pulled away. "Jane! I know it's unexpected, but something's come up and I won't have another chance to come by again," she explained.

Jane's smile faltered. "What is it? Are your aunt and uncle all right?"

"They're fine. Everyone is fine. It's just that I won't be able to make the hats and things for the children because I'm to be married in the morning. Oh! I don't think I was supposed to tell you that. I'm sure I was supposed to say I was off to be a governess. It's all right if you know, you won't tell." Hot tears rolled down her face before she could stop them.

Jane pushed her into the cool confines of the church. She hummed soothing words while ushering Orabella past the pews and into the back wings, the living area stopping at the well-used kitchen table. Settling Orabella into a chair, Jane let her cry for a few moments while she put water on to boil.

"It's all right, tell me everything, calm down," Jane said as the kettle went off.

Orabella sniffled, focused on the crisscross cuts in the old wood. She traced them with fingers and eyes to soothe herself, stop the tears. She thought of St. Martha's false black waves, imagined going under them, finding quiet.

"Drink this, it will help," Jane said, shoving a cup of tea in front of her.

"Thank you," Orabella said, hiccupping and closing her fingers around the offered drink, heat sinking through porcelain into her fingers. Jane had already added sugar, and she stared into the still-swirling liquid, embarrassed over her outburst. "I'm sorry," Orabella said, "I don't know what's come over me. I was fine just a moment ago at the Hanovers'."

Jane sat down across the table and the story spilled from Orabella's lips like a wave.

She couldn't hold any of it back, no matter how secret it was meant to be. This was a church, Jane her priest, and her confession was as honest in the kitchen as it would be in the confessional. *I am to be married, I am going away, my husband is a stranger who won me for a debt.* Jane listened.

"It just seemed like there was no other way to answer at the time," she finished.

"You poor thing. That uncle and aunt of yours! They had no right!" Jane exclaimed.

"I couldn't stay there forever. Something had to change, and it looks like it's this now. Maybe it won't be so terrible. He seemed . . ." Orabella paused, her fingers dancing over the gouges left in the wood, looking for patterns by touch. Hoping for arcane secrets that would force the strange creature of her life into sense and finding only the history of consumption. "Fine. Odd. But like a man who would treat me well enough."

"You cannot tell how a man will be from a single meeting in a garden, Orabella. I'm sure he promised that but he all but bought you! No one will uphold this, we can keep you here, I'll talk to Father Peter, he'll understand." Jane gripped her hand, tightly, warmly.

"Jane, you are a true friend. I think I should go through with things, though. Unorthodox as it was, my uncle wouldn't have invited anyone who would hurt me, debt or no. If not him, there will be another. And anyway, I did say yes, and one must endeavor to follow through on one's commitments."

"No! You're a good person and you don't have to settle for this! You deserve a proper suitor who cares for you and to have a real wedding with your friends and family! Like anyone else! And besides, you'll be trapped."

Orabella bent her fingers into claws and raised them above her head. "He'll be a murderous duke out for my fortune, like those stories in *The Candle*? Don't be silly!" She laughed. "I have no fortune. And you're the only friend I have to speak of, and besides, it was my family who made this match. It will be fine."

The tea had gone cold, untouched in both their cups. "Are you sure?"

Am I? Does it matter? "Yes," Orabella said anyway. There was nothing else to say. Nothing would change what was to come short of running away in the night, but Orabella was not so bold. There would be no lords to take her in and fall in love with like in those stories in *The Candle*. No, this was real and she must be married and leave in the morning.

"Well, the children will miss your hats and mittens this year and I'll miss you. Will you write?"

"Of course, I'm sure I'll come back to visit. I think my husband has some business here."

"What does he do?"

"I'm"—she hesitated—"not sure. He looks like he works. My uncle said they were a well-off family, the Blakersbys. Maybe he was only rough from traveling and he doesn't work at all. Perhaps we'll spend every day staring at each other over books in front of a fire."

"Don't get lost in your fantasies," Jane scolded.

"It's fine, Jane. I promise I'll write. Please don't worry."

"Oxbury, you said? There's a small parish there, I think. Maybe I'll be able to visit you," Jane relented. There was nothing else to do, too late—Orabella had made up her mind or it had been made for her.

We'll still be friends, I will still have this. The idea comforted her, as she tried to provide answers to Jane's questions—answers she did not have. What is your new home like? The family? What will you do there? How long will you travel? When Orabella left, the sun was nearly gone, the last few rays of it orange and drowning under the blanket of night. By the time she reached the building that had served as her home for most of her memory, the sad creature it was, the sun, too, was only a memory. Everything was ending.

She stood at the doorway and stared back out onto the street, at the neighboring houses, their curtains drawn but slivers of light coming from the edges where they failed to meet. Her neighbors—she knew their names, faces, as they knew hers. And now she would go to a place where no one knew her save a single man. They shared no history, no bond, there would only be the commitment to keep him honest, to keep her company.

The door opened. "Orabella?" Mary, one of the maids that worked for the family, asked, annoyed, impatient, ready to go to her own home.

"Yes?"

"Dinner's already set and your uncle is complaining. Your aunt returned some time ago. He has plans for the evening."

"A card game? So soon." Orabella bit back whatever else she might say. It wasn't proper to speak of their vices before the help.

Mary looked at her strangely. "I wouldn't know, miss, it's none of my business."

"I suppose not." Orabella swept past her, steeling herself to be lectured for her lateness. The maid took her shawl. Orabella went straight into the dining room, where a modest meal of roast chicken and vegetables waited along with her aunt and uncle.

"It was such short notice, we couldn't do more to mark the occasion," he said as she sat.

"It's lovely, thank you for thinking of me," she replied, as expected. She had already cried and raged and quieted, so again she smiled. Showed the face she had learned so well, the expression that Elias called false, but it was the only way she knew to be.

Her aunt and uncle waited for a moment, searching for a break in her mask, but she had learned very well. The maids served them and they ate in silence. Orabella forced herself to swallow every bite.

Chapter Three

Orabella sipped at her tea, hoping to calm her nerves and settle her stomach. The organ twisted and tumbled, mimicking how she had passed the sleepless evening. In the dark, alone, the mask had slipped, fallen to nothing, and there were only worries and nightmares chasing each other back and forth through her like mice all night. Exhausted, she sat at the dining room table, toast and jam untouched, the sweet smell only making her more nauseated. The tea was not helping.

An anxious fog filled her mind and she fought to keep it from rising into a cloud that would become rain down her cheeks. *I'm just exhausted, I should have come home earlier, to rest*, she chastised herself in place of her aunt. She wished she had stayed out longer, wished now that she had gotten lost in the setting sun. But there was no time to do anything different now. Breakfast was ending. Everything was ending. *He'll be here soon*, she thought, standing and smoothing her skirts before joining her aunt in the parlor, the very same from the day prior, when everything had changed. This time she sat, taking the seat next to her aunt.

Her hair was combed and pinned away from her face. Orabella had made herself presentable. The dress had been worn only once before, by her cousin to a holiday party before she married, put up for storage and forgotten afterward. The color, a deep forest green, nearly black, looked suitable for a wedding and would be easy to travel in, as Elias had requested. The waist, fitted but not too tight, suited her figure with a low neckline and loose sleeves that were cut too long and reached her wrists. The cream-colored shawl Orabella wore over it was her own. She knit it herself two summers prior. Idle hands being the devil's playground, Orabella fiddled with the tail of the yarn left untucked. A small detail, forgotten and now made useful for her fidgeting fingers.

Her aunt snatched her hand, brought it to the green skirts and held fast. "I was nervous, too, on my wedding day. I know this must seem abrupt, but I have always thought of you as my own, since you came through the door hanging on your father. I hope you know that we truly want the best for you." Her aunt's words were sincere, but her appearance was the same as on any other day. Graying hair pinned up proper but her clothing plain.

Orabella's cousin's wedding had been a different affair. But then, Constance was different from Orabella. The older girl had fit so easily into the roles of society. Perhaps because her parents had always been part of it, and it had been expected of her. She hadn't been raised, however brief, by a flower seller and a man known mostly for telling a good story around a table. Orabella had always struggled to match her and failed; she lacked something, some quality, that her cousin had in abundance. Control, tact? She wasn't sure, but with its absence she knew she became too different to fit in well enough. As children they had been happy playmates, but as they grew, so did the gulf between them until it seemed there had never been a closeness at all.

Constance's wedding had been held in a church, a gathering of two families, with the bride's and groom's relatives from the surrounding country. Everyone had worn their best clothes. Constance and her groom, Marshal, had been happy, in love. He had courted her for a year, everyone knew of their plans after the wedding, and Orabella heard things were still well between them. Constance had never written to Orabella after leaving. She had a son now; sometimes Orabella's aunt spoke of her daughter's new life, in passing praise. When her aunt and uncle went to visit, they did not take Orabella, and for those weeks alone in the house with just the maids she breathed easier. There were no engagements. No visits with the Hanovers or Morrisons. No disapproving glances from her uncle. *Do they summer in the country, Constance and her husband? Will Constance be curious now and come seek me out? Will they come to Oxbury, her husband and little baby? Whisper about how odd my new family is, how odd I am?*

The questions kept her occupied. She cared for Constance only because she knew her, and Orabella knew so few people, really. They were all idle daydreams, a story to unspool while she waited, her aunt's hand on hers as if she would run off as soon as their heads turned away. The woman played at soothing her, surrounding Orabella in the scent of powder and rose water. The touch, the scent, was not like Elias's. His had been constant movement, reassurance, and something more that she couldn't let herself name. This was not that. Her aunt's hand was pressure, constant pressure.

"There's nothing to fret over," her aunt hummed. "In a year you'll be settled, things will be well, you'll see." The words did not reach into the churning pit of Orabella's belly, but she smiled, played at thankfulness to please the woman who'd given her shelter and claimed her as family even if Orabella hadn't felt true

acceptance. "And you can visit with the Taylors, they're Mrs. Hanover's relations, her cousins; remember, she was telling you they
summer there. I'll write them and make an introduction. It will
be good for you," she said.

"Let her go, Caroline. She is not a child," her uncle huffed as
he entered the room dressed in much the same manner that he had
the day before. The day was like any other: a morning visit. The
morning dragged on, impossibly long, or she had been awake too
long. A normal day, only it wasn't, not at all. "Where is that man?
I don't have all day for this," he grumbled.

"The hour is still early, Worrell. She's frightened," her aunt
snapped at her husband.

"Frightened?" He snorted. "Of what? She's old enough and I
have heard of her walks alone, her dalliances."

"Those are rumors," Caroline hissed, her hand pressing on Orabella's, not quite pain, not yet.

"Yes. Please, Uncle, don't say such things. I have been careless
at times but never crossed any lines." She was thoughtless, dull,
everyone said so, but she kept herself well from those scandals save
for the ones that existed due to her very existence, which she could
not help. There were already so many reasons to reject her, why add
to them?

"You have agreed to marry her off to a stranger! You couldn't
even be bothered to give them time to know each other a bit!"
The older woman was red in the face, working herself into a fever
pitch, her hand tighter and tighter in her anger. Orabella held
it still, ignored the discomfort pressing into pain that her aunt
called care.

She glanced to the entrance, tired of their arguments. It didn't
mean anything, a show her aunt put on to feel better about what
was happening, to soothe her own conscience. Orabella spotted a

dark form and her heart jumped thinking it was Elias come to collect her, but it was just the skirts of one of the maids disappearing around the corner.

"Listen to me," Worrell said, voice low and angry, drawing her back to their argument. "This is for the best. They are a good family. We have done everything we could for that girl, and I will hear nothing more of it."

They spoke as they always did, as if she weren't there at all. They expected her silence and a brave face, and she performed it. Readied her lips and tongue to form the words they wanted. *It's all right, it's for the best.* Her uncle had not lied: she was agreeable, the world was easier, gentler on her that way, and perhaps, she reasoned, it's what her new husband would want.

The bell rang, ending the argument—they needed their own masks. Elias had arrived.

Her heart beat against the cage of her ribs, sending blood rushing to her ears, filling the world with the sound of her panic. Orabella tried to control her breathing, but it was too fast. She would be lightheaded in a moment. *This is no way to start things,* she scolded herself the way her aunt would have.

Her aunt gripped her hand tightly, as she had throughout her life. A warning, a punishment, pain. Not like his touch. For the first time in her life, Orabella pulled free. It was too late for such warnings, everything had been decided, there was nothing she could do to ruin it. Even if she cried and wailed now, threw herself on the floor, she didn't think that it would stop anything. There was an inevitableness to her situation. It was what she had tried to explain to Jane, there was nothing she could do. It would be this or some other.

It wasn't Elias that filled the doorway.

An older gentleman, dressed in black, his high collar slightly yellowed behind a crooked cravat. Sloppy in the way that powerful men allowed themselves to be sloppy. He swept off his hat, his eyes passed over the small party, landed on Orabella. The Registrar. Her own gaze had long since left his person.

A man followed him.

An assistant, before he was close enough to recognize. The same eyes that had met hers in the parlor the day before stared at her now. He had cut his hair, the tips of it curling, brushed along his collar, and his face, shaved free of the beard, was pale and younger than she would have thought. A strong jawline and chiseled features with lips that seemed too soft by comparison. Tall and broad, he fit his tailored gray jacket and vest well. His pressed shirt shone bright, and his cravat fell elegantly about his neck. His clothes were much finer than they had been the day before, finer than the borrowed dress she wore now.

Elias, she realized, *is handsome.* He stared back at her, his expression relaxed, amused even. *Surprised?* he asked silently. She tightened her shawl around her shoulders to keep her hands from trembling. Everything in her twisted tight, nerves stealing what warmth desire attempted to spread in her. This was worse somehow, that he was handsome and clean and Orabella was still only herself.

Herself. She'd lost it. Forgotten what she was meant to show. Hands smoothed over skirts, shawl straightened, and she was again presentable, but less so than he, for a wedding.

"Is this the bride?" the Registrar asked, frowning at Orabella.

"Yes," Elias answered.

"And you're agreeing to this? You want to marry him?"

The Registrar had spoken, had asked her something, but the world was slow, the air thick. She looked at her uncle and aunt. They stood side by side, united in this at least and waiting. Only

Elias still looked at her with gentle eyes. "Yes," she said. "Yes, I am agreeing."

"Bring a table," the man commanded, taking the seat that her uncle had occupied the day before.

There was no need to call for one, the maids had been in the hall listening. The room was so quiet, the air so thick, the click and clack of their shoes was the only sound. A moment later they appeared, the table held between them. They settled it in front of the Registrar.

Orabella kept her seat on the couch, unsure of what she was meant to do. Her uncle had settled on the opposite side of her aunt and motioned with his eyes that she was to stand. But Elias was there, hand out, waiting.

She took it as she had in the garden and faced the Registrar. Elias held her fingers in his, rubbing his thumb over her knuckles, soothing. A nervous habit of his own? She wasn't sure, couldn't be sure, she knew nothing of him. Orabella tried to read something in his manner but there was nothing to read, good or bad. He was proper, as expected of a man on his wedding day. Her own feelings were a tangled ball of yarn and she couldn't find the end, couldn't hope to unravel it, to begin making sense of them as man and wife.

"What am I supposed to say?" Orabella asked, the words a breath, the taste of their foolishness stale on her tongue.

The Registrar answered with his own question. "Do you two agree to take each other on as husband and wife?"

"Yes." She knew the lines, it was only a reminder she needed.

Elias squeezed her hand, the press warm, no threat of pain. "Yes," he agreed.

"And you two, are there objections against this?" The Registrar pointed at her relatives, clear he expected their responses quickly.

"No," her uncle barked.

Her aunt, who had been full of accusations and objections, made nothing of it now. Before the man to whom her objections would matter, she said nothing about them. She shook her head, smiled, wiped a tear. With that, Orabella's life and whatever would become of it passed from their hands. No longer an unwanted Mumthrope, she had become a Blakersby, legally, unquestionably.

Elias reached into the right pocket of his coat and removed a small cloth. He untied the bundle, revealing a gold ring. A thin band, nothing inscribed, no jewels adorned it. "This should fit well enough," he said, taking up the hand he held and maneuvering the band over her left ring finger, where it settled at the base. "How is it?"

The gold was an unfamiliar weight on her skin. She turned her hand; she'd never worn rings and the color was closer to her own skin. "It fits well, how were you able to match my size?"

"A good eye." Elias's voice rolled over her soft with praise.

"Sign here." The Registrar, voice gruff with reality.

Orabella signed her name quickly before passing the pen to her husband. She looked away as he signed, searching his face for his feelings, but his expression was neutral. The Registrar gathered the pages and folded them, save one, which he passed to Elias.

"Keep that for your records. I will file this one by the end of the day." The Registrar's job complete, he placed his hat back on his head. He took his leave and it was done.

She looked back to Elias, her husband but still a stranger. "Are you ready?"

She wanted to laugh. *Ready? Ready for what? How can I ever be ready, everything is changing so quickly.* She said nothing, she'd been raised well. It was what her aunt expected of her, what her uncle expected. She held the tremor inside her, kept it from her hands by gripping them tightly in front of her. "My trunk is waiting in the foyer."

"Ah, so you did find something you couldn't replace after all." His voice was low, playful and, she thought, pleased.

Elias removed an envelope from his breast pocket and presented it to her uncle. The older man floundered, embarrassed. The transaction had not been meant to be seen but it hardly mattered. It didn't stop her uncle from taking whatever it was that Elias handed him. His eyes went cold again, and he accepted the envelope.

"Then we are finished," Elias announced with a nod, reaching for her arm.

"Goodbye, Aunt Caroline. Goodbye, Uncle Worrell. Thank you for caring for me. I will write when I am settled." Clouds where her brain should be, worms again in her belly. *I am a dead thing to them.* There was no room, no time to spend on grief; she had to follow this handsome man and hope his goodness was more than his face.

Her aunt and uncle, the only parents she had known for the better part of her life, said nothing to her goodbyes. Said nothing as Elias took her arm, pulled her close to the door. *Ah, I see*, Orabella would have said if there had been any time to say anything else.

"Your luggage is likely already on the carriage. Your uncle seemed . . ." He paused, choosing his words. "Anxious to see this through. We will take the train for a time." One of the maids approached, Mary again. She held a package, wrapped in plain brown paper and tied with twine, in her arms. "Then we will go by mail coach for two days to Korringhill."

"Korringhill? I thought it was Oxbury." The name seemed pleasant, bright.

"Korringhill is the name of the manor. My home, your home now."

"All right," she said. She felt like crying but if she started it would never stop. She would fill this new house with her tears. A sort of sadness, a sort of excitement struggled in her and she couldn't tell one from the other. She couldn't let him see it. "I've never been on a train. I haven't gone anywhere at all since I came to this house. We used to live in France, my father and me. I haven't thought about it in ages. I've forgotten the language, I think. Isn't that strange?" Her voice sounded too high in her ears.

"It's all right, Orabella." Elias's breath tickled her ear; his scent, ginger and smoke mingling with the wool of his jacket, flooded her nose.

He stepped away abruptly, took the offered package from the maid, and untied it.

"My apologies, there wasn't time for a better presentation," he explained, shaking out the fine woolen cape in a mulberry color, trimmed with gray and brown fur. He stepped forward, wrapping it around her and tying it at her throat. "It's not strange you've forgotten. It's been some time, we forget things from our childhood, it helps us survive growing up." His fingers lingered at her throat. "It is still cold outside. This is not much of a wedding present, I'm afraid, but I hope that it is of some service to you. The fur is rabbit."

"Presents are given by the guests, not the groom," she said, turning her eyes downward to the gift to avoid the force of his gaze. *I shouldn't have said that, I sound ungrateful.* She was forgetting herself, her manners. "I'm sorry, I don't know what's come over me. Thank you. This is lovely." She ran her fingers over the thick fabric, the soft fur, collecting herself.

Closer now, she could see the flecks in his irises, a white scar across the bridge of his nose. His nostrils flared and his eyelids rose, just a hair, for a moment before he replaced the distance between their bodies. His cheeks flushed pink. "You're welcome. We'll miss our train if we wait much longer."

She followed him out. There was nothing else to hold her in her uncle's home. She didn't turn as she walked down to the street, where a hired carriage awaited them, her trunk strapped to the back, just as Elias said it would be. The driver held the door open. Elias helped her up, climbing into the seat next to her. She looked past his body through the window back at the house. There was no one there, the door was shut, the curtains closed.

In the close quarters, there was only his nearness, the sound of his breathing and her heart pounding. Small things made huge, they drowned out horses' shoes on cobble, the shouts and sounds of the world beyond. She could smell him, the same scent she had caught when he held her in the foyer, ginger and smoke, the only scent in the world.

"I was not expecting to be . . ." Orabella started but the end of the sentence wasn't there—the thread of words fell away, lost, and she let it drop. She clasped her hands tightly, tried again. "Everything has been very . . ."

"I know this is all sudden, but I think you will settle in well once we arrive." He covered her hand, untangling her fingers and wrapping his own between hers.

"Yes, I'm sure I'll soon find my way under your care," she replied.

Stroking her knuckles as he had the day before, he continued. "We will travel for three days before we arrive at Korringhill. I shouldn't ask this of you, I know you are unsettled, but may I have one thing from you? A small indulgence."

"I can't imagine what that could be, sir, I have nothing." Her voice came out a whisper. She wanted to lie down, cover her head with the quilt she hadn't taken until she had time to sort through her own heart. But there was no time, would be no time. Her husband wanted something from her *now*. He lifted her hand and pressed his lips to the digits, the touch warm and brief, an answer to her question, a warning of his coming actions.

His free hand slipped under her chin and angled her face upward. He tilted his head and kissed her. *It feels different*, she thought before thinking became impossible.

She had been kissed before. Quick, wet things that made her giggle in night gardens during parties. A curiosity for her and them, a moment of physical contact that left her feeling warm but unsettled and was not often repeated, and never more than that. His touch was different. The motions were familiar enough that she knew how to respond: she parted her lips for him, and he took entry. But it was *different*, not the hurried stolen intimacies of before. Elias's kiss was slower, deeper. A rush of heat through her body, a silent response to touch. A hungry need that sent warmth to every extremity, chased the winter she carried all through herself, and turned it to a bright spring, bursting with life.

Orabella wrapped her fingers in Elias's fine jacket, pulling him closer. A low, lusty sound emerged from his throat and spilled into her mouth.

He tastes sweet, she thought as he pulled away.

"Dear heart," he murmured, his face still close. "In three days, I'll introduce you to my family and we will make this a proper marriage. Until then, this is as much as I will ask of you."

She sighed, her pleasure in his touch a softer thing. "We have some time, not much, but some, to learn of each other. That's thoughtful of you."

"It would not be right for us to begin things in the bed of a rented room. You deserve something better than that. Let me show you that I'm sincere in my affections."

She wanted his kiss again, but he released her, leaning back against the seat. That would be all there would be, then. "Thank you, that's very kind of you. I have had hardly any time to think."

"We'll be at the station soon." His expression seemed to hint at some other meaning, but she couldn't grasp it. A reminder of where she was, a carriage, traveling to her new life, with her new husband in the seat beside her.

Her skin tingled where he had touched it. Her tongue too thick for her own mouth. Inside her, amid the tangle of her emotions a hungry, animal thing woke. Orabella turned to her window and tried to smother it while Bristol moved past and away from her.

Chapter Four

The carriage that met them in Oxbury was the finest thing Orabella had seen in days.

Aged but stately, kept up well enough, as were the two horses that drew it. Dark paneling but a sturdy build, it was more luxurious than the mail coach had been and large enough to sit at least six people inside. It stood in the center of what Orabella had been told was Oxbury. There were only a few people and they walked close to the shops, giving the carriages a wide berth. Everything was quieter than it had been in the city. She would have thought the arrival of the coach would draw stares but the people walked past without looking. The driver was elderly and he nodded at Elias, spared a glance at Orabella, and then turned back to his horses. Elias held her door and helped her into the seat, taking up his own across from her.

It was early afternoon, but once inside the carriage, the air turned twilight-dark. The windows were covered. Elias sat across from her, a valley between them. Nothing like the cramped confines of the mail carriage. The carriage lurched to life and Orabella lifted the fabric that blocked the light, tried to catch more of the town, but the carriage picked up speed quickly, turning the buildings into a blur that her tired eyes could not follow.

"Are we in a hurry?" she asked, releasing the curtain.

"In a way, I suppose. There's dinner tonight, for the family to greet you, but there's plenty of time before that. You should rest first," Elias replied. He removed a candy from his pocket and stuck it in his mouth. Ginger: he'd been eating them since they'd been together. Travel upset his stomach, he explained.

"Your family? I wasn't expecting to meet . . . but of course, your parents." So soon, no time to rest or be settled. She hadn't thought it would happen so fast, the introduction to his family, and part of her whispered that it wouldn't. That when they arrived there would be a little room for her to sit in, like a princess. Like a prisoner. Like the orphan she was.

"My father and sister, yes, when we arrive. My mother is dead. I suppose I hadn't told you that. But later, during dinner, the rest. Aunts, uncles, cousins. I assumed you were aware of what makes a family despite your own."

There was a bite to his words. A joke, mean-spirited and unlike how he had been with her so far, or had she been overlooking things? He had been sullen when she asked questions to learn more about him but he seemed pleased when she spoke of herself, so she did. But perhaps that was not what she should have done. *Maybe*, she reasoned, *it was how I asked him.* "I'm sorry, I didn't know about your mother. I should have asked of your parents." An oversight, and maybe now he saw how deep her faults ran. Her mastery of society was only surface-level. It did not take her long to make a mistake and her mistakes had begun days ago. She spoke too much of herself, of their travels. Her mouth ran too freely.

"Apologies, that was uncalled for. I didn't mean to . . . I didn't mean that. I'm nervous as well. It is not every day a man brings home his beautiful wife. And you have nothing to apologize over. I didn't tell you and you would have no reason to assume." Charming, as he had been at the garden.

"It's all right. I'm sure this is a time of change for both of us." She looked down at the bunched fabric of her skirts and smoothed them before folding her hands in her lap. *I'll ruin all my dresses at this rate, Aunt Caroline is always warning me about that, but I suppose I'll have to remember on my own.* She moved the curtain again, found the ghost of her reflection in the glass and fiddled with her hair.

"It's all right to be nervous. It's good that you are attempting to compose yourself. This is proof I was not wrong in my judgment of you."

"And what judgment was that, Elias?" It was clear now her error, she was too chatty. But the change in his manner, that biting remark, maybe it wasn't just her bad habits. *No, he's nervous, I don't know him well enough, and I speak too freely when I am not careful.*

Elias's teeth were blue-white in the dark, the only sign of his smile. "Did you think I didn't know? I wasn't to meet you until later, no doubt so that your uncle might obscure much of you from me for as long as possible. He would not have told you who called. It was by your own design that you came to the parlor that morning, and I am glad of it. It shows that you are clever and brave. But it seems that I saw the best of you then and will not be shown it again."

"Am I supposed to be clever and brave? I thought a wife was well mannered and soft spoken. That is what my aunt taught."

"Korringhill is large and lonely. It is a very old building. It's easy to be frightened and even easier if you're bored. But I think you'll be able to entertain yourself. You did so well in your uncle's home. So, have I seen the best of you?"

"I'm not sure I know what you mean, but it's different now, isn't it? Before, it was more familiar. I acted out of self-preservation. I don't think there was anything I could do to change my fate, but I wanted to know. I wanted to see things with my own eyes."

He leaned forward, his gaze like a dog's on a bone, meat still clinging to it. "And what did you see in me? Why did you say yes? I know how I looked."

Elias's interest was sharper than it had been on their journey when he asked about dresses and hobbies. He had never asked about their meeting that day.

"You . . ." She paused. His nearness made it hard to think, the memory of the first carriage—the act not repeated since, but now they were alone again and it stirred in her. "Surprised me. You did not seem as you looked, Elias. You are not a bad man, I don't think." She could feel her nerves rising in her, her aunt's voice telling her to bite her tongue, but she pressed on, spurred by his rawness to match it with her own. Asking the questions that had scratched at her mind, that she was sure were the root of her unease. "I don't know anything about you. You've taken care not to leave room to speak of yourself, or perhaps I am not as practiced in conversation as I thought. What do you do? I know nothing of your business. Or of you, for that matter."

He shrugged, a movement more the sound of his jacket scraping against the seat than seen. "I deal in imports. I own a few ships. It's all very boring. There is simply not much to know of me, Orabella."

"Nor of me and yet I've dominated our conversation these past few days."

"There is more to you than you give yourself credit for, wife.

But for now"—he leaned and pulled back the curtains, flooding the carriage with light—"you should see your new home."

Korringhill Manor stood behind a carpet of rolling emerald hills, nestled in dark woodlands. The building itself rose like a gate for the forest beside and beyond it, the trees tall and ancient. The manor was covered in ivy, turning the slate-colored stone green and alive. The slow creeping of the woods had begun to swallow the building but parts of it still stood bare of leafy tentacles, which ate the light that would have otherwise illuminated the angles of it. Orabella could just make out the glimmer of windows and the door that led into the depths. Something queer happened to the sunbeams as they passed over the steepled roofs. They trapped the light in pools, like water, and it could not pass the shadows, leaving the façade of the massive building deep in darkness, despite the bright sky above.

How will I live here? She had expected bright brick, handsome gardens, but approaching it now realized there was no reason for her to have had such thoughts. It was just a story she told herself to make things easier. *I should have asked*, but she didn't know she had reason to ask. Korringhill Manor towered with an obvious prestige but lacked all pretense of leisure, of joy. Not a place that people lived in, instead it had the feel of a place that people couldn't leave.

The dark, imposing building, the dark, wild woods behind. The scene spun from a dream, a fairy tale. She leaned back into the carriage; the manor, too hard to look at.

"It's a bit overwhelming. Or maybe"—Elias paused, tilting his head in question—"underwhelming?"

"It's not what I expected. I thought it would be . . . something else."

"I should have told you."

I should say something. He would be insulted; the fault was with her and yet her tongue stilled, her eyes drifted down to her skirts.

"Orabella, things will be different here, for you. I'm sure you'll find your footing quickly."

She looked up, tried to find the words to correct her mistake, but Elias had turned away. The carriage slowed to a stop.

The door swung open and Elias descended first, extending a hand back for her. The moment Orabella's feet touched the ground and her skirts cleared the door, it closed. The driver was already taking his seat. The horses moved as soon as he settled. Their hooves followed the path disappearing around the house.

Escorting her closer to the massive structure, Elias said, "Your trunk will be delivered to your room."

The door creaked open, revealing an old woman in a slate-colored dress, her iron-gray hair pinned above her face.

"Elias," the elder woman said, her voice much sturdier than her appearance, "you've returned! And is this the wife?"

The woman was tall and thin. Her face held sharp creases where the skin had wrinkled with age, and she held her hands, fingers and knuckles thick from arthritis, curled in front of her like talons. The woman's lips twitched before she lifted them into a smile that softened everything about her. "She appears quite healthy. Come in, come in! The air is still too cold."

"Mrs. Locke, this is Orabella, my new wife," he introduced her as they passed through the threshold into the entranceway of the house.

It was nothing that she could have imagined.

She stood in the massive hall of a home larger than any she'd ever been inside in Bristol. Light streaked through high windows and onto tiled floors. A large staircase divided the hall into two halves and led up to a gloomy second floor. To her right the door was closed. To the left was another hall, streaked with sunlight, the shadows brown and blue where it didn't quite reach. The door shut behind her, a dull, final boom that echoed in the high, empty space. Orabella, startled, turned back expecting to find a hidden doorman but it was only the old woman.

"Show her to her room," Elias instructed. He placed a hand on Orabella's back, directed his words at her. "I'll see you for tea after you've had a chance to clean up and settle."

Panic fluttered in Orabella's guts. He was leaving her alone, in this impossibly large space, so soon, in the foreboding house.

"No. The Old Master and the Lady are waiting to meet her. Before the dinner," Mrs. Locke explained, crossing from the door to join them in the hall. Her heels made clicking sounds on the floor, and Orabella looked down to find the tile woven with cracks and missing squares. Not as grand as at first sight.

How difficult it must be to clean, she almost said, thoughtlessly. How rude it would be; she bit her tongue. It would embarrass her husband, embarrass her. But a question remained. "Who?"

Elias took her arm instead. "We'll meet with them, then. And then she can rest. Her room is ready?"

Orabella fixed her smile to her face and did not press.

"Of course, Elias. We're all so happy that you've returned." Mrs. Locke said.

She is so familiar with him. I thought they would be more distant, less personable in a house like this. She thought of her uncle and aunt's maids. Mary had been with them, but the other girl, Anna, was new; Orabella hardly knew her. Before that there had been another girl. They sometimes laughed with her aunt and she asked after their families. They were just the help, there for a service, and beyond that, there existed no relationship.

It was as Elias had said in the carriage; things were different in Korringhill than they had been in her uncle's home.

"They're waiting for you in the garden room, Elias," Mrs. Locke said.

He turned her towards the sun-splashed hall, lead her away from the entrance.

Orabella's body stiffened, breath caught, waiting. For the floor to open, the sun to disappear, a trap to spring around her, but her foot touched the tiled floor and her heels clicked against it just as in any other home. *And this*, she reminded herself, *is my home now*.

"Orabella, about my family. Their manner may appear . . . difficult. I believe you'll do fine, but do not lose yourself."

She had been to countless teas and meetings. Polite when spoken to and quiet otherwise; at least, that is what had always been expected of her. She imagined her face with the perfect, still expression, swallowed the rolling, sick feeling in her guts. She kept step with her husband. She would give him no cause to be embarrassed by her. She would not embarrass herself with a misspoken word, a bundle of skirt in her fist. Later, when she was alone, she could fall apart, wilt like a flower. Now she must be who Elias expected she would be, a good wife.

Arm in arm they walked through the entranceway and into a smaller hall. The light that spilled from the windows made oddly shaped pools on the floor in front of the open doors, the beams caught and trapped by the formations of furniture stored within. Elias moved past the rooms quickly, but Orabella turned to peek in each one, helpless to stop herself. There was no theme, no plan to them. Each held a collection of items that must have been relocated from all over the manor. It was the only way that made sense.

Beautifully carved shelves and alcoves adorned the walls, covered in dust, along with everything they held. All the furniture was made from heavy wood, clearly expensive, but left stacked with no order or care. Chairs with fraying threads and stuffing bursting from holes. Tables with chests and boxes on their tops. A bed, sorry mattress shoved against a wall with crates and bags piled atop it. Paintings on the wall of unknown people, landscapes, still lives, but they were all so covered in dust and cobwebs that it was impossible to make out more of the art than just an impression. Parlor, office, library, she could only guess at the former lives of the space, all of them now made the same. All of them storage. Everything dust covered, the cushions moth- and mouse-picked. The doors open only to provide light that came through filthy windows into what would have otherwise been a black hall.

"What?" she breathed and stopped. His eyes were turned towards her, careful. *An old family, didn't my uncle say as much?* She fixed her smile. This was her family. They would talk later.

A last turn and the magic she had hoped for was there. She looked into a different world apart from the cracked floors and dusty rooms.

Orabella blinked the brightness from her eyes and stepped forward into the light. It could be her own parlor again, where she had met Elias. It could be the homes of her aunt's friends. The air smelled unnatural and sharp, stung at her nose.

Her fingers dug into Elias's arm, she bit the inside of her cheeks. In front of her sat the most beautiful woman and a corpse.

Chapter Five

"This is my wife, Orabella of the Bristol Mumthropes," Elias said as he placed a hand on her back, gently presenting her. "Orabella, this is Hastings and Claresta Blakersby."

He's mad, he's mad and I'm trapped, he's mad, he's mad. The words spun out in her mind but in her mouth there was only her good, thoughtful breeding. Her husband was introducing her. "I am pleased to meet you," Orabella said. Her stomach felt tight, her throat thick, but her eyes were steady, her voice even. The scream was building, expanding in her.

The corpse and the woman were seated upon new, fine chairs. The wood was shiny and the emerald-green cushions smooth upon them. To Orabella's left sat a matching couch that could fit three, but Elias stopped them at the edge of it, creating a distance between the newlyweds and the dead man. Only a single teacup, a silver bell beside it, sat on a round table between the corpse and the woman, who Orabella was doubting, as the scream clawed at her throat, was a woman at all. Still as the body next to her she was a statue, a doll. *Paint, they've just painted in here.* That sharp smell filled her nose and she grabbed at the detail because it was a physical reality she could understand, to distract from the impossibility that sat in front of her. The walls were bone-white but the two bodies on the chairs were whiter still.

The sunlight through the glass doors lit the two from behind, casting long shadows across the carpet. A garden through them, unkept, covered half the door with dry stems, winter-dead. The gold light picked up their blond and white hair, the shadow gave their skin the bluish sheen of fresh milk while creating a strange halo around the pair, ethereal and terrible all at once. Hastings, the father, the corpse, was in black. Just like the house, his clothing ate the light. Everything in him was sunken. His eyes were the ivory yellow of old paper, of bone, still wet enough to shine. But in the jaw, the cheeks, the unbroken nose, she could see her husband. Where Elias was handsome, time had pulled away any fullness that may have been in Hastings and left only a thin, skeletal version of her husband's vitality. A fly lit upon his skull, at the edge of his white hair.

It's too early for flies; the spring has only just begun. A silly thought. There were always flies where there was death, rot, and here was a body. In a chair. Elias, her husband, was introducing her. And she must not embarrass her husband. The fly danced and buzzed and the corpse moved. Hastings's hand brushed away the insect and Orabella felt the cracks in her, the weakness of own lips before sense took over. Hastings was merely old. *How horrid of me,* she thought, to entertain such stories.

Her fingers relaxed on her husband and the fly flew to the woman, landed on her moon-white hand, and she did not move.

Claresta was stunning. A cream-colored dress that looked yellow by comparison to the skin covering her body. Her face held Cupid's bow lips under a nub of a nose and large true-blue eyes. Twin pools that looked straight ahead viewing nothing at all.

Everything framed by blond tresses that tickled her dainty wrists, the hands folded in her lap. Claresta did not seem young but wasn't old; ageless, she hovered mysteriously without years.

A bride and her groom. Death and his Lady. Even without Orabella's fantasies, they were fantastic. Strange, royal creatures that bore only the passing resemblance to herself and the man who brought her. They were visiting a court, paying respects to a still king and queen, and the rest of the gallery would burst through soon. Their court of fairies and monsters to come through the glass doors, through the overgrowth that lay beyond to dance and welcome her. The fly crawled across Claresta's hand and she did not move.

Past them, through the doors, the garden of Korringhill waited. Thin branches that may have once been flowers or bushes lashed across the glass that led out. Hidden below them, the hint of a stone walk leading deeper into the mess of weeds and brambles that would burst to life in a few weeks and block out much of the light currently gracing the room. It would become as dark as the halls if nothing was done with the plants.

Hastings shifted, his forehead wrinkling over the sunken orbs of his eyes. "Are you Worrell's or Peter's girl?" he asked, his voice a deep clatter.

"My father was Peter, sir," she confirmed.

"And your father agreed to this marriage?"

The more he spoke, the more Orabella relaxed, the more she thought herself foolish. The scream died in her chest, shriveled into a hot coal of embarrassment, but that was fine because it was hers and only hers. "He's passed, sir. When I was a child. My uncle introduced us."

"Your uncle? Worrell? And he knows Elias has brought you here?"

"Yes. He thought this would be a good match for me. He said your family was a fine one." *I am a good and worthy girl*, her smile said.

Elias's thumb moved along her back, the slightest touch. *Does he know how my thoughts ran from me?* The small touch wasn't enough for her to read warning or praise, only that he was there, that he was watching.

"Come here, Orabella." Hastings said her name slowly, trying the strange syllables on his tongue, frowning as if they did not suit him. "Sit here, let me get a better look at you, child."

Orabella took a seat on the couch closest to the old man. The scent of dust and mildew rose from his clothing, the fresh paint not enough to obscure it in close proximity. It mingled with something medicinal on his breath. He leaned forward, close enough for her to see the pores on his papery skin, hear the rattle in his chest. No, not a dead man, not yet.

"There was another girl. She was better suited I think, more like Claresta." Hastings gestured at the stone-still woman. Looking at her again, Orabella could see how her cousin favored her. "Didn't Worrell think we were good enough for his daughter?"

The familiar shock of it. Of course, they wanted her cousin but she still carried the right name. A consolation prize, a curiosity. "I'm sorry, sir. She was married last year."

"Last year," Hastings repeated, leaning back into his chair. "The time is getting away from me. And you agreed to this?"

"Yes," she repeated.

"I suppose it wouldn't make a difference even if you hadn't. If nothing else, she will make a companion for Claresta." He lifted the silver bell, released a high, sweet chime.

"Excuse me?" Orabella asked. "What do you mean?"

"Orabella." Elias. Her name, sharp, as warning.

Orabella took in the room once more. An old man on his seat, a sitting room with a garden beyond it. A husband to remind her of herself. Everything was different but it was all familiar, all the same. *How strange*, she mused but said, "Apologies. I'm fatigued from my long trip. I look forward to knowing my beautiful sister-in-law better."

A young woman dressed in the same uniform as Mrs. Locke came through the side door. She kept her head bowed, folding her hands before her. She had the same white-blond hair as Claresta but the resemblance stopped there. She was short and stocky, red in the face when she looked up. "Yes, sir?" she asked in a small voice.

"Take Elias's wife to her room, and then straight back to the kitchen with you. We have guests. Sit, Elias, we have matters to discuss," Hastings ordered.

Claresta soundlessly stood from her chair and walked past Orabella without pause. Her first sign of life, to leave. Orabella watched her as she slipped from the room. The sunlight clung to her until it could no longer and the shadows they'd walked through swallowed her whole.

"They've arrived, then?" Elias asked.

"Of course, they were here by the evening of your departure. They want to see the wife you've brought back to us."

Elias reached for her, offered his hand. Orabella took it, letting him help her to her feet.

"One moment, sir." Elias took a position by her side and walked her into the hall, the maid in front of them. He bent and whispered, "Hastings is an old man. Do not trouble yourself with what he says. You're tired. I want you rested for our wedding night. I'll see that you're comfortable after I'm finished here."

His hand slipped from her back, his fingertips pressing gently against her before he went back to the room, taking the seat Claresta had vacated.

"This way, ma'am," the maid said, reminding Orabella of her presence.

Orabella followed the maid down another hall. The air smelled stale, all the windows were closed and didn't seem like they would be opened for the spring, not with the mountains of discarded furniture that blocked the sills. Peeling wallpaper decorated her path, fallen like leaves in places and swept to the side. For all the work that had been done in the garden room, nothing at all had been done past that. Not even to maintain the space. The rooms they passed were like the ones before, overflowing with priceless, pretty things that had been made ugly through neglect. The maid's near-white hair floated above her dark uniform like a ghost lantern in and out of the slanting pools of light.

"Miss? One moment, please!" Orabella managed to call out. Her voice thudded oddly against the walls.

The maid stopped, turned. "Is something the matter?"

"No, I just—" A lie. She could feel the fountain of words building in her, the prattle that it would become. She breathed in deeply, mold and dust filling her nostrils, and she sneezed. "Could you give me just a moment?"

The maid pursed her lips and looked about the hall. "All right, just a moment, though. I'm needed back in the kitchen."

"Yes, I understand there's a dinner tonight, guests," she tried.

The maid only nodded and looked away, ready to be finished with the task of escorting her.

Orabella peeked into the nearest room, curious. The air was clearer, a broken window allowing a current. From the door she could see the damage the rain and cold had done. The walls had bare spots where someone had tried to save whatever paintings had hung there, but along with the strips of fading and falling wallpaper, there were black blooms of mold. She placed her hand on the door frame to lean in for a closer look but pulled it away quickly. Her palm came up covered in sticky gray dust. The print of her hand was clear on the wood. Disgusted, she wiped it on her skirts to remove it from her skin, sparing the cloak she still wore. *It's an old dress, it won't do any harm.* She had been afraid of the home from the outside but now, seeing the guts of it, it seemed sad. A stately manor, fallen into ruin.

And like the home, there was nothing to be afraid of in her odd in-laws. An old man, and maybe her sister-in-law was only slow to warm up to new people. *I'll do my best to be friendly with them. We are all here together, after all.*

"Ma'am? I have to get you to your room."

"Yes, I know, your other duties," Orabella replied, wiping her hand on her skirt again, the touch of the mold still crawling over her palm.

The hall ended in a staircase, and her escort ascended the steps quickly. The pity that had crept into Orabella's heart evaporated as she stared into the void of the second floor, which swallowed the ghost lantern of the maid. No light waited at the top, but the maid moved without pause.

Orabella stepped forward, looked down at the floor. The wooden slats showed through the worn carpet of the stair. The dry sound of paper leaves of wallpaper crunched under a heavy foot, and she turned back, expecting to see Elias, but the hall was empty. *The wind*, Orabella thought, remembering the broken window.

"Ma'am?" The maid's voice floated down the stairs to her.

"So sorry! I'm coming!" Orabella placed her foot upon the first step, testing it, and then swept up them, one after another.

She followed the girl into another hall lined with more rooms, the doors open to let in the light, which seemed to be how things were done there. There were turns that Orabella tried to follow but the place was a maze of rooms and halls. She looked into the them as she passed, hoping for landmarks, but there was nothing to see, they had been cleared out. Some had holes in the floor and broken windows, and she shivered at the ghastly place that was now her home. The rooms took a change suddenly. Still empty but in better state. No carpet and the floors had mismatched spots where boards had been replaced. Here, too, repairs had been made. The maid stopped at a door at the very end, and knocking once, pushed it open.

And there, beyond the door, was magic.

Korringhill had been lovely once, and in this room, her room, it still was. Or had been made so recently. Had been made opulent. The walls were covered in fresh Chinese wallpaper depicting a beautiful garden where exotic cerulean flowers bloomed from branches that were dotted in jewel-green leaves against bright green sky. Still birds with rich golden-brown feathers hung in the air or stood with ripe purple berries in their beaks all along the walls.

The furnishings were new and shined with care. Everything was formed from a soft, pale wood that brightened the space, made it more like a fairy tale. Her bed sat, headboard against the wall, in the center, covered with a forest-green comforter that matched the thick rug. Here, too, the planks were mismatched, old and new but sturdy.

On one side sat a vanity, her combs unpacked and already neatly arranged next to a tea tray. Opposite this sprawled a wide window. Next to it in the corner stood a wardrobe where another young maid worked hanging her dresses. Mrs. Locke watched from the door. Orabella turned to thank the maid who had helped her but she was already gone.

"We're almost done with your things. Sloane will help you

change into your dressing clothes so you can rest," Mrs. Locke explained. "Your cloak," she said, holding out her arms for it.

Orabella handed the heavy bundle to Mrs. Locke, who passed it onto the chair waiting at the vanity. Hugging herself, the world wider and colder than it had been, she crossed the room to the window, thinking to close the curtains to stave off the draft. Outside there was a courtyard garden as unkept as the other.

I should ask them to leave, she mused, but the idea made her nervous. Then she would be alone in that strange old house. "I think I might like to take a walk. I'm a little lost in all of this, I'd like to get an idea of my new home."

"That won't do," Mrs. Locke said. She reached out for Orabella's elbow, steering her towards the bed. "You are fresh here." Her voice was smoother now. "You'll get lost in the halls and there's no one to lead you around at present as the entire staff is occupied with our guests. It's better that you rest."

Sloane finished in the closet and joined Mrs. Locke at Orabella's side. "I've already set out your gown for your rest, ma'am." Orabella took special notice of her face and name. She wanted to remember them so that she could be on good terms when they met again; she didn't want to give them a rude impression of her, and forgetting their names so quickly would do that. Sloane had mouse-brown hair and wide eyes, skin the color of the underside of a mushroom, with pink cheeks. She seemed to be about the same age as Orabella, maybe a little younger.

"Thank you, but I'm really not tired." She moved away from the window and reached for the cloak, unsettled by the house, wanting air and a moment to think. Restless.

A hand on her arm. "No, there's not any time for that today. You'll regret missing your chance to sleep tonight. It's your wedding night."

Orabella swallowed the protest that waited on her tongue at the crass reminder and then the heat of embarrassment because the old woman clearly meant the dinner. Meeting the family. *It's a celebration, I'll be up all night.* "You're right, I should get some sleep. I've been traveling." She moved to the bed and the young maid followed.

Orabella gasped. Sloane's fingers efficiently undid buttons and laces, leaving Orabella in her shift and stockings before she could utter a complaint. Nearly bare, Orabella snatched her robe from the girl's fingers.

"This is fine, thank you," she sputtered as she covered herself, pulling the sides closed tight to chase away the feeling of being exposed. It did not work but she tried. "I can manage on my own."

"If you're comfortable," Mrs. Locke said, either not noticing her discomfort or ignoring it altogether, "please come and have a cup of tea. It's at the perfect temperature now. Sloane, turn down the bed."

"Wait, I was supposed to take tea with Elias!" He had said in the front hall, she was sure, that they were meant to have tea together. But then in the garden room he'd said he'd be up later, no mention of the time. And she was already in the nightgown. There was such distance between them still, he couldn't see her like this. It wasn't proper even if it didn't matter.

"He wasn't thinking. There's so much to do! He won't have time. Don't fret, you'll see him at dinner. For now you've had a very long trip. Please, a cup of tea will soothe you."

Orabella sat in the chair, trapped in the course of the afternoon. Tea, then rest, then the wedding dinner. Mrs. Locke went about the business of making the tea: here is the cup, the spoon, the water, the leaves.

"Would you like some honey? It's best taken that way." There was no room for an answer, the glistening, fat spoonful had already made its way to the cup, the heat turning it liquid smooth, Mrs. Locke's hands adept at the task.

She sat the cup in front of Orabella. Sweet steam floated up to her with a bitter note underneath it all. Carefully she took a sip and found the taste to match the smell of it, sweetness followed by bitterness. The liquid on her tongue, she realized how thirsty she was. She hadn't had anything to drink or eat since breakfast, and that had been hours before. The tea was too hot to be refreshing but she drank it anyway, just to drink something. She sipped again, her tongue honey-coated, the taste only sweet. She tried to pick out the flavor: it was familiar, but different, wilder, not exotic. *It must be local*, she decided. "It's very good."

"I'm glad it is to your liking. We'll leave you to get some rest."

"Actually," she asked slowly, shyly, "can I have a little lunch? I know everyone is so busy, but it's been such a long time since breakfast. If it's not too much trouble."

Mrs. Locke smiled. "I'll send something up. Please be patient. Everyone is so busy today."

"Of course." She wouldn't be a bother. It was all right to ask. To eat.

Sloane picked up the teapot and tray, leaving the cup for Orabella to finish. The women exited quietly, shutting the door with a hard *thud*. Alone, Orabella closed her eyes, took a deep breath, and opened them in her new world. Her face stared back at her in the mirror, unchanged. Her marriage, her relocation, had made no difference. There staring back at her was the same face that looked at her the morning before she met Elias, and the evening after. The difference was only the place, a different little room.

"What am I to think? How am I to be? How am I supposed to behave as wife?" she asked her reflection. There were her aunt and uncle but the model seemed wrong. Elias was more controlled than her quick-to-anger uncle. And she wasn't her aunt, who moved though society so deftly. Orabella cared only for the opinions of others insomuch that they impacted how much she could bear of her own life. The ladies her aunt spent time with seemed to have husbands that existed somewhere in the shadows, much spoken of, little seen. The women her own age disappeared from her circle of society after making their matches and did not call for Orabella to visit. There was no one to mimic.

She turned deeper, picked at the little-considered memories of her own parents. Fragile, transparent things, almost faded to nothing, it had been so long. She'd been four when her mother passed, nine when her father followed. An eternity. She closed her eyes and tried to pull the bits and pieces of them together. *We spun in the living room.* Her mother's face laughing, eyes closed, a beauty mark next to her bottom lip. In her memory, her mother's face looked too much like her own for Orabella to be sure of its truth. Her father's image was stronger. She had stayed with him longer. Short and stocky, his face red with laughter, she remembered that clearly. Her parents sang a song in French but she no longer recalled the lyrics or what they meant, so she hummed the melody, the only thing she had left. *Were they like that always?* Was it real or just another story to make her smile in her life? Her mind didn't often turn to the past. It was almost as if her parents never existed at all, but she was there in the world, bone and blood, skin and hair, so they must have been too. *Will Elias and I be like that? Can we be?* A flickering but bright spot of hope at the question.

"I'm sure my life will become lovely here," she said to her reflection.

Orabella drank the last of the strange tea. Leaves settled at the bottom of the cup and she tried to find shapes, turning it this and that way, a drop of brown liquid following her direction. Her future hinted at in strange shapes. *A foot, a mouse, and a . . . candle, I think?* She replaced the cup. She didn't know how to read the leaves but she liked the game of it.

I should write my aunt and uncle, let them know I've made it. It was the proper thing to do; perhaps they weren't done with her, maybe it had been hard for them as well to send her off in such a way. A letter was expected. A letter would give her something to do for a little while. First them, then she would write to Jane. She would want to know how Orabella had got on with the trip, her new home.

She would have, but alone for the first time that day, exhaustion settled around her. Like the thirst and hunger, it came on quickly, powerfully. She touched her head, her reflection frowning back at her, the light dancing, shimmering at the edges. "I'll lie down first. Maybe everyone was right after all."

She left the vanity and slid into the bed, pulling the blankets over herself. She had never closed the curtains—there was still a draft but the blanket was thick, the pillows soft, and the light wasn't enough to hold her.

Chapter Six

"Wake up, ma'am." A voice fluttered softly over Orabella, pulling her out of dreams that smelled of spices she couldn't quite name. A groan rumbled up her throat but her lids were stone, refused to lift.

"Please, ma'am. You must be dressed quickly and down for dinner." The voice was nervous, fluttery and high; it came paired with a hand shaking her shoulder.

Dinner. The dry, musty scent of the house filled her nostrils, bore down on her. In her sleep there had been hands, the dusty darkness of the staircase a throat that pressed around her, swallowed her endlessly. The blanket fell back from Orabella's shoulders, allowing the chill of the room to slide over her skin. The lingering fog of sleep refused to lift, held tight.

"Ma'am." Sloane, the girl's name was Sloane. She stood over the bed, hands wringing, eyes darting. "Dinner has already started. We have to get you dressed, quickly."

Orabella slid to the edge of the bed, placing her feet on the floor, the rug strange and new to her toes. Information came as muted sensation puzzled through a moment. The kiss of cold on her breast and belly: *I have been undressed.* Slippery, wet, warm, floral scent, too early for flowers, *I am being bathed.* Orabella couldn't cross the distance between herself and her body. Still sleep-tangled, she couldn't find the words to send the maid away, to let her gather herself, her own nudity an afterthought where, dully, there was the memory of embarrassment.

Past sunset, the room was all shadows and orange light. The oil lamp cast hazy, dancing ghosts on the wall that congressed with the birds, glinting gold, rippling on their branches. The girl rubbed a soft cloth over her skin and sensitive spaces. The touch was far away, ticklish; was she standing? Sloane moved Orabella like a doll, and Orabella moved along, lifted arms, turned, no questions. The air pulled goose bumps from her skin but it didn't feel real. A dream of too-early flowers and dew.

"Is everything all right?" Sloane asked. A question.

I must answer when spoken to. "Yes." Her voice came out creaky, dry. "It's cold, I'm thirsty." Orabella looked down at her body again, in confusion; why had she allowed the maid to undress her? But then Sloane was lifting a chemise over her head. *The dinner, my wedding dinner. It's started already?* A nightmare, late for her own debut.

The moments flickered past Orabella. A chemise, blink, corset, blink, now she moved to a chair, blink. Blink. Blink.

The brush tugged at her curls, a sharp pain. Enough to pierce the fog, a moment of clarity.

"Please." Orabella held her hand out for the brush. "Let me." The words pressed blunt edges against her tongue, the roof of her mouth. Too many, they spilled clumsily from her in mumbled waves.

Eyes downcast, Sloane handed it to her. There was panic in her voice. "I'll learn. So that I can do it proper."

She tried to grasp the brush, but the wood was jelly, her fingers water, weak, and the brush tumbled from them.

Sloane retrieved it from the dark sea of the floor where the lamp's dancing light did not reach. Orabella's feet sank into the murkiness, absorbed by the carpet and wooden floor. "I'm sorry, ma'am. You're tired, I'll be more careful."

A tug, gentler. Another and another until her hair was a cloud. The fog of sleep settled around Orabella again. The scrape of pins and combs on her scalp, tiny pricks and stings.

Have the streetlamps been lit yet? She looked out the window to sky and the tops of the trees. No neighbor or lamps to go by, it could be just past sunset or midnight, she couldn't tell. "I've forgotten," Orabella croaked at the dark square of glass.

"I'll help you into your dress, ma'am." Sloane held up a white garment for inspection.

"That's not my dress."

The gown was from at least a decade prior, by the look of the pleated sleeves. Adorned with glass beads, thousands of them, all along the skirt, creating a multicolored garden of flowers like the ones along her wall, beautiful and false. The colors were bright and garish like a carnival dress. A costume, a mockery.

"It belongs to the Lady," Sloane explained.

"Am I the Lady?" she asked, grasping at memory. A beautiful doll.

"You're the bride." Hesitation. Sloane's hands faltered, fluttered like butterflies against the closures.

"Yes, I know. My husband is Elias. We were supposed to . . . it's so dark." The words fell away and she snatched at them, trying. Everything was too light, the world shimmered. She couldn't collect her thoughts. "My aunt will," she started, but stopped; her aunt wasn't there, she remembered, it was just her. With no one to be upset, she must remember to be good. "I'm the bride, yes," she agreed. It was easier to agree.

The beads caught the light and sparkled against the fabric. Smooth, cold silk, rich against her body but the smell made her sick. Dust and mildew, old, improperly cared for, like the house. The maid pulled the dress tight, and the bust crushed Orabella's breasts, cut her breath.

Orabella slipped into a pair of silken slippers which were, blessedly, a truer fit than the gown. She looked in the mirror and saw herself but not herself. Borrowed finery, hair still in tangles, threatening to loosen itself from the pins. Her skin gleaming from oils and her eyes sunken. *A ghost.* She reached for her reflection to see if she was real.

"We have to hurry," Sloane said as she turned to the vanity. She took a stub of candle from her apron pocket, fixed it to the waiting holder, and lit it.

Orabella took a step, her body unsteady in the constricting dress. The air was water around her, a cold force that worked against her, but she pushed forward, following the waiting maid into the hall. She held the dress in her fist after the first few stumbling steps, glass beads pressing into her palm, threatening to cut. Her other hand pushed against the wall, brushed dried paper and more feathery things as they traveled from her little hall to elsewhere.

Sloane moved quickly, eager, taking the pool of light with her. Orabella tried to speed up, forgetting to hold the dress, the skirts dropping, her feet tangling, body pitching towards the floor. Her palm caught the wall, which shifted, slid under her hand, before holding her.

"Wait, please, Sloane!" Orabella cried, sure that the walls would swallow her words. "I'm sorry, I know we're late. I need . . ." But she didn't know how to finish. Didn't know what she needed. Never knew what she needed. It was easier to say yes.

Sloane offered her hand, suddenly beside her, no space between them.

Like a child, Orabella took it, the two of them led on by a single, flickering stub of candle through the twisting halls, the staircases, until they were back on the first floor. The rooms were all dark with night. The halls were tunnels.

A burst of sound, raucous laughter, broke the silence. One more turn brought them to the edge of an entirely different place. A different world. Another trick of the house.

Here again there was magic.

The wide windows of the room, alternated with mirrors, showed nothing but flat, black panes, no grass or patio or anything of the world that must be. There was only night beyond the manor, and in the manor the light danced, tricky before her eyes.

Candles, rows and rows of them in mismatched holders, sat on tables spaced throughout the room. Tallow, thick and greasy, filled the air, chasing away the must and mildew. White wax spilled haphazardly downward, covered the table and pooled on the floor. The smoke stuck to her skin, oily and slick. "My tea," she mumbled, the memory already far away. A different Orabella read the leaves, not her.

A tug on her arm and Orabella stepped forward at Sloane's urging. Meat and heavy spices mingled with the dusty scent of the house as she moved towards the table that waited in the center of the room. Long, impossibly long, it was covered by the remains of a meal. A carcass, animal, picked over, flesh still red clinging to spine and ribs. Spilled bowls, cast aside, and half-eaten scraps of bread and fruit surrounded it. Nearly every seat was taken by some member of her new family.

A collection of illustrations from her book of fairy tales made real.

They matched the Blakersbys she had already met, Claresta and Hastings. Tall, pale, with ice-blond hair and varying degrees of beauty. If Claresta was a fairy queen, then these were her court. Their features shifted before her eyes and she couldn't decide what to make of them. Drooping lips, noses pressed to near snouts, eyes too far or too close. And then a blink and they were ethereal. Magnificent. Handsome as Elias was handsome, beautiful as Claresta was beautiful. Marked more by their similarities than their differences and divine in their strangeness. Maybe twenty, maybe thirty guests, she couldn't tell, and the mirrors reflected them, endlessly repeating. A court that spanned forever in a single room, their laughter filled her ears, echoed in her skull.

In the center, an empty chair next to him, her husband.

"She's arrived!" A man's voice rose through the noise.

Heads swung to meet her, sparkling jewel eyes focused, their laughter falling silent. Orabella clasped her hands in front of her, found her smile, and waited for direction. It was how she'd been taught. To wait, to smile, to be led, and all would be well, but their eyes were bright and cold and made her want to cower, to run, to hide.

Elias was at her side, the space between his standing and meeting her arm missing, but she rested into the hand that clasped her elbow. The flow between moments broken, steps missing. Now she sat. Smiled, nodded. Did she speak? Should she speak? A plate appeared. Red meat cut into cubes, bite-sized.

"I'm thirsty," she thought, but the words, dull edged, slipped past her tongue, out of her mouth.

A cup of wine floated in the air in front of her, droplets fell from the rim, bloomed on the dress. "Drink," the room said, drink the candles and dancing darkness said, the hard bright eyes said.

"And make merry," she mumbled through parched tongue and throat. She took the cup, looked into the swirling sweetness of it, and drank. Gulping, unladylike, but she was so thirsty. The world teetered and spun, the air grew sharp little legs and walked all along her arms.

Laughter, high biting. "I like this one, what wit!"

"Bring her water," Elias ordered, taking the cup. More flowers bloomed on the borrowed dress, bruise-red all along the gown. "Eat."

Like the brush, the fork was a slippery thing. She held it in dumb fingers, stabbed at meat and vegetable, ate as she was commanded to. Gamey on her loose tongue. She took another bite.

"We're having venison in your honor! Hunted her just this morning," someone said. Orabella found the source, fixed on it, a man with a pig nose and icy blue eyes. "A beautiful thing, just for you. Have you ever had fresh venison before?"

"Deer." She looked at the perfect cubes, saw no animal in them. "No."

The man grinned, revealing a sharp canine as he raised his cup. "You should know, then, what it's like. You can taste the forest in the meat. I'm sure you'll come to appreciate it." He laughed then, deep and loud, joined by the rest of his table.

"What a good girl," he said wistfully. "Can this pretty girl do any tricks, Elias?" He drank, the table laughed. High, barking, biting.

"Can she sing? Did our little robin bring us another little bird? It would be lovely to have another voice in the family. Or can she dance?"

"Or did you marry her for her penmanship?" another man from down the table inquired.

They laughed, braying whoops and guffaws, table slaps, squeals. The edges of Orabella's smile faltered but held. There was a joke there, cruel, the knife edge directed at her. She was herself enough to catch that, but she held it still in her teeth, refused to swallow it, to let it weigh down her lips. Her smile was her only shield and she held it against them. Even in the haze of tallow and wine she could do that.

"Tell us, Elias! Why'd you marry this one?"

This one struck her muddled brain and stuck. An insult? Or was there another? But then he was praising her, and she clung instead to the sweet words. Did he think her lovely? Did he think her beautiful? It's what he said. The wine was heavy in her belly, pulling her back down.

"Stand up, girl, let us have another look at you."

A hand pulling her from her seat, raising her arm for all to see. And she followed, agreeable, posable, yes. Below her, the dress shimmered, the candle flames played on the beads, the spilled wine a haphazard path down her front. Too loud, too bright, she closed her eyes. Their whispers drowned in the sound of her own blood, howling through her skull, filling her ears.

Their hushed voices rose like a wave, became clattering shouts and yells. She couldn't follow them; if they spoke English, it fell foreign on her ears. She wanted to push the chair back, return to her little room, but she couldn't, it wasn't proper. *It's my wedding dinner*, she thought. The air crawled along her arms, she drowned in tallow, her blood howled, the family howled back.

Elias's voice, the only one she knew, broke through. "I trust there are no objections?"

Silence. Eyes were on her husband before passing over to

Orabella. Glistening, focused, the eyes of weird, secret creatures, brighter than they ever appeared in her little book.

"Wait! A gift! For the new bride!" the man with the upturned nose shouted from his place down the table. "A gift from the forest!"

"A gift." Orabella snatched at the concept. It was one she understood. Gifts were given at weddings by the guests. She was the bride. It was right they should receive something. It was expected.

"Orabella." Her name a warning from Elias's lips but she was turned away, her hands were free, the scattered petals of her attention on the man who had spoken, whose arms were full of a wooden bundle. A puppet. A toy. A strange gift.

"Thank you," she said, because it was what she was supposed to say to gifts, all gifts. She held her arms out, accepted it.

A fawn. Smaller than she imagined, its pelt was covered with white spots over brown fur, whorls of dried birth and blood all over the body. A long neck and legs topped with little golden hooves that had never touched grass hung from her grasp, lifelessly.

"Your husband cut it right out of that doe's belly this morning and called it a gift for you."

She was meant to reply, meant to say something. Her stomach churned, the room spun with it, their laughing, pale faces, their tooth-filled smiles. *Run*, the fawn in her arms said. *Run*, the blood in Orabella's own veins repeated. But she could not. It would not be proper. "Thank you," she heard herself say. "It's lovely."

A roar, a flare of candles, and the room was pleased. The fawn disappeared, there was music, there was cheer. The world spun, the night went on and she was lost in it. Then there was Elias, finally, pulling her up and away, the room echoing with the barks and screams that her new family called laughter.

He was pulling her, fast, too fast, and she tripped on her skirts, her feet tearing at the gaudy dress, ripping age-thin fabric, scattering glass beads. He traveled in the dark, no light for their way, and so she was lost, his hot hand dragging her forward.

"Elias." A plea, Orabella didn't know for what: to stop, to leave, to scream. She couldn't breathe.

He stopped and hushed her; the world was a silent, black maze all around. There was only the press of his hand, their breathing.

"Elias," again. She couldn't think, couldn't speak to say more than his name. Something had happened there at that table but it was all mixed and blurry in her mind.

He cradled her cheeks in the dark. "Orabella, I'm so sorry." His voice seemed far away.

The air smelled of wine still, from his mouth, and mildew but she didn't know if it seeped from her clothing or his. "For the gift?" she asked stupidly, confused and lost, and reaching for the only thing she knew.

Elias's kiss came as hard and as unexpected as it had in the carriage.

Chapter Seven

Golden birds, brown birds, holding purple berries in their beaks, stared silently back at Orabella and she wondered how they sang without dropping their meal and why they were so close until the heavy fog of sleep fell away, left her bare in the morning light.

Her pretty new room with its pretty new wallpaper. Not a forest surrounded by curiously bold songbirds. A bedroom in a curious manor. The singing came from outside, the real forest. She turned away from the birds and found her bed empty, the sheets untouched. "He didn't stay."

She lay back, her head aching as she pushed through the molasses-thick puddle of her memories. It was all laughter and tallow. Sweet dark wine. Strange bright things. "Silly, silly, I was drunk and tired and seeing things. I've been letting my imagination get away from me. Bodies in a garden room and fairies for a family. What was I thinking? I should have had water."

Orabella ran her fingers like combs through her hair, finding tangles fit for a bird's nest. "Changed into my nightgown but too lazy to care for my hair," she hummed at the cotton gown she wore. "Or did Elias?" She couldn't recall more than his kiss in the dark. Whatever came after was lost. She didn't want to think on what that gap meant; everything had already been too much. It was better to ponder the little room, her own carelessness. But her mind wandered back to the time gap, and breathing deeply she tried to feel some difference in her body but she felt as she always felt.

Next to her bed on the little stand was an oil lamp and her little book of fairy stories, opened and turned to save the page. She picked it up, looked at the illustration of Rapunzel, hair trailing down her tower. "Was I reading last night?" She closed the book, replaced it on the stand, and sat up.

Her body protested, rested but tired all the same. A late night after a long trip. "The wine, my stomach was empty. How foolish of me, I know better than that."

The clothes she wore were clean, but the scent of the evening, greasy tallow candles, spice, meat, all clung to her and mingled with the decaying odor of the house. *Flowers*, she remembered dimly. The soap. The too-early scent of spring was gone. She sniffed again, the tart smell of her own sweat. It had been cold, her body remembered the cold, and she couldn't place why she would perspire save for one reason. It was her wedding night. But her memory was as dark as the hall where Elias kissed her. She shifted, winced.

Aching, she pulled herself up, pushed the thick comforter down. Her gown covered her legs and she felt her thigh over the thin fabric, found a tender space on her. Reminded herself of what the night had been, pulling the gown up, revealing the run of her skin and finding it marred by three thick, long bruises. Orabella touched them gently but didn't know what to make of them. She tried to push the thoughts away, there was nothing to be upset about. It was her wedding night, her husband.

Her husband who towered over her, whose hands swallowed hers. She shivered. "It's only a bruise. An accident, I'm sure."

Orabella climbed out of bed, made for the bowl of water and pitcher that waited on the table from the night before. It swirled gray with old soap and filth but the pitcher had been left, still half full. She took the bowl to the window.

The curtains were unchanged, letting in the morning light. She pushed open the window. Cool air flooded the room, and the birds were louder, different from the streets of Bristol. She looked at the sun, guessed at the time. Still morning but later—there were no workers, no business to go by. Only the light and the placement of the shadows on the floor.

She dumped the gray water and closed the window. The draft was still there: her ankles and feet, bare, were cold. "The curtains." She fingered the thick fabric but dropped her arm back to her side. With the curtains closed, there would be no light.

There were oil lamps but she had no matches to light them, and besides, she was tired of lamplight. The draft was a small thing; she could survive it.

A new bowl poured, she washed away the sticking stench of the night and donned a blue dress. Simple enough for any occasion. "We'll meet proper today, the family and me. I hope I wasn't embarrassing last night." But then, everyone had been full of the same wine from what she could remember. Laughter, shouting, there was something else there, wet and heavy, but she couldn't hold on to it, the memory slipped past her, dived back into the puddle of the evening.

She sat at the vanity and looked at herself. A little ill from too much drink and her hair a mess. She took to fixing what she could.

She plucked the pins from it and worked at the tangles until they were curls. She pulled it up into a respectable bun.

Satisfied with her reflection, she turned her attention to the door. It was time to brave the house.

Even in the confines of her uncle's home she had been allowed to come and go as she pleased. The manor, she reasoned, would be the same. A larger building, but she would learn. Smoothing her skirts, checking buttons and sleeves, she made a plan. The kitchen for a breakfast and then Elias. They would talk. As husband and wife.

The first step was to leave the room.

She stood, swept across the floor, and turned the knob but the door held fast. Locked.

Orabella tried again, yanking harder. An old house, the wood swells, doors jam, she told herself, but it did not release. A jittery, cold feeling through her teeth as she lifted her fist to knock on the door. The memory of the twisting, empty halls, and her own island of fresh wallpaper and new furniture.

No one would hear her.

"Hello?" She knocked and called anyway. "Is anyone there?"

She pressed her ear to the door. Small scraping noises, rodents, she was sure, but then after a moment, something larger in the hall.

"Hello!" she tried again. "The door is stuck!"

The creaking of floorboards, uneven and not quite like steps. Then the doorknob, a press on the door. It didn't move.

Orabella's stomach twisted. "Oh, I guess it is locked!" *Elias? Why would he?* The night tried to inch into her memory but she pushed it back, no, there was some reason, she needed patience to understand. "My husband will have the key. Could you find Elias?"

It was late, we all had too much to drink, maybe he's still sleeping it off, she tried to convince herself. The door rattled again, the knob twisting and turning while whoever was on the other side pushed. Big enough that the door shook.

She jumped back, startled by the force. "It's locked!" she called again, sure they hadn't heard her through the thick wood.

The movement stilled, then steps and they were gone without explanation.

"What a strange house," she mumbled, stepping back from the door.

Restlessly she paced, until bored Orabella went back to the vanity and opened the drawers. A box of ribbons and some false jewelry. The bundle of her knitting needles. Her combs arranged neatly in a row.

And finally, her stationery set.

"This place is so large, it'll be lunch before they come back." Orabella sighed and placed the paper and ink on the vanity. "But maybe it's a blessing. I would have forgotten to do this if I hadn't been forced to wait." Taking up the pen, she began her first letter.

She started with her aunt and uncle. An obligation that, once completed, wouldn't need to be repeated until she heard back. Done now so it wasn't forgotten again. There would be so many other things to fill her time here, Orabella was sure. The manor was huge, there were lands. Families summered nearby; they must spend their time on something.

She captured only the most important details for her family. It was all they would want. *I am fine, the trip was long but the weather was good. Everyone here seems* . . . She paused at this, not wanting to lie, but the words didn't come easily. Orabella thought of Hastings and Claresta, the Old Master and the Lady, tried to remember what they were like at the dinner but they did not come through the haze of the evening and she could not for certain say they had been there at all. *Refined*, she settled on. *They held a dinner for me and everyone seems well pleased with the union.* She wished them well and put the letter aside.

A fresh sheet and she began, *Dearest Jane.* This letter flowed from her truer but still she held back. She didn't want to make the woman worry—she had chosen this path, she would figure things out, make the most of it. *His family is very lively, they are much different than I expected. Everyone says they are old and I thought they would be more withdrawn but the dinner was cheerful.*

Orabella's pen hovered in the air. She picked at the dark space in her mind, her husband's apology and then nothing after that but weight like waves pushing her under and down. She couldn't tell her friend about that so she moved away from it, back to the dinner.

Tallow candles and venison. Bright eyes, a family that looked like a family, more alike than different. The strange meat and . . . the fawn. *A practical joke, it must have been.* She shook her head to chase away the horrible image of the dead thing in her arms. *It was . . . stuffed or false. I was drunk, and even sober did I not mistake his father for dead? I am a foolish woman and they're a bawdy bunch; perhaps that sort of thing is common in the country. I should be in better humor.*

A knock on the door broke her from her concentration. A rattle of keys and the door swung open, easy as anything. Mrs. Locke, key still in her hand, and the younger woman, Sloane, eyes downcast.

"Hello!" Orabella said brightly. Quickly she scribbled her name, folded the letter, and put it in the waiting envelope. "A moment." She addressed the missives, ready for the mail. She wasn't sure how long it had been but she looked at the slant of the sun on her carpet, its position shifted from before.

"We thought you would sleep late. Elias should be in the dining hall by now, please hurry, he's waiting," Mrs. Locke said.

Orabella bit her tongue. She mustn't take the old woman's words too personally, she was late, it was late. She held her question for the same reason. Saved it to ask her husband, sure there was a reason for the locked door.

"I'm sorry, ma'am. I should have been here to help you with your dress sooner," Sloane said.

"It's fine! I can dress myself well enough. I'm sure everyone was very busy with all the guests. I don't want to be a bother." *It must have been her at the door but the old woman is the one with the key.* It was fine, a mix-up.

"Come along," Mrs. Locke said.

Orabella followed the women into the hall. Beyond her door, the hall was a line of darkness punctuated by rectangles of weak sunlight that spilled in through the open doors of the vacant rooms that shared her small area of the manor.

Only then did it occur to her that even if she left her rooms, it would have done no good. Following the two women, Orabella tried to recall landmarks but there had been none to speak of, or if there had been, she had passed them so quickly in the dimness that she did not catch them.

"I'm sure I'll learn my way here soon, so I won't take up too much of your day." Orabella spoke up from her place behind them as they left the portion of the halls that she had already come to think of as hers.

"You shouldn't walk about without an escort, ma'am. These halls are confusing."

"Very good, Sloane. Miss, Sloane will be your personal girl."

"I don't really need such treatment," Orabella said, flustered at the attention. "A few days to acclimate myself, learn my way around, I'll be fine."

"That is not the way, ma'am," Sloane replied, the simple explanation the only one given.

"The way?" Orabella pressed.

"Of Korringhill. House rules, ma'am. The women are cared for," she said.

"But you're a woman," Orabella tried again, stopping her with a hand on her arm.

Sloane turned to her. She stood in the shadows while Orabella was still in the light. "No, ma'am. I'm your personal girl."

There was no humor in her face. She was determined, serious, and Orabella fumbled for what to do, what to say. She'd never had this sort of help, she didn't know what was expected.

Is it because of my sister-in-law, Claresta? she thought. Maybe the mother had had some illness too. *Were the women of the family of weak nature?* "Claresta!" she remembered. "I saw Claresta leave the sitting room where we met on her own. I'm sure I can be trusted."

"When you become the Lady, you may do as you please as well," Mrs. Locke said, tersely. Her manner was harsher than it had been the day before.

Stress, things are not going as they should, Orabella reasoned. Her own internment in her bedroom was proof enough of that. They came to a split hall.

"I'll leave you two now, I must attend to my other duties. As I said, Sloane will help you throughout your day."

"Thank you for taking the time," Orabella said. "If I could trouble you to put this with the outgoing mail for me?" She presented the letters, the top envelope slipping open.

Mrs. Locke took it from her hand. It disappeared into a pocket. "I'll see that it is taken care of. Enjoy your day." She turned down the hall, vanished as swiftly as the letter had.

Orabella and Sloane turned the opposite way. There were open doors hidden in the dark. In the light she saw the beads that had scattered from her dress. They twinkled like stars all along the floorboards. She stopped, picked one up, and rolled it gently in her fingers, careful of the sharp edges while she tried to remember the dinner, the dream. Laughing, their laughter, her arms full.

"Ma'am?" Sloane again.

"Sorry, I got distracted. The beading from my dress needs swept up. Maybe we can save them, but they shouldn't sit, they're sharp."

"Don't worry about it, ma'am."

"It was an old dress," Orabella replied slowly. Sloane didn't respond, and while she sorted out what to say next, they met the stairs. The same that she had traveled with Elias if the beads were any indication.

I should draw myself a map, Orabella thought as she followed Sloane down the passageway.

Her fingertips trailed along the wall, scraps of peeling wallpaper catching them. Orabella stared at the steps, watched her feet disappear, swallowed by their descent. They reached the bottom and she paused. The rooms that were likely once meant for servants were filled with discarded furniture, boxes, books, all manner of things. Windows and doors open for the light. Wherever the maids stayed, it wasn't there. She had seen no other rooms fit to live in and her own were disconnected from anything else.

"This way, ma'am," Sloane called gently, bringing her attention back.

She nodded and followed her past the kitchen, the scent of baking, sweet and warm, filling the hall. Orabella peeked in and caught sight of a middle-aged woman and the blond from the day before. *The cook,* she thought. She and the girl remained focused on their work. Orabella's stomach grumbled at her, reminding her that she hadn't eaten, not really, not well, since early the day before. She moved faster, closing the growing distance between herself and the maid.

Sloane walked into the dining room; the same room from the night before but different now, the magic was gone. The smell of the tallow, flame, and fat lingered and Orabella stopped at the doorway, the one she had left by, and closed her eyes. They were there, that strange, laughing family. Her arms felt full, she felt sick.

"My wife," Elias called, drawing her back. He stood at the table alone, his lips curled in a smile, hand out, waiting. A dream.

"Yes. Good morning, I think, Elias," Orabella replied and stepped forward to join him.

Chapter Eight

The sunlight laid bare what the candlelight hid. The worn floor. The cracks in the windows. The dust on the mirrors. Even the table was dull and shabby, the cloth that had covered it for dinner removed. The meal sat directly on the bare wood with only one guest, her husband, but it was not set for the party of two nor was it the breakfast she expected.

Three small frosted cakes sat in the center surrounded by plates of tarts and cookies like a fairy meal, all laid out in shimmering sugars. Maybe it was the light, maybe she needed more rest, but the edges of everything seemed softer to her than they should be, bright and glimmering just past where the world was clear.

"Come sit beside me, wife," he said, pulling out her chair.

"This is . . ." She paused, glancing back at the desserts before flicking her eyes up to her husband. A bolt of heat shot through her center at his smile, his long fingers tapping the back of the chair. She felt it rise to her face, spread featherlight shivers through her. Orabella looked away, embarrassed, unsure if he had taken his liberties with her. Unsure if as husband and wife there even was such a thing. Unsure how she would feel if he had.

His hand slipped warmly around hers, and lifting it, he kissed her knuckles. His touch was gentle, as it always had been, and she wondered at the bruises. Wondered if that same hand left them, if Elias in passion was a different thing, but he was talking now, and she needed to listen, to follow. "It's a bit formal but this morning we have so many treats to taste. Tomorrow we'll have breakfast in the garden room instead if that pleases you?" At the last word he tilted his head, the question genuine.

"Pleases me?" she repeated, feeling dull, but he only smiled and nodded.

"Yes, I want you to be comfortable and this room is too much for just us but the cakes wouldn't have fit on such a small table."

She didn't remember a table in the room. Just the little one with the little bell. Orabella hadn't looked carefully—maybe it had been moved against a wall. "If it is just us then a smaller table would be better, you're right. But won't your father and sister join us tomorrow? I know I am rather late today." Her thoughts spiraling, spinning, question after question that she swallowed because she must control herself. A repeat of the garden and the carriage. He made her nervous and charmed her in equal measure.

He squeezed her fingers and led her to her seat, where she obliged him and placed herself. "The cook," she finally said, finding her words. "She must have spent hours this morning making all of this."

"It's no trouble. It is what she's paid to do, and for our first morning together here, I think a little fanfare was called for."

"I don't think I've ever seen this many treats on one table." She could smell the sugar, close to cloying but not quite.

"No?" He cut into the nearest cake. White frosting, and inside a cake to match. He placed the slice on her plate. "There was a pie last night but I'm afraid that my family, your family now, didn't save us a single piece. We'll have to make do with this."

Elias picked up her fork and speared a piece of cake, presenting it to her lips as an offering. He leaned close, his scent, ginger and smoke, mingling with the cake that hovered just at her mouth. He waited. Orabella tried to read his expression, remembered his touch in the garden again.

Hunger, she named it and felt it in herself. Twisting and hot all through her body. An intimacy between them that had grown from before. Strange and compelling. She'd not been taught her response but Orabella understood it on instinct.

She opened her lips for him.

He placed the fork delicately onto her tongue, and she closed her lips around it. Sweetness exploded in her mouth, and he cut another bite from her slice, eating it from the same fork before starting the cycle once more.

I should feel embarrassed, ashamed, she started to think, but the words left her as she recognized the warmth in her face, the steady spark that ran along her skin, for what it was. Pleasure. She liked it, she wanted it, and it was all right for her to indulge. Elias was her husband. She turned her face more fully towards him, bold as she'd been in her uncle's sitting room.

Faint stubble ran along his chin; he hadn't shaved but he had groomed. His hair was combed, swept back from his face. His eyes were different than his family's. Pale, not the gems of his sister and father but washed-out sky, nearly glass-gray in the sun. Gray-purple half-moons under them. She lifted her fingers and touched his bottom lid gently. So intimate, thoughtless.

He smiled wider, showing bright teeth before turning his face so that his lips met her palm. He placed a kiss there and the warmth that flowed through her burst in her chest. She tried to remember anything that had happened the night before but there was only that one, crushing kiss in the dark, and everything that came after, anything that came after, was lost.

He captured her hand, nestling his cheek against it, keeping them close. "Orabella." Her name was a breath between them, heavy. His stubble tickled her palm. "Will you kiss me good morning?"

She drew in a sharp breath, her back pulling straight against the chair. The clink of the fork on the plate and then the feel of his arm, snaking around her waist. His body closer now, so close she could see the fine hairs just over his lip. His pale eyes were darker, cast in the shadows created by their bodies.

His thumb stroked the fingers on her captured hand, a familiar touch. She parted her lips to speak, his desire weighing down the air, but there were no words in her throat. Brows pushed together, a frown pulling at her mouth. Elias's lashes rose, and his hand dropped away, releasing her.

"Last night . . ." She stumbled with her words, knowing only that she needed to say something but not what. "I'm not sure, I had too much to drink, and I don't . . ."

"Last night?" There was laughter in the question.

Orabella's stomach sank. She was inexperienced and drunk.

"Last night," he repeated, "you did nothing. We did nothing. You could barely stand, and I am not a monster."

And there, finally, was the hot jittery roll of shame in her. Her first test as his wife and she had failed. "I'm so sorry, that wasn't . . . I don't usually behave that way!"

"Yes, my Orabella is careful. She watches herself, holds herself. And maybe I am rushing things. There will be other mornings."

Her center tightened. Not a thought but an emotion, brief and strong; she had displeased this man. She slipped her hands over his cheeks, her fingers numb with nervous cold, and pressed her lips against his, determined. Bold as he saw her.

There had been men and kisses before, stolen in gardens and corners, but she was not adept at it: Orabella had been kissed, she had not kissed. Her attempt was clumsy, artless, but Elias responded. His arms flew around her, drawing her from her chair to pull her body to his.

He tasted like the cake. Sweetness flooded her mouth and under that was the ginger of his candies. Elias's hand tilted her head, changed the angle at which their mouths met, but he didn't release her. His tongue, hot and slow, moved over hers, rewarded her efforts with his own. Hunger met with hunger, birthed pleasure between them. A flood of it all through her that pooled low in her belly and spilled tickling drops lower still. She shifted and, gasping, he released her, a smile on his lips.

"So, my wife does want me." Purring, pleased as she was pleased.

"I-I'm sorry. I'm not used to this," she stammered.

He silenced her with the press of his lips. "I look forward to you being used to me, then. I can't wait to see more of you. But for now you'll have to return to your seat or I will not wait."

She scrambled off, graceless; searing pinpricks of *want* traveled over her throat and cheeks. She settled in her chair, tried to pull herself together. "You are very forward. I wasn't aware you would have any passion for me when I agreed to this marriage."

"Did I not make my passions clear to you in the carriage when we were finally alone?" he teased.

Orabella smiled at the memory of it, that first touch of warmth. "Before then, I meant."

Elias picked up the fork again. Holding it to her lips as if nothing more had passed between them than words. She opened her mouth and leaned forward, taking the bite without pause. Humming, satisfied and low, vibrated from him. "This is a marriage of convenience," he admitted, taking a bite of the cake before offering her the next, "but I would not have sought you out if I did not want you. I told you, you have been at the back of my thoughts for these past two years."

"Then why did it take those two years to court me?" The question came out more accusing than she meant it, still jittery from the kiss. She reached for the cookies laid out on a tray to keep from looking at his face. To help her calm down. "And the room? You clearly meant for someone to come here with you; what if I had said no?"

"Do you think I didn't try?" The question came flat with that sharp edge she'd heard in the carriage, with his family, but never again directed at her.

"Did you?" There had never been another suitor, not a serious one. Elias had been the only man to come to the house for her hand. There was no reason for him to be denied, and if he had come before, there would have been no reason to rush their marriage. They could have courted, had at least a small wedding, a dress of her own. Time to understand each other better.

"I did. It was a simple matter to find out who you were, you are . . ." He paused, a playful smile on his lips. "Quite distinctive. But your uncle rejected my request. It wasn't until he needed what I could provide that he agreed." He pressed a tart into his mouth.

"That makes me sound as if I am property. Traded for goods and services."

"How your uncle treated you is not how I will treat you."

"You intend to spoil me beyond measure, I believe is how you said it." She bit into a cookie, the buttery body flaking onto her tongue as she turned to him.

"Yes." In the sunlight he nearly glowed, the gold of afternoon, and she realized she didn't know what time it was, earlier or later. "The only woman I would have brought here is you. If you had said no to me that day, I would have come the next and every day after until you said yes."

"And if I never did?"

"You would. I had your room prepared in advance. I, too, needed to prepare for you."

I wonder why he hid such a face behind a beard? The parlor felt like it had happened years before, not days. Guilt that she could not say the same pushed her eyes away. Regardless of her attraction, Orabella had said yes because it was the only option, and she could not see a future where her choices would be better, not worse.

"My door was locked," Orabella said quickly, changing the course of their conversation.

"For your safety," Elias explained. "I didn't want you wandering in the night. You don't know the house, you'll be lost. As you said yourself, you had too much to drink. Imagine what could have happened. You must keep the door locked at night. To keep it shut, for your safety."

"My safety? I understand why you didn't stay last night but surely that will resolve itself soon and you will be there, won't you?" She knew the truth as soon as she asked. There was only one closet in the room. It held only her clothes.

"It pleases me to hear that you want me. But no, even after we are together, I will not stay with you. I have night terrors and I will keep you up all night if I do."

"I don't remember you having any issue on our trip."

"I have a certain medicine to control them, but I do not like the effects of it and would rather not rely on it if I do not have to. It upsets my stomach. It is easier to spend our evenings apart."

A tidy excuse that she had no reason to doubt—still, it struck

Orabella as odd. The same oddness that she felt when he signed his name. She thought back to him on their trip. "Is that why you didn't speak much while we traveled?"

"Yes. But your conversation during that time made things easier for me."

"I wish you had told me. I thought you just had a fondness for ginger candies. There was no reason to keep it a secret. But that doesn't explain why I need to lock my bedroom. Are there bandits wandering the halls?" She chuckled, rolled her eyes.

"No! The only people who walk these halls are the family and those that serve us," he said, matching her with a laugh of his own. "It's a practical matter. The house is old and drafty and a gust can push the door open. The bolt from the lock will keep it closed. You don't want to leave space for night creatures to slip in and nibble on your toes." Teasing, charming.

"I've felt the draft. I have to remember to close the curtains tonight." It made sense, showed his care. She took small bites out of her cookie and turned what he'd said over in her mind. There was nothing wrong, but it was all so different than she'd thought it would be. "Will you lock me in every night?"

Elias's expression was soft, gently troubled. A frown. "Every night that I leave you, yes. But"—his voice dropped, quiet and unsure—"I have a key for you. Keep it on your person, so you can escape if you need." Elias reached into his pocket and presented the gift.

It was a match for the one that she had seen Mrs. Locke use. A deep iron color, nondescript in every way. She picked it up from his palm, turning it in her fingers, surprised at its plainness. *What a strange choice of words*, she wanted to say but instead she said, "I don't know why but I expected it to be silver."

Elias surprised her with a kiss. His deep, consuming, needy kiss.

Hungry lips and tongue searched for hers and she let him consume her, happy for the touch, wanting more of it. In the fist of her hand, the key pressed into her palm, secret, safe.

"Keep it close, it's important that you don't lose it and don't let anyone else know you have it. Your maid, that girl, Sloane? She will come to your room with Mrs. Locke in the morning. No one else."

"All right," she said, confused. He seemed so serious, and she missed the ease of things before they spoke of the door. She was sorry to have brought it up. She turned the conversation again, clumsily, as she slipped the key into her pocket. "How did you know about my uncle's debts?"

A different smile stretched at his lips, played in his eyes. He handed her a glass of juice, waited for her to drink before he spoke again. "I like to play cards too. There are only so many games in Bristol. And I would remember the man that kept the woman who haunted me locked away."

"You accuse my uncle of locking me up and you've really done it." She meant it as a joke; thoughtless and clumsy as it was, she wanted the ease back between them. He looked away and she remembered why she had changed the subject to begin with. "I wasn't locked away," she continued quickly, "I visited with other families quite often. I went to church. I wasn't some sort of princess from a fairy story." *But perhaps I am now*, she thought, drawing her back up straighter. "So, should I expect one day to sell my own daughter to pay off my husband's debts? Tell me now, perhaps I can start hiding away whatever spending money you give me."

He laughed and bent to her, kissing her cheek. "No, dearest. That is nothing you have to worry about. I like to play cards, from time to time. Your uncle had a different relationship with them. And I do not lose." He took her hand in his, placing it over his heart. "Our daughter would be precious to me. But if it settles your mind then I promise never to play them again."

It seemed too easy, the answer too compact, and her free hand twisted in her skirts even as she forced her next question out. "If you are so well off then why must we live here? Why not back in Bristol? Or London? Or anywhere else?"

"Do you not like it here?" he asked softly, his thumb working as always across her fingers.

I don't care for it, should I say? We've only just been married, will he be upset? "I don't know," she answered, finally, keeping the truth to herself. "It is very different than what I am accustomed to, and I've only been here for the one night."

"It's just a house. You will settle and be comfortable, I'm sure of it. You'll find things to fill your days." As he spoke he swept a hand over her cheek, catching a stray curl and tucking it behind her ear. "I prefer your hair down. Will you take it down for me?"

He released her hand and lifted his arms. Curious, she stared as he reached over her head and unpinned the bun she wore, placing the stray bits of metal on the table next to her plate. The curls fell over her shoulders and down her back to float, like a cloud, all about her. "This is not what you were expecting, I don't think." She laughed as she looked at him for approval, expecting him to mirror her amusement in the thick tumble of hair that made its own way about her shoulders.

His expression remained soft. "Wear it out or in a braid from now on. I won't make any other requests on your appearance, but I do love to see your hair. Your eyes are beautiful, you are beautiful, more so when all these curls are framing you."

"Elias," she breathed, flattered. "You don't have to say such things."

"I do, you're my wife. Your comfort is all I care for."

The night scratched at her memory. His words had a falseness, a sort of conditional truth to them when played against it. He had said such words before at that table but it had been different. The same but different. In the light now, alone, she wanted to take them for what they appeared to be. She wanted him to be what he appeared to be. They were already married. Orabella had already come to this place. "We should get to know each other better!" she reminded him.

He smiled and presented her with another tart. "We will. I'm afraid there's no one to visit here but the renters, and they're all hard, solitary people. No card games or teas. There's little to do but talk to one another."

"Is that why you spent so much time in Bristol?" she asked, matching his light tone.

"No, it was my work. I'm afraid I'm quite boring, Orabella."

"I don't think so, but wait! Mrs. Hanover, my aunt's friend, told me that there were people who took summer here. Her cousins. I can't remember their names but I'm sure my aunt will want to make an introduction."

He pursed his lips and a cloud came over him before clearing, and the smile returned. "Yes, there are a few families that come here to escape the city but their homes are farther away than you would think. Oxbury is a small town but the lands that count towards it stretch quite far. Most, actually all of those families are across the woods. By the time your carriage reached them, it would be time to head for home. We do not spend much time visiting."

"I see," she said. "It's fine, I suppose. I am not known for my affection of visiting."

"Are you disappointed?" he asked.

"No, there's no reason. I don't know them. Am I to eat all of this?" Clumsy still, but trying. She had no knack for charm or coyness. Her ears burned, and she turned back to the table, focused on the fairy buffet of sweets, and tried to sound composed. "I thought there would be more people at breakfast. You have such a large family."

"They will be up and about soon. They'll finish this off before they leave, I assure you. We were up late celebrating, and besides, the morning meal will always be for us. You will take lunch with Claresta and we will eat with Hastings for dinner."

"They're leaving so soon? I thought I would get a chance to meet them personally. There wasn't any time for introductions last night. I'm sorry, I was so late to dinner. I overslept."

"You were fine," Elias said, dismissing her apology. "Everything was fine. Think no more of it, Orabella."

His words had the weight of an order, given gently but still given.

"Claresta . . . I'm sorry to ask this, I don't mean to come off as rude, but she didn't seem very warm when we met before. I don't think she likes me very much."

"She'll have to get used to you." His voice was hard, all the charm gone from it. "Eat more," he said, the gentleness returning as he dropped the matter. "It's already late as it is."

"Can you sing?" she asked suddenly.

"What? I suppose so, I'm not very good." He stumbled, caught, for the first time, off guard by her. He was flustered but soft and she liked it.

"Last night they said . . ." She tried to remember. "They called you a bird, a robin!"

He shook his head. "Think nothing of that, a joke."

Orabella started to apologize but a forkful of cake stopped her.

Chapter Nine

Orabella stared at the needlepoint in her fingers and tried to make sense of the pattern. There were flowers but no way to know what it was ultimately to be. She wasn't sure if the bit of brown was meant for a tree branch or a basket or a little animal. The maid or nurse who had started the project had not copied any image to the cloth and left behind the orphaned stitches, unfinished and forgotten.

"Finish it however you wish," Mrs. Locke said when she shoved the work into Orabella's hands, wrongly assuming that she would be skilled enough to make something of it. But Orabella was no good with embroidery, she was a knitter. If it had been a blanket square or sock she could puzzle it out on her own but the hoop and its colorful stitches were a mystery. It had been hours, she was sure, and she had only managed to add two more stiches. Plucked them out, tried again.

Time felt strange. She was sure it had been late, near afternoon when she shared cake with Elias—if not already the second half of the day—but she'd been sitting in the room with her sister-in-law and the sun was still the cold white of morning and did not move across the floor.

Claresta sat in a rocking chair that did not rock in front of the window, and like the sun, cold and white, she did not move either. In the light she looked delicate and false. Like a doll, silent and still, waiting for a child to come play with her. Her hair, shimmering in the sun, fell around her shoulders, spilled down her front. Her eyes stared straight ahead, unblinking, over just parted lips. If not for the rise and fall of her chest, Orabella had been wrong that first meeting. It was Claresta who was the corpse.

A piece of unfinished needlework rested on Claresta's lap as well, her fingers folded and still over it. Hers was meant to be much simpler. A child's learning piece. Something even Orabella would have been able to work through.

Orabella looked out the window, the same one Claresta stared through, and tried again to figure out the time. They were alone, there was no one else to ask, no clocks on the wall, and Claresta hadn't responded to her greetings. Questions about mystery needlework and time of day would likely go similarly unanswered.

There was almost nothing to the room at all. Decorated sparsely, no vanity, no wardrobe. Claresta's sheets, pillows, and blanket were all a downy white color. No rug on her floor but it was smooth and kept well. The glass in the window she stared so intently into was clean and unbroken but there were no curtains to cover it. A hospital room in nearly every way but for the wall.

Three of the four walls were painted stark white. The fourth, though, was entirely different. Straight across from the foot of her bed was a mural.

A forest where magical creatures hid behind trees and played with people shrunk down in size, with winged fairies and elves and children that grew from flowers. Fantastical, nonsense things. Everywhere

Orabella's eye landed there was something new and unexpected. Little stories inside the story. Impossible to take in the entirety of it, it was too much detail. She settled on the small stories, got lost in them, and finally decided not to look at all. But Orabella couldn't help but peek as she waited for the morning to end and each time she found a different little creature, a different little story. After the eternity in silence with her sister-in-law, she was no longer sure whether the painting wasn't really moving when she looked away.

The artist had spent so much time and had such skill. If it was not life, then it was a close proxy for it.

The painted trees were thick and dark, covered in lush green leaves where an impossible assortment of fruit grew. Oranges next to melons nestled in a ring of berries, apples and pears on the same branch. Songbirds in wild, bright colors flew between them, mingled with birds of prey that held protesting mice and rabbits. Gems instead of rocks covered the ground below between mushrooms with beautiful caps. There was no sky, only the forest. And between all the stones and trees and fungi there were the animals and the fairies and all the small people.

Cats lounged on branches and hunted below mushroom caps, mice scurrying along gripping tiny lanterns, holding hands in long lines for safety. Foxes prowled and danced, joined the hunt and avoided the dogs at the far edge of the painting. Others were more fantastic. A unicorn who sat getting their mane braided. The scaly wing and rolling neck of a dragon with a plume of smoke. The lion-and-eagle combination of a griffin. And many more she could not name with bright eyes and sharp teeth. Orabella did not remember ever reading about such things but it had been years and years since she'd read children's stories.

And among them all, the fairies.

They were pale and done with such variety no two were alike

though they did all have the same look, the same manner about them. The artist had managed to make them, with paint, glow against their surroundings. Their small features, done with care, bright eyes and stained-glass wings. They wore strips of cloth or nothing at all and flew around the animals. Played among the trees, the flower children, and shrunken proper people.

It was beautiful. Even so, she couldn't look at it for long, The image was too much all at once and threatened to swallow her attention whole, so she stole glances, worked on the piece in her hands, and forced her attention to find other things to hold her.

"The sun is very nice," Orabella tried, again. "Spring will be here soon."

A doll. A mannequin. Claresta did not answer.

Careless in her annoyance, Orabella punctured the cloth with the needle, its tip penetrating Orabella's finger, lodging itself in her thumb. "Christ!" she snapped in pain and frustration, dropping it all on the floor, giving up.

She brought the injured digit up and inspected it as a bead of deep-red blood formed on the tip. She licked it off, salt and copper. A flash of memory, a plate with little cubes of meat. *No*, she thought, and went to the window. Colder in front of the glass than it had been in the chair. The same draft that plagued her room, that swept through the house according to Elias, was there too. She made a note to bring a shawl even though the Lady of the house did not appear to need one herself.

Claresta did not stir at her approach, and for a moment, Orabella thought of snatching the useless needle from her hand and stabbing Claresta with it as she had stabbed herself. In her mind, the needle sank into Claresta's skin like wax.

Orabella lifted her hand and gently passed her knuckles over Claresta's cheek. To prove to herself that Claresta Blakersby was a living being, flesh and blood, just like her. The skin was cool but alive under Orabella's touch.

"What are you looking at?" Orabella sang, pulling her hand away, embarrassed at her intimacy.

The room overlooked the garden she had seen through the sitting room where they first met. From the vantage point on the second floor, she could see the lay of it, more of its hidden expanse.

Her uncle's garden was nothing compared to the massive space that spread out below her. Multiple paved walks that turned and twisted between many plots meant for an abundance of flowers. Statues, like the ones her aunt had never quite purchased, were spread throughout. Gods and mystical creatures in silent play. There were walls and from above she could see the many private spaces that they created. The garden went on beyond the curves of the manor. There was magic. A fairy-tale garden, fit for a princess. The mural made real.

But it had all fallen into the same disrepair as the manor. There were no flowers, only twisted branches, bare from the winter, that might have once been beautiful but now were brittle fingers that overgrew their assigned spaces. The walks were cracked and broken. For every statue that stood in one piece, there were two that did not, parts scattered all over the ground.

"Oh, how sad. Do you remember when it was kept up?" she asked, turning back to her silent companion.

The woman had moved.

Not much, just her blue eyes focused on Orabella before moving away. Just her eyes. *Follow me*, they said, and Orabella, good girl, good wife, good sister, did.

She turned back to the window. The forest.

Tall, thick trees with heavy branches. A trail led from the garden proper into them. *There must be a space to picnic*, because it was all she knew to do in a wooded place, but the idea left her cold. It didn't seem like a place where people would eat. Again her fairy stories—she remembered wolves and bears and that there were more things that could eat you, as she looked for whatever it was Claresta was so intent on.

Nothing but green, celadon and malachite, evening mist in the afternoon, and then, "A deer." Whispered as if her voice would startle the creature from two floors up, through glass and stone.

A doe, tawny brown with thin legs and graceful neck, head held high and still but for her ears, which swung slowly from side to side. She bent, lowering her head to the grass and growth at the edge of the forest.

Hand to belly, nausea rose with memory, couldn't be avoided now. Orabella could see only long, limp legs and neck, golden hooves. The fawn. The wedding night. Her thigh ached with memory. The forest churned, turned from green to sparkling black. Tallow, melting, dripping in the air, turning the spring oily against her skin.

An explosion, a cracking boom that scared the birds from their branches. The doe reared, turned, took flight back to the forest.

Too much cake, she thought at her rolling stomach, pushing away from the legs, the hooves, the single dark eye. Let that be a dream, let that be too much drink. Let it stay in the past. A man holding a rifle came into view. His brown, nearly black hair was uncovered. Orabella couldn't see his features but the hair alone said he wasn't family. Elias had the darkest of their hair and his was cider light, only a few steps away from blond.

"A groundskeeper," she said, pressing herself closer to the glass to get a better look at him. The old panes shifted under the pressure of her fingers. Loose, in need of repair like everything else in the manor. Orabella pulled back for fear of falling through them, tumbling out of the window and ending on the paved ground below.

"Not a very good one." She laughed to try to bring some lightness back into the room, the morning.

"Not a very good what?" Mrs. Locke asked.

Orabella pressed back against the shuddering window, swallowing her startled scream, the glass making shrieking protests in her stead but holding all the same. She jumped back before it had a chance to give under her. "Apologies, I didn't hear you come in. There was a man. In the garden."

Mrs. Locke sniffed the air. "That would be Cullen, more than likely. Pay him no mind. It's time for lunch."

"I meant groundskeeper!" she said, wanting to clear things up before they got the impression that she was unfair to the help. "But it's a good deal of work. I did not consider my words and I'm sure he's a fine gentleman."

Mrs. Locke sniffed again. "He is none of your concern. Have a seat. Your lunch is ready."

Her words were hard, formal, an order, and Orabella stiffened at them, offended and unsure in her offense. She had only just arrived, the woman was old and, she reasoned, likely just blunt. "I'm sorry but I'm still full of that delightful breakfast and will simply not be able to eat another bite."

Sloane had returned, the first time Orabella had seen her in the days, weeks, endless moments since she'd deposited her for her visit with Claresta. Her arms were heavy with a serving tray and another girl trailed behind her. *Amanda*, Orabella reminded herself. That was the girl.

"You need more than cakes. You must have meat," Mrs. Locke said.

She took her seat; she was new, she shouldn't argue. A flurry of activity. Tables appeared from the air, a place was set before her, another for Claresta.

Sloane sat a covered dish in front of her on the table and lifted the lid.

The scent of meat filled the room. Rich, savory, laden with spice, the whole of the night tickled at her memories, teased her with nausea. Swallow, swallow. "It smells lovely." Cubes of meat, cut just so, suspended in a stew.

Across from her, the maid picked up Claresta's spoon and began to feed her. The woman opened her mouth obediently, her eyes straight ahead.

As Elias had fed Orabella.

No, that was affection. I have to stop all these stories. I'm making things up. She picked up her own spoon. The food filled her mouth. Sloane waited by her side, hands clasped in front of her. She ate until the spoon hit the bottom of the bowl. "I suppose I was more hungry than I thought." She laughed but no one joined in. The dishes were collected, the tables removed.

"Please wait a moment, we'll return with tea and then you and the Lady will both take your afternoon rest," Mrs. Locke explained.

"No, thank you." The words rushed from her mouth, stumbled over one another. There was a system here, she should follow it, learn its rhythm. She knew that, and still—"I slept very well last night."

"Dinner is late here. You'll need the rest," the old woman said.

"No." Orabella stood, smoothing her skirts. She was being difficult; she smiled to seem less so. "I do not wish to interrupt Claresta's schedule, of course, so I'll take my leave now." She turned to Claresta. "It has been such a lovely time. I'll see you tomorrow."

"Where are you going?" Orabella jumped at the old woman's voice. Even in her uncle's house, where the help cared nothing for her, they did not question her. More disturbing than the surprise came the sick realization that she did not have an answer.

"A walk," her lips supplied. "In the garden to see what can be done to bring it back."

"Absolutely not! The garden is not fit for—"

She searched for the drive that led her to the sitting room in her uncle's house, the boldness that Elias praised. "I used to walk the streets of Bristol on my own. I'm sure I can handle this garden. I'll run if I see any bears. I'll find my way downstairs. I should learn the lay of the house."

If I can make it downstairs it should be simple enough to find my way out. She stood at the threshold already, a breath and she'd be in the hall, away from the doll and the window.

"Wait, miss!" Sloane, tray still in her arms, hurrying to catch up. "I'm to accompany you!"

"Of course, that's fine," she said as Sloane joined her, and it was. She was glad of it: the halls, now that she stood in them, were darker than she thought. "Mrs. Locke, you should get a cart for the meals from now on. Instead of making the girls hold them." To endear them to her.

"A cart?" The woman's cheeks were red, her lips a tight line.

"I'll speak to my husband on the matter. It is such a small thing." She smiled, hoping the old woman saw it as friendly, saw her efforts to help, not to be above. "I'll take my leave."

Orabella turned, nearly dashing from the still room and down the hall.

"The fastest way to the garden is that way, ma'am, but," Sloane said, pointing down the hall, "we'll have to stop and get your cloak and that's in the other direction. We'll take the kitchen door. I have to go there anyway." She turned away and began to walk.

Chapter Ten

This place is full of twists and turns, isn't it? I've been trying to get my bearings but I haven't had much time." They walked past more open rooms made storage and others that were closed tight. The light came through the dusty windows, leading them on. The hall split off but they stayed straight. "This is a different way than how I came up."

"Yes, ma'am. It's very difficult at first but if you just stay on the main paths, you'll be fine. The other parts of the house aren't safe, you know, in bad repair. Just stay to where the doors are open. If you see closed doors, more than open ones, then you shouldn't go there." Polite, stiff. A version of Mrs. Locke.

Orabella laughed. She couldn't help it. "Keep to the path? It's a house, the woods are outside! I'm sure it's not as bad as you're making it out to be. Just a little polish and some new boards and this place would be a wonder. Besides, that first night you took me down a way with no open doors, I think. It was very dark. And please don't call me ma'am. My name is fine, I'm not so much older than you."

"No, there were doors open, ma'am, but some of the windows up here are boarded up. They try to repair them when they break on the front part of the manor but back here, no one will see if it's just panels. And it wouldn't be proper to call you by your name, ma'am."

"Then 'miss' for now, until we're better acquainted." A fair compromise. "How long have you worked here?" They reached the steps. A square of afternoon light waited at the bottom.

"Since I was sixteen . . . miss. I'm twenty-two now." Sloane took the steps quickly, sure of her footing.

Orabella followed, reaching for a railing that wasn't there, her hand landing on the wall, her foot on the first step then carefully on the next. "No wonder you're so used to this place. I'll grow familiar with it in a few weeks."

"I'm sure, miss," Sloane agreed, stepping down into the hall.

Orabella blinked in the bright light. She had expected to come out near the kitchen and dining room but she did not recognize the paintings on the walls of the first room they passed. She broke off from Sloane, too curious not to stop, to stare. It was kept better, the floor cleaner, but the window was covered—the light came dimly from the hall, stolen from the room on the other side. It was enough.

She remembered them, like a dream. Realized in oils was Elias's family, her family now. Jeweled eyes, curious features that all seemed alike. More people on the walls than had been around the table.

There was a large picture missing, the space lighter than the wallpaper around it. *It must still be here. They don't appear to sell anything, I wonder why they moved it*, she thought idly, her eyes dancing from face to face before settling on one.

It was a man. He looked closer to Elias except his hair was true gold and his eyes were the same bright blue as Claresta's. The painter had done the job well, the same perhaps who had done the mural in Claresta's room, the skill was there in both. She reached out to touch it, expecting it to be, somehow, warm, but on contact it was just paint, dusty and cracking. The illusion shattered.

Is that what his nose would be? She hummed, tracing the line with her eyes. The man in the painting had the same jaw as Elias but the mouth was different, thinner. His cheeks were broader and held more color than her husband's. *Well, maybe that was the painter's prerogative.*

The door slammed shut, the room turned midnight.

Orabella spun, moved against the wall in fright, a frame pressing against her back, biting into her flesh through the fabric of her dress. She shifted, it fell with a thunk onto the floor, and a squeak, high with surprise, squeezed out of her throat.

A draft, she reminded herself. *The house is drafty, it's why I'm to lock the door at night.* She pulled in a deep breath, filled her lungs with dust and mold, the house, and stepped forward.

Something moved, thumped. *Rodents*, she thought. Elias had said as much over breakfast. They sounded huge but mice always sounded larger in the walls than they were. She took another step.

Her hair caught, held her. After it was freed by Elias that morning, she'd never gotten around to doing anything else with it, and she'd forgotten until that moment that it was still out. Now it snagged, pinning her to the room. She held perfectly still, began to reach up to break the strands and free herself. The air felt alive and thick, smelled of dirt and age.

Something shuffled, closer. Hot air on her check, a breath.

Orabella screamed then. Jerked away from whatever had captured her hair, felt strands ripped from her scalp, but she ran for the door, where she thought it should be, and met only the wall.

"Sloane! Sloane!" she screamed as she felt along the wall, searching for a knob.

Straight in front of her, the door swung open, pushing her back onto the floor. The light so weak before blinding bright then.

A man stood in the frame, towering over her. A specter. "You shouldn't be here," he said.

Orabella's heart pounded and she felt another scream in her. Recognition came swiftly. *Hastings.* "I'm sorry, sir, I didn't mean any harm, I was just—the paintings," she tried to explain. Her skirts were covered in dust, filthy.

"Ma'am!" Sloane's voice shot across the room. "I'm so sorry, sir, she wandered away."

"Keep track of your charge. What are you doing in this wing?"

Orabella looked at Sloane, tray still in her arms, face red. "It was my fault," Orabella said. "Sloane's taking me to the garden, I need some air. This was the best path. I wandered off."

He snorted, a wet rattling sound. He looked different in the hall. His eyes were wet and rimmed with red from illness or just age. A smell, medicinal and slightly of mildew, rose from him. His back was bent forward, his head seemed too heavy for his neck, and the wispy strands of hair that adorned his crown hung limply around his sagging face, revealing a pale dome under it. His hands were large and she could imagine they would have been as strong as Elias's when he was a younger man, but now they were age-spotted, with thin fingers to match the rest of him. "Yes, it's good for you to get outside. Healthy. It's fine."

He held out his hand for her. Orabella took it, watched hers disappear. The grip was stronger than she would have thought. Strong enough to leave bruises. Her thigh ached, a reminder. Hastings said nothing as he helped her to her feet. Standing, steady, he released her, clearing the path for her to leave the room. He closed the door behind him, stalked back through the halls, no farewells.

"You weren't to go into the rooms with the closed doors!"

Sloane scolded, her voice low and panicked. "It's dangerous! The floors aren't stable in some of them."

"It wasn't closed! The door was open when I went in, the draft . . ." Orabella whispered back, guilt rising.

"You're lucky you weren't hurt. You could have gone through the floor! But the Master says it's all right for us to come through here and it is your first real day. Just be more careful." Sloane calmed.

The title sounded strange. Her uncle had been "sir" or "Mr. Mumthrope." *You're the bride*, the wedding night again, her memory was falling, bits and pieces, back into place. *The Old Master*, they called him but she wouldn't. She refused. "Is there a basement?" she asked, ignoring it. She would call him father, father-in-law, sir, anything but that.

Sloane shrugged. "I've never been down there."

"I see." Orabella nodded and looked back to the room. The light, weak, was enough once again. She looked back at the door while she smoothed her hair. A draft, a nail, a few mice, nothing to be afraid of. The house was old, she shouldn't let her imagination run away with her. She pulled the curls back, twisted them into a quick braid. "The tray must be getting heavy," she said, turning back to Sloane. "Let's hurry on, then." She wiped at her face where her mind said she had felt breath. It had only been a draft. "I won't get lost this time, promise."

Sloane looked doubtful but continued their journey despite it.

"Is this where Elias spends his days?" Orabella asked, looking into the room where the light came through. An office, mostly empty but still functional. The area of the house kept up, like her rooms. *Is there a library? Maybe I could find something to read. Or not. All the books have probably gone to mold if there are any.*

"Of course not. Mr. Robinson is tending to the renters."

"Robinson?" she asked. *A little bird.*

"Oh, I suppose they've changed it to Blakersby now, my apologies. I've been calling him Robinson for so long. A mistake."

"Is he not what he says? Is this not his family?"

Sloane turned, eyes big and round on her face. "Oh no, ma'am! He's of the family! The Master's son! I don't know much about the history. He's always just been Mr. Robinson. I'm sorry, I don't know anything, and Mrs. Locke did correct me, I'm careless."

"It's all right. I understand, I'm very careless myself, so please, don't worry too much over it. I'll ask him. Families are complicated things."

Sloane smiled, nodded in agreement, and it felt like Orabella had gained some ground between them. Sloane looked behind her every few steps as they made their way through the halls of the lower floor, moving away from Hastings's offices, in and out of ownerless halls in varying states of disrepair. Only a few minutes passed but already Orabella was tired of the walls, the floors. There was a sameness in their tattered state that bored and suffocated her.

The smell shifted from dust to something more pleasant. Bread and seasoning. As sudden as any other turn in the house, the kitchen.

"I'm returning this tray, Maggie!" Sloane sang, setting the tray down on the large table at the center of the room.

The kitchen was larger than the one she was used to in Bristol. The oven was in use, the smell of baking filled the air. Bread, but it seemed late in the day to make it. In Bristol the bread was made in the morning but it was not Bristol.

There were multiple work stations; the room was clearly meant to accommodate a robust staff for the types of large parties that a manor the size of Korringhill must have been created to hold, but those days were long over—but not in that room.

It was maintained.

The walls were dark and spotted but not with mold or mildew. It was soot; the smell was fire and good things. Bread and meat.

A woman came out of the pantry, arms full of foodstuffs meant for dinner. She had a stout form, brown hair shot with gray and pulled back into a wiry ponytail. "Manda just went to fetch water to do the washing." She paused, eyes settled on Orabella. "The wife."

"Yes, my name is Orabella. Are you the cook? It's nice to meet you. Your cakes this morning were lovely. I wish I could have eaten them all."

"They'll be eaten, everything in this house is." Maggie put her bounty down, sorted out the vegetables, and began chopping. "Don't get used to it. I hear you're from the city. We're well stocked here but nothing fancy, not like for the wedding. Mr. Robinson had enough ordered for the night but we don't have it in the larder for cakes and tarts every morning."

Robinson again. "I wouldn't dream. I'm sure whatever you're used to preparing is more than suitable for my tastes." Orabella didn't want to impose, didn't want to make any more disturbances in the house past what she'd already caused. They would already gossip about her; it wouldn't do to give them more to speak on.

"It's getting late, miss." Sloane, free from her burden, appeared at her side again.

"It was nice to meet you," Orabella said as Sloane pulled her away, eager to continue on.

In the halls again, Orabella could see that it *was* late. Not yet evening but later in the afternoon than she would have thought a moment before. Time was so strange, and without the movement of deliveries and streetlamps, she couldn't track it. She was losing minutes, hours.

"Where are we?" she asked, her shoes making tapping sounds

on the bare wood floor. Carpet, she was learning, was sparse. Removed in patches by time and the neglect that covered the manor like a blanket.

"This is the northwest wing. We keep the coats here. There's an exit straight to the stables and servants' quarters."

"Ah, so there is order to all of this. Maybe I can draw a map. You don't all live here? In the house? How odd, there's more than enough space."

"No, we stay in a smaller building, about a mile away. We leave after dinner is cleaned up and no one is back until Maggie and Manda come in the morning." She paused for a moment. "I suppose I'll have to come up with them now too. To help you with your dressing."

"You don't have to. I get along just fine on my own." The idea made her uncomfortable, to have the girl at her beck and call. Orabella didn't need it; she didn't want it.

Sloane stopped, her hand on a door. "No, miss, I have to. I'm to be your personal girl."

The matter had already been decided, probably before Orabella had arrived, when it was clear that Elias was going to bring back a wife. It was true, then, he really would not have taken her refusal.

The smell came down the hall, slow and thick, chased away the last of the bread and seasonings. Dusty, a little like rot but dry, a little like mildew but not. Overwhelmingly old. Orabella coughed, waving her hand in front of her face, which did nothing at all to stop the air from filling her lungs and mouth. A film covered her tongue, soaked up her saliva, and she fought the urge to spit on the floor to be free of it. Sloane walked forward without stopping, into the waiting room, straight for a closet on the other side of the entryway while Orabella stood gasping at the door.

Wide windows stretched nearly to the ceiling letting in bright sunlight. There were no curtains and the despair was laid out for anyone to see.

On tables, chairs, and in an old bronze tub were piled coats. Jackets of all makes for men and women alike. Coats and cloaks in different colors, with linings of silk and trimmings of fur. What seemed like hundreds of coats, all thrown together on every available surface and spilling onto the floor. As fine as the one Elias had gifted to her but left to rot, unused and forgotten by owners who were no longer there.

She walked to the nearest one. Thoughtlessly, impulsively, she ran her finger over the dark wool collar. It fell apart, turning to dust and threads. A coat made of dirt, the enchantment all worn off. The source of the smell was no longer a mystery: the coats were rotting where they sat. Gently she turned the topmost one over, a man's jacket, younger than many but still out of fashion by a decade. It seemed orange at first but the hidden side of it was brown, close to her skin. It had sat so long the sun had washed the color out.

The pile moved. She stumbled back, dragging the coat with her, the lapel trapped in her fists, exposing the horror underneath. The coats rippled and shifted, threatened to tumble down and slide across the floor to where she held their brethren in her fingers. Pink and gray tentacles reached from them, whipping through the air before disappearing.

"Mice!" Orabella nearly screamed. Their nests disturbed, they scrambled from the pile, found tunnels in the cloth, and disappeared again.

"Are you all right, miss?" Sloane asked, returning to her side, quickly.

"Sloane, what is this place?"

"It's the coat room, miss. I imagine every rich house has one."

Sloane took her hand again and pulled her to the coat cabinet, the only one in the room. Made from wood, cedar by the smell, earthy but sharp.

Not like this, she started to say, but the maid had turned back, plucked the cloak that Elias had given her from the rest, and shook it out.

"I think this one is yours, miss? I heard it was a very fine cloak Mr. Robinson gave you," she said, presenting it to her.

They're already gossiping. "Who do all these others belong to? I thought it was only myself, Elias, and my father- and sister-in-law. This is too many even for the guests." *And too old.*

Sloane shrugged, walked around her back, and placed the garment over Orabella's shoulders. "The family has already gone, miss. These have always been here. The Master and Mr. Robinson put theirs in the cabinet and there's no need to worry about these others."

Orabella sputtered. "They're a haven for rats."

"I haven't seen any," Sloane said.

"But there was just dozens of them," she said, turning back to the coat pile. The still-dark side of the coat she'd grabbed faced the sun but the mice were gone, quick as they had come. "Were they that fast? How did you not see them?"

Sloane smiled apologetically and shrugged again, the movement her answer and explanation for everything. Orabella clenched her teeth, frustration making her muscles tense, chasing the rattling shock of the mice away.

Orabella fiddled with the tie at her throat. She sniffed; her nose had begun to run from the dust. The smell was receding at least, or she was growing used to it. *Good, I'll have to survive here with it.* She sighed.

"Show me the gardens," she said, resigned, needing to move

away from the frustration of it all. The day was not going as she imagined her first in her new home would.

Pressing for answers about the rules, the house, and the people in it would do no good. Sloane would just shrug, tell her that things were always like that. Orabella wanted, needed air free of dust, needed to breathe air that had never touched those walls.

Sloane smiled, nodded, eager to please, and Orabella nervously looked back at the pile of coats and wondered what other small terrors waited for her in the bushes of the garden.

Chapter Eleven

Orabella breathed crisp air, full of the promise of dirt and growing things. Eyes closed, she sucked down lungful after lungful of the garden, the forest. Free from decay and mold and the rot was the good, mulchy kind that promised new life. "It's so different," she said, opening her eyes finally, "than the air of Bristol."

Sloane smiled shyly in return. "I wouldn't know, miss. I've never been past Oxbury."

Orabella started carefully down the path, the tiles that should have lined it broken and waiting to twist an ankle or cause a slip at any moment. Even so, her feet were more confident on the fractured path than the stairs in the manor. The stones she knew, she understood their breaks and faults. There was no fear they would splinter and fall under her.

Free of windows, the sun shimmered in blue sky. Afternoon.

"Time is so strange since I met Elias," she hummed as she walked. "Everything is so fast or so slow outside of the city. But you, you were born here?"

"No. I was born in London. My ma, my real ma, passed when I was a little baby and her sister took me in because they didn't have any children. My aunt and uncle rented land from the Master, and when they passed on, he gave me work here."

"Oh!" Orabella stopped the girl, hand on her arm. "A coincidence! I was raised by my aunt and uncle as well. I was older when I lost my father, but still, I know what it's like to live like that." A hope, a desire, a nervous flicker of a proposal. "We should be friends. We're not that different in age and it's so lonely here."

Sloane's eyes went wide in shock. "Oh no, miss! It wouldn't be proper!"

"Please," she insisted, embarrassed for asking, anxious at rejection. "I need a friend more than I need a personal girl. Even if it's just for times like now when we're alone, let us be friends and not a lady and a maid."

Sloane blushed, her checks turning pale, rose pink against fresh cream skin. She nodded, quickly, shyly. "All right, miss, I mean Orabella. That will be . . . that will be nice."

"Grand!" Orabella exclaimed, releasing her and walking again. "We'll have such fun when the weather turns, I'm sure of it." She couldn't seem to stop talking, relief washed through her: she wouldn't be alone. She had a friend in this strange new place. Someone who could show her the grounds, help her find her footing.

"Tell me about the city," Sloane asked, nervous. "What's it like away from here?"

"It's nothing really, like any other city. I'm afraid it's not very exciting. Just buildings and afternoon teas. You know."

"I don't." Sloane's voice was low, sheepish.

A guilty pride took hold in Orabella, sprouted roots. In Bristol, no one would think her interesting for her thoughts and stories, but here, here it was different. She had something that at least one person did not.

A history of somewhere else.

Excited, Orabella spoke on everything she could recall. The most mundane things, the lunches and walks along the river, the balls and tea parties, the dress shops and bookshops. Anything she could remember. Sloane listened brightly, devouring every detail, hungry for more.

The two women passed through the garden, arm in arm, heads tilted towards each other. Around them, the tangled branches and vines sprung, unkempt but showing the first, small signs of what would be leaves and blossoms.

It was nothing like the orderly rows of her aunt's garden. It was wilder, more intimidating, and more private than that garden had ever been. The walls, crumbling in some parts, opened into little patios adorned with benches and trees spilling bare wisps of branches. The walkways were hills under each step. Brown grass that would be replaced with green when the weather turned poked out between cracks and cobbles, blending plot and path into one. Trees, decorative once, had grown feral, mimicking their neighbors in the forest just beyond, their branches a promise to hold back the sun in the coming weeks. The paths would be dark, shaded. Like the halls in the house that presided over it all.

From the ground it was impossible to see where the edge of the garden and the forest met. Everything was green and brown and crumbling, dotted here and there with sunlight.

The statues left intact stared back at them as they passed. Orabella took small note of them, thought them gods, and then moved on. She didn't bother to ask Sloane, who had made it clear that she knew nothing, everything in the manor was what it was, what it had always been.

Orabella turned back to see how far they'd come. Through the branches and thin, bare vines she could see Korringhill. The plants were eating at tall windows, one she was sure, if her sense of direction was to be trusted, belonging to the room they called the garden room. Where she had first been introduced to her sister- and father-in-law. But they could all be called the garden room, there was no window where the garden couldn't be seen. There were hidden doors and paths that led closer to the house but the weeds had grown tall and thick and it would be a trial to reach the glass. If there was still glass at all.

"Did you have gas lighting? I've heard about it. It must be nice not to have to carry candles and matches everywhere," Sloane said, drawing her back to the walk, the day. Her friend. Different from Jane but still, a friend.

"Yes! It was nice. Especially at night. Everything is so dark here when the sun sets. And quiet. It will take some getting used to. But you! You have to walk home in this darkness. Through all this? It's on the other side of the garden, isn't it?"

"There's another path. If you leave through the kitchen there's another way that goes past the stables and up a clear road."

"Is it in the forest?"

Sloane laughed. "No! Past the garden there's hills and such. Farmland but mostly people keep sheep here. The ground isn't good for growing."

"The wool must be nice. I suppose I can expect more mutton dinners."

"Yes, but in the spring and summer they hunt too."

"Who hunts?"

"The men."

To the point and not unexpected. Of course it was the men who hunted and of course they would hunt, being in the country. She'd seen it herself just that morning, although he hadn't been as lucky as the hunter the day before. The memory of meat made her mouth water. The deer from the dinner that had become stew at lunch. Wild and rich, like beef but different, and nothing wasted. And then she was sick with the memory. She swallowed, focused back on the day. "What about the groundskeeper?"

"Who?" Sloane asked.

"I saw him from the window before lunch. He must have been hunting deer. So much meat! I can't imagine that we would need more already." The carcass on the table, the candlelit dinner, the family all teeth. She shivered. "Or not, there didn't seem to be much left from the dinner."

"There's not a groundskeeper, not really. That was Cullen, probably. He and Mr. Grey do what they can to keep the paths safe but there hasn't been anyone to tend the garden for years. Cullen's really here for help with the stable."

"I see," Orabella said slowly, looking again at the landscape. They had turned, the house was hidden behind trees. A new discovery, a hidden pool. Closer, the air turned swampy but still good, natural.

"Are there fish?"

"I don't know. I suppose there could be. I wouldn't eat them," Sloane replied, joining her at the edge of the dark waters.

"They wouldn't be for eating. They're to look at," she explained.

Sloane's face fell, embarrassed.

"I was thoughtless, I didn't say which, and people do keep pools to catch fish. For sport. I read about it in *The Candle* last year! Lord

Ullsworth had fish brought in for his pool in Rome one afternoon in the summer last year."

"You're teasing." Sloane wouldn't look at her.

"I'm not! The paper said it smelled horrible after three days because it wasn't meant to be a pond and the fish started to eat each other. And then everyone refused to attend his parties or visit until he had the whole thing drained and cleaned. It was really quite embarrassing for him."

Sloane laughed, convinced, and Orabella relaxed. It was all right. She leaned forward. The dark water below was a mirror but her face was obscured by debris, she could barely see herself.

"What's the candle?" Sloane asked.

"It's a society paper. It's mostly gossip but there are stories too. I guess there's nothing like that out here. My aunt said that there are summerhouses here but I didn't see anything."

"There are!" Sloane said brightly, happy to contribute something. "On the other side of the woods. It's quite far to walk but there are some manors, not as large as Korringhill and they're empty right now. You'll be visiting when the city people come, likely."

"Elias said that we wouldn't. That the Blakersbys weren't close to other families and it was too far."

Sloane shrugged. "I guess that's the way it will be, then. I really don't know. We servants, we just keep to ourselves, most of us don't have family or anything."

"I guess we're all orphans," Orabella muttered at her reflection. She reached down, brushed a bit of fallen bark gently to reveal her own face. Her hair, loosed by her husband, disappeared in the dark waters and left only the soft brown of her face, undulating on the surface. She touched the reflection with the tip of her finger, watched her water self ripple.

"You shouldn't touch that," Sloane said, her reflection appearing in the water.

"It was just a finger," she sighed, wiping it on her already dust-covered skirts.

"We're late. You'll need to wash up before dinner."

"Is it late?" She looked towards the sky, tried to find a sun, setting or otherwise, but there was only a cloudy blue expanse. "Just a little longer before we go back," she said, taking up Sloane's hand and tugging her towards the bench. "Let's sit and talk more. You tell me about yourself, or I can tell you more funny stories from the paper."

The maid chewed on her lip, glancing back towards the opening. "All right," she relented, "but we can't stay too long. It'll be dark and there are boars and foxes in the woods."

"I thought you carried candles everywhere," Orabella teased.

"A candle will not help us against a boar."

"I wouldn't know. I've never seen one. Tell me about it," Orabella prodded.

The birds sang above, and for an afternoon they were just two women, enjoying a garden walk.

"Wait!" Orabella hissed, grabbing Sloane's arm on their way back.

"What is it?" she whispered back, quick, wary.

Orabella pointed, silent, at a fox sniffing and pawing at the ground. Hunting, she thought. Its coat was red, but duller than she expected, more like orange. She'd seen fox fur but in her mind she had always thought it would be brighter, like a cardinal. *But then*, she thought, watching the animal nose and dig, *they wouldn't be very good hunters.*

A loud screaming, crying sound rose from the forest and she gripped Sloane's arm as the fox's head shot up, eyes yellow bright. It opened its mouth, yelled back, took off after the call.

"Is that what they sound like?" she said, awed, the wedding night again knocking at the edges of her memory. The barking laughter, the bright teeth.

"You get used to it. They howl all night here." Sloane sighed. "Come on, it's too cold to stay out here longer." She sounded like a nursemaid but Orabella, shivering, nodded and followed her back into the great old house at the edge of the woods.

Chapter Twelve

They took dinner in the same mirrored room that had held the wedding party. There were far fewer candles, the table set for a smaller affair. Only three diners: Orabella, Elias, and Hastings. Claresta was, as Elias warned, missing from the table, and Orabella wondered who would feed her, as the servants were all gone. Even Sloane had left once she deposited her at the table. A day worker in her way.

Orabella's reflection stared back at her, as it had in the pool, only this time it was repeated endlessly, ghostly and dark in the cave of the dining room. Close but with the feeling of something vast just beyond the flickering light.

It felt different than it had the night before. Made the evening just past feel more like a dream, and maybe it had been. She hadn't been feeling as well as she was now at the table, and had drank the wine on an empty belly. Exhaustion, overwhelmed with the newness of it all, wine straight to her head—all things that made a story of her memory. Punched holes in it and there was nothing on the other side but a wide dark eye that she turned away from.

Sloane's manner had retreated as soon as they turned back to the house. The blank mask on her face returned. Orabella took her tea, rested once again, drained from her walk, the long night, the days of travel. The sun was gone when she rose. Again, Sloane helped her change. Though she felt better than she had the night before, she woke groggy and slow. One of Orabella's own dresses this time, a cold sky blue. Not her color, it had been bought for her cousin and passed on to her, but it didn't matter. There was no one to show off for; Elias didn't seem to care at all.

He sat across from her, a smile for whenever their eyes met.

At the head of the table, between her and Elias, sat her father-in-law. Hastings Blakersby, she thought, was not long for the world. He looked worse than he had in the hall. She wished he wasn't there at all. She wanted to ask Elias about his name, his standing. But it wouldn't be right or smart to do it in front of his father. That was a conversation for when they were alone.

They ate in silence, their silverware clinking against the plates with each bite. She stabbed at a slice of chicken, cut just so, as her meal from the night before had been. The vegetables, too, had been chopped into small pieces, the right size for the tines of the fork to hold, almost small enough that she did not need to chew at all. Across from her, Elias used his knife to cut his own meat. Her place setting did not have one. They prepared food for her as they did for Claresta, easy, without fuss or flair. To be swallowed, barely chewed.

"This chicken is so well cooked and the vegetables so fresh!" she tried, forcing the nerves from her voice, hoping to start some conversation between them. Even with her uncle, there had been talk over a meal. The silence felt heavy against her, a fourth diner, sitting too close.

"Does that surprise you? That we have adequate food? What

did your husband tell you of your new home?" Hastings replied, his voice gravelly and low.

A misstep but she couldn't see where she had gone wrong. "No." She laughed. *I am harmless*, she tried to communicate with the sound. "It's only that I didn't see any animals here, or a vegetable garden. But this all tastes as if it were gathered from right outside the kitchen. It's never this fresh in Bristol."

"Our renters," Hastings supplied, clearly meaning for it to be the end of things.

"I learned of them today. Sheepherders. I look forward to their wool, I knit! I'm afraid I don't know much more about them than that, though. Elias and I did not have a chance to speak overly long before our wedding. I'm sure I'll learn more about this lovely place." Complimentary and bright. Across the table Elias smiled, pleased.

She wished she were better with words but she knew she lacked the skill. Could barely manage deceit in the smallest of things and often said too much. Was rude and thoughtless so it was better to be quiet usually, but tonight, she was trying. Careful. Thoughtful. A good wife. A good daughter.

"As part of their debts, our renters provide the food we eat here," Elias explained.

"We own everything on this land," Hastings interjected.

"Elias has told me what an upstanding family I have married into." She clutched her fork. *I have no talent for this*, she chastised herself, as if that would make it better.

A smile, rare and fleeting, touched Hastings's lips. "Yes. A great family, very old. You will learn more. You're one of us now, for better or worse." He paused, regarded her again, and she shrank under his gaze. "Not the first. Not the last."

What does that mean? What do I say to that? She picked up her wineglass to look away, to gain some time to think. Sipped at the dark drink. The sweetness lay thick on her tongue. *Careful,* she cautioned herself, *it will go straight to my head.* She sat the glass farther away from herself, to tamp down the temptation to reach for it to have something to do with her hands. "I'm sure I'll get my feet under me quickly."

"You seem to have some trouble with that. Staying on your feet," Hastings mused, a glimmer of cruel humor in his eyes, and in that moment he looked the most like Elias. Like Elias from the carriage where she thought before she could stop herself that it was perhaps the moment Elias looked most like himself. The old man drank from his own glass, but it wasn't to make space for her comments, he was simply done with the topic, with her. She stayed silent, toyed with her fork and kept her smile.

"I had hoped there would be someone more familiar with our ways in your seat," Hastings said suddenly. "But the boy tells me that you were the best. If Lovell were able or even if I could have gone myself, a different wife would be sitting here."

"Is he an uncle or a cousin? I didn't catch anyone's names last night. Did he attend? I'm sure I'll remember him if you describe him a bit," she said, ignoring the note of disappointment in the man's voice. She wasn't what he would have pictured. A Black woman, when they wanted, she reasoned, a woman who looked like her cousin. "I thought I would meet everyone today but I haven't seen anyone at all."

"They've all returned to their own homes. They left while you sat with Claresta," Elias explained.

"Next time then," she said. A good wife, a good daughter, she let the matter drop. She would try to win them over. Try for their acceptance.

"Sir." Elias's voice was even. "It was Orabella I had set my eye on, and it was Orabella who I returned with. She is dutiful. Do not discount her so quickly."

"I do not but I do think her clumsy. I found her in the halls today, wandering around without an escort."

"I took a wrong turn!" she interjected quickly, hoping to draw any blame from Sloane. It had been her fault, after all. "I was distracted. There are such lovely things here." She touched her hair, in a single, thick braid now, swallowed the memory of the dark room, her panic. Overreacting and too easily scared by wind and nails.

"Yes," Elias said, his gaze turned towards her. "These rooms hold many surprises. But what were you up to today, my wife?"

"I went for a walk in the garden. I think it would be quite beautiful with some care."

"You went out?" Elias asked, the question hard.

"Yes. For a while, after lunch. Perhaps once it's warmer Claresta might like to sit with me out there as well. I think it will be very nice in the summer, it looks like there is ample shade, and if the pool is drained and refilled that would be magical—"

"No."

"I suppose it would be quite costly to improve the pool but that's fine! I'm not very good at recognizing plants but I thought I saw something that could be lilacs. Maybe a tea garden?" She tried steering clumsily away.

"Claresta is not to leave the house. You may walk the gardens as you please, I'll have workers out for your pool if it pleases you, but Claresta must stay here." His jaw was a hard line.

"Of course, I'm sorry, I didn't mean—her health . . ." She reached for the glass then. She didn't know what else to say. Sweet and thick, the wine burned in her belly, lessons from the night before forgotten in her panic.

"You should concentrate your efforts on the space outside the ballroom. The family would like that." Hastings spoke through a mouthful of chicken, meat moving over his tongue with his words. But Orabella smiled at him. She had said something he liked.

She pictured what she had seen of the manor from the garden. The second tall window, perhaps. "I haven't had a chance to explore these halls and I've only seen a bit of the garden but everything looks so lovely," she said slowly, her words like her steps on the broken garden path earlier in the day, light and unsure. "Perhaps tomorrow I will venture there."

"Oh no, dearest, it isn't safe for you in that wing. It needs extensive repairs, I'm afraid. Concentrate on your garden for now," Elias said quickly.

"Yes, and you concentrate on your work. The rents are due. The week is drawing to a close," Hastings said gruffly.

End of the week? She counted back quickly in her head, matching the dates with the travel, the wedding. "Wait. No, I'm sure it's only Tuesday."

Hastings shook his head. "It's Wednesday."

"Wednesday! I seem . . . to have lost a day."

"Traveling, dear, don't worry yourself over it. You'll get back on track," Elias soothed.

"Yes. I must have lost track of things. And with the wedding. Wednesday it is, then," she agreed, eager to please. She tried again to find her day but it remained hidden. *I miscounted somewhere, lost track. Today is Wednesday.*

A clatter of metal and a chair scraping backwards. She looked towards the sound as her father-in-law stood. "Good night," he said without warning and was gone, leaving the room and disappearing into the hall.

"You've finished?" Elias asked after a few quiet moments between them.

Her chicken was half eaten, the vegetables were gone. "Yes. I don't have much of an appetite this evening. I ate a good deal earlier."

"Good." Elias rose from his chair, met her around the table. He pulled her chair out.

Dinner, it seemed, had ended.

"Come now," he said, holding out his hand. Playful smile, handsome face. He really did look like the painting. In the dark, anyone could make the mistake. Now that Hastings was gone, the question was bursting in her.

"Elias," she said softly, looking around. They were alone, nothing but their reflections, a thousand replicas of their own forms, left in the room. "I wanted to ask you about something."

His brows creased; the smile wavered. Worried.

I've made it seem too serious. I'm sure there's a reason. "Your name," she breathed, nervous.

"Elias?"

"No! I mean Robinson. The staff told me that it's what you've gone by, and I wanted to know the truth, I want to understand. I'm sorry, I should have thought of a better way to approach it."

His hand was hot on her face. "Is that all? You worried me. I thought you were unhappy. Robinson is my given name. I was a bastard. I've always been a part of the family, but I have been formally acknowledged so we are both Blakersbys now. That's all there is."

He pulled her closer, wrapped her in his arms. In her memory he said he was sorry, but there in the dining room he said, "You have married well, dear wife. You have nothing to fear, not from me. What a fine pair we make, an orphan and a bastard. Will you divorce me now?"

Elias's words were honest in their roughness. Orabella should have been appalled, she knew that—it was what her upbringing dictated in response to his crassness—but she wasn't. It was thrilling and easy. There were no tricks in his language, just the harsh words, his teasing question. His hot breath tickled her neck, finding a space between the high collar of her dress and her throat. The smell of his skin and clothing, wool and ginger. Pressure in the curve of her neck, through the fabric, his lips. A kiss but it was his language that warmed and shocked her.

"No." She sighed, his touch pleasing but dulled by the layers of clothing between them. The heat held back but the pressure all around her. Different from the night before. He had held her tighter then, nearly crushing. He was more careful now.

"Orabella." Her name a song.

Her head felt light, too much wine again, she'd forgotten herself. Heat pooled in her belly, coursed all through her, made the space between her thighs tingle, speeding along the desire that Elias stirred. His mouth moved close to her.

"My wife," he sang, his tongue sneaking into the shell of her ear.

She gasped, flinched, and was presented with his laughter. "It tickles," she said.

"I'll do more than that."

His kiss caught whatever words she meant to say, her open mouth covered by his. His tongue begged no entry, it took what he wanted, explored what he wanted, and she was powerless to do anything but reject or return his passions.

Orabella chose to return them.

He tasted like the wine. His kiss was slippery, boiling. Not confined to press and touch, he nibbled and sucked, teasing her lips, chin, and jaw. The world was only hands and mouth, and when he did release her, the candles seemed brighter than they had before.

"Will you let me take you to bed, Orabella, or is there something more you wish to know?"

The world spun, her stomach filled with fluttering insects. Butterflies or the fairies from the painting. The space high between her thighs pulsed, begged for more, and there was no reason to say no. No reason to stop him, to decline. He was her husband. "Bed," she breathed, shy and lusty all at once.

He moved in the darkness, confidently pulling her along through the halls cut with moonlight. His hand burning like a torch around hers. As before, their wedding night only momentarily interrupted by the day.

Chapter Thirteen

"How can you travel without any light? Even the maids use a candle." She asked to hear him speak, as he lit the lamp in her room. Strange that he would want light now, when she was sure that they meant to do something usually confined to the dark. The moon provided some through the open curtains and she watched him as he worked, nervous now that she was free from his hold.

"I am used to it," he replied. He was a creature of the manor, like Sloane, like Mrs. Locke. Like Orabella would be, she supposed, given enough time.

He followed different paths than Sloane. Orabella hadn't seen the little beads on the floor. She'd looked for their twinkle but found nothing. The path didn't feel like the one she had traveled down to reach the dining room, but she couldn't be sure of how many halls led to hers. The light came to life, reminded her where her thoughts ought to be.

The bed had been turned down, made ready. Orabella's night-gown lay on it and her combs were set out on the vanity. *She came back*, Orabella thought, picking one up. Cold against cold fingers.

His work done, Elias had returned to her, reached for the buttons of her dress. The world felt like it was covered in a thin layer of wool. Nervous, unsure, her eyes danced over the vanity looking for something, anything to stall the moment, and finding it, she moved without thought.

"What's this?" she asked, lifting the oil lamp that Elias had lit, turning it carefully in her hands. It was not the one that had been there before; she wouldn't have noticed at all if they weren't so incredibly different. The others had been lamp bodies, glass tops. This one was a genie's lamp. The bronze body was stamped with swirling patterns mimicking smoke.

"A gift," he murmured over her shoulder, his face in her mirror. "I told you, I work in imports. It's a matched set and was sitting in storage. I saw your little fairy-tale book and thought you might like something like this. I've already sent for a copy of *The Thousand and One Nights*. I thought you would like something else to read."

She rushed to explain, to keep him from thinking that she was childish, "The fairy book is a keepsake. From my father. It's nothing to . . ."

His finger was firm against her lips. "It is dark here, I know, but there is light, Orabella. You bring light here. I like your fairy books and your little ways. When the weather turns, I'll have workmen here for the rest of these rooms, to turn them into a suite, and you can fill them with whatever you find. Whatever pleases you."

Orabella put the lamp down carefully. "I think it would be better if you stayed closer to me. Will you move into one of these rooms?"

"Do you really want that?"

"I think you please me."

A laugh and she bit her lip, embarrassed to have said something so intimate, but he leaned closer. "Then yes," he replied, his lips brushing the cusp of her ear. "But not before there's a room here for me. My nightmares are too much to sleep by your side."

"Where do you sleep now?" Nervous at his fingers making quick work of her buttons. Shivering as they ran over the now bare skin of her chest. Elias's gaze was focused on the space below her vision, his fingers sliding under wool and cotton to find sensitive flesh. His hand making its way past the barriers of garments, she found herself shy, jumpy, near panic.

"I have a bedroom on the third floor in the opposite wing from this. It's not as kept up, the wing, but it keeps my nightmares to myself." He pushed her dress away from her shoulders and down her arms. She moved in response as she thought she ought, pulling her hands free from the sleeves and letting the gown drop to the floor. A puddle of blue fabric from which she in her white chemise and plain corset bloomed. He smiled, pleased, and began to work at the next layer.

We are all little birds, nesting in the rafters, she thought madly, unsure of where to put her hands as he undid lacing, quickly, expertly. "You've done this before." She didn't mean to say it, couldn't help but say it.

His laugh was warm as his tongue had been on her ear. "Yes. I'm a man of a certain age, and good for you because I at least know what I am doing."

He was kissing her. His hands had left her body, only a thin layer of cotton covered her. Elias's hands were on her cheeks, pressing her face upward, and his mouth swallowed hers.

Orabella reached forward; her hands, nervous, eager to be of use, found his jacket and shirt, soft but not skin, under her fingers.

She pulled back, too aware of their differences, of her own vulnerability.

"Wait, wait," Elias tutted. Slipped free from his coat and pulled his shirt off in one motion, dropping them to the floor with her dress carelessly. He didn't stop there, his hands went to his belt and she looked away.

Her stomach jumped. "I'm sorry, I don't know what I'm meant to do."

"Do whatever you want, love. In this bed, in this house, whatever gives you pleasure is my pleasure," he purred. "Orabella, look at me."

She forced her face up to meet his and her vision filled with his form, completely bare, before her. He stood still, his arms relaxed at his side, his head tilted slightly, watching her. Setting her jaw, she reached for the strap of her chemise and he moved forward, one long stride to place his hand over hers.

"Don't," he said softly. "Just look at me for a moment. Touch if you like, but at the very least, look. It'll help your nerves."

The warm, low lights of the lanterns cast deep shadows over him but they hid nothing, all of him revealed. Her head stood at the height of his chest and she glanced over the flat plane of it to avoid his eyes. Brown hair curled at its center, the muscles well defined, and she wondered at what he did, what he really did, day to day, out in the world. She lifted her finger and traced a thin line on him. *Scars*, she thought, frowning. The white lines, ragged and long healed, ran all over his chest and shoulders. She turned her head and found them down his arms as well. Entranced, she followed them to his hands, noticing that they, too, showed the trails of injury.

Distracted by the strange map of her husband, she followed it to his legs, and meeting his cock, stopped all at once. He touched her face, urging her forward so she kept her eyes on it, on him. His shaft sat nestled in a thatch of dark hair and ended in a bulbous, pink tip, just peeking out of the skin that surrounded it. The whole of it stood as he did, straight and before her.

Elias cupped her face, forced her to look at his eyes. "I'm just a man, you should know what a man looks like."

"Is this to be the only time I will see it?" Her voice sounded small, she wished it were stronger or that she had something wittier, more confident to say.

But he laughed, a real true sound, and taking her hand, led her to the bed. "Come here, wife. My Orabella, let me please you."

His mouth pressed hard against hers, wine and heat and the dark came with her fluttering eyelids. His hands turning her until she was in his arms fully. His passion pressing out any thought of the dinner, the house, the future, the world itself until there was only his touch.

The last of her garments fell from her quickly, disappearing onto the floor as Elias pulled her into the sea of the bed, placed her against the pillows before she could protest. To say no, to decline was all she had been taught, and now she wasn't sure of anything but the heat that poured from him over her. She gasped as his mouth ventured farther, down her chest until it found her breast.

The shock of teeth and tongue on her nipple made her push her thighs together but they wouldn't close, Elias lay between them and he laughed around his mouthful of her, delighting in her flesh.

Orabella didn't know what to think of Elias, what he was doing to her, only that she wanted more. That her body pulsed and ached for his touch, and he, without her words, knew by some instinct that she didn't understand to provide it. She craved the experience.

Everything in her, her spinning thoughts, the coil of her guts, her fingers twisting in the sheets, everything, repeated only one word, *more*.

Heat ran through her, dropped into her belly, and made her body shiver and tighten. Orabella's head felt light, a buzzing in it. *The wine*, she thought, touching her own lips, already swollen and sensitive from the welcome violence of his kiss.

"Is that what my wife wants?" His voice, a low growl of sound before he kissed her, pulled her into his embrace and tumbled through the sheets so that she found herself atop him, her legs spread, that pulsing apex between her thighs settled firmly against his belly. The demand that she had always said no to whispering *yes* with every heartbeat.

Orabella faltered, unsure, and Elias spread his fingers over her stomach, ran them upward until they reached a fat breast where he squeezed her nipple, gently drawing a squeak from her.

"Beautiful, my Orabella, beautiful. Kiss me."

And she did. Easier this time because she was wine filled, because she had more practice. Because they had gone so much further than she had ever allowed. A period in her life was ending. Orabella was not becoming a woman, she had been one already, it didn't feel like maturity, only a blossoming.

Is this what marriage is like? Is this what I thought it would be? Orabella on her back again, Elias at her neck, her breasts. The air heavy, her body tingled, her thoughts slow and wet with pleasure. *Had I ever thought about any of this?*

She ran her hands over his back, crisscrossed with scars. The question of what happened to him drowning under another, more present one: *Had I ever thought it would be someone as beautiful as him?*

Elias Robinson or Blakersby *was* beautiful and he was hers, and then there were no more thoughts because his fingers were pressed against that part of her that pulsed and begged, stroking and rubbing.

Orabella wrapped her arms around his shoulders, pulled him closer and pressed her face into his neck so that every breath was filled with his scent, no longer wool but earthy and wild. *He smells like the garden*, she thought, and then, *no, the forest.* There were sounds, animal cries and low moans, and she recognized them as her voice only when she stuttered out, "More." But she didn't know what it meant, only that she wanted.

Elias obliged, his fingers slipping through the wet folds of her, finding her entrance and pulling a high gasp that turned into a moan from her throat. He laughed, light and easy, and she wondered at what she felt for him before settling on that he was beautiful and kind to her and that was enough. His fingers did wicked work against her. They teased and pressed, and a queer ball of nerves built under them and all up through her torso. Her own hips rocked in response, knowing by instinct what was coming. Elias kept the pressure on her, in her, until the ball in her broke, split open, and her body was heavy and warm and liquid. She thrummed, passage contracting and releasing around his fingers. That low mouth hungry, a promise to swallow him, hold him inside.

"You're ready for me," he announced.

He moved swiftly, boldly, his fingers slipping from her entrance, replaced seamlessly by that organ she had seen before. His cock slid into her without resistance, one smooth thrust and she was filled, no space between them.

Orabella sucked in a quivering breath, shocked at the suddenness of it.

"There, there, love, it'll feel better in a moment," he comforted, but his voice sounded like praise.

"It doesn't feel bad. Sudden," she replied, her own voice foreign in her ears.

"Good. I want you to feel only pleasure in my arms." There was no more talk to be had, Elias was moving, thrusting between her thighs. Orabella had no history to compare it to, there was only the measured, deep movement of her husband.

She drowned under him, didn't realize that he was speaking through his moans and cries. "This is our night, Orabella, we are one, love, you are mine," he said like a chant until she kissed him to have something to do with her mouth.

He cried out, pulled himself from her, and she felt his seed, hot liquid on her belly. Elias kissed her brow and eyelids, sang her praises as she tried to collect her breath. The impossibility of pleasure lingered over her skin, in her body.

"Are you all right, love?" he asked.

"Yes, I think, I mean I feel all right," she said. "It wasn't how I thought it would be."

"Did you think it would be awful?"

"I didn't, I mean it couldn't be or else no one would."

A deep chuckle. "Yes." He pulled away from her, stood from the bed.

Orabella's arms emptied of him, and she tried to collect herself. *I need,* she started but the list of tasks didn't come to her, only the tingle of memory from what had just transpired. Her husband returned, a glass in his hand.

"Where did this come from?" she asked, its oddness enough to snap her back to attention. Her wineglass from dinner.

"I brought it up. Drink the rest, it will help you sleep."

"I don't think it will be an issue. I'm fairly worn out. As you must be, it has been an interesting few days." *More days than I thought,* she reminded herself.

"More, for you, it's been more," he said, pressing the stem of the glass into her hand. "And you have a mind to comfort me when it should be the other way around. You are good, and I will never be a man who is worthy of it."

His praise sent a rolling warmth through her. She took the glass. Drank as he asked.

"Let me help you." He hummed, pleased.

Orabella couldn't muster the energy to argue. She let him clean his leavings from her belly and thighs. He stopped, fingers hovering over the long streaks of bruises on her thigh. "What's this, love?"

Dreamy, soft from pleasure, she didn't know what he meant until his fingers pressed and the dull ache of it rose again. She pulled away. "I don't know. I must have fallen into something. The wedding dress was very hard to move in."

He kissed the dark lines. "I'm sorry, I should have taken more care."

A dark hallway, the crush of him and mold and rot and . . . "No, I was clumsy, the dress was long. I should have thought to pin it at least. Let's not think on it now, it's in the past." *It wasn't him, Elias is careful, I fell, I must have,* the tickling rumbling roll of the recent pleasure moved through her and she stopped, let herself settle in that memory instead. Let Elias help her into the gown left out for her. Let herself be pushed back into the bed. Watched with drowsy eyes as he dressed himself. The world blurred, golden flames, dusty shadows, she was slipping away. Then the weight of him on the edge of the bed, the edge of the world, his arms on either side of her.

"You need your rest. The door," he reminded her, kissing her forehead.

"I remember," she answered, her voice already heavy with dreams.

She struggled up to watch him leave. The door stood open past his shoulder. The hall behind nothing but darkness, looking back at her as she looked into it. *The moon has decided to hide from me*, her mind sang, drawing a forest where cats batted at a low silver globe that dipped and dove to avoid their paws. Her head was heavy, everything so heavy. Too much wine. He was there again, in front of her. The smell of the house in him now and there was a kiss, like the kiss the night before, too heavy, crushing, she couldn't breathe and then it was over.

The door shut, the lock turned, and she was alone. She wanted sleep but something held her.

She had forgotten her hair, the thought came to her suddenly, and she pushed herself to wake, to move. *Just a moment, to comb it and tie it or it will be a mess in the morning.*

He had left the light burning near her bedside. Alone, she sat up. She took the lamp and moved to the vanity, shivering slightly. She settled it on the table next to its match. Orabella took a moment to inspect the other, an exact replica, both beautiful in their craftsmanship. Tired, fading, her vision was blurring and they looked even more magical, the light making them glow just so. "I'll have to ask them to water my wine down," she mused to the flickering lights. To the softly shimmering woman in the mirror with her bronze skin, her dark eyes but the gift of kiss-swollen lips. The cold woke her more.

She crossed to her wardrobe, rustled through it and found her shawl. She wrapped her shoulders, happy for the extra warmth. The room, outside of the blankets, held a chill, the winter still clinging to the walls and no heater had been set for her.

Should I ask? she thought, combing her dark locks, working out whatever tangles and knots had arrived through the day, clumsily, quickly, each pull reminding her of that moment in the dark room.

The picture, the nail. *My mistake, there's nothing. I'm just clumsy and thoughtless.* Orabella's hair was a soft halo of curls around her face. She braided it, twisting the strands together to keep them from gaining knots while she slept.

She blew out the lamp and returned to the bed, keeping her shawl for warmth. She closed her eyes, waited for sleep to find her again. It did not keep her waiting long. In the walls and halls she heard movement. *Mice.* Half dreaming already, she saw them dancing and singing.

The knob turned, the door rattled gently. *A draft,* she dreamed. The space where Elias had been still warm between her thighs, foxes laughing in the trees.

Chapter Fourteen

Sloane stood behind Orabella, who wished that she would go away. They had become fast friends over the three weeks that she had spent in the manor. The routine had been steady. Breakfast with Elias and as the cook said, nothing so fancy as the first one. A morning with Claresta but now she brought her knitting or the little fairy book to read out loud. The kitchen girl, Amanda, the one everyone else called Manda, often came to sit and listen, and it wasn't so lonely. Then a walk in the garden. Dinner with her father-in-law. Night again with Elias. She was growing used to the wine he insisted on, to help her sleep and soothe the night sounds.

And then it rained and there was nothing to do but rest in the afternoon. The second day in a row, she wished that Sloane would leave her be. But the girl hovered around the bedroom, fidgeted with the yarn and needles until she confessed she was better with thread and Orabella suggested she finish the project that she herself had given up on. So now she sat, second day, in a chair pulled from one of the endless rooms turned storage, watching while she made designs in fabric.

"Oh, Sloane, you don't have to wait for me. I'm just writing to Jane to let her know how things are going here." She wrote to her a few times a week, to have something to do, but hadn't heard back yet. Hadn't heard from her family either but Orabella was not surprised by this. She didn't expect it.

The maid nodded. "I'll just wait here to help you with whatever you need."

Orabella bit the inside of her lip to keep from frowning. It was the same as the day before. She yawned.

"Oh! Miss, are you tired? I'll turn down the bed!" Sloane jumped to the task, ready to be useful.

"Yes!" Orabella agreed. "I'll take a rest right after I'm done with this letter. You may go, you know I would prefer to rest alone."

For three weeks there had not been a single moment in which Orabella was not attended save for when Elias locked her into the room at night. The door rattled and the mice scampered through the walls and ceilings. The third and fourth night she found it frightening but now it was just like the halls and closed rooms, usual, expected. It was her home now.

"I'm not supposed to leave you during the day, Orabella," she said. Her voice trembled.

Orabella turned to her, took up her hands. "I know, but I never have a moment alone here. I'm not going to run away. You can do your needlepoint in one of the other rooms, can't you? I'll just be right here, resting. And it's not as if anyone will know, no one comes here."

Sloane looked down at their intertwined hands and squeezed Orabella's gently. "I'll leave as soon as I've readied you for bed. You promise to stay? I'll return at the normal time, when you usually rise." She waited for Orabella's answer, brows pressed together, worried.

"I promise," Orabella swore.

Sloane smiled, nodded, and released her. Took her usual place again, just over Orabella's shoulder.

"Do you mind waiting somewhere else, please? It feels as though you're reading my letter as I write it."

Sloane moved silently away to stand in front of the door.

Sighing, she bent towards her paper, pen in hand. She always thought she didn't have much to say, she didn't do anything different from day to day, but when she started the words poured out of her. *The draft in this home is driving me mad, the mice in the walls. I've never had a pet but I've thought of asking for a little cat to help. Or maybe a whole herd of them. A pride like they were little lions hunting the savanna of my corner of the house. Wouldn't that be delightful? But then I suppose it would smell of cat instead of mildew.*

I know Elias would grant it, he is very indulgent, he often leaves gifts for me. Orabella glanced at the small pile of books on the table, the new pen and pretty leather journal he'd given her. *But I think he's at as much of a loss as I am as to what I am to DO here. He has his work, and although I talked about taking on the garden and am bursting with ideas the truth is I haven't the slightest idea of where to start or how. There's no groundskeeper here, I've told you that, I think. Just a boy I've only seen from a distance. Sloane says that his name's Cullen.*

There's no sign of anyone else from Elias's family. If I hadn't been at the dinner I would have thought I dreamed them all. It feels like a dream, that night. I suppose they aren't close. That's all right, it's not as if I can speak poorly of such an arrangement. I do wish I had more to do here. I didn't think I would miss the sounds of Bristol so much. There at least was always somewhere to go, but here, there's only the garden or another room. I miss reading The Candle. *Can you send me some old copies? They've probably started a new serial by now.*

She finished the page, signed her name, and tucked it into the envelope. "All done," she sang, standing and passing the letter to Sloane to put into the mail. It disappeared into her apron.

"Here, here, let me get you ready for bed!" There was a nervous energy about her as she fussed with Orabella's buttons.

I've barely dressed or undressed myself since I came here, she thought. After the first morning Sloane had been there before she rose, with Mrs. Locke by her side, unlocking the door to let her in. Every night it was Elias who stripped her down and then pulled a gown over her head before he left. But it did no good to argue, someone else had created the standard and she was too fresh in the manor to change it. So she surrendered, let herself be dressed and undressed in turn.

The maid removed her skirts and jacket, leaving her in the shift and stockings. She moved to lift the thin cotton piece and Orabella stopped her. "This is fine, Sloane. I'll have to get dressed again for dinner, after all."

The maid helped her into the bed, and she settled beneath the blankets, her head on the pillow. Orabella closed her eyes and listened to Sloane draw the curtains. Waited for the door to open but there came no more sound.

"Sloane?" she called.

"Yes, Orabella?"

"I thought we agreed? You don't have to wait here while I sleep. I'm sure there's something else you can do with this time."

"I know I said I would, but I can't leave you here. Mr. Blakersby doesn't want you alone with the door unlocked and I haven't got a key, only Mrs. Locke does. I have to stay."

"Is that all?" Orabella jumped from the bed, reached into her top, and pulled out the key Elias had given her. In his gifts, a chain, plain and heavy, had come for it. Orabella was unsurprised that Sloane hadn't seen it. She seemed trained to ignore things she hadn't been told to notice. "I have a key. I'll lock the door right behind you. So, please, allow me to get some rest."

She met Sloane at the door, holding the key up like a talisman. Sloane bit her lip, the flesh moving in and out of her teeth, torn as to what to do next. She was being told to leave and there was no reason not to, no reason to stay, the conditions set by Elias, the earlier commands, had been met. Orabella had the key to the room, she was in charge of her own destiny, as far as her afternoon was concerned.

"Oh," Orabella startled, remembering. "It's supposed to be a secret so don't tell anyone all right? So we both have a little secret and we can hold each other true."

"All right, I won't. I won't tell but I'm not supposed to leave," Sloane looked away, brows pressed together.

"Please," she said more gently. "I just need some rest and I will do so better alone."

Sloane melted and in that moment Orabella was reminded that Sloane was good and earnest. Smiling and ushering her maid through the portal, she shut the door behind her. Orabella put the key in the lock, turned it, took it out. She held the key in her fingers, held her breath, and put her ear to the door.

A gentle knock at the door. "Miss?"

"Yes?" she called back.

"Your tea, don't forget to drink it."

She turned to the cup on her vanity, cooler now in the time it had taken her to write her letter and convince Sloane to give her peace. "I won't."

"I'm going to take the letter down and visit with Maggie in the kitchen. I'll be back in at the normal time, enjoy your rest."

"I will, thank you," she said.

Muffled, she could hear Sloane's footsteps receding.

Alone for the first time in what felt like weeks, Orabella let out a breath. She leaned against the door, letting the experience wash over her as the rain washed over the manor outside. Her shoulders dropped, her entire body loosening as the air settled over her. She breathed deeply, clutching her key to her chest.

The cold crept into her slowly. Through her stockings and over her shoulders and down her legs. She shivered, placed the key back around her neck, and went to the wardrobe, pulling it open and shuffling through her clothing, organized differently than she was used to, until she found her dressing gown. She put her arms through the worn mint-colored sleeves and took a moment to look at her clothes while she tied it, chasing back the cold. So many of her dresses were green or blue. Colors that had flattered her cousin.

Well, it doesn't matter now anyway, she thought and closed the wardrobe.

More awake, she opened the curtains again, looking out into the rain, down into her garden. She hadn't found an entrance to it, her exploration confined to whatever rooms she could glance into as they passed. She had tried to convince Sloane to go off the path but she refused and so far would only go to the main garden.

Below her the rain pushed down the remains of the bushes and weeds, hinted at the cobblestone of a path exposing what could have been. *There must be a way*, she mused.

"What a miserable day," she said to the view.

She walked back to the bed, sat on the edge of it, and thought about lying back down. Her feet dangled over the side and a breeze blew over them.

It's so drafty, she thought, grabbing at the covers, readying to lie down, then stopped. *But this is a wall.* She frowned. She sat still, sure that she was mistaken, that the air came from the direction of the window or the door, but it blew gently over her feet.

She slid off the bed and followed the air back into a tiny slit along the edge of the wallpaper. Curious, she ran her finger along it, finding a small edge. The paper resisted her nails and determined, she went to the vanity to fetch the pen. Carefully she inserted the tip into the crack and slowly leveraged it upward, cutting the thin line in the paper. A little past the height of her knees the groove stopped and became another edge so she turned, following that line with the pen until she had cut three sides of a square from the wall.

Oh, I've ruined it, she realized but still she was curious and couldn't stop now that she had started. She worried at it, digging her nails in, careful of the paper, to see if she could find a latch or some trick. *It's probably just a patch in the wall and you've made it worse with your busy mind*, she scolded herself. Orabella pushed against the panel, releasing the latch that held it on the other side and opening the small door into a dark void that spilled cold, dusty air into the bedroom. In the opening sat a pack of wax crayons and a stack of papers, yellowed with age. A child's hidey-hole, only it stretched farther than a child would like. Storage, then.

Was this Elias's room? she mused as she swept up the crayons. There were only a few of them, well used and stumpy. Not proof that he had ever stayed in the room, but then, why did he put her there? Why was it so kept up? Someone must have slept there before her. She dumped the crayons in the drawer where she kept her stationery. Taking up one of the lamps Elias had given her, she lit it and turned back to the dark.

She had intended only to peek inside but the hidden hall stretched much farther than her light. Curious, she crawled inside and found a space tall enough for her to stand, wide enough for her to walk through. She turned back to shove her feet into the slippers that waited beside her bed and then ventured forth down the hall in the wall.

The first few meters were finished, roughly, but that stopped after a short distance. The plaster disappeared and left only the bare wood and brick. She heard skittering that must be mice but they fled before her light. She took turns following the dark paths, a sort of maze inside the space between rooms, the way she had come disappearing behind her swiftly. Fear overridden by her own curiosity.

Like the day she met Elias, there was no reason to say no so she said yes. Nothing stood in her way forward so she moved in that direction.

I should go back, she thought after she had walked enough to realize that the hall went on longer than a few meters and she did not know the manor. She wondered at how her bedroom was the end of her hall but then she thought of all the turns and passages, all the rooms with their closed doors, and thought no more of it.

The house was an unknown thing built without logic or care, and now she was inside its darkest parts. She turned back, taking the turns she thought she had come down, finding more than she remembered. Orabella realized quickly she had lost the way. Her heart pounded, panic setting in, but she forced herself to be calm. She had only walked a few meters. There had to be a way out, other than the way she had gotten in.

She covered the lamplight and closed her eyes, letting them grow accustomed to the darkness. She opened them, keeping the light away and focusing back on the floor, and began walking again. She let out a soft, delighted cry.

Along the ground, a streak of light.

She bent and, not bothering with care, pushed the portal open. She climbed out into a room she had never seen before.

The windows were open, though their panes were broken, letting in the rain. The door also stood ajar. According to Sloane, that meant safety but the room was in such neglect that it was clear no one came there. The air smelled earthy, like soil and rotting leaves. Woody, natural in a way. She stepped forward and stopped, her feet landing on something soft and wet. She looked down to find a ring of mushrooms growing from the floor. Little brown and white caps that sprouted all around her. She stepped carefully over them and looked closer at the room.

Furniture-filled, like the others, storage; it would never be of use again. Uncovered, the dark wood was rotten, home to the mushrooms that grew with abandon on the arms and legs of chairs. The embroidery on the seats, once likely quite fine, had been eaten through by moths and mice, the stuffing ripped out and turned to nests by the same animals. She thought of Claresta's wall and the mice that ran along the bottom, holding hands for safety. *I wonder if it was inspired by life; all we need are a few cats and we're nearly there.*

Shelves that should have held books and decorative knickknacks had turned verdant with moss. Everything in and about the room had been left to rot. Like the garden.

I have to get back to my room, she thought, picking up her skirts, making her way to the door. She peeked out and found an unfamiliar hall, the doors open. No wallpaper or carpet remained. The entire length was mossy, like the floor of a forest. A window waited at the end.

She walked towards it carefully, her feet sinking into the false carpet with every step, and looked outside. She had come, somehow, to the back of the house. The window overlooked the garden, but it was not her sister-in-law's hall that she stood in. That one, like hers, was kept, not well, but serviceable and neat. This hall had fallen to ruin. Was rotting and, despite the open doors, clearly not safe.

She turned and stopped. A stairway to the next floor.

The wood above her creaked. *There's someone there*, she thought, and wondered who, briefly. Surely not her father-in-law, he was far too old, but it could be Elias? Or a workman? *Or a fat rat ready to bite me. I'm not supposed to be here, I need to find my way back.*

She turned away from the stairs and walked down the hall, stepping carefully, remembering Sloane's warning, the danger of falling through the floor. The doors were open, spilling gray light out into the hall, keeping parts of it clear, but the advance of the decay was impressive. What wasn't rotted was green with moss. The hall seemed not the inside of a building at all but a strange wood where she would meet something fantastic.

Presently she came to a wide stairway, adorned with wooden angels and faded carpet. The spread of the moss seemed stopped by God's messengers. Tall windows stood in front of it, casting light onto them, giving them a glow. *This isn't the main hall*, she thought but walked down the steps, turning on the second landing and then finding herself on the first floor again.

Here the hall was dark save for one weak light farther down that spilled from an open door, and she was glad she had not blown out the lantern. She moved forward carefully picking her way past piles of rotting lumber and building materials. The most evidence that she had seen that the manor had ever been under any repair outside of her mismatched floor. She hugged her arms through the thin gown, tried to pull warmth into them.

She reached the source of the light and gasped.

A grand ballroom unfolded before Orabella. The mirrored walls had silvered with age and made the room seem soft and alluring. The smooth floor was still intact, though worn in some places. The high ceiling still held its angels and clouds, even chipped and faded they were delightful; she could still see the way they danced and played above. A piano waited to one side and she went to it. The keys were covered in dust but she itched to press them down, to see if it still played.

She gave to her curiosity one ivory key and a tone, clear as a bell, rang through the room. She pulled her hand back and waited, wide eyed, for someone to come, to follow the sound in what should have been an empty room, but no one appeared.

This room, with its silver walls and piano, wasn't abandoned only waiting to be used again. Somehow it had escaped the ruin that crept over the floors and up the walls. Alone though she was, it felt like there was someone else with her, pressing against her, watching. *The mirrors*, she mused, her distorted reflection ghostly on their silvered surfaces. *A trick of my own imagination.* She let out a breath and put the lamp down on the piano. Hands free, she turned to the window, ignoring the feeling. *This must be the place Hastings spoke of.*

It still rained; the light that came into the room was weak and shadowed but she could see the garden through the glass doors. Could see what had once been a beautiful pavilion that was meant to lead out into a fairy land of flowers and trees and now sat blocked by its own overgrowth, hidden and unused, and she knew where she was. Relieved, the urgency drained from her. There was plenty of time.

She tried to imagine the room when it had been finished, new, full of life and music. She hummed a melody to herself and began to sway and spin, remembering the parties she had gone to with her cousin, the ones she had held herself back from enjoying too fully. The bright taste of joy in her would only ever be a taste and never fill her belly. But then Elias had come.

The memory of their passions was physical, the heat sparked all along her body, her mouth watered for his kiss. How he affected her, how quickly she had lost herself to him. How it made

everything seem bearable. Her silent sister-in-law, the constant ob-
servation, the falling-apart house. It all made sense now that she
had seen it for herself. Elias wouldn't let someone he cared about
wander through that dilapidated space and he had shown over and
over that he did care. What were the gifts and his gentle nature if
not care? She would be a better wife, more trusting of him.

She closed her eyes, found herself spinning to her made-up
song, her arms held out in a mock dance, and wondering a simple
wonder: What if Elias had spoken to her those two years ago when
he first saw her?

Would she have let him court her anyway? Would they have
run away together? Would she have come to care for him as a true
wife and not with this twisting desire she found in herself that only
happened to align with the convenience of their situation?

Humming, she swayed, let the fantasy answer her questions. A
reality in which she and Elias were in love, in which they danced
that night that he had seen her. A fantasy where there was something else besides this place of dark, rotting halls and abandoned
fairy gardens. Something more than just her fantasy.

The room creaked, echoed all around her.

She stopped, her eyes shooting open, and she spun, trying to
find the source of the creaking sound, but there was only the rain
outside. The ballroom was as empty as it always had been. Her reflection and the silent angels above the only things with her. Even
the rain was fading. *I have to go, I have to get back*, she thought. She
didn't let herself say the real reason, that it would be dark soon and
she would be alone in those halls.

But she knew where she was now, could navigate at least back
to the main stairs by the line of the garden. She went to the door,
looked back once, checking all the ballroom over again to find
nothing at all.

She moved quickly down the hall, the ballroom's the only door that was open, and the space became dark and closed as she passed, the faraway light of the ballroom fading with each step. In the dark, she reached a set of doors. She found the knob by touch, swallowing any growing panic in the darkness, refusing to make a fool of herself again. It was an old house, there were rats and mice and that was all. She pushed the doors open, hoping. The house rewarded her, and she spilled out into the entrance hall she had come through on her arrival.

It was empty. She quickly made her way to the main steps. She knew enough of the manor to find her rooms. She flew up the wide steps, followed the halls, found the glass beads still glittering on the floor like a constellation, and after just a few wrong turns, made her way back to her room that overlooked her little garden.

She unlocked her door, slipped inside, and locked it again.

The small door that had started her adventure stood open, dark as it had been the first time. She hurried over to it, closed it, the latch catching. The pattern of the wallpaper hid the slit she had made. She breathed a sigh of relief as she removed the dressing gown.

The light green fabric was soiled with dust and dirt from her journey. She walked to the mirror and found that her face was the same. Cobwebs had caught her hair, and flecks of yellow and white dust like snow covered her.

"Oh dear," she mumbled.

She stuffed the filthy robe under the mattress. She would have to think of something to do with it later but for now she needed to care for her face. She dipped the waiting rag into the water and washed herself. Then she combed her hair, removing the webs and tangles.

A knock at the door. Then, "Miss? Are you awake yet?"

Sloane. "Yes! Just give me a moment!"

She looked herself over, checked for dust on her shift but found it clean, protected by the robe. She took a step and then stopped. There were dirt tracks on the carpet. *The slippers*, she thought. She kicked them off and hid them under the bed, and ground the dirt into the carpet until it, too, was invisible.

Finished, she went to the door. Opened it with a smile she hoped looked rested and well. She let Sloane in.

"We'll have to get you ready for dinner," Sloane said, walking to the vanity. She paused. "Miss, you didn't drink your tea."

A cold spike shot down Orabella's back. "No, I'm sorry, I just laid down."

Sloane looked stricken, betrayed. "Orabella! You promised! I'll be punished!"

"No! I wouldn't let that happen! It's not your fault, it's mine," Orabella said, closing the door and crossing the room to Sloane.

The maid looked like she would cry, her face fallen, lips trembling, eyes red. Orabella took the full cup from her and walked across the room. Throwing open the window, she flung the liquid outside, emptying it into the garden. "There," she said, turning, "no one will know."

Orabella lifted a finger to her lips. The room filling with the cold wet air, the smell of the garden below, of a world outside filling her nostrils.

Sloane smiled in return, repeating the motion. A pact between them. Secrets and secrets.

Only then did Orabella realize that she had left the lamp in the ballroom.

Chapter Fifteen

I don't want to go to the garden today. I should learn the house more," Orabella stated, lightly, as if it didn't matter. A change of pace. "I'm bored," she added for good measure.

Sloane wrung her hands next to her. They were in the hall outside Claresta's room and the girl looked back, worried.

"No one is listening," Orabella said, taking her arm and bending towards her.

"Someone is always listening, miss," she responded, a whisper. "And we're not allowed, you're to go to the garden and your room. That's all."

"Says who?" Orabella teased.

"Mrs. Locke!" Sloane answered quickly.

"Well, Mrs. Locke is not in charge of me and Elias said I can do whatever I want." He didn't mean what she meant to do, she knew. He meant she could buy dresses or read all the little stories she desired but there was nowhere to buy dresses. No papers delivered with the mail. There was only the house. Orabella began walking down the hall, not the way to the garden but in the opposite direction. She took the first turn, was met with a hall full of closed doors save one at the very end. "You know the house well, don't you?"

"Of course! I know the places where you should go and shouldn't. We don't come down this way much, it's not . . ." She stumbled over her words but Orabella didn't argue. Elias had said it was all right for her to do as she wished and the hierarchy of the house was law.

"I know, we have to be careful. I've seen the disrepair of the place and I won't go into any closed rooms, as you've said. I just want to know what else there is in this dreary place." She smiled brightly at her, hoping to impart some sense of adventure in the other woman without revealing her true motives. She had to find the lamp. A gift from her husband, it was important. He would notice it was missing. She would find it. "There's this little space, under my window. I just want to get to it."

"I'm not sure, Orabella, that wing is . . . we're not supposed to, it hasn't been worked on." She couldn't forbid her, as Orabella suspected. "Mrs. Locke will be upset. We have a schedule."

A weak excuse and Orabella smiled. They came to a staircase, the darkness not one mass but many cloudy creatures, turning over one another. "Where does this go? You have candles if we need?"

Sloane nodded slowly and Orabella, smiling, took the first step. Bold. The face she showed Elias she'd use here, hope Sloane believed it as he did. The wood held and she followed with another until she was fully inside the maw of the staircase. Sloane, timidly, following after. The world was made of nothing but their creaking steps and breath.

Orabella trailed her fingers down the wall, her foot searching for the next step as she descended, but her body knew well enough how many steps there were and this staircase did not prove different. At the bottom to one side, a wall. On the other a hall where the doors, all of them, stood open pouring dim light onto the floor.

"You see, Sloane! It's fine. Look how much light there is!" But it was not where Orabella wanted to be. She knew the ballroom was across the main hall and that was where she had left the lamp, she was sure she had had it till then. *Curse me for losing my head, afraid of nothing.*

"I suppose, ma'am, and we can look for a bit this afternoon if you really want but we're on the wrong side of things here," Sloane relented.

"Are we? This place is built so strangely."

"Yes, I don't know exactly what door you need but I think I can get you there. Just this once, all right?" She looked nervously up the stairs they had come from before taking Orabella's arm again. "We'll go back through the house on this floor."

Orabella grinned. Things were different, they had formed a new bond between them. They had secrets; they had broken the rules together and now they continued. *We can trust each other*, Orabella thought happily. They were friends.

The rooms were different.

Still storage, as the rest of the house, but they were filled with *things*.

"Sloane! Come look!" Orabella sang, stopping in the first one, bright with sun and filled with dishes. Years' worth of china, switched out with the seasons and never passed on.

"We shouldn't touch it, someone might be upset," Sloane warned, standing at the door while Orabella moved through the towers of plates and bowls, stacked like porcelain castles.

"Wouldn't it be nice if they were in the garden? Like little fairy houses, wouldn't that be a delight?" She giggled, lifting a white

cup, blowing the dust from it, revealing a still smooth and shimmering side.

"We have to be careful, what if something breaks?"

"No one cares, there's been no one here in years. Look at the
dust! We could smash up this whole room and no one would be the
wiser for years and years. Grab that crate," she said, a quick, liquid
idea coming over her.

"For what?" Sloane asked, lifting the wooden box.

"We're going to take some, for the garden." Orabella picked up
a plate, brushed it off, found pale pink. Into the box and then another in blue, green, cups, bowls. A rainbow assortment. "All right,
let's go," she hummed.

"You're very strange," Sloane said.

"I know," Orabella replied, thinking of Elias telling her he liked
her quirks, of the empty halls with only her maid. "It's all right here
though, isn't it? It doesn't bother you, does it?"

Sloane shook her head.

"Good," she said, feeling bolder, lighter. She'd escaped her
room, she'd come to this place and no one was the wiser. They were
strange and the house was what it was but it was all right, everything was all right. They moved to the next room.

All vases, their flowers long since gone. One put into the
box. Another room, small glass figurines that someone, one of
the portraits that had no name, must have collected with great
enthusiasm, their efforts left to gather dust and moss and mold.
The windows here were broken; the wind came into the room
freely. The mushrooms she had seen before grew under the sills,
hiding from the light; the wood of the floor farther back was
stained dark with rot. Delighted, Orabella stepped carefully over
the threshold, and knelt to the floor where most of the surviving
figures waited. Many had been broken, knocked over by mice or

the wind and rain that came in. "Sloane, come here, pick some! I think these are made in Italy, in Venice."

She did, laughing, her fears put to rest. Together they picked among the glass, so many of the fine little things broken. Legs and heads missing. They made a game of it, guessing at them, imagining the sounds of animals from faraway places neither of them had ever seen.

"It's getting later," Sloane said suddenly. "We should go, if you want to see the garden."

"Yes! I'm sorry, I still can't keep time in this place. I'll follow you, no more stops, besides, our box is full." The crate was topped with little treasures.

They passed more rooms, bursting with other things. Covered in dust, covered in moss, blocked by heavy doors. Halls of peeling paper, carpet only a memory, forgotten by everyone. But they laughed and chatted and the sound echoed down the dark stretches, at each twist and turn.

Orabella tried to make sense of the place from the windows. They had turned so much she had lost her place. She saw the forest and then a new turn and there was nothing but another view of the manor and then a turn again and there was a pond, small and hidden like the view from her window. Korringhill was large, sprawling, and held a quiet world inside it.

The light came suddenly, and she looked back at the space they had passed through. Saw the shadows of closed doors and nothing else, but she, impossibly, recognized where they were.

"The Master's rooms," she said softly, forgetting that she had sworn to call Hastings anything else. "How do you navigate this all?"

"Yes, we shouldn't stay. Please, Orabella, don't dawdle here." Cagey again. They were back in the domain of Mrs. Locke; a threat there, one that a few minutes outside wouldn't overcome. They were friends, but other things too, and those other things between them still mattered, no matter how much Sloane and she had laughed in the halls.

She passed the room where she had seen the portrait, the door still shut tight. The painting likely left on the floor to rot, like everything was left in the house. It didn't matter. It was only a painting like so many others covered in dust. For a moment she considered going back, replacing it on the wall. She'd promised Sloane though. She kept walking.

Their chatter had slowed, become quieter, when Sloane suddenly sighed. "I don't know why you want to see this. You'll be disappointed, miss, it's just another garden."

"It feels personal, like it's mine. Maybe if I can think of something to do with that one, the other won't be so overwhelming," she mused.

Sloane considered her words before nodding. "That makes sense but what did you want this stuff for? You don't need these plates and cups in your room."

"I want to see if we can really make a little fairy town. Wouldn't that be fun, don't you think?"

"It's a little childish, I think," Sloane said shyly, afraid to insult.

The words stabbed at her anyway. Little knives turning in her gut, her throat. Orabella forced a smile, an explanation. "I'll have children eventually. It would be nice to have something to do with them when they're old enough."

"I didn't think!" Sloane relented and a silence fell between them. A guilty, embarrassed sort of silence, each unsure of what to say.

They entered into the main hall where the staircase waited and all the walk-throughs to those other, wild spaces that the house hid. Sloane crossed the steps. "This way, miss," she whispered as they reached the double doors opposite where they had come from.

Orabella's heart skipped. This she knew, the silver ballroom. *My lamp*, she thought to herself. She had forgotten, distracted by the idea of making the little make-believe town, by the rooms with all their odd, pretty things. But she mustn't forget.

"Be careful, we're not supposed to be here at all. It's being worked on. Or it will be again, eventually, when the Master decides."

She remembered the moldering wood and dusty bricks from her first trip. They were exactly the same, untouched even by her passing. *Everything is waiting in this house.* "I'm in no rush, there's plenty of time."

They turned away from the dark hall that Orabella thought would lead them to the ballroom. The doors here were open and the sun came through the windows that hadn't been boarded over for broken glass. It shimmered on the ground in what were otherwise stripped rooms.

"My bedroom is above this?" Orabella asked as they passed another room.

Sloane nodded but offered nothing in the way of explanation.

The sun splashed across the floor in the gray halls, making soft contrast. Dust motes danced in the light and Orabella saw potential. A sad beauty, near to the kind that existed in the garden, in the ballroom. Freed from the oppressive darkness, something could be made of them. The house looked back at her, the weight of expectation on her skin, pressing into her blood.

More people, a better family, she mused. She touched her belly. Elias hadn't left anything behind in their lovemaking. *I wish to know you better*, he said, cleaning himself from her thighs when she asked. The memory of a warm weight in her arms made her shiver. Every night that passed made that first bruising heavy kiss, that horrible drunken dinner, seem more like a dream. More unreal. They were only a sad family in a sad house. Everyone would make a better impression when she met them again. If she did. Elias hadn't said anything about it, and when she was with him he was kissing her and she could not remember the things that worried and troubled her.

Orabella collided with Sloane; they had stooped. A shut door but on either side windows, the dry grass and weeds reaching to the panes from the ground.

"Is this it?" she asked excitedly. Orabella reached for the doorknob, her hand curving over the cool metal, and she turned. Disappointment rose in her when it didn't move, but then it released, the mechanism in the door shifted, and she pulled it open.

The rain had stopped. Cool air blew away the dust and, shivering, she stepped outside, laughing.

"Sloane! Come on! Come out with me! This is such a lovely little space!" Excitement coursed through her; the mystery solved, she hiked her skirts above the ankle and stepped over rocks and grass. *It's all overgrown but a bench and some care, oh, how lovely this could be*, she thought. *Not a garden, not really, a courtyard. I could manage this.*

In the middle of the hidden space she turned, as she had in the ballroom. Laughing, she took high, stomping steps in a circle, beating down the tall grasses. Satisfied, she called Sloane again, reached out for the box and settled it all on the ground. "From here, we'll be able to see it during the day, see?" she said, pointing up at her own window where it had stopped raining outside.

Sloane, confused but willing, joined her on the ground. "We should have gotten your cloak, I wasn't thinking. It's so cold and you'll get ill, it's damp."

"I'm sturdier than that." Orabella laughed as she moved the

pieces from the boxes. "Besides, it's better if we can anchor them in the mud."

They placed the dishes and vases, stacking them to form little mock homes with the glass animals around. A little village, as Orabella had said, laughing. Their hands were covered in dirt and dust, Orabella's skirts made filthy in their play, but her smile was real, her laughter genuine, and if Elias could see her, he'd be pleased. So pleased. The sun crept over them, the air cooled, and even Orabella, lost in time as she was in those halls, could see that the hour was late. She looked at the windows that looked out onto her garden from the first floor.

The windows stared back at her, dark as midnight despite the sun. *Closed rooms.* She stood, gathered her skirts, crushed the dry grass between her little fairy town and the glass with her steps.

She cupped her hands over her eyes, blocking out the sun as she had the flame in her lamp, and pressed her face against the window. The panes creaked in their frames but held. A bedroom fitted with sheets and pillows. *Elias*, she wondered, leaning closer, searching for some hint of her husband. *No*, she remembered, *he said he was on the third floor.* She looked closer: a bedroom, set as a bedroom, not storage but meant for use. And the door was open.

She pressed her face closer, trying to find what waited on the other side of the hall, and saw a face, ghostly white, staring back at her.

"Sloane!" she shouted, jumping back, turning to find the girl as she scrambled away from the window. "There's someone there!"

"We've been caught!" she moaned in return.

Of course, it's just another maid or Mrs. Locke, I'll tell them that it was my fault. But the woman didn't appear to be in the dark gowns of the servants and her face was pale. She pressed herself against the glass again, even as Sloane yanked at her arm.

The room was empty, the door closed, but there was one thing.

Catching the light, just so, sitting on an end table, was her lamp. "There's no one." She stumbled over her words. "It must have been my reflection,"

"Come on! We'll be in trouble."

There wasn't time to look again. Sloane, fluttery, nervous, was too frightened now and it was late, really and truly. She had taken too much time in her games, forgotten why she had come, and it didn't matter because the lamp was there, waiting, just on the other side of the window in a place she had never been. Orabella nodded, her hands cold, her head throbbing suddenly. The little garden didn't seem as sweet any longer and she wanted away from the space. *But you can never be away anymore, you live here now*, she thought, twisting her hands into the skirts she held. *No.* She pushed the sticky, sick fear away. *It was moved, someone was cleaning and found it, I'm jumping at nothing.*

Sloane grabbed her hand and pulled her back into the house. She kicked the door closed gracelessly as they passed through.

"Sloane!" Orabella laughed. "It's just tea! I'll say I made us late."

But Sloane didn't answer, she dragged Orabella, her grip tight, Orabella's steps tripping, running to keep her arm from leaving the socket. They were back in the hall and together they ran down it, avoiding the abandoned construction. They arrived at the door out of breath but slowed and walked through, as a proper lady and her maid. Orabella opened her mouth to tell Sloane that there had been nothing to worry over, that everything was as it should be, that she was allowed to wander in her own home, but stopped herself.

Across from them, over the wide expanse of tiled floor, was Mrs. Locke.

They were struck still by the old woman's presence, and she

moved across that space violent and focused. Orabella tried to find her voice but it was Sloane who did so first.

"Please, ma'am. I'm so sorry, I know we're not permitted, I was only doing my duty." Sloane shrank as she spoke and Mrs. Locke was upon them.

"You've let the wife be late for her tea," Mrs. Locke said to Sloane but the words were meant for Orabella. "We never let our Ladies miss their tea."

The old woman turned and Orabella, wordlessly, followed. Orabella looked back at Sloane but she wouldn't meet her eyes.

Later, when she was wrapped in the ginger, wild scent of her husband, covered in blankets, the room dark as it often was now that their bodies knew more of each other, he laughed close and husky. "You're giving Mrs. Locke a hard time."

"Is it so important? I'd rather spend my time as I'd like. I do not always care for tea in the afternoon, or a nap. I understand Claresta has some needs but I am perfectly healthy."

He hummed in thought, his hands roaming lazily over her, teasing and toying. "You are that. You may do what you wish, my Orabella. You are good and careful but please try to follow the schedule of the house. Skip your afternoon rest if you must but do try. Things are better when we try. I trust you won't be any trouble."

But in the morning, proved a liar, she woke with a sore throat and an aching body, a divine punishment for playing in the mud when she should have been at tea.

Chapter Sixteen

The air outside was warm, not quite hot, a beautiful spring day still early enough in the season that it was rare and the nights were cold. Early enough that when it rained, the chill stayed in the air, but it had been days since the last downpour and the world outside was alive and green.

It had been days, too, since she left the house. Her bad luck, her poor planning to run out without a cloak or shawl in a too-thin dress. Orabella's fever had been sudden and high, her cough wet and wheezing. She begged to have her window opened, for air, but Sloane, Mrs. Locke, even Elias said no, that would make her worse. They gave her tea, thick with honey, heavy with herbs, for her throat, for her fever.

The dreams were wild and haunting beasts that slid over her mind, drowned her in their depths. The fawn pranced on air, golden hooves and dark eyes dripping thick fluid, and she, body heavy and foreign, ran after it, convinced it knew where her little lantern was. Barking laughter following her down halls until she was caught, pinned down, and teeth met her throat.

After days, the fever broke and the world was bright and warm, utterly transformed into true spring. She recovered under the sun, wrapped in a blanket in front of her window. Her husband read to her in the afternoon and she thought of Claresta, wondered if the gentle care she felt for Elias for staying with her was how Claresta felt towards her.

Days blended together until Sloane came to the room, vibrating with excitement.

They were to go out.

The carriage was the same one that had brought her to the manor. The driver was already in his seat, holding the horses. Another man, dressed plainly as Elias had been dressed at their first meeting, waited at the door. He spoke quietly to Sloane but at Orabella and Elias's approach, he stopped, pulled himself up, and she saw his face for the first time.

So this is Cullen, she thought, a greeting on her tongue. She had seen him again since that moment in the window roaming the garden, but Sloane had said that he worked with the old man, Grey, in the stables. Here was the proof.

"Good morning, ma'am," he said softly, shyly. A young man but not so young that he should be shy. Older than Sloane, closer to Orabella's twenty-six years. But he had a sharp, good-natured face. Clean shaven but there was a roughness to him. His chestnut hair was too long and oily, his clothes were clean but worn.

"Good morning! You must be Cullen. I saw you from the window when I first arrived."

He looked confused. "I'm sorry, I don't recall—"

"It's all right, you wouldn't. I think you were hunting. There was a deer. I'm afraid you missed." She laughed and he joined her.

"That was a good while ago now! You have a good memory!" he said.

"I wish I did! But no, I had just never seen anyone hunting before, not really. It was new."

"Well then, I'm glad I provided you with some enjoyment because I surely failed to provide dinner!"

Even Sloane laughed at the joke, the mask she usually wore in front of the other members of the family slipping.

"You're very funny, Mr. Cullen. Are you coming to town with us?"

"Yes, ma'am. To help with your packages and such."

"I can't imagine I'll have much. I'm really just going to look."

"You may purchase whatever strikes your fancy. There is nothing there that you can't have. If you want something you can't find, order it. Don't hold yourself back, Orabella," Elias interjected.

She'd forgotten he was there at all. His face was hard, his eyes cold and locked on Cullen even though he spoke to her. Hostility. Elias took her in his arms and kissed her fully on the mouth. When he let her go, both servants were looking away, embarrassed. "Elias!" she squeaked.

"You are a Blakersby. You do not need to worry about such things. Whatever you desire will be taken care of."

"Am I?" she asked. She meant it to be playful but the tone did not match.

"You are my wife. Do as you wish," he said.

Cullen held the door of the carriage for her and she climbed inside, Sloane following after. The curtains inside were tied back and Orabella waved at Elias but he did not return the gesture. She sat back and twisted her skirts. She had to say something to Sloane, turn the mood.

"What a nice surprise for the day!" she sang.

Sloane kept her mask. "Yes. It is very nice for a trip."

"Oh, Sloane, please! I know I got you in trouble and I didn't mean to but it won't happen again," she burst out. "Please, I'm sorry, don't be cross."

Sloane giggled. "You sound like a little girl, younger than me! It wasn't so bad. Mrs. Locke just scolded me on the danger. Said I should know better and she's right! We can't do that again."

"But we know the way now and we know it's safe. Besides, Elias said it was all right, Mrs. Locke won't be a problem anymore, I promise." She couldn't say that they had to. That she needed to retrieve her lamp before Elias noticed it and everyone knew that she'd slipped out. *But what am I so worried over?* She frowned, thinking that for the first time. Elias hadn't ever been harsh with her, not really. Even in anger, Mrs. Locke didn't direct her venom at her, so what, then?

"But it's not Mrs. Locke!" Sloane stopped, looked away. "I'm sorry, it's nothing. If Mr. Robinson says that it's all right, then it must be. Mr. Robinson is so generous. You'll have a nice day today."

"Blakersby," Orabella corrected her, and regretted it. It placed the line back between them. Lady and maid. "We must try to be careful about such things, all of us," she added hurriedly. *We're friends, we must be careful, please*, she wanted to say.

"Right, of course," Sloane responded, her lips pushing downward.

"Tell me what shops there are," Orabella said quickly, hopefully, dragging Sloane back into the casual space of their friendship.

The ground changed under them as Sloane described the small town storefronts. Dressmaker, accessories, she ticked things off her fingers and Orabella relaxed, happy that they were talking again. It became smoother than it had been and she looked out the window to see the town buildings moving past, the horses slowing, their destination reached.

Orabella hadn't really seen it before; she had been preoccupied with her husband, her new home. Her eyes swept over the quaint buildings again and it all looked more welcoming. The light, or her own settled mind, she wasn't sure, but everything was smaller and cozier than it had been in Bristol. The streets were well kept and the people bustled here and there on their business, only turning their heads to gaze at the carriage that had appeared in their midst. Single- and double-story brick buildings with shingled roofs surrounded them.

Again she was in the center of Oxbury, the carriage taking up all the available space, out of place, a dark blot on the quaint town.

"Where would you like to go first, ma'am?" Sloane asked.

A baker, a pharmacist, a copper market for pots and pans. But there was also a dressmaker, a jeweler, and other accessories. A small stationery shop and another that appeared to sell curios.

"I wasn't expecting such nice shops." Even through the window she could see the quality of their wares. In sharp contrast to the threadbare manor. The wealth they, the Blakersbys, claimed to have. Everything about Oxbury was small but incredibly wealthy.

"For the London people." Sloane shrugged.

"The London people?" Orabella repeated. "Is that what you call them?"

Sloane nodded. "Yes. Will some of your friends come? I've heard that ladies like you go visiting."

"I'm afraid that I don't have an awful lot of friends." She stopped before mentioning Jane but a sudden and sharp sorrow filled her. It had been weeks, no letters had ever returned to her. "Do we get mail at the house?"

Sloane shrugged. "Yes, it goes to the Master's rooms. I don't have any cause to pay attention to it. I can ask Mrs. Locke for you, if you'd like. Are you awaiting something?"

She had seen Orabella write every letter, taken the envelopes herself, but it was Sloane. Once the duty was done, she would not think on it. "No, I was just curious, I suppose. I'm sure there's nothing to be said about it. I need to decide on where we're going, don't I?"

Her thoughts were broken and distracted. She wanted to know why there had been no letters, even just to say that hers had been received, but there was no way to press the issue; she was very far from Bristol. The demands of her day were more present and she tried to focus on them, pull herself back. "A dressing gown, I think, for the evenings. The house is chilly." And the one she had was still stuffed under the mattress. *Should I tell the truth, maybe not about the door, but that I went out that day? No, she trusted me and I betrayed her.*

Sloane nodded and led her into the dressmaker shop. The inside was more spacious than it had looked from the street and more smartly decorated than she had thought it would be. A velvet up-holstered chair for the shop's guest to sit in, for her, and a table for tea and pastries. The walls were lined with fabric, a single, glorious dress was displayed on a mannequin but for all its beauty, even Orabella, who had not been in society in over a year, could tell that it was an old style, out of vogue but still gorgeous. Wealthy but behind the times. She did keep up with the papers.

Sloane greeted the shopkeeper, a middle-aged man with thin-ning brown hair and tight, pointed features. Slender with an im-peccable suit jacket and trousers, every bit of him in place. Orabella expected his smile to turn, to see a flicker of doubt in his eyes as she was used to when she had a chance to visit the shops in Bristol, but none of that happened. Instead, the owner showed them to seats, livelily chatted, and called for her measurements to be taken.

"All this fuss, I really only came to look." Orabella sighed.

"Sir will be upset if you don't get at least one dress."

Orabella looked at her curiously. Sloane was sure, firm. It was not optional. "How do you know?"

"Mrs. Locke told me that the Master said so."

"If he wanted me to buy a dress, he could have just told me himself. I know my wardrobe can use a few updates, no need to dance around it."

"Oh no, I'm sure it wasn't that. But please, ma'am, pick something."

The owner nodded, agreeing with Sloane and motioning to the selection of fabrics. When Orabella didn't move, Sloane reached forward, sorted through them like a parent with a child. "This one, I think. It will be nice. It suits you."

A dusty color somewhere between rose and peach. A sunset color. Orabella ran it through her own fingers, the feel soft and luxurious. "It's beautiful. But where would I wear something like that?"

"Why do you need somewhere to wear it to?" Sloane asked, confused. "The Lady, Ms. Claresta, she never goes anywhere but all her dresses are fine."

"Yes, that's right. I suppose I've never thought of it. A dress, then, something I can make use of. Your style books?"

Cakes and tea were served while Sloane and Orabella flipped through dress books. The seamstress came out, made pleasant comments and helped them select fabrics. She suggested evening gowns, garments for fancy outings, but Orabella declined.

"I'm afraid that I don't have plans for anything like that. I'm sorry to disappoint," Orabella said sweetly, a little overwhelmed at their demands. "I think my wedding was the last thing of note." She stopped, too late realizing how it made her sound, made the family sound. "I am just getting settled in the house, I imagine I'll be staying home to get used to things for a bit longer." She laughed but her body remembered how the dress, covered with cutting glass, felt pressing into her skin. Too tight, too long.

"Of course," the dressmaker said, all smiles. "Then I suggest these styles, they're perfect for receiving guests."

She nodded, eager to move on from her slip, eager to move on from those memories of barking laughter and that horrible, horrible gift. "These are all so lovely. But just these will do," she said, indicating the styles she had chosen. Just two—her clothing was fine, she didn't want to be greedy even though excitement snapped in her with each turn of the page. "I need a new dressing gown," she said, finally closing the book to cut off the desire.

"I think we have one ready that may work for you. It's an older style but the color would be lovely. It is a fine piece, would you like to see it?"

"Yes," she said quickly. The mood had shifted, just so, and the day didn't seem so bright any longer, but it wasn't the fault of the dressmaker or Sloane or anyone else. Just her own guilt.

The dressmaker went to the back and returned a few moments later with the robe over his arm. "Will this do for you, ma'am?"

The dressing gown was made from a peach-colored material with lace trim and bow accents. She touched it and found the fabric to be light and soft, smooth against her skin, silk. A beautiful piece. The shop was old-fashioned as the dress it displayed out of season, but it could not be faulted for its work.

"It's lovely," she said, forgetting she needed something heavy to replace the first.

"I'll have it resized for you. The summers here get so dreadfully hot and the color suits you. It will serve you well."

"It is beautiful. I'm—"

"I know who you are," he said, cutting her off quickly, unsettling her, drawing attention to her misstep.

"How silly of me, the carriage is very distinct." She laughed. "When do you think the robe at least will be ready?" Orabella asked.

"In a few days. It's no large matter. Please do feel free to request anything else of us. We have your measurements, no need to come all the way back here." His tone was lighter, friendly again, but he had moved to the door as she spoke, his hand hovered over the knob.

She shook her head. "No, you have been most thorough."

"I'll have everything sent," he replied, sweeping the door open to allow them to pass.

She stepped out, Sloane following close. "Everything will look so lovely on you! You have such a good eye. It must be because you're a real lady. You need a hat! And some shoes!"

Orabella let herself be led to the next shop, where they tried on hats, picked two and then the shoes to follow. She stumbled in choosing, there were so many options, but she settled on styles she thought would suit, fed on Sloane's excitement. She gifted the girl a hat for their walks, but she wouldn't agree to a new pair of shoes. She said it wouldn't be proper.

"Where next?" Sloane asked when they left the shoe store. "I think Coral and Brass is open. They have the loveliest accessories! You'll adore them, ma'am!"

"I'm a little tired of clothing and such. I need, I mean I would like, to get some yarn and a hook or a set of needles. A pattern to follow." Orabella spoke haltingly, embarrassed for asking after such a small thing. In Bristol, she used only whatever was on special, made hats and socks for children who did not have them. Made shawls and mittens for herself. Nothing really thoughtful or fashionable. There was no reason, no point. But now there was no reason not to indulge.

"It's been so long since we've come to town! The Lady has all of her dresses sent in. She never comes out. This way, ma'am!" Sloane nearly sang, clearly pleased to be away from the manor.

"Claresta is the Lady, then?"

"Yes." She frowned. "But you're here now. I suppose that changes things."

No, I'm the bride, she remembered, vaguely, like a dream, and her mood soured more. "I don't think so."

"Are you tired? We should get home, you're recovering still," Sloane said suddenly.

"I'm fine, I would really like some yarn." *Maybe I am just tired.* The shopkeeper seemed to be missing in the shop Sloane had led her to, but the store was open, and although empty of patrons save the two of them, it had no shortage of stock. Crammed in every nook and cranny there was something for sale. Empty tins for sweets, old books, some fabric that wasn't nearly as nice as what the dressmaker displayed, wooden toys for small hands. It reminded her of the manor with all its little treasures. A set of little wooden dolls, new denizens and decorations for her fairy town built in her secret garden, grabbed her attention. She considered them, turned their simple figures over in her fingers, glancing down when she replaced one with others. They rested on a worn stack of books. Fairy stories. She moved the cat and opened the top one. She hummed, content, reading the first few sentences.

"Over here, ma'am!" Sloane's voice sounded like a shout in the empty store. Her eyes were bright, her smile wide, and Orabella stopped, hopeful. Happy to see her happy after days of blankness. She pointed to a basket of yarn. Skeins of beautiful colors, rose, a deep mulberry, not quite black.

"What nice colors," Orabella sang, crossing to her, the book still in her hand. With her free hand she reached into the basket, brushing her fingers along the hanks of yarn. Soft but sturdy. Quality.

"Isn't it pretty? They would all look so nice for you."

"A cardigan," she agreed. She nodded towards a small pile of books, the top one featuring two crossed knitting needles. "Look there for a pattern, would you?" She picked up a hank of the dark purple, it reminded her of the wine served with every dinner. "Do you think Claresta would like a shawl? Or a blanket for her lap?"

"I wouldn't know, ma'am. She's never been in my care," Sloane replied without looking up from the book she flipped through. "Do you like this one?" She turned the pages towards Orabella.

The statement seemed strange, the family was too small, she'd been there too long, how could she not know? "I'm sure it's fine. Oh! What's this?"

Behind the little display, folded neatly, was a small stack of knitted goods. Likely from the same family that had made the yarn itself. She dropped the purple yarn back into the basket and reached for the knitted fabric of the same color, pulling it free. She shook it out, revealing a lap blanket with squares made of a repeating leaf pattern.

The door swung open and she turned to find a woman bustling in. Red faced and middle-aged, her hair, which once must have been a red-blond color, was now streaked with gray. She had small brown eyes and thin red lips. A solid, full woman.

"Sorry, sorry," she said as she rounded the counter and settled herself behind it, placing the length of wood between herself and Orabella. "Do you see anything you fancy?"

Her tone was bright, friendly as everyone's had been, but Orabella could still hear the wariness in it. *I shouldn't be surprised,* she thought, it must be her, she was new and it was a small town. She smiled warmly in return, ignoring the coldness from the woman.

"Yes, I'd like to buy all the yarn you have here, that book of patterns, a set of needles, and these," she said, holding out the blanket and the book of fairy tales.

"I keep the needles back here," the woman mumbled, turning and retrieving them from a hidden crevice. She placed them on the counter and held her hands out for the rest. Orabella moved to pass them over and the woman pulled back suddenly, grasping her own fingers. "Just put them down, on the counter. I'll wrap them up for you."

Orabella smiled, attempting to show the woman that she was harmless, friendly, but the air was cold around them, colder than the weather. She held her own hands out in front of her. The woman wrapped the items in brown paper and tied it all with twine.

"Oh no, ma'am," she said. The package secure, she motioned for Sloane to step forward and passed it off to the maid. She didn't ask for payment. She knew who she was.

"Thank you." Orabella forced the words to come out bright and clear. And she was thankful that she had found the yarn, it felt like something for her, really and truly, and made the trip worthwhile. "Good day, ma'am. Thank you again for the yarn."

Her steps lighter, she followed Sloane out to the carriage, happy to have come but ready, she admitted silently, to return. *I've rushed out of bed too soon, I think.* The cold had gone but in the warm sun she felt weak and sleepy.

A church bell rang. She'd never heard them before, not in the manor, and she looked around, finding the stone building, the steeple jutting above the house line, just a bit farther into the town. "The church!" Jane filled her thoughts with each clang of the bell. Noon already; the morning had passed quickly, much more quickly than it ever did in the manor's halls.

"Sloane, I want to go to the church."

"Why? Do you pray? You've never asked to go on Sundays," she said, passing the package to Cullen, who waited by the open door of the carriage.

"No, I mean, yes, well, not really. Not as well as I should. My friend Jane, she's a nun back in Bristol and she said she would write to the local parish. I should introduce myself."

She didn't give Sloane time to protest. Like with the trip to the hidden garden, she started walking in the direction of the church.

"Wait! Wait, ma'am!" Sloane called, and Orabella slowed, turning back to see the maid and Cullen coming towards her. "We shouldn't wander away alone."

"Are murders common on the streets of Oxbury? Is there a madman snatching up women in broad daylight here?" Orabella laughed.

"I'm sorry?" Cullen asked.

"*The Candle* always has a story like that. A poor girl disappears because she walked alone at night. But it's daytime. I think we'll be all right. Nothing can get us in the light." She laughed again, bubbly, hoping to pass the mood, forced as it was, along to her companions.

"No, it's just not proper. You're a lady," Cullen explained.

"I suppose it's like that even here." She sighed. "Well, come along."

"What's *The Candle*?" he asked.

Sloane jumped in, excited to explain, and the three of them made conversation under the watchful eyes of windows as they passed. In time they left the streets and found a worn path. The church was a small building on a small hill. One single steeple and enough room for a small congregation. Plain in a rural way. Simple stone, no stained glass. A squat house off to the side where the Father stayed. Between it and the town, the grass grew tall and green.

Just as they approached, the priest left the house by the back way and waved at them. An elderly man, clean shaven with his gray hair cropped short. Portly in his dark cassock, he looked friendly under the spring sun.

Orabella picked up her skirts and sped up, Sloane and Cullen slowing.

"We'll wait here, ma'am," she said. "You'll be taking confession or something like that, won't you?"

"Perhaps," she said slowly, eyeing the two. "I won't be long."

She crossed the distance alone. "Hello!" she called brightly.

The priest's eyes flicked from her waiting servants back to her. "You're the wife."

"Yes? I'm Orabella Mumthrope, I mean Blakersby. How did you—"

He laughed, a full-belled, kind sound. "Don't make anything of it! It's a small town and news is news. I'd heard the younger one, Elias, had taken a wife."

"Younger one?"

"Of the family." He waved his hand, dismissing the question. "I'm glad you've come to see me, but I'd rather see you on Sunday. An example for the rest of them." He chided gently.

"I'm sorry, I don't know your name, Father."

"Forgive me! I'm so used to this little town. My manners! Eugene. Father Gene to everyone around here."

"It's nice to meet you! I was wondering if you'd happened to hear from my friend Jane."

His brows creased. "Jane, the Browns' girl?"

"No! Sorry, I suppose you would know her by Sister Jennine Ignatius. She's a nun in Bristol, she said she would write and I hadn't heard from her so I thought maybe you had or would know if there was some trouble at the church?"

He smiled kindly and patted her shoulder. Warm, fatherly. "Don't trouble yourself. I'm sure your friend is fine. The mail doesn't run often or regularly. There's a coach but it doesn't come around much unless it's the spring and summer. When there are more people. Outside of that it's once, twice a month."

"Then my letters are probably at the post, waiting. I wish someone had told me!" She laughed. "Overeager as always. My aunt is always scolding me to be more patient."

His brows moved and he glanced over her shoulder at her escort. When she looked they were speaking to each other, heads tilted close. "Do you," he asked, his attention back on her, "want to come in for a cup of tea?"

"I would like to but I'm very tired. I'm just getting over a fever and I think I've used all my energy. I only came by to introduce myself."

Worry rippled across his features. "I don't know much about that family. I try not to involve myself in the gossip of the town. If you need anyone to speak to, remember that the church is here for you. Always."

Orabella paused, turned over his words and looked back at Sloane and Cullen. "Thank you, I'll remember that, but I'm treated very well. I'm sorry to trouble you."

"No trouble at all. Be well."

She said her goodbyes and walked back to her companions, who ended their conversation quickly, nervously. *There is something else between them*, she mused, and wondered if Sloane would tell her, if they were really still friends.

"Did you have a good morning, ma'am?" Sloane asked as they neared the carriage.

"Yes," Orabella answered, but she was exhausted. Overwhelmingly so. "Mrs. Locke will be pleased to know that today I think I'll nap."

Sloane laughed and started to talk about the dresses they had seen in the style book, the hats and shoes they'd left behind. How nice it would be on their next trip. Hopeful and bright while Orabella stared out the window, idly daydreaming.

Home again, Mrs. Locke waited for them, Manda by her side. "I hope I'm not too late for lunch. I got Claresta a gift while I was out!"

Mrs. Locke narrowed her eyes. "We expected some delay today. Come, then."

I wonder if she'll like the blanket, I wonder if she likes anything, she thought as they entered the halls that led to Claresta's room. She forced herself away from her pointless questions, tried instead to focus on what little joy a gift could bring.

A hollow moan carried lightly down the halls, sending a freezing jolt of fear through her. Like wind, like a dying thing. Pain. Her pace quickened until she moved at a run.

In some part of her mind she heard Mrs. Locke calling for her to wait but she ignored the imagined voice, quick to jump, and barreled down the hall and around the corners until she was stumbling into Claresta's room. The terrible sound had become sobs without the buffering of the walls but Orabella didn't hear it at all anymore.

The only sound she could hear was the beating of her own heart as she stared at the scene before her.

There, writhing on the bed, half tangled in sheets, was a beast rising from a dark pool where there should have been only the makings of a bed. The smell was thick, sharp. Bile rose in Orabella as she watched the slick, furred creature pulse and writhe in front of her. Long white fur dripping red, body all hanging skin that clung, too long, too much, from its bony form in wet, slick strips. The beast howled, open-mouthed, all sharp teeth.

Orabella screamed.

Chapter Seventeen

Orabella's mind ran too fast for her to catch her thoughts, to piece together what she saw. *Blood.* One word but nothing to withstand the horror of it. Under, the part of her that was all instinct and drive told her to run, to leave the house and halls, go back to the church, beg sanctuary, but her limbs did not listen.

Her body, foolish deceitful flesh and bone, took her to the blood, the thrashing creature.

Pain. The beast howled broken and wretched and Orabella, powerless, thoughtless, ran to it. There was so much blood, it darkened the sheets and formed shiny black eyes that reflected nothing. The smell rolled over her, coppery and sharp.

It was only when she held the gnashing, howling beast that she realized it wasn't a beast but a doll. Her sister-in-law finally come to life. She pulled the soaked sheet from her, heavy with sweat and blood, found her form under it. She tried to calm her but there was no calming her. Orabella could only hold her own screams as she tried to find the source of the injury that would surely be fatal

if not treated, but the woman was fighting her, fighting everything
in her pain.

Claresta stopped suddenly, turned her face, high red spots on
her cheeks, mouth a perfect *O*, and for the first time, Orabella
would think later, the woman noticed her. Claresta's nails, sharp as
claws, dug into Orabella's arm, breaking her hold. Quick as a cat
the woman turned and reached for Orabella's face. Her eyes were
bright and mad but they saw her, focused on her as she turned,
impossibly strong.

Nails, talons, dug into Orabella's skin, dragged, cutting through
the meat of her arms that she'd used by instinct to cover her eyes.
"Claresta! Stop! It's me! It's Orabella!" She yelled but she didn't
know if it mattered, she didn't know if the woman had any idea
of who she was at all. "I only want to help!" she screamed, lamely,
worthless against Claresta's rage, her pain.

And all the while the woman was howling, sobbing, barking,
screaming. A fox. A beast.

"Miss!" Sloane yelled, and there she was, helping to hold the
wild animal who looked just like a woman. The maid, slight and
mousy, grabbed her around the middle, hauling her off Orabella,
panic giving her strength.

Orabella dropped her hands, took a deep breath, and lunged,
grabbing Claresta's wrists, holding them in the air, keeping them
from reaching for her own face or turning and going after Sloane.
There was nothing human in Claresta's eyes.

"Oh no," she said softly, barely a whisper, impossible to hear
under Claresta's howls.

"Mrs. Locke! Mrs. Locke! We need help!" Sloane yelled.

It's too late to help. The thought slipped into Orabella's head as
she looked at the woman's face. She couldn't make sense of it all,
her vision had been reduced to red and white and black. White

arms, white shift, white skin. Pools of black, blooms of red that appeared where there should have been white, white, white.

"It's all right, ma'am, it's all right." A voice, soothing like a mother. Her entire being numb, her arms and hands aching from holding back the red-and-white beast that had been such perfection. Perfect as if she had been painted by that mystery hand that made the mural. A breathing portrait without flaw; now she was wild, rage twisting her features.

Maggie from the kitchen. The one time Orabella had met her she was short, curt with her, but this version was gentle and loving. Strong hands covered with burns reached for the wild thing Orabella held. She tried to explain that it wasn't Claresta, that it was a wild animal wearing her face, that she'd attack, but all she managed was "She's hurt."

"I know, ma'am. I know. You've got to let go," Maggie insisted.

But that was all wrong. If she let go the beast would be free, would attack and rip away more of the doll that she understood the poor woman to be. She shook her head, her eyes back on Claresta, who had morphed even more. Her howls were screams now, wordless and wild. A banshee, haunted, terrible music that echoed in the small room.

"Please!" Maggie was pulling at her fingers and Orabella released Claresta. The strength of the people that held them both pulled them apart, and Orabella tumbled into the arms of Maggie, who dragged her to her feet. But the feet that had been so eager to run into the room would not listen, would not cooperate, and stumbled over the floor. Her body caught in a chair. Claresta's chair, where she was dropped, unceremoniously. "Don't move!" Maggie said now, an order from servant to Lady, the world upside down. *But then, hasn't it always been like that here*, the thought came with laughter, the dark eye of the fawn staring back at her in her memory. How quickly things had turned. From the lovely day, the lovely town, her time in the garden to something else, something truer. Impossible to ignore, impossible to forget. Terrible, bubbling laughter filled her that she couldn't keep down, the whole thing so horrid and absurd and real.

Her laughter mingled with the screams of the woman in the bed. All red and white now and thrashing against the servants. *A fox*, she thought, remembering the sound of them from the forest on that first walk. Barking, screaming calls. *She's a fox, not a doll. She doesn't know how to move in her human skin so she sits and sits and sits*, Orabella thought madly, mind spinning from the violence of it all.

Cullen was there, so quickly from dropping off her hats and yarn, the trophies of her day. Who had told him to come? Who got Maggie? How had help been summoned through all those dark halls to that terrible room? Maggie and Cullen held the madwoman down, and there was Mrs. Locke with something sharp in her twisted hands. A needle gripped between fingers locked in the perfect position to do so. The old woman was bending towards the bed. She was speaking but the words were lost in all the noise.

"Drink this, miss." Sloane, sweet, steady Sloane.

She pushed a cup into Orabella's hands, which she took, wrapping her fingers around the fragile porcelain form, expecting warmth and finding none. The smell was familiar, though. A cup of tea.

"Drink, miss, please." Urgency now as the maid pushed the cup gently upward.

She opened her mouth and the cold tea, thick with honey, poured into it. She gagged but swallowed it in gulps because what else was there to do but drink? Empty, it slipped from her shaking fingers and landed in the cradle of her lap, the dregs of it spilling on her skirts. Leaves forming a fortune that she couldn't decipher.

"It's all right, miss." Sloane again. But no, it wasn't, it was all wrong, why was Claresta in bed? Why, when they were to have lunch as they did every day? But then, she had gone to the shops and the day was so lovely but now muddled and ruined. The details hard to hold—blending, mixing into a nightmare reality.

She turned away from the howling woman. Found the mural. Her head spun and a low sound like wind through the halls filled it. The painting swam in front of her eyes, the small figures moving among the branches. She shook her head but they didn't stop. They caught the mice and popped their heads off. Pulled the cats' tails and ears. Mischievous little things. The foxes watched them all.

She let out a cry but no one could hear. She closed her eyes, wished it all away. Her body felt heavy, her head light. She turned back to the bed.

The world moved slowly. Her sister-in-law had calmed, stopped her fox howls, and another chair had been brought out. Cullen was carrying her, blood on his shirt and vest now, but Claresta was still again, the doll again. He put her in the chair carefully and she looked more like herself, madly like herself all streaked red. Her mouth hung open, her little pink tongue exposed, and her hair hung in tangled strands, stuck to her face. Glassy blue marble eyes and all Orabella could see was the fox woman. Cullen looked at Orabella, his face dark and tight and then gone as he turned back, stomped out of the room just as quickly as he had come.

She watched as Sloane and Manda pulled the sheets from the bed. Blink. They were carrying a tub of water. Blink. Maggie spoke to Claresta in low, hushed tones. Claresta crying, water falling from still eyes. Blink. Manda was bathing the blood from Claresta. Sloane washed the scratches on Orabella's arm with the same water. Blink. Claresta sat naked, still, covered in blue and yellow flaws where there should have been nothing but milk. Off-color blooms dappled her skin. All along her thighs, breasts, and even her arms and shoulders. Like flowers, they had bloomed and lay dying all over her body.

Mouth honey-stuck, no matter how much she swallowed. It trapped Orabella's questions, her words behind the wall of teeth and lips. The honey flowed through her, making her sluggish and numb. The weight of her own limbs pulled her down. Her head full of honey. She closed her eyes, let it fall back.

"He'll be after her again, she can't bear it," Maggie said.

"Maybe he won't, she's here now," said Mrs. Locke.

The bride. She tried to lift her head but she was so tired, so heavy. *Someone is hurting Claresta*, she thought, holding on to the words. Orabella had to remember.

"We shouldn't speak, she needs to be put away. Sloane!" Mrs. Locke again.

Who is Mr. Locke? Orabella wondered in her stupor. She tried to pull herself up, her body refused. *Was Mrs. Locke ever a Bride?*

"Come, miss, it's best if you return to your own room now." Sloane's voice wavered and shook.

She tried to stand but again her feet failed her, her body too heavy, far heavier than it had been. Maggie came to assist, kitchen smoke and spice overlaying the blood, and hauled her up. Between the two she was light.

Dimly Orabella was aware that she was being dragged, forced away from the horror of Claresta. Back to her little room. Orabella couldn't hold her head up. The air pressed against her. Drowned her.

In this house, Orabella was another charge. Her wedding night repeated, Sloane stripped her, dressed her, put her to bed.

"Rest now, miss. It'll be all right. The Lady just had her monthly, that's all. It gets so terrible for her sometimes when it comes, you don't have to worry about anything. Just get some rest. Mr. Robin-son will be by to check in on you. Just get some rest."

There was no moment of transfer. The bright day to the deep honeyed halls of dreaming. Her wedding night again.

In the toiling, thick darkness she couldn't breathe in the too-tight beaded dress. The same scene but this time she stood on the table and her arms were full of fawn, long limbed, honey-colored coat, big dark eye staring up at her. Sticky, sweet. That wild, half-seen family who laughed and made references to history that remained as obscured as the room they dined in. The candle flame never reaching far enough. Claresta was there this time, she sat next to her father, her fingers wrapped around fork and knife, and every time she opened her mouth to laugh a bark came out instead. Above them all the fairies from the mural spun, eating mice and plucking the beads from the gown. The family laughed when the little ones did obscene things alone or with one another. And through it all she stood, still as a statue, a doll put on display just like Claresta.

Orabella stared into Elias's pale eyes sparkling in the dark as he looked back at her, his expression stormy and cold. He reached out his hand for her, as he did after every meal, ready to help her down. She took it, grasping at his fingers, eager to be away from the pale, fae court of his family, her family now.

The table fell away. She fell down, down, down, the dress becoming tighter. She clutched at the fawn, pressed into its soft body, felt it buckle under her as she fell. Through the table and the halls—the house itself had become a living thing and it swallowed her, took her in. The walls were red and fleshy. A throat. The little ones followed her, sprinkling white and yellow fairy dust all over her, tying her in cobwebs, a parade of mice running past holding hands. The darkness was soft as she passed into it. It tangled around her, left her gasping.

Chapter Eighteen

Orabella woke gasping, clawing and kicking at the crush of blankets and body that held her down.

"Love, love, calm down! It's all right." Elias's voice was panicked, and when the halls cleared from her eyes, his concern was on his face. He gripped her shoulders, only freeing them when she stilled, rubbing her arms, soothing. "You're all right."

She looked past him to the closed door, the room, familiar now, cloaked in night. "Is it very late?" she asked, voice cracking and breaking. She tried to swallow but her throat was dry, papery.

"Yes," he answered. "Very late, my love." He sat back from her, brushed her hair from her face, fussed over her thin nightgown. He wore his pants and a work shirt, loose at the collar. His shoulders were draped with the blanket she'd bought for Claresta.

"Is she all right? Claresta, is she . . . herself?"

"She's fine. How sweet you are to think of her." He kissed her knuckles. "You have no need to worry, try to focus on your own care. You were knocked around some."

Her arms were crisscrossed with wounds. She tried to recall the attack, but the details were flashing, sun-washed, twinkling shards of memory that cut her whenever she tried to grasp them.

"You've missed dinner. You must be starved," he hummed. Her wedding night, again and again. In the dream, in her room. Orabella looked for fairies over his head but there was nothing, just the light of the oil lamps placed on the tables in the room.

On her vanity sat a covered dish on a tray. A decanter dark with wine and an empty glass. "I'm thirsty."

"Yes, you must be." He stood, took up the decanter and the glass.

"No!" she squeaked, pausing him. "The wine is too heavy, can I have some water, please?"

He looked like he would deny her but then stopped, smiled. "Water, then you'll eat some and the wine to settle you. You were having a nightmare, I think."

"Yes." The fawn stared at her from the edge of the bed. Blink. The animal was gone but the wounds on her arms remained. Elias filled the space, holding a cup to her lips. She drank until he took it away.

"Now you must eat something." He went back to the table, fussed with the tray, and turned, presenting her with a plate of pastries, sugar thick and crusty across the tops.

"Where did these come from?"

"Maggie made them, special for you to have. Said they would hold better than dinner." He plucked the one from the top and, settling on the bed, presented it to her.

She knew what to do—had she not watched Claresta be fed for weeks? Had Elias not done it himself the morning after the wedding dinner? She opened her mouth; his pleasure was clear. One pastry, all fruit and dough and sugar chewed and swallowed, followed by another then another until the plate was empty. He presented his fingers, she licked sugar from them, mindlessly.

Orabella could feel his laugh through his kiss. Different from the hard possessiveness of their last kiss before her day in town. Another time. As far away from the nighttime house as Bristol was from Oxbury. As far away as the morning she said yes to him.

Her husband was at her neck, kissing, mumbling, humming over her. The familiar jittery feeling of pleasure stirred in her. A ticklish warmth in her belly and between her thighs, an anticipation of his touch. His hands caressed her breasts through the thin fabric of her gown, and she sucked in her breath. He growled against her and she froze, reminded of her dream, of his barking, screaming family. His barking, screaming sister.

Elias pulled away quickly, guiltily. "I'm sorry, that was thoughtless of me. You need to rest, to heal."

"It's just some scratches," she said, her head still swimming from the surge of desire in her.

"There shouldn't be a mark on you. Take tonight to rest, you've had a fright."

"No one's told me what's wrong with Claresta. I thought she was just . . . that something had happened to her, but I'm not sure anymore. Please, won't you tell me?" Orabella felt unlike herself, floating, unreal. The feeling had been there for a long time now. Days. Weeks.

Elias kissed her forehead. "Claresta is not well. Her mind is gone, it's how her mother died."

"An affliction passed down."

"Through the blood on her mother's side. A madness, I'm afraid. She is not like that normally and I'm sorry you had to see that."

It was all so simple, it made so much sense, but she remembered the awful garden all over Claresta's body. Petals of bile yellow and violet blue. Flowers where there should only have been snow. A lie.

"I should have asked sooner, it was thoughtless of me."

"No, you've been perfect. And now you must sleep." He stood and poured a glass of wine for her. "By the way, where is your other little lamp? I see only one here."

Her fingers froze around the glass. "I don't, I mean I'm not sure what—"

Elias pushed the glass on her and kissed her, stopping her half-formed excuses. "I'm sure one of the maids took it without thinking after turning down the bed. That girl of yours, Sloane, likely. It's probably in the kitchen or coat room."

She hadn't thought about the horrendous coat room since the weather changed, happy to be free of it, but she remembered the terrible mice now, the rotting garments. *He knows*, she thought and knew then that she had convinced herself that he was like her. A person who suddenly found themselves in this strange place free from all its history. But Elias was a Blakersby too, and he tolerated all their strangeness.

The way she was learning to tolerate it.

She drank the wine, handed him back the glass. Pleased, he smiled and kissed her, his tongue taking on the taste of hers. Sweet, fermented grapes, thick honey. Honey in everything they drank but water. He settled her in the bed, turned down the lamps, and, still draped in the blanket, turned to leave.

"It's for Claresta," she said, her teeth floating, head light.

Elias turned back, he had no face, just a shadow. "What is?"

"The blanket. I got it as a gift."

He shifted, looked down at himself. "She won't mind if I borrow it for a little. I'll ensure it makes its way to her. Sweet dreams, my Orabella."

The door opened and shut before she could form the words in her mouth to respond. The key twisted in the lock. She pulled air over her tongue, threw the blankets off, and let her body be laid over with the cold, letting it shock her awake. The fawn watched from the bedside.

The darkness swam in front of her, her eyelids felt heavy as did her arms and legs. Dizzy and drowsy she stumbled across the room, her feet catching on the carpet, tripping her. The dark ocean of the floor rushing up to meet her, she reached her arms out, stopped her descent.

Crawling now, the fawn dragging beside her, golden hooves hovering, scraping the floor, she made her way to the window. Light streamed from it, the moon was bright, beckoning. She struggled up to her feet. Swaying, she fumbled at the sill, found the lock, and pushed it open. Cold air struck her face, pushing back the rushing darkness that bubbled up in her brain. Honey thick, it pulled at her limbs, dragged her down into it. A cacophony of screaming, dying barks from the woods echoed in the dark.

She breathed deep, a single breath, and then stuck her fingers as far into her own mouth as she could, devoured her fist past her knuckles until her own body forced the intrusion out along with everything in her stomach.

She spat, empty, and turned, leaving the window open and sliding down under it. The smell of night filled her room. She leaned her head back against the wood under the window and took great, sucking breaths from it. Her head was clearing slowly. She let herself lie there under the window shivering, the taste of vomit in her mouth, until her breathing evened out and her head felt the right weight on her neck. The fawn was gone.

Slowly she sat up, thoughts turning in her. *The wine*, she realized or maybe finally let herself see, *had something in it*. Her tongue felt unnatural against the roof of her mouth. A bad fit. Through wine and pastry it still tasted of the tea that she had sucked down after the attack. The familiar tea with extra honey that had calmed her so quickly. Tea in the afternoon, wine at night.

Something to help her sleep.

The same tea they gave to Claresta. A vision of the woman filled her mind, not the howling banshee that had fought her but the other, after that. The naked statue of a woman drooling into her own lap, waiting for someone to care for her. Covered in bruises.

They're doing something to her. She reached through the honey-thick waters of her mind for the thoughts, held them to her chest. *They'll do it to me, I have to . . . help her.* Her belly trembled as she pulled herself up and crossed the room to the little secret door. She traced the outline where she had broken the paper, the soft, cold kiss of air tickling at her feet.

"I'll be lost," she mumbled. There would be no light to help her find new doors. There wouldn't be anything but dark wall after dark wall.

She wavered against the bed, thought of lying down, giving up, and then called herself a fool. The key lay against her chest, heavy and warm.

There was no Sloane waiting on the other side of the door. It was night. The halls belonged to her and the mice.

She turned to the door; her hand settled on cloth that was not the comforter. She clumsily lifted the mattress and dragged her neglected robe from beneath it. Crumpled and still dirty, but she slipped it on, its dark color covering the starkness of her nightgown.

She held her breath and put her ear to wood. There was nothing. No scratching, no steps, shifting sounds, nothing at all. She took a deep breath and unlocked the door as gently as she could. The click of the lock sounded like a gunshot.

She stopped, her body rigid, but there came no reaction from the house.

She slipped the key out and hung it from her neck. Gripping the chain tightly, she opened the door.

The hallway stared back, the light of the moon cutting slices in the darkness. She stepped forward.

Her footfalls, covered in soft slippers, made no sound as she moved, slowly, cautiously at first but then quicker, hopping from one pool of moonlight to the next. In between each the darkness seemed closer. Cold and crushing.

She turned down a hall and trailed her hand along the wall as she traveled down the steps. Her fingers pulled at the old paper, made it flake and fall. Her trail would never be found, the steps were dark, no light would touch them. She went down them, entered a familiar back hall, saw the lost beads glittering on the floor.

She moved through the pools of light, peeking into rooms filled with stored furnishings and old paintings. Nothing moved. There was no one there.

She passed the dining room and followed the path of the halls back up another set of stairs in the wing opposite hers to her sister-in-law's floor. *It's strange*, she thought idly to keep her mind from making up ghosts in all the corners, *that they do not mirror each other, that every floor, every wing, is so different from the one that faces it.*

She crept along the hall, her breath held, waiting, unsure for what. Nothing. Just her and the house.

She knew Claresta's room from the end of the hall. The door was shut but light slid from a crack along the bottom. She cursed her oversight then and clutched the key that hung between her own breasts. The door would be locked tight, as her door was every night. She had come for nothing at all. Softly she stepped towards it and put her ear against the wood, holding her breath and listening.

A hushed voice from the other side, so low it could be mistaken for one of the house's drafts. She pressed herself tighter to the door, willing more of the words to travel to her fully formed, but it was only the shape of them, the hint that they were voices and not some other, nightly noise, that made its way to her.

More than one person spoke. A deep male voice and a high ringing one. Claresta was not alone in her room. Two voices. There and awake in a room that should have darkness and dreaming, just like hers.

Quietly she slid to the floor and, closing one eye, looked through the keyhole.

A sliver of the room but enough. It was orderly and lit by flickering oil lamps. She knew the bed was to the right of the door and in it would be Claresta because her chair, in front of the window and clear from Orabella's vantage point, was empty.

The man said something. The creak of steps, and she held her breath in case the low sound betrayed her. The figure came into view and she gasped, forgetting herself. The sharp intake of air seemed loud enough to pierce the barricade of the door but he didn't hear it. He didn't turn to what she was sure, so sure, was a familiar sound to him by now. He had pulled such from her nearly every night under different circumstances. He still had the blanket about his shoulders.

Elias, beautiful Elias walked across his beautiful sister's bedroom. And then he was gone from her limited view. *They're just talking, he's visiting*, she thought even when her guts turned and called her a liar. The bed creaked, loud as the lock on her door. She couldn't move, couldn't breathe, as she waited for him to reappear, to take his place across the distance again.

The light lowered, disappeared. A bitter scent filled the air. Elias was staying in the room. His sister's room. The sighs she knew from her own mouth came through the door.

She stood, her body still protesting, weak from its ordeal. Her hand hovered over the knob, so close she could feel the cold pouring from the metal. With a jerk she pulled it back. *I should not be here, I was not meant to be here*, she thought, stepping back from the door. *It's my own fault, I'm making stories of it, I don't know anything, I couldn't see.* She rationalized the thoughts firing quickly one after another. They were siblings, she was sick, perhaps they were just comforting each other. *That's what brothers and sisters do*, but she wasn't sure, she had no siblings whose behavior she could compare it to, and that was her husband.

She covered her mouth to hold in whatever sound threatened to rise from her. Shaking her head in the darkness, she turned, lifted her skirts, and ran to be away from them, from that door and its terrible mysteries. She ran, following the streaks of light until her breath came too loud from her chest. Her hands shook; she stopped, steadied herself on the wall, took gasping breaths until her body settled.

She looked around. She had made it, free from the cursed hallway, but now she stood in some other space, one she had never been to before. There was a staircase that went up to the third floor.

Wait, I'm being foolish, I've come too far, but in the darkness, among the settling sounds of the old house and mice in the walls she heard a door open. Heard steps. She took the stairs upward.

Dark, no light here. She might have been, she realized, inside the walls themselves, in all those twisted passages. *Why am I running, it's my husband, he's said I can do as I like, what fault have I committed?* There was nothing, no mystery. It had been Elias all along and she had been foolish, so foolish to follow him. Overeager, her aunt would say. But she kept moving forward.

Foolish, just as she had been foolish to run up the stairs that led her there, she moved forward, unable to go back.

She stumbled, there was no step where there should have been. She would need to be more careful. She must have reached the top but there was still no light. Forward, no choice, the dark closing around her, cold and vast, she reached her hand out, felt the wall, centered herself, and stepped forward.

The wall dipped and rose under her fingers. Doors. She stopped at each, felt for the handle and tried it, but it wasn't until the fourth door that one finally gave and creaked loudly as it opened, spilling light into the hall.

She froze at the sound, sure that she had been caught, but there was nothing. Her eyes adjusted to the brightness and it showed an empty hall lined with closed doors.

She slipped into the room, shut the door, closed her eyes, and breathed deep. Earthy scent filled her nostrils. *Moss, a forest*, she thought, *another ruined space.*

Opening her eyes, she screeched, the sound passing through her lips before she could stop it. Staring back at her was a fox. Teeth bared, tail up, it stood on a table, ready to pounce. Too scared to move, she stared at it, and it matched her stillness.

Stuffed, she realized. *How silly, of course, what would a fox do here? How would it get here?* There was no way up to the third floor from outside, the windows were still sound. Not a real beast, an old hunting trophy. She relaxed, took in the surroundings. Another storage space. Old beds and tables too heavy to carry down the stairs. The room was its own forest. Birds in frozen song, possums and badgers, creatures from the woods, hunted, stuffed, and displayed for no one. She needed to sit, to think.

She stood at the portal, her back to the wood, and breathed. Dust and mildew filled her nose. A familiar scent now. She moved forward, gazing back and forth over the objects left to rot, her feet landing lightly, testing the floor. The door had been closed after all.

She reached the covered tables and the jumble of chairs, meaning to sit in one and rest, but the fox drew her.

What is happening here, is Claresta a victim? Am I? I don't understand. If I am a good wife then will I be safe? No, I need to get away. She touched the fox. Old fur under her hand, she smoothed her fingers over its teeth, to prove it wouldn't bite.

The door clicked. She snatched her hand away, the teeth biting into the palm as she passed, drawing blood.

Panicked, Orabella dove behind the chairs as quickly and silently as she could, pulling her skirts about her as the door opened, slowly to limit the sound of the hinges. Trusting the shadows to be enough, she held her breath as someone entered the room, their steps heavy and uneven, a scraping sound. Their breath wet with every exhalation.

Memory pulled at her, the scenario was familiar, and she touched her hair, still loose and tangled. Remembered the ripping loss of those few strands in the portrait room. It hadn't been a draft. Whoever it was moved around the room and she tried not to make a sound as she tracked their shadow along the floor. Sweat broke out against her skin, her body hot and cold all at once. A rabbit in the brush while the fox nosed through the leaves for her.

The man—from the weight of the steps it had to be a man—came closer, and because it had to be a man, it could only be Elias. But the scent, not unpleasant, that filled her nostrils was not his. She couldn't place it. Sweet and spicy. Like wood but not. Bitter.

Like the tea. He reeked of it.

He stopped just past the shadows that covered her, his breath even, and she fought against her shuddering body. Made herself small and quiet.

"Wife," he growled. His voice was deep and familiar. *Elias.* She shuddered in a different way from the sound of it. A flush of heat passed through her that tightened at her nipples and filled her stomach with the fluttering of wings.

No, she thought again even as the honey dripped in her mind. She couldn't move, couldn't be seen. But she wanted to be. Wanted to tumble out of that hidey-hole and present herself to him, a gift on all fours. The image came so vivid and violent she nearly cried out. A wild thing, infected and awoken by the wildness of Claresta. *Here I am, husband*, it sang in her, daring her to take him back from his sister.

She would not move.

The man stopped, so close now that she could reach from her hiding place and touch him. He let out a breath, annoyed, and then turned. He stepped past her, crushing rotted wood under his foot and filling the room with the scent of soil. His foot went through to the ankle before, snarling, he pulled it out. A scraping sound. His shadow moved farther away until the door shut and she was alone.

She sat still, holding the position until her body ached, afraid to move at all. Finally, she willed herself to look just outside the safety of the forest of furniture legs.

Nothing but the room, bathed in pale moonlight, stared back. Elias, it could only have been Elias, was gone. The door closed.

Slowly she pulled herself up, body aching, and crossed the room. She listened at the door for some other sign of life but she heard nothing. As she had heard nothing when she climbed the steps, but she had felt something then. Had felt it all throughout her body as she did now. The hallway wasn't safe. She turned back, panicked, trapped, and saw something had changed.

The fox had been turned. No longer facing the door, the snarling snout pointed to where she had sat hidden. He would be waiting on the other side to catch her. Make a real game of it.

She moved away from the door slowly, careful with her steps, careful of the spongy carpet of wood rot. She wouldn't leave tracks for him. She took to the wall, desperately hoping. She felt along it with careful fingers until she found the familiar catch and eased the small door open.

As with the one in her room, a cold breeze met her and darkness that seemed impossible. She heard the floor creaking. He was still about, in the next room over. *A better hiding place*, she decided, and slipped into the void, closing the small door behind her.

She meant only to wait but she reached her hands out, feeling for her space, and found that under her, just to her left, there was no floor. She bent over the hole and blinked because there, a room's length away, came a single strip of light.

A way out.

She bit her lip, considering before she slid her feet over the ledge, planning to lower herself carefully, but her toes met with another step. Carefully she felt downward to find a steep staircase built into the space. She took it, climbing down like a child, her rear bumping quietly on each tread until she had met the final one. Breathing a quiet sigh of relief she fumbled with the locking mechanism she knew must be there and the door swung open.

She emerged gulping air, pulling herself free before turning and pushing the door shut.

She blinked in the moonlight, shivered in the wide-open space, and realized where she was.

Somehow, in all that darkness she had rounded the house and made her way back to her own floor, her own rooms. Quickly she stood and fled from the room, back to her own bed.

The room was just as she had left it, all things in their place, her window still open. She locked the door. Pulled off her robe, exhausted, dropped it to the floor, and then climbed into her bed. She kept the window open, needed the air. Orabella curled under the blankets and waited for her husband, who she was sure was coming to punish her, haul her into a dungeon, break her to pieces. Above her she could hear the sounds of movement, stopping scratching searching, as she heard every night, and knew they were not mice at all.

Her will faltered and then failed altogether with the rising of the sun, when she finally let the comfort of sleep take her.

Under its light she dreamed of Elias calling her name, calling her his, and biting at her neck while she made new scars all along his back with her nails, as Claresta had scarred her. In her dreams he filled her belly with barking, yowling kits that clawed through her skin while the long-limbed fawn stared with one huge black eye.

Chapter Nineteen

"Miss? Miss?"

Orabella woke slowly. She couldn't make sense of the room at first, her room; the light was all wrong. Her thoughts were scattered, the vision blurry at the edges. Her body felt too heavy, still moving through the honey of her dreams. She focused on the girl, something was wrong, her hands were full. She blinked sleep away. Sloane held her robe, all dirty from the walls and floors she had traveled. In the light her crimes were clear. "I overslept." She reached for the only thing she could, the obvious.

Sloane nodded. "Sir told me to let you sleep longer but you've got to get up now."

She saw him again, crossing that floor. Remembered his growling voice when he had her trapped. Not a dream but she couldn't make sense of it. Something was wrong in it all. She didn't want to believe it but she couldn't not.

Sloane folded the robe in her arms, quickly, efficiently. "I'll have this washed for you." It was Sloane. Her friend.

"I took a walk, early this morning. I was having some trouble sleeping. I know the place well enough now, I went out to the garden, just at dawn," she stammered. "The light was so lovely. But I tripped and made such a mess of things. I came back without getting very far. It must have been before everyone arrived."

Sloane nodded, eager as always to please, to believe. "You shouldn't be out by yourself, miss. It's not safe, you understand, don't you?" Her tone had turned, dropped into a whisper. A hint of desperation as she crossed the room and took up Orabella's hands. "At night there's even more danger. I shouldn't say, everyone knows, but Sir, he wants you to feel safe and you are safe, just stay in your room at night because—"

The sound of a throat clearing stopped the words spilling from Sloane's mouth. Only air remained in Orabella's hands as the girl stood, turning, sweeping up the offending robe with her. She stood like a shield half blocking the sight of Mrs. Locke at the door. With her, head bowed, was another girl, one she hadn't met before or at least didn't recognize. A young girl, younger than Sloane. She held a breakfast tray in her hand.

"You must get up now," the old woman said, her voice coming out wet. Like Hastings's. Like that of the man in the dark who wanted her to come to him.

Orabella closed her eyes. *A cousin or nephew. A night watchman, something, I can't let my mind run away with things. It couldn't have been Elias. I am making up stories, my mind is making boogeymen of mice.*

Had the fox turned? Had the door opened? Had someone spoken to her? She couldn't be sure now in the sunlight.

"Close that window! The air is still too cold," Mrs. Locke snapped. Sloane moved to obey. The young girl sat the tray over Orabella's lap. Toast, sausage, and tea. The scent that rose from the prepared cup was different. More earthy.

"Does she have anything she can put on? Where's her robe? We can't have her falling ill again, not now."

"She spilled wine on it," Sloane said quickly. "Last night, it's still damp, needs washed. But it's fine! The other just came."

A package on the vanity. Sloane hurried to it and unwrapped it with care, pulling out a peach gown with all its pretty lace and ribbons. The one she'd ordered from the dressmaker the day before. The day that passed from delightful to horrific, all at once. "But how did he finish so quickly?"

"There's not much work yet," Sloane said simply. She slid the robe over her shoulders. Smooth, soft fabric. Luxurious and beautiful.

"We'll be back soon. Eat your breakfast, you've been called," Mrs. Locke said.

Orabella looked at Sloane but her eyes were on Mrs. Locke's retreating back, the shutting door. The sound of the key in the lock.

"You've been called to the Master's rooms, to speak to him," she said quickly.

Her stomach twisted, her shoulders pulled tight. She'd been caught. *Was it Hastings?* But the idea was ridiculous. Hastings, large as he was, was far too old to chase and she had been chased. But then, what did he want?

"Is it about Claresta? About what happened?"

"I wouldn't know, ma'am. I don't know anything about what the Master thinks or wants. But, forgive me for speaking so plainly, I think you should be careful. Not everyone will appreciate the way you are."

She didn't need to ask questions, she did understand that. She nodded at the food, choking it down quickly. Just in time for Mrs. Locke to return with a dress draped over her arms. This one was a noncolor that had maybe been lavender but over time had faded into a sort of gray. Plainer than the one she had worn to the wedding dinner but just as out of style, this one older by decades.

It smelled of storage. She smiled, pulled herself slowly out of bed, and let herself be stripped to her shift, sweat stiff from the day before but it didn't matter.

The dress didn't fit any better than the wedding dress had, it was just wrong in different ways. The billowing fabric had been tailored for a woman with smaller arms and a tighter waist. Or perhaps her undergarments had just shaped the dress that way. The bust scooped low, revealed the bruises from her sister-in-law's attack.

She pressed her fingers into them, jumping at the sharp shock of pain.

"What's this?" Mrs. Locke asked, her fingers reaching for the chain.

Orabella recoiled. "A charm. A gift from Elias."

The old woman sniffed and let it be, Elias's name enough to ward her away. She motioned for Orabella to sit. She followed directions like a child and Sloane took up her hair. She styled and pinned it, clumsily. She had never learned correctly. Elias liked it down. The end result was fine, acceptable enough to meet her father-in-law, covered in bruises as she was.

Dressed, she followed Mrs. Locke, Sloane at her side, down through the now familiar halls. She'd been to the Master's halls, had never come up with something better to call them. She'd seen the little office, and now she was led inside and shown to an overstuffed chair beside a merrily burning fireplace and sat before Hastings, the Master of Korringhill.

"Hello, sir," she said, still unable after all those weeks, all those dinners, to be familiar with him, to be comfortable.

He sat casually, his chin resting in the cup of his hand. "So, you've seen Claresta."

The air was hot, stuffy, the fire too warm. Sweat dripped from her into the borrowed fabric of the dress. "Yes. Yesterday. Is she well?"

Hastings chuckled, sat up straight, and sighed. "My, he did bring such a dutiful wife here. Any other would have left. Gone to that little church. Written back home to get away. But not you."

She smiled, unsure. "I don't follow you, sir. She's sick. Isn't she?"

"She's a Blakersby."

Orabella thought of the wild family, their barking, screeching laughs. The fawn. Wild, jewel-eyed family, beautiful and strange. She shivered. "Aren't we all here," she said before she could stop herself, mouth too quick. It could be taken wrong.

He laughed, too wet a sound. "I suppose we are now. Tell me about yourself, then, Orabella." She could hear the rattle of his lungs with every word.

"There's not much to tell, I'm afraid. You know of my family. I've been in the care of my aunt and uncle. I attended lessons when I was young. I've kept myself busy with charity work."

"You must be very bored here, after your life in the city," he supplied, his tone even, nearly friendly, hinting at the man he must have once been, someone of society. Someone who could make conversation.

"No, it is nice here. The garden is beautiful and the town is cozy. The air is so fresh. I hope to spend more time with my knitting. In the city there were always visits to be had. Here it is so much quieter." She chose her words in praise, tried to endear herself to the old man.

"You are very clever, I'll give you that. A clever little wife for my clever little boy. I thought it was your look that pulled him to you. He's young and young men are foolish for that sort of thing, but no, I don't think it was."

Insult or compliment, she couldn't tell. "I don't think someone like me can sway anyone when you've Claresta."

"A rare thing she was. But . . ." Hastings paused, his anger tapering down as he regarded her again. "You are very clever. So perhaps you have more to offer of your person than I thought."

"I must thank Claresta for letting me borrow such fine dresses," she responded by way of accepting the compliment. Let her gratitude shine brighter than her vanity. "Elias and Claresta are so lovely, I am so plain and surprised that I caught your son's eye at all."

The old man made a sound that could have been a laugh but came from his lungs filled with phlegm and struggled from his lips as a cough. He held a handkerchief to his mouth, took a few moments, his back bent and heaving with each cough that followed. Finally, he wiped at his mouth, tucked the cloth away. "You seem fit and well. Clever. I almost wish I had known you before. Maybe that would have been better."

"What do you mean, sir?" she asked as he stood slowly, shuffled up from his chair and to his desk. She wiped sweat from her forehead while he was turned away. The room was so unbearably warm.

"There is nothing worth your curiosity in this house. You will be doted on, you are a bride. Keep your schedule, abide by your duties. Do you understand, Orabella?"

Hastings held, in his hands, her little lamp. Shined bright, it sparkled in the flame of the fire. The lamp she thought she'd left in the ballroom. The lamp that had shown up in the window across from her secret garden. A gift from Elias.

"Yes," she said, holding her hands out. "Thank you, I understand."

"The family is old and there are things that you do not understand, that you do not need to understand. I think you know that very well. You will be a very good bride, I think. Elias has chosen well."

She nodded, forced a smile.

"Good. Then I think we can end here. Unless you have something you wish to ask me?" he said, brow raised, waiting. Testing.

There were questions. Thousands of them. She took a deep breath, saw the fawn in her mind, and smiled, shook her head. There was nothing to ask, not of him. "No, thank you for calling on me today. We have never really had the chance and I treasure this. Thank you."

A little silver bell and there again were Mrs. Locke and Sloane, ready to take her back.

"I think she should have some rest, don't you?" he said, dismissing them.

Orabella gripped her lamp to her chest as she went, unsure of what it all meant. Did that mean that Elias knew? That he knew what she saw? She chewed her lip, copper taste touching her tongue. No answers in the small, sharp pain. The only thing she did know was that there could be no questions. Not unless she was careful.

Her door hung open and on her bed sat Elias, flipping idly through one of her books. He smiled, stood at their approach, holding out his hand to take his wife.

"Thank you, Mrs. Locke, and Sloane, is it? You can wait in the hall."

Sloane looked nervously at him. "Sir, I don't mean to be disobedient, but the hall."

"It's fine. Shut the door behind you," he said.

Fine, fine, of course, you're here, Orabella thought. *Then, no, no, it wasn't him, it was a dream, a misunderstanding.* But the lamp was in her arms.

Her refusal was subtly written on every part of her but in the end she nodded, did as she was told.

"Elias." She would ask. Clear things between them. But she saw the robe, left on the chair, folded and filthy, the lamp in her arms, and knew she couldn't. Because then he would know that she had disobeyed him. That he had asked one thing of her and she could not control herself well enough to grant him that. And then what would become of her? *I could be mistaken, it was late, the wine, yes, the wine.* There was something in the wine. In the tea.

"You've found your lamp," he said softly, plucking it from her hands, setting it on the vanity.

His face was different, less at ease. He reached for her, hand on her cheek, and everything in her wanting to pull away. *Did he touch her with this hand? No, I mustn't think like that, I don't know, I didn't see.* Her mind spun, a different face showing at every turn, angry, hurt, confused, disgusted.

"How was your talk with my father?" he asked, voice low, soothing. No anger.

"It was fine. He was concerned over how I was settling in here, being away from the city," she answered.

"And how is that, love?" he hummed, toying with the lobe of her ear.

"Fine, the town is lovely. Thank you for yesterday."

"I'm sorry, you were never meant to see that." He sighed. "Your ears aren't pierced."

"What?" she asked, confused.

"I'll have to do it myself." He pulled out her stool, settled her on it.

She covered her ears with her hands. "Do what?"

"Pierce your ears. It's a simple thing. Take a long needle and press it through." He squeezed the lobe and she jumped. "Just like that."

"A needle," she repeated. It was what they used on Claresta, it was what he would use on her.

"You look like you've hardly slept at all."

"I had some trouble. Bad dreams," she said. The memory of the man in the room, the stalker in the halls. Was he real? Was he her husband?

"You'll rest today. Maybe tomorrow too. I've brought something to convince you to stay in bed. I know how much you like your walks."

Her stomach dropped, breath stopped in her chest. Caught.

Elias was turned away, picking up the bundle he had dropped on the bed. "I'll have some workmen come in for the garden. A little late in the season to start planting and cleaning but you seem to have kept your interest in it and I do so want to be a good husband to you."

The garden walks, he means. "What did you do with the blanket?" she asked, the words a rush.

"The blanket?" His fingers hovered above the knot on the parcel. "The gift!" he said, memory coming back. "I gave it to Claresta. I checked in with her before I went to bed myself. I'm sure she will love it when she's more herself."

And who is that? The fox or the doll? "Good, that's good," Orabella said out loud. *What I saw, a dream, a misunderstanding.*

He finished unwrapping what he held. "Don't think on it, love. Here, surprise!"

Mail. Two letters and a stack of papers.

"*The Candle,*" she gasped.

"Mail runs rather irregularly, I'm afraid. I should have warned you of it before. I've had the Bristol office collect the papers for you. You enjoyed reading them, yes?"

"I, I did. The stories, I liked the stories. How did you . . . ?"

"It's no large thing. You received some letters as well."

She picked up the two envelopes. The first was from her aunt and uncle. Short. She sat it aside. The second she held, tears brimming. "Jane."

"She'll get all your letters in a few days. The post hasn't run since you've arrived."

"Then how do you keep your business steady? This can't be sustainable. Not that I know anything about that." She laughed, feeling foolish for having been afraid at all.

"You do not have to worry over such things, Orabella. It is fine and well, you won't end up on the streets or begging your aunt and uncle to have you back. You will always be cared for."

Overeager, jumping to conclusions, imagination running away with her. *This is a marriage of convenience, why do I need—* She could not stop herself.

"Then I am the only one?" The question tumbled from her, quiet, begging, needing. *Console me, make me believe*, it said.

"The only one. My love, no other." Elias's voice came low, lust curling along his tongue with every word. He slipped from her ear, crouched at her feet, a willing subject. His eyes wide and bright in the light. He looked the way he had in her uncle's garden. "How could I want anyone else? Why would I not want what is my own?"

Orabella looked away, she had no answer and it felt like honesty, what she knew of it. And she wanted to believe. Needed to. "Thank you for the paper," she said finally.

"No need, but you're welcome, my darling." He turned her palm to kiss it as he was fond of doing, but he stopped, staring at the skin. A fresher scar in its center. "What happened to your hand?"

A fox bit me, she thought. "I fell. I must have cut it on the sill."

He looked at her more closely, searching her eyes, but she kept her face blank and still. Like Claresta. He pressed his lips to the cut. "Be careful, these floors, these halls, it's easy to fall. Now you need to rest. I'll send your girl in to help you change. I'll take dinner with you here, in your rooms, tonight."

"Thank you," she said. She was tired. *How silly of me, what was I thinking last night?* And what would she do? Where would she go? Her fear was only waking dreams in those dark halls, brought by exhaustion and alcohol and stress. Dispelled by the sun.

The morning light met Elias across the room. She hadn't seen him from that angle, in that light, since they'd come to Korringhill. She'd only seen him in the shadows of the house. "You look like that portrait."

He stilled. "What portrait?"

"The one downstairs, in your father's hall. There was a young man on the wall, he looks just like you, is it you? There were so many paintings in that room but I didn't think any were of you and everything is so old here."

"There aren't any paintings of me," he said softly. "Forget you saw it." He turned away, his shoulders tight.

Elias slipped from her room without another word, replaced by Sloane, who shut the door quickly behind her.

"Sloane! Come! Come! Look!" Orabella sang brightly, holding up the paper.

Whatever upsets the maid had were forgotten along with propriety when she picked up the top paper. Sloane took a seat on Orabella's bed and dove straight into reading.

Orabella opened the letter from her aunt and uncle, scanned it. Perfunctory, simple, quick. *We wish you well in your new home, do write if you need anything, we'll be sure to visit once you're settled.* Nothing but the most expected reply.

Finished, she sat it to the side and opened the envelope from Jane. Her handwriting was bold and blocky, little grace but legible. The letter was dated a week after Orabella's departure.

I asked your aunt for your address. She came by with the last of the hats you'd made. I think she knew I was disgusted with them, what they did, but I didn't say anything directly. You wouldn't have liked that. Orabella could imagine her look; happiness, warm and familiar, flooded her. She hadn't been forgotten, it was on the slowness of the mail. She read the rest of the letter. Jane had written to her early, sure that the mail would be late. She said she also contacted the Father at the local parish to look out for Orabella in case she ever came to church. She imagined her friend bent over the scarred table in the kitchen writing the letter. She was not forgotten.

"Are you all right, Orabella?" Sloane asked.

Orabella wiped the tears from her cheeks. "I'm fine, sorry, I don't know why I'm so emotional. I guess I'm just tired." She reached for the bundle of papers and found the issue after the last she'd read. She skipped past the society pages and straight to the story she'd left behind.

When she relieved herself later the world made more sense. The red streaks on the cloth, another sign of her irrational nature. *I am always off around this time*, she mused. It took her by surprise as always, she was never good at keeping track of her dates and she'd been so out of sorts since she'd come to the manor. Days had slipped past her, unnoticed, but her body kept time despite her.

Chapter Twenty

I t's such a lovely day," Sloane nearly sang as they walked, following the same paths that they had followed before. A schedule,
left to falter and that they were finally coming back to now after
days and days. Elias at breakfast, as he had been before the terrible
day. All smiles and charm. Just as he had always been with her. The
stone and dirt walks that had been made safe by their footfalls.
Orabella and Sloane came to the center of the garden, where they
always sat and chatted.

The walk, familiar, drained Orabella. Her body felt heavy and
her head buzzed and throbbed softly. It had been four days since
the attack. She was ordered to stay in bed for the first two. She
took her meals buried under the covers and Elias came and kissed
her but nothing more, her monthly bleeding holding him. Orabella tried to knit, to follow the new patterns in her book, but
she couldn't keep the stitches straight, lost count of them, made
holes. The yarn, beautiful and soft, became a mess of tangles in
her hands. She read the paper and slept too much. In and out of
dreams, everything seemed far away. It had stopped quickly, her

bleeding. The cycle ending almost as soon as it had come. Sudden like the arrival of spring. Then she had been allowed up to resume her life but given a reprieve from Claresta.

Orabella sat down heavily, placed a hand over her too-fast heart, and let out a long breath. "I'm feeling a bit lightheaded. I think I need a drink of water."

"A drink? All right, we'll go back. I'll take you to the sitting room and we'll have lunch there," Sloane suggested, reveling in the freedom they'd been given. They were allowed now to go to the garden room, the sitting room, the little garden if they liked.

Orabella shook her head. "No, I just need to rest, I'm not ready to go back in yet. The air is good for me and I just need some water. You'll be faster without me. It will only take you a moment. And then after a drink I'll be ready, I think."

Warmer out than she expected. Than it should be for March? April? She wasn't sure. She hadn't seen a calendar, there had been no reason. *I've slept too much, I need to walk more*, she thought, stretching her legs. She'd needed so much rest recently, it was no wonder she was so tired. Even before the incident, the walk in the town had worn her down, made her sleepy.

Sloane frowned, biting her bottom lip, torn between following and following, stuck in the impossible contradiction of being both the servant and the caretaker in one moment. Finally she relented, young and eager, so eager to please she nodded. "All right, I'll be right back. You'll feel better after a drink. Your color is already coming back." She smiled, friendly, warm, and Orabella was struck, suddenly, by how pretty Sloane became when that genuine smile graced her face. How it brightened her features, took her from mousy to lovely in one simple movement.

Then Orabella was alone. She swept her eyes upward, to the house. Every empty window stared back at her, the darkness of the manor hiding whatever might or might not have been in the many rooms. She searched each one she could see quickly, looking for the white figure of Claresta, but there was nothing. She stood, turning her gaze to Sloane's departing back. The girl was fast, had already put distance between the two of them.

Orabella stood, stretched, looked for shade. The sun beat down on her, she wore her cloak, they wouldn't let her leave without it for fear another cold would overtake her, her constitution weakened by everything else. She moved to a broken pillar under a tree that had regained its greenery. But then, a hint of red caught her eye and she went to it to see if it was a rose or something else. A trail of little observations, small questions, and she was at the edge of the forest, staring at the thick trunks.

Like an invitation, a path.

She had never gone this way, never gone so close, and she hadn't meant to now but the forest looked cool and the birds were singing. She stepped onto the path. The shade wrapped around her with a cool breeze and she sighed.

She hadn't meant to go so far, her feet stumbling over broken stones that made the walkway, heels sinking into dirt and mud, but once started she couldn't stop. Her feet carried her and she tripped along with them, the only witnesses the broken statues and the birds that stood guard from those heights. As she moved closer the distinction between wild and tamed blurred and she was, before she realized, in the forest, no more broken path, no more plots. Only ancient dark trees and undergrowth.

I should stop, she thought even as she took the next steps, finding a new way carved in the dirt itself. *It must be safe*, she reasoned but she had no support for this and she did not stop to question herself, thinking on some level that the path must be used by Cullen, who hunted game for their dinners. That he must come out here often enough that it was safe. That she would be safe if she followed the path.

As in the house, so in the forest.

The forest path and the dark, hidden halls in the manor, the little door in her room. Then, like now, curiosity drove her, impulse. She was alone, no one would mind if she indulged, she'd turn, be back in her little seat before Sloane returned.

Birdsong, high and bright, spun down from the branches to her. *Can she sing?* her memory asked in response. "No, stop, it's lovely here. Elias is . . ." She hummed, thinking of her kind husband. Her prince who read fairy tales to her while she rested.

A good match, a kind husband. A prince. Her laugh matched the birdsong. *A prince? For me?* It seemed so long ago that he told her of how they came to meet. Trading an introduction for a card debt. How foolish to think him a prince or herself even worthy of one. Korringhill wasn't a fairy castle. And yet . . .

In the wood there were birdsong and moss-covered logs topped with beautiful mushrooms. Everything shimmered in the light. Like the ruined rooms, beautiful and mysterious, and she wanted to go farther, find a little clear spot, sit under the trees, and dream.

Should I find a patch of grass and lie down so the moss can grow over my body, the leaves can be my blanket? Or maybe I'll sprout mushrooms and a new little hall will grow here from what's left of me. A new little house for a new little wife. Her thoughts were morbid and whimsical, strange, like the halls she had left behind. Muddled. It had been all right for the first day but then something changed in her and she couldn't quite find her footing. Everything was suspicious and questionable but wasn't that where one found magic?

She kept walking.

The path turned and wound like a snake, the trees sentinels that stood against the bright light, the underbrush closer with every step. And then, at a turn just like any other, she found herself in another garden made from stone.

The cemetery was as run-down as the garden and the manor. The stones that weren't broken or tilted were covered with lichen and moss. The individual plots had become grass and weeds, forest flowers sprouting where they could. The gate was eaten by creeping vines, part of the forest.

Beyond that there was a building that had once been a church but now, caved in, all that remained were the supports and crumbling stone walls, which were nearly overtaken by the forest. A temple for the deer, a choir of birds. The foxes, she knew, prayed elsewhere.

She walked towards it anyway.

Stones, bright white, dug up and washed for markers. Carved only with a single roman numeral, stopped her journey. There were twelve in all, clustered together in a sad order. A children's grave-yard for children that had never breathed. She looked up, saw the fawn floating, lowering its head, dark eye still on her.

Orabella pressed her palms to her eyes, willed it away.

"You should go, miss. You should run straight to the church and beg them to take you in. Beg your people to take you back because this place is cursed. That family is . . ."

She whirled around expecting a ghost but the speaker was real. Solid as the trees or the stones. Cullen.

"Listen, miss, Orabella," he continued, reaching for her, his hand cradling her elbow. Familiarly casual. "I don't mean to talk so plain to you but you have to listen. What happens in those walls, it's not Christian or right. And I shouldn't say but you need to know. It's something evil. Go look at them, go see what they say."

"What are you doing here?" Too shocked to pull away, she was unsure if he was real or if she was still dreaming.

"I saw you leave the garden, I followed you here. Sloane asked that I try to help you. You should leave. Go back to your people."

"Elias is my husband," she tried again, attempting to ignore what he was saying. But she had seen what she saw. *A dream, a dream*, she tried. "Sloane is my friend, if she were worried why didn't—"

"There's always someone listening in that house. The walls are—"

His hand left her arm, snatched away by a brutally fast shadow. Bristling, angry, it swallowed Cullen in its fury, pulled him down under the thick thudding of violently pounding flesh.

A boar! Backing away, she tripped over a hidden stone, tumbled to the ground while Cullen tussled with the beast.

"I'm sorry!" Cullen cried, but animals don't understand apologies. Orabella knew that and now Cullen would too.

There was a wet, cracking sound, it rang through the air, stilled the birds, stilled her heart. She felt it in her guts, in her chest, all through her, and Cullen was quiet. No screams, no pleas. He cradled his arm, mouth wide in the kind of sudden wild pain that makes no sound at all.

And above him towered the boar. Towered Elias, red faced, angry, tusks bared. Handsome features twisted into something still beautiful but grotesque and wild as Claresta had been. A Blakersby.

He reached for Cullen, dragged him up from the ground, stood him on his feet. Cullen's face was swelling, eye bruising, limp limb held to his body. His reward for trying to save her. Elias released him and he ran, leaving her on the ground.

Elias's face was wild, red at the cheeks. Teeth bared. Her prince, a beast towering over her.

"What are you doing out here? Did he bring you here? Why did you come with him?"

Orabella raised her hands, a physical wall to stop his questions, hold his fury. "I didn't! He followed me! I was only out for a walk!"

"A walk? In the forest?" Face softening. The beast recognizing his mate.

The world spun. She tried to match his voice to the one who had given her the papers and teased about piercing her ears just days before. Who had made her smile, promised nothing but joy, delight. Her prince. Strange, so strange that he would come like a prince should come, in the enchanted wood, but he was the beast. She couldn't make sense of this magic, this story. "I've just gone for a walk."

He crossed the distance to her, held out his hand, face still red, in shame now. She hadn't been meant to see it, that part of him. "You should still be in bed."

She let herself be settled on a tombstone like a bench. And he in the grass.

"How did you find me?" So quickly they had looked for her. Did Sloane run straight to the house? Was she in trouble? And she had tried to warn her, was her friend.

"Were you running away from me?" An honest question, what she knew of honesty. But then Cullen had said he was horrible and she had seen him, seen the monster in him. The scars that she traced in pleasure made sense then. His voice was sad and low, with none of the growl that it had before. There was no real accusation but his eyes were fixed on her. A weight there, in his words, just the same.

Had she been running away? Her thoughts were hard to hold, slow, and although she was driven to walk into the forest, she couldn't say why she had decided to leave the garden. Not really. He hadn't asked her that, though. He had asked if she were running from him.

Elias was always so kind. Visiting in the day and at night. He held her hand, petting her knuckles. Read her fairy stories while she had her tea, that thick, sweet tea with the bitter end. Loving, doting even. No hint of that other man that lived in him. The man that attacked Cullen. "No," she answered, truthfully.

"Then why did you come here?"

Dark circles hung under his eyes and she could only see the ghost of her reflection in the darkest part of them. A dusting of small, nearly invisible hairs covered his cheeks and chin. She lifted her fingers, touched his jaw. "I don't know, I'm sorry, I didn't think," she said, frazzled over what she'd just seen. "I feel like I'm in a fairy story here sometimes."

"This is not a fairy tale, love. I'm real and so are you." The words came out a whisper and his eyes fluttered closed as she smoothed her fingers over his jaw until her palm met the bone, forming a cradle for his face. He leaned into it, into her. Utterly tamed. Harmless to her.

"Then why do I dream of you?" The words slipped out. She should run, screaming, as Hastings had said, eager to escape, but she sat with his head on her lap.

"Dreams?" he asked softly, his hand on her thigh.

Visions of teeth, the crush of the darkness while the court looked on. Her dreams from that bitter honey sleep that lasted for days and days. "Yes. I dream of you."

"You sound upset. Is it so unpleasant to see me in your dreams?"

"Upset?" She dropped her hand, broke their connection. "No. Yes. I mean I haven't thought about it." But she should be upset, not about the dreams but what she had seen.

All the things she had seen. *It's real, it was all real.* But she smiled because she was a good wife and he was a prince and a beast and she didn't know what else to do.

Mine, his voice from the dream called her as he turned her face back to his. He placed a chaste kiss on her lips. "Of course, you were upset, darling. After what you saw. It was only natural that you would be."

She couldn't follow his answers. They didn't seem to match what had happened to her. Her days of dreaming and he had held her hand. When? All night? Was it only night? Honey dripped in her mind, weighed it all down, and she couldn't press through to form any meaning.

A shift and he was holding her, the weight of his hand stroking her back through the thick fabric of the cloak, his other wrapped around hers, his thumb over her knuckles. *What did I see? What happened in that room?* She couldn't answer, not for sure. Everything was so fragmented, her body ached from the attack—had it been an attack? Could she even call it that? Her attempt to help Claresta had already been too late, hadn't it? The bruises and the blood. And hadn't it been Claresta who attacked her? Red and white and the screaming. *Fox bride,* she thought. *No, wait, someone is hurting Claresta.*

The memory shot like lighting through her. The bruises, as old and older than hers, covered what should have been porcelain white skin and fought for dominance in her mind against that other wild and red thing that screamed and howled and dug sharp claws into her.

Elias slipped a finger under her chin, pushed her face up to meet his. "You saw my sister in one of her fits. And now you know."

Then there was Hastings, returning her lamp, reminding her there was nothing to be curious over in that house. Her house. Elias looked like Hastings.

"I know what? I know something happened but I can't . . . This place is . . ." She stopped, unsure of what she meant to say, how she meant to finish. Unsure if she should have spoken at all.

"You know my sister is mad," he said softly. He leaned forward, wrapped his arms around her. "But you are not. You are whole and mine."

She's a Blakersby and Elias is a Blakersby.

The pieces of it all fell into place. The answers, the real answers, the things she should have just known but didn't. Why he had chosen her with her family and its gambling debts and its gossip. Why he hadn't chosen one of those London girls whom it would have been no doubt a simple matter to swoon with his own success, with his own handsome face.

It wasn't her. *It's them*, she thought. *And now I am them.*

He clasped her hands together, held them to his chest. Between the grave markers and the high grass he seemed so earnest, so simple in his desires. The heady scent of the wood, dead leaves left to rot, and the hint, the smallest hint, of new growth filled her nostrils. She understood his desires, the want that burned in his sea-storm eyes, because he had taught her night after night. He craved the place he could hide, could bury himself, and she had become it.

Sickness rose in her and her mouth watered because his desire lived in her too. Saw him in the true night and she still wanted his touch, starved for it as she was. His passion, his kindness. *What did I really see? He says he wants me.* Proof of his passions in his attack: Hadn't she seen the looks that he gave Cullen for simply being near her? Was that jealousy not proof of his love?

A wife? No, what he needed, wanted, was a place to hold him and his secrets. A little hidden door that led to all kinds of hidden places in a woman, and she had agreed. She had come and let him fill her. "All right," she whispered, tired, her head full of buzzing, her tongue honey-thick.

"Thank you." He released her hands and took her face. "Thank you," he repeated, pressing his lips to hers, pressing her lips open so their tongues met and his taste filled her mouth. Ginger and smoke, always the same. Not like that night. Was there another? She didn't know, couldn't tell anymore. "I knew," he spoke quickly, pulling his mouth away but keeping his face close, so close. "I knew, I knew, oh, Orabella." His moan came low and deep along the cusp of her ear.

She shifted, wrapping her arms around him, and he lifted her, easily, and placed her astride his body. She could feel him, his desire given flesh, pressing against her own through the confines of their garments, her own thin drawers the only thing barring him entry, his woolen pants holding him back. The stone bit at her knees as she balanced above him, steadied by his right hand while his left felt under her skirts, searching for the warmth and wetness of her flesh.

He used this hand to break that boy and now and now, she thought through the vibration that settled all over, competing with the hot, tickling flush of his touch spreading through her. His mouth on hers, his tongue and teeth against hers, he swallowed the laugh that bubbled from her. Took it for pleasure and moved his kisses to other parts.

His mouth traced lines on her face to her neck, his touch breaking only momentarily to free her skin from the confines of her dress. He pressed his mouth to her throat, first one side and then the other, laying gentle kisses along the bruises. "Oh, what have they done to my love," he murmured, dragging wet lips against the garden of violence on her skin.

They? No, just her, she thought, her memories and words jumbled, forgetting the long streaks of bruising on her thigh, forgetting the barking laughs. The memories blurred, lost shape and meaning. From her mouth came only gasps.

"I should mark you mine, you are mine." He groaned before dragging his tongue back across her throat, his teeth nipping at the skin.

The dream spilled back into her, her belly full of his kits scratching and biting at her to be free, but then so close to his heat, his need, she didn't care. Couldn't care, as his cock pressed against the space between her legs, rubbed against that hidden bit that made her shake and purr with his attentions. With each wordless plea she felt wicked and filthy. She had seen, she had *seen*. But her body begged for his touch. Needed it.

"Tell me you're mine, Orabella, promise me, now, and I promise I'll keep you. I'll give you your dreams. I'll do anything, just promise me."

His words filled her ear, urgent whispers between them, demands. He left her neck, brought her eyes back to his. She couldn't make sense of his words. She heard him in her dreams, *Mine, mine, mine*, over and over as he bit her. Over and over as she ran down dark halls taunted and blessed in turns by little winged creatures. His? But he had already married her, already taken her. Would he give her those dreams forever? Those twisting terrible dreams that suffocated her and made her burn with need in equal measure.

His cheeks flushed with pleasure. "I'll bring your smile into your eyes," he whispered. "I'll give you everything that was always denied you, just say you're mine."

The fantasy could be hers, she could taste it, so close. She closed her eyes. The world smelled of earth, her tongue tasted of honey, but she saw the silver ballroom. Saw her husband's smile, all teeth, felt the fox children in her belly. But her husband, a beast real and true, was no fox. He was something else, like she was something else, and they were both there, in that dark house, together. "Yes," she said, pleasure-drunk, fear-foolish. "Yes."

Elias leaned her back, fumbled with belt and skirts for a moment, and then there was no space between them. Broken, sharp-edged stones pressed into her back, grass and flowers crushed under their weight.

He kissed her, took her hips in his hands, and rocked her against him, hard, his cock pressing against her just so, just right until the pleasure broke over her, chased away all her thoughts. Rolled heat through her body, leaving behind a spinning wasteland in her mind, the connections between her thoughts and body broken.

He gasped, held her close, and she felt the wetness of his own pleasure all over her underthings.

He stroked her back for a few moments, the only sound the breathing that came too hard. A languid tiredness slipped over her, her body weak and odd. He lifted himself from her; the air bit coldly between her legs before she snapped them shut. Elias reached back for her, settled her on her feet before putting some distance between them. She knew his motions, had learned them. The way he tucked his shirt, reset his hair. Made himself presentable. In the proper order of things he would clean and dress her but they had not done things in the proper order.

This was not her bedroom. They had not had dinner.

She looked down at her skirts, violet, stained from grass. She reached up to her hair and plucked leaves from it. *How long have I been out? How long have I been awake?* She wasn't sure, time felt slippery and faster than it should. Did she walk down the forest path moments ago or had it been hours, days?

"It grows late and colder. Let's get you back in before the last of the sun." His voice sounded different. None of the heat, the desperation of a moment ago. It was the man she had met in the garden again. Well mannered, even tempered, and she wondered where that other was. The beast who smelled of tea and boxed stablehands for their smiles at her.

Cullen had come to warn her, Sloane had asked him to. *No, it's gossip, servant gossip. I'm fine. I didn't see anything. A dream.*

He said he would give her dreams to her. A promise made in passions. "Do you know what my dreams are?" she asked, staring at his palm.

"Your dreams? Of course." The smile was in his voice. "I'm your husband, why wouldn't I know?"

Because you've never asked, she thought but said nothing. What was there to say? He was her husband and her dreams were not so special. Not so unique. To be happy. To be loved. To be herself.

He stepped closer, took her hand, threaded his fingers through hers. "You're tired, you need rest. You've seen things I had not meant you to see. There have been too many episodes for you recently, my love."

She turned quickly, catching his eyes. They were gentle, loving. His lips curved into a slight smile, handsome and worried for his wife. *It was not my episode*, she thought, and stopped the words from coming. *Wasn't it?* The details were already tumbling. It was Claresta who had attacked, been attacked, but she had been attacked too. She had been distraught. She had slept. She had dreamed. *Someone is hurting Claresta*, the words hummed again, tickling at her. A reminder. She looked at her husband, remembered the wet crack of bone.

Her head had begun to ache. *Too much excitement, too much blood*, she thought. "I feel so strange."

"You shouldn't have come so far today. Not in your condition," he replied, taking her hand.

He pulled at her gently and she followed, turning back as they left the lonely garden, the little cemetery.

"It's all right for you to come here, once you're well again. The path is well walked, there is no danger this close to the manor, but I will ask you to wait until the weather turns fully. It is too cold under these branches, you'll fall ill."

No danger? But I saw a beast. She nodded. "Should I come back here?"

"It's quiet," he responded.

She opened her mouth to say that the manor was quiet, that it was empty and lonely, but held the words. The house was never quiet in the way the forest had been. There was always some rodent movement in the walls, some servants whispering just out of sight so low that all she could hear were the shapes of the words, not enough to decipher their meaning. But there, in that space it was quiet, so quiet. Only her own heart. "Yes," she agreed.

"Wait, I almost forgot." He released her, jogged back to where he had been a boar. Bent and pulled a treasure from the grass.

Oilcloth, a dark stain spreading through the sack. She could smell the blood and one eye saw a bedroom before she shook the vision away.

"What is that?" Her nose wrinkled, a grimace formed on her lips.

"Rabbits. The traps were lucky today. I have to get these to the kitchen or it will only be vegetables and potatoes for dinner," he teased, but the blood scent cloyed around him and made her stomach churn.

"I'm afraid my constitution is too delicate for the reality of what keeps me fed." She smiled weakly. She heard her sister-in-law's fox screams drawn by blood and pushed them away, a bad memory.

"A lady," he said, and pulled her forward, back into the wood.

A bride. She stayed silent, let herself be led.

The walk back was different than the one there. It happened faster, the trees a blur of darkening shadows. "There's time yet before dinner. Darling, why don't you have a bath?" Elias suggested. A normal walk in the woods, a normal evening ahead.

She looked at the sun, tried to figure the time but she hadn't gotten the hang of it. Couldn't read it for later or earlier. *Dinner? Wasn't it just lunch?* She shivered.

Together they walked down the garden path. She looked for Sloane but didn't see her anywhere.

Closer to the house Elias slowed and looked up.

She followed his gaze back to the house and up to a window. She found Claresta, small and bright, staring back down at them. She couldn't make out her features from the distance, but she smiled and waved anyway. *There is no anger between us, we are both held here*, she thought, remembering the woman's bare body. Remembering the blood and fear and pain of it. *A fox in a trap. No, I shouldn't think that way.* She hoped the gesture communicated across the distance, that the still woman understood. The late afternoon sun caught the pane, made it sparkle.

Elias stood for a moment, his focus on the window before coming back to her. He took her arm and walked by her side. He made idle chatter about the garden, asked what she thought to have done with it, encouraged her to decide quickly.

Everything is all right, she thought. "It's good to see Claresta up again."

"She's still in bed, sedated."

"But she was at the window." Orabella smiled, confused. She was sure she had seen her, a woman in white—who else could it have been? Who else had it been all those times? Claresta wandering, aimless and mad. In those rooms next to Orabella's secret garden. As she moved through the halls. Claresta in her nightgown and milk-white skin, who felt no cold.

"The window? No. There was no one in the window."

"I've had enough teasing. When we were coming back in, I waved. I'll only be a moment, just to say hello and then goodbye again."

He shook his head. "But there was no one in the window. It would be impossible for her to be there right now. She will stay that way until the morning, at least."

"But I saw her, in the window." She didn't like the childish whine in her voice but couldn't stop it.

He brushed her hair behind her ear, kissed her temple. "You didn't see anyone, love. The light was playing tricks on you. There was no one there."

But I saw, she thought. *Didn't I?* No longer sure, she tried to pull up the image, the memory, but there was only a window, a figure that may have been a person or a shimmer caught at just the right moment.

"I've let you up too early. You should still be in bed."

"No!" she stopped him. *If he puts me to bed again, I'll never get up*, she thought frantically, the idea filling her mind with urgency, but she couldn't say why. The fear, the danger, they came to her quickly without reason that she could find in that moment. No, there was only time to act. "I'm fine. Really. My mistake. I'll have my bath and join you and your father."

She turned and they closed the distance to the door. They passed into the dark maw of the house together, into the hall, just like all the halls. One of them hers, one of them his.

It would have been better if there had been crying, some warning before they turned the corner into the kitchen, that normal, living space among all the decay and disuse, but the only sound was the fire already set to boil water.

The thick, sharp, cloying, coppery smell of blood was everywhere. Orabella rubbed her tongue against the roof of her mouth to try to stop it but she couldn't and she wished for honey, for anything that wasn't that.

On the cook's table was Cullen, glassy eyes, waxy skin. The shirt was cut open, removed, leaving only the horrible thing that had been an arm, broken savagely. Now Maggie worked to set the bone, to make sense of it. Sloane stood silent, eyes wet across from them, holding cloths, uselessly.

They all turned to them in the doorway and Orabella looked up at Elias to see if the same man she'd seen in the graveyard was there. His face was impassive, unconcerned. "Here," he said, raising the bloody bag. "The traps were good today."

Maggie stopped in her work, accepted the bag, sniffed. "Rabbit." She sat them next to Cullen, turned back to her work in dressing his wounds.

"You," he said, turning to Sloane. "Heat some water. My wife wants a bath."

Sloane nodded, wouldn't look at her. "I'll get the other girl, sir."

"I'll walk you to your room and then I'll need to clean myself up as well, I suppose. It won't do any good to leave my wife dining with a woodsman." He led her out into the hall, away from the blood. Away from the broken man.

She nearly missed that it was a joke, missed her cue to laugh. She did, and caught Sloane's look, her betrayed face. But there was nothing she could do, he was her husband and she couldn't risk his anger. He was all she had in that house.

Little secrets, little doors. But he keeps his secrets too.

"Is everything all right, love?" Elias asked, bending close so his lips tickled her ear as he spoke.

"Yes, I'm just tired. This afternoon has been more than I expected."

"Selfish me, I shouldn't have taken things so far with you." He kissed her temple. Not that he had destroyed a person, not that he had shown her such terrible violence in him.

His hand wrapped around Orabella's. The familiar sounds of the house settled around her. The mice in the walls, the whispers of servants, and now, tickling at her nose ever so faintly, the smell of blood.

That poor rabbit, she thought, *to end your life in such a trap. My poor sister-in-law.* She focused on the two, the dead rabbit, the woman. Spared no thought for herself and couldn't bear to think of Cullen. Couldn't bear to think of herself. Trapped in the halls just as thoroughly as they, she followed her husband back to her room.

Chapter Twenty-One

Sloane shook out the dress and presented it. Like the wedding dress, it was out of fashion, not just by a year like the dress that had been displayed in the town's shop, or even by a decade. No, this one was much older, from maybe twenty or thirty years before. But it had been well kept, the smell of cedar filled her nostrils—it had been taken out of storage and not given any time to air out, like the wedding dress.

It was a light, near golden color with a matching sash and lace trim around the low collar. The sleeves were short and meant, she assumed, to be worn with gloves but she hadn't any, not the long type that would have been in style then.

"What is this?" Orabella said. She sat on the bed, still damp from her bath.

"The Master asked for this," Sloane said slowly. As she had before. On the wedding night so long ago. "The family has come again."

Orabella's fingers gripped the sheets. *Elias didn't say, no one said.* "I must make a better impression this time," she said brightly.

As before, Sloane helped her into the garment. This one was too long as well but it fit better, the lower cut giving way for her breasts, the wide skirt for her hips. She sat in the chair before her vanity and let Sloane brush and pin her hair in place.

The low neck showed the bruises along her skin but in the flickering candlelight they looked not like violence but an accident of birth. Just an unfortunate flaw of her skin. She touched them gingerly. They were fading. She was fading. How often had she done this? She touched the glass, the mirror met her fingers and she wondered if that meant she was real.

Standing, she gathered the skirts and followed Sloane from the room. Weary, bone tired. She wanted nothing else but to crawl back under the covers, sleep for a hundred years so the vines could finish growing up over the building and another prince could find her. But she was due for dinner with her husband, her prince and the beast in one, and she would go.

She walked down the hall with Sloane ahead leading by candlelight and Penny, the new girl, brought up to help with the bath, trailing behind. The night was just like her wedding feast. *But then, hasn't every night been the same?* It was always Sloane with her candle, leading her from her bedroom to the table. But this time, like before, she wore another woman's dress. *Claresta's*, she reasoned as she made her way into the halls. Like the last one must have been, but it seemed so old, too old for a woman Claresta's age.

They came into the dining room and she smiled at Elias, who stood and met her, taking her from Sloane for the night. He held her hands and bent, brushing his lips against her cheek. He had shaved, his chin felt smooth against her skin, and he smelled of soap, but she remembered the blood. He wore a vest and proper white shirt. Not for her.

Hastings sat at the table, at the head as usual, but with him were others. The family had come again, as Sloane had warned. Not all of them. A man with an upturned nose like a pig that did not match his cold eyes and thin cheeks sat next to a woman with dark hair and sallow skin. And across from him the woman with the small jaw.

Orabella turned back to Elias, questioned him with her eyes. *Why didn't you tell me?* But he only took her hand, stepped back, led her to the table, and helped her settle into her seat across from him, next to the other woman. Like the first meeting with Hastings and Claresta, she was expected to know how to behave, to act accordingly.

Hastings watched her from his place at the head. She smiled as she sat. "Good evening, sir."

"You have been well, I take it," he said.

There are no mysteries in this house. "Yes," she agreed.

He turned away, back to his plate.

The dinner had started without her. Like before, on the wedding night.

She looked at the plate in front of her. Perfectly cut squares of meat, impossible to tell what it had been, no existence before the plate, where it waited for her mouth. Drowned in a mushroom sauce, it smelled fragrant, delicious. Bite-sized vegetables and potatoes beside it. Like the wedding night, like every night. But she had seen the rabbits. She couldn't stomach it.

"Hello, dear family. It's so nice to see you again," she said softly.

The woman with the dark hair turned to her, pupils swollen, almost no iris. Deep, black voids. Like the fawn's eyes. Like the halls.

"I'm sorry, I don't know your names."

"That's my uncle, Charles," Elias said. "His wife, Elizabeth, and my aunt Alice. Hastings's siblings."

They seem much younger, she thought. They were middle aged, the same age as her aunt and uncle, but Hastings was ancient. *A second wife, then, later children.* There was no telling how old the frozen Claresta was. She tried not to think of what she looked like with her features distorted in her madness.

"Pleased to meet you, Elizabeth," she replied.

At her name the woman blinked, tilted her head like an animal summoned. Waiting, like a bird, to sing its song. "It's so easy to get lost here. So easy to lose your way in the forest. I was young. I had a daughter."

"Eat your food," Charles said, picking up his fork, spearing a dripping piece of meat, and shoving it into his mouth.

Elizabeth stopped, turned back to her plate. The fork she lifted held little cubes of meat, just like Orabella's.

They ate, with none of the revelry of the last dinner. Charles did not laugh or make lewd jokes with Alice. They were all respectable but silent. Quiet. The only sound the clink of forks. The lifting of glasses. Orabella left hers on the table. She pushed the meat around and nibbled at the potatoes, the vegetables.

"You should try the rabbit, dear," Alice said. Orabella turned to face her. "The mushrooms are local and delicious. Well, almost everything is but even we sometimes must settle for imports." She stressed the last word and Orabella tried to figure out the meaning. Was there an issue with Elias's business?

Local, she thought, at that table eager as Sloane to please. She picked at one cap, cut into pieces. Her stomach jumped. She thought of the hallway she had stumbled down. *No, no one goes there. I shouldn't have been there.* She placed the fork in her mouth, deposited the mushroom. A taste that matched the memory of the hall, mingled with spice and blood. She forced a smile to her face and swallowed. "It's very good," she said. "Everything prepared here has been delicious."

"Is something wrong?" Elias asked. Cold eyes. No shelter there.

"No, I'm fine." *He'll put you in bed, lock you in your room, you'll be like Claresta and Sloane will feed you from a spoon if you don't, if I don't . . .* She blinked, fighting back the drone of words in her mind. She'd seen the beast in him. Her heart beat hard, filled her head with the sound. Orabella sipped at the wine, smiled.

Alice smiled too. "It's a shame that Claresta couldn't join us this evening. I had a lovely chat with her."

"A chat?" *How? She doesn't speak, she doesn't do anything at all except for howl and scream and no, no. A turn of phrase, then; they sat with her, as I do.*

"Yes. She misses your visits. But I heard you had fallen under the weather. All better now, I hope?"

Orabella nodded. "I'm fine. It was nothing. It's nice of you to ask." *They must've seen the bruises, they must've seen the scars on her arms. They must have known what happened to her.*

"Good. Eat, dear. You must keep up your strength." An order. "Don't let the meat get cold. Your husband trapped it so well. It's good for your health."

The words made her shiver. Her husband had shot a deer, trapped a rabbit, shattered a man's arm. Bile churned in her but Orabella picked up her fork. She speared the meat, placed it on her tongue, and chewed it slowly. She sipped the wine carefully, small tastes, not enough to cover the other. Still bloody, still fresh.

"It's time, then," Hastings said suddenly, his voice deep and wet. Orabella could hear the rattle of his lungs with every word.

"There's no point in waiting. Spring is here, it'll be summer soon." Grease dripped down Charles's face, caught the light and made him seem wilder.

"Summer?" Orabella said. "But it's only just April?" She turned to Elias, looked for some support but found none. "Surely I couldn't have lost track of things so quickly!" She laughed.

Alice considered her. "Do you keep a journal, dear?"

There was an unused one, from Elias. An early gift. "No," she admitted. "I didn't have much to write about, the days are much the same. I'm grateful and my life is good here," she hurried to explain. "It's easy to lose track of things, in the country. My fault for being too leisurely."

Alice sat back. "She is very well mannered."

"As I said before," Elias agreed. "Orabella is a lovely woman."

"Well suited for the family," Alice said.

"I was well suited. My darling was well suited. Charles said, he said. When I was Liza," Elizabeth said.

"Quiet," Charles said.

"Do you remember our baby, Charles? Do you remember her upon the stairs in her little white dress?"

"Elizabeth," he said, voice knife-sharp.

"The stairs swallowed her right up. This place swallowed her, swallowed. Charles, do you remember me? I was Liza."

He took her hand and Orabella knew the touch, felt it in the small, delicate bones of her own hand. Elizabeth silenced, turned back to the plate. Picked up her fork, held it as if it was new, never seen before.

"A shame we couldn't have more children after that."

"Yes, and these old halls miss children. We hope to see yours soon," Alice said.

"It's only been—" She meant to say *a month* but stopped. It hadn't been, had it? "A little while since we were married. We're still learning about each other."

"The blood needs to be refreshed."

"Yes," Hastings agreed. "And some blood has stayed too long. Perhaps this will be a new age."

"I'm sorry about your daughter," Orabella said, lost in the

conversation, grasping at what she understood. They had lost a child. They hadn't had more.

"Rosette. My Rosette. The birds in her room taught her to fly. The birds lied," the ghostly woman said and then started to weep.

"It's all right, dear," Alice said in place of Elizabeth. "All family is blood."

Orabella nodded, unsure of what to say. The house itself. It swallowed.

The old man coughed, the action heavy with phlegm, drawing the attention back to him. He held a napkin to his mouth, took a few moments, his back bent and heaving with each cough that followed. Finally, he wiped at his lips, dropped the cloth back on the table, and looked at her with wet eyes. "All family is blood," he repeated.

She watched Elias grip his utensils in his fist, but he stayed silent. Orabella thought she had made an error, that she was not meant to speak, but it was too late to take the words back. She sipped the wine, forgetting herself.

"You'll keep to your duty. You're blood, one of us before all," Hastings said. No lantern this time but she knew what he meant. He wasn't speaking to her but he was.

Elias's fingers twitched on the table, curling into themselves but releasing before they formed a fist, lying back flat. "Yes, sir."

"That is what it means to be family. What it means to be blood," Hastings said, eyes hard, voice stronger than she had ever heard. He looked at Elias but sounded like he was speaking to himself.

"I wouldn't do otherwise," Elias answered.

Hastings nodded, turned away. "It's been so long since I've seen the garden."

"Forty years at least. Do you remember how it was?" Charles sounded joyous.

"And so it will be again," Alice sang. "Spring is here."

"Don't have children. Everything gets lost here." Elizabeth looked at her then, her eyes big as the fawn's had been and just as dark.

"I need to put my wife to bed," Charles said, standing.

He'll hurt her, Orabella thought. She wanted to tell him to stop, to give Elizabeth over to her to take to her room and hide away like a little mouse, but she said nothing. He was her husband and she was clearly unwell.

"Tomorrow you and I can sit in the garden. The air will do us good," she tried.

Elizabeth looked at her strangely. "Are you the new nurse?" she asked before looking around the room. "Charles, I'm tired."

She rose, like a dream, and Charles gripped her hand, holding her at the table. "This is not our home, darling."

"It's late," Hastings said and stood, taking his leave without goodnights.

"I will visit with you more, Orabella. Tomorrow, perhaps. Good night," Alice said. Together with Charles and Elizabeth, she left the dining room, leaving Orabella alone with her husband.

"Drink the rest of your wine. Let me put you to bed."

There was no use in arguing, it would do her no good to take a stand on it. He was her husband. Something had happened. Something had changed. The animals were clawing their way out of the family bit by bit.

She picked up the cup and drank from it, slow sips and then long swallows until it was gone. A throbbing hum started on her second sip, turned to the irritating purr of wings by the last. Her head felt light as the cloud of her hair but her body was heavy, so heavy.

He rose from the table, took her hand, led her through the dark.

In her room he turned down the lamps, but before then she saw in their flickering shadows the birds on her wall flap their wings. Elizabeth's strange words.

Elias said this room was meant for me. Elias is a liar. When he came to her, she opened her arms and held him. There was nothing else to do.

The door stared back at her, dark against dark, a mouth, no, just the throat. The curtains in her room had been drawn but she could see the difference between her space and the space beyond that beckoned and called.

She had let him love her, as he had in the sad little graveyard. Moaned and sighed under him until he was panting, spent above her. And then he dressed, kissed her head, and slipped out the door as he always did. Just the feeling of heaviness and now the throat of the house, one of the hundreds, thousands of openings. A tangle of throats and no stomach. A many-headed snake twisted in on itself. She would rot in its esophagus.

Something had changed.

A dream, she thought. The door couldn't be opened. She slid from the bed. Her head felt too light, her body too heavy. Slow to respond, slow to turn, but it moved. The wine. Her body had grown accustomed enough to wake. With clumsy fingers she lit the lantern that waited and turned back, sure she would see the door locked tight and it was, just as it had been left.

There was an option, though. Her little secret door. The family was there, they'd be about the halls, they were night people. The walls would be her passage. She would travel them as the mice traveled them.

She left the lamp and crawled inside, cold air swirling about her, and she shivered. She closed her eyes, took a deep breath. The world spun and her thoughts came to her from under the thick coating of sweetness in her mind. *I should be afraid*, she thought, but the fear that should have been there wasn't. To be afraid was too much to bear. Instead, she was left with broken thoughts, a jumble of near feelings, and the quiet sense that something was very wrong. *It's a dream*, she thought again. It was the only thing that made sense anymore.

She didn't think, she walked the dark path, searching the ground for strips of light. She'd been there long enough to know that the house would carry her, show her the way. No light, a dark thing, she was like the rest of them. Under her bare feet, mouse skeletons splintered, turned to dust. Ahead and behind her, the ones that lived chattered and wrestled, no fear in her presence.

Why should they be afraid? I'm no fox, she thought as she took the twists and turns of the tunnel. She would find her way out, or be swallowed. *Would they find me? Or will the mice eat my skin, fill my bones with my hair, and make a fine nest of me? Then I'll become the ghost of the house. A scary story for the next bride.*

She thought of Elias at another house, another family with a poor ward and too many debts.

A slice of moonlight, not just along the bottom but all around, her height. *A door? Of course, they would have to have them some-where, they can't all be for children.*

In the dark, she felt along the wall for the latch, the trick of it, and found it, pushed it open. A room, like all the other rooms. Furniture stacked from top to bottom. Chests that had held secrets for so long the leather straps were rotting away. She smelled a hint of earth on the air and knew that soon it would sprout mushrooms and toadstools like those other places she had found.

She moved through the room, touched a dish set that hadn't been used in decades—a thick layer of dust on it, left forgotten. And then there was a portrait. She lifted it, twisted it to the moon. A little boy with storm-gray eyes and a solemn expression. His hair was shaggy and even dressed all in finery he seemed out of place. A trick of the artist. The only child Orabella had seen in the entire manor.

Elias is a liar, she thought again. There existed one portrait of him, and even standing alone he didn't match. A bastard child—her heart ached for him, the sad little boy. She sat the portrait down, leaned it against a waiting mirror, and made her way out of the room.

The door stood open and led to a stunted hall. She hadn't traveled so far in the walls, maybe she was only on the other side of her little wing now, she couldn't be sure. There was only one other room on the floor, the door closed, and a staircase that led upward.

Light spilled down from above and the stairs were well worn. She followed them up.

A tower. She tried to remember what the house looked like from outside. A single door at the top of the steps stood open and led into a small bedroom.

She stood in the room, eyes dancing over it, a familiarity to it all. *It's like my old room, with my aunt and uncle.* The little room with its little desk. She turned and found a small single bed with a stand next to it. A simple wardrobe. The bed neatly made, not slept in. A small stack of books on the desk and next to them a stack of letters.

"This is Elias's room," she said to hear it. The place he went to sleep was not so far from her. Connected by a passage, a staircase. Above her the entire time. *Is that what I've heard? Has it been him this whole time, moving around in his little room? Elias is a liar.* But it was late and he was not there. Orabella crossed the floor to the wardrobe, pulling it open to reveal his clothes. She touched them with shaky fingertips, their owner confirmed when she pulled a sleeve to her nose and breathed in his scent. Wool and ginger and the woods. *His room but he's not, he's not . . .*

She couldn't put the words together, couldn't form the thoughts. He was not where he was meant to be. She knew where he was. The blood boiled in her and she sank deeper into it, her world becoming shadows cut across by shadows. Darkness in and darkness out.

She spun around the room again, looking for something else, anything else, and found the letters. She picked one up, took it to the window for the light. It was unsealed and she pulled out paper, the feel familiar on her fingers.

Dear Jane, it read. "No," she breathed. Reached for another, found the same. *Elias is a liar.*

She looked out the window, could see over the whole garden, shimmering under the full moon. She almost turned away but the scene caught her. The dark pool. Where she sat with Sloane. They were down there, like little wooden toys, so small. Alice and Charles and Hastings and Elias too. She watched as Hastings climbed into the pool.

She watched as Elias drowned him.

Heard a chorus of foxes barking, screaming, laughing from the woods.

"I'm mad. This place. This place. No." She put the letters down neatly, orderly. *A dream*, she thought, kneeling before the desk, *I am in a dream and this is how things go.*

She couldn't stand it, the little room, all her letters. The horrible thing in the pond. No, a nightmare. She fled. Back down the little stairs and then another hall, she lost and found her way through the manor by the sparkling light of glass beads, the long lines of her fingers' tears in the wallpaper.

Found her way back to her own little room. Locked the door, shut the secret one, and buried herself under the covers.

Chapter Twenty-Two

She shifted, moved away from the light. Open curtains. Morning again.

Orabella woke with a start, looked around the room wildly. Sloane sat in her little chair, worked on embroidery.

"You're awake," she said coldly.

Orabella nodded and looked down at herself. Her hands were filthy, her gown as well. She kicked off the blanket, and her feet left dark smudges on the sheets. "Sloane, I—"

"Sir said you were not to be woken this morning. That it had been a late night for him and you needed your rest."

"Sloane, I'm sorry, what happened to Cullen, I—"

The maid lifted a finger to her lips. "A horrible accident. Sir has already paid him compensation, given him time off to heal. Accidents happen, it is nothing to worry yourself over, ma'am." She put down the embroidery and stood. "You need to freshen up for the day."

She wanted to say that she understood now. That she knew what Cullen was trying to tell her, what Sloane was trying to tell her, but there were always ears in the manor. She let Sloane help her change, let her wash her feet and hands.

"I had a horrible nightmare last night," Orabella said slowly as she climbed back into the sheets, freshly shaken of the dirt and grime of her nighttime excursion.

"It's morning now, don't think too much on it," Sloane said softly, stronger than Orabella had ever given the bubbly girl credit for. She brought the basket holding her copies of *The Candle* to her. "Read a little. I must get breakfast." And she left her alone.

She never leaves me alone, they never leave me alone, she thought. *Something has changed.* Not in the house but in Sloane, and she was sad for it. She picked up the paper to have something to look at.

What I saw could not have happened. There would be some notice, some to-do. And I am meant to be in bed.

There was no order in the basket. They had picked through them in their excitement, she and Sloane. The papers were slippery, hard to hold. Her hands felt weak. She couldn't concentrate on the words. She had wasted all her words on letters that were never sent. Wasted them on waiting. She forced herself to focus, to find something to hold her. The top paper had a date for the end of March, the one under that, a month later. "Wait," she said, cursing herself for the dull girl she was. It had been there, he had shown her himself.

She dug through the basket, looking more closely; the newest paper was for the end of April.

"I've lost track of so much time." It seemed far away, unimportant. She was changing, the house was changing her. What was a month? Her husband was a beast, she was kept well, did it matter? But her hands were shaking. She couldn't let herself think of what happened in the forest. What she saw in the night. They were all dreams. Her imagination. It was almost summer. Spring was nearing its end and she couldn't leave.

There was nowhere to go and her husband wouldn't let her leave. There was no world outside of Korringhill. And no mysteries in its halls. She must survive there.

The door opened and there was Sloane with her breakfast and the new girl, Penny, and Manda carrying dress boxes in their arms. Behind them trailed Mrs. Locke.

Sloane settled the tray on her lap. Tarts and lavender gummies. Sweets baked specially by Maggie at Elias's request. They'd had a long night. The sweets tasted sour on Orabella's tongue but she ate them.

Manda, free from her packages, swung open the door to the wardrobe. Without a word she began to pull Orabella's clothing from it. She handed it to Penny, who folded it quickly and stacked it on the bed. Sloane worked through the packages, carefully unwrapping them while Mrs. Locke watched.

They were taking her clothes. "What are you doing?" Orabella nearly screeched, the panic pouring into her voice, forcing it out louder than she meant it to be. She would be like Claresta in her light gowns, fit only to sit by the window. Or haunt the halls.

"Clearing the way for your gift. A waste, I think, but I will do as I'm told," Mrs. Locke said, sniffing, clearly annoyed by the entire affair.

"I don't understand."

"We must clear the old to make way for the new."

Elias drowning Hastings.

Laughter came out as a snort then a cackle, ringing and mad. "This family doesn't let anything go," she said before she could stop herself. "What am I to wear? My nightgown? Even Claresta is allowed clothing!" She had spoken too much, lost hold of herself, but she was exhausted and unsettled. Her tongue was loose.

The offense Orabella thought she would see was missing from Mrs. Locke's face. Instead there was a curiosity, a calculation.

"Finish your tea, miss," Sloane reminded her from where she worked. The first package unwrapped, she shook out a dress. Brand-new, beautiful dress. Finer than anything she'd brought with her, finer than anything she'd ever worn. The color suited her, a warm magenta trimmed with bronze. Sloane hung it in the wardrobe and moved to the next package.

Dresses.

No more secondhand ones in colors that did not flatter, did not suit except by coincidence. Instead, she was met with sub-dued oranges near gold, stripes in pretty greens and ivory whites, soft reds and blushing pinks. New undergarments to match, in silks and cottons. Stockings and garters that had never once been mended.

"Wait! Stop!" Orabella called, and the three maids paused, turned to her. "That's my shawl! I made that. I'd like to keep it. Put it back, please."

All three of them looked at Mrs. Locke and for a moment she thought the woman would refuse, would force them to toss it with the rest. Mrs. Locke nodded, motioned for them to put it away, and the shawl was set, gently, down on the bed to wait.

Penny moved a pile of the folded clothes from the bed and left the room as Sloane unpacked the next one, a light yellow, like the sun, and hung it. Manda repeated the same process as Penny, dis-appearing out the door. Alone. Pinks, creams, golds, and violets. Dresses and jackets, blouses and skirts. More than three women could carry. Orabella's head swam.

Small boxes of pins and jewelry. "Just glass," Mrs. Locke in-formed, her eyes on the three women who handled the pieces. "Playthings."

They glittered in the sun, clear stones and milky pearls. A box designed with intricately inlaid mother-of-pearl patterns was produced and the jewels, glass or not, were put inside. The box made full was set on the vanity before the mirror.

All manner of expensive, lovely things.

The work was done and the maids stood, their hands folded, waiting for Mrs. Locke's next order.

"Clean up the breakfast, Penny. Amanda, take care of this paper. Sloane, finish with the wife."

What the man in the dark had called her. The hunter. Elias. The beast. The murderer.

She wanted to send them away, to puzzle through all the things that she had seen in the dark, but Mrs. Locke was there, watching. And what would happen if she did?

They changed her nightgown. A light, ethereal thing spun from seemingly nothing but mist, the fabric was so fine. The sleeves were short and the neck low, lower than anything she had brought with her. New like everything else. It showed off all her bruises and scratches. All the things that had been done to her in that house. Sloane replaced the peach dressing gown over her shoulders, tied it closed under her breasts, and put her back into the bed.

"Oh, miss, you look so lovely," she nearly sang as she tucked the covers back around her. Sloane moved her hair, set it prettily around her shoulders. She grabbed the hand mirror, one of the gifts, and handed it Orabella. "Look how lovely you are!"

Orabella took the mirror and considered herself. Her hair was down, as Elias liked it. As it was always now since she'd been in the manor. She looked pale, bags under her eyes. Washed out and gray. Tired. She looked like herself, not herself.

Her clothes were gone. Her husband spent the night in the bed of another woman. *His sister, his sister, that was the worst of it, is the worst,* the wings sang as they pushed her down into that thick sludge of memory where it was easier to float and let the sweetness choke her. She fought against it. *What I saw, I could not have seen.*

"Look at my lovely wife."

Elias at the door, leaning against the frame, the hall a gray square behind him. He had dressed well, his shirt neatly pressed and brilliant white. His jacket, brown, shimmered gold where the sun caught it. "Elias," she said, the only word her tongue seemed fit to form being his name when she supposed there should have been questions.

He crossed the room to her, looked at her more closely. "You look so beautiful. Nothing I purchased even compares. Don't you think, Mrs. Locke?"

"We are all thankful that you have brought such a lovely bride into this house," the old woman replied, and the words cut Orabella like a knife.

"This is all too much," Orabella said, unsure if she meant the gifts, the praise, or the crush of bodies in the room, but the words seemed right. Like a thing she should say to such gifts. She looked up, met his eyes, tried to remember the heat of her anger, tried to find that piece of herself to hang on to but she felt it all slipping away. This man could not have been who she saw in the night. She wanted to lie down, to run, to move and be still all at once. His gentle touch, his eyes so filled with need, even the slight pink of his cheeks at the sight of her chased away the cold in her and she was drowning in a different heat altogether.

"Everything else has been too little," he said, standing straight.

"Where did these clothes come from?" To change the subject, to keep from crying.

He smiled, hid his teeth from her. "The dressmaker."

"In town?"

"Yes." He leaned forward, his mouth at the cusp of her ear.

"The jewelry is not glass. I would never put anything false on you."
His voice was a low growl. The voice of the beast. The voice of her
husband.

Desire, thick like honey, flooded her mind. *A dream*, it hummed.
But still. *A warning.* "What am I dressing for? Are we going out to
town? To meet with another family?" She pulled her hand away as
she pulled guesses from her memory. Places she had gone before,
moments that had been before the manor, before the marriage.
Normal things that a husband and wife would do in the world
beyond Korringhill Manor.

"There's nowhere to go here, I'm afraid. Just the town, and
you've seen much of that. Perhaps we can go on holiday later, after
you've found your footing here. The dresses and the jewelry are
because I wish to see you be lovely," he said softly. He met her in
bed, slid close to her so that their heads touched, intimate, gentle.
"Orabella, my love, I wish I could let you lie here all day. I wish we
could spend the day in bed."

The door opened, the maids returned. Sloane and Penny.

Elias kissed her forehead, slid off the bed. "I'll see you after
you've dressed."

"For what?" she asked.

"Hastings's funeral," he said, with all the gravity of suggesting
an afternoon picnic. "I'm afraid he passed during the night."

It was real, the nightmare.

Chapter Twenty-Three

The room was different. It was the one she had first met Claresta and Hastings in; the dead garden had burst into life and cast green shadows into the room. A table had been moved in and the family sat around it, playing cards with grease-covered fingers. The remains of a boar sat on a platter against the wall; bones lay bare where the meat had been ripped from them. The head still sat, tusks and all, undisturbed. Cut fruit waited in sugar and honey, glistening. Bread, golden and slathered with butter, flaked crumbs over the table as greedy hands reached for it.

Those who couldn't fit at the table lounged on couches and chairs, their voices too loud with the drink that flowed from every cup. Wine, sweet and savory, spilled down their chins, chunks of flesh, fruit and boar, showing between their teeth with each laugh, each word.

The family. More of them than at the wedding dinner. They had risen from nowhere, like little white mushroom caps after a fresh rain, and come to the house. They filled the room pale faced and jeweled eyed.

Alice—she remembered her from the night before—dashed from her seat to lay claim to Orabella. She pulled at her arm and Orabella turned to search for help from Sloane, but it was past the time when Sloane could help. The maid's face was blank and she turned away, retreated into the house. Alice pulled Orabella in, sat her at her seat and wrapped her arm through hers, holding her to it as she sat to one side. On her other waited a heavy, middle-aged man with thick blond hair and a boisterous laugh. He elbowed her roughly and showed her his hand with every new deal of the cards.

Orabella's eyes dashed around the room, searching for the familiar, settling on Elizabeth, who sat on the couch with more of the strange family, her black hair stark. She held her hands in front of her and smiled, nodding at their jokes, whatever they were. Playing her part as Orabella played hers, mimicking the only other wife she could see in the room.

"Here, look, give us a kiss for luck," her neighbor said as he picked up his fresh hand.

"Leave the girl alone, Patrick! I'll give you a kiss!" Another man shouted from the couches, and then a tussle as some cousin or other wrapped their arms about Patrick and mocked the act with loud smacking noises to the delight of everyone around them.

The sun made no difference, they were as they had been on the wedding night: loud, brash, and strange. A fairy court, and their queen, Claresta, watched them, silent and still. Ageless in a dress so blue it looked like the sky. Pure, untouched. She sat next to the table where her father was laid out, truly dead this time, the corpse Orabella had imagined made real, and she wondered how she could have made the mistake before. Now in his black suit, settled on the table, his cheeks were sunken, his skin already taking on a green color.

Orabella wore dusty gold, a gift from Elias with jewels to match. Sloane and Penny had done the work. Her hair floated around her like smoke.

Alice pulled her closer, just a breadth farther away from Patrick, and loudly whispered, "These men and their games. I've never had the knack for it—cards, you know—but these men do so like to play."

"You are all so lively," Orabella agreed, speaking because she thought that was what was required of her, thinking of her uncle. She touched Alice's arm and the woman smiled, showing sharp yellow teeth, and Orabella wished with everything to look away but she returned the smile.

A hush settled over the room and in walked Elias, returning prince. A king, his father, was dead. He smiled at Orabella, took the empty seat across from her, blocking the door. "Am I too late to play this round?"

The noise resumed. The cards were dealt. *Didn't he promise?* She couldn't remember all that had been said in the carriage, in the garden, in the bedroom. Everything was so long ago, the world was so loud now. She drank the wine that was handed to her, lost track of things. It was all right. Elias would never hurt her.

They played for wooden tokens produced from baskets that lined the table. "Just for fun," Alice had said, showing her one. A *B* was carved in it artlessly. *Blakersby*, she thought, handing it back.

Elias smiled from across the table, his eyes catching hers for a moment, and then turned to laugh at some joke. The tightness that had been in him the night before was gone. Here he was loose and good-natured, comfortable among his fellows. None of the anger that he had shown at the wedding, at the dinner. But things had changed.

Claresta sat like a doll in a blue gown. She didn't eat, she didn't laugh, she sat at her father's arm like a statue. No evidence of the violence that had happened days before existed on her face and Orabella wondered if she had only imagined that the woman had clawed at herself. Or if, if she bent close enough, she would see a map of thin white lines all over her delicate skin. If it simply did not show as well on her as it did on Orabella, who still carried the wounds.

"Is the bride everything you thought?" A nephew, perhaps? Orabella couldn't quite place his age but his jowls hung low while his eyes seemed young. He made thrusting motions towards a woman who laughed and pushed him off. *Drunk*, Orabella thought as the man went slamming to the ground, still laughing and saved by another man with a clatter of plates. Food spilled and drink dribbled. No one minded. A servant cleared it.

"She is," Elias started, and a hush fell over the room. She felt their eyes turn to her; the heady drunk feeling evaporated suddenly as they all waited, breaths held, for Elias to tell them, to judge her. He waited, thinking over his words as he moved cards in his hand.

Who is he comparing me to, his sister? She is perfect, perfect, nearly magical, and I am just a silly human girl who no one wanted. Is that what you'll say, husband, is that— She stopped herself, forced the poison thoughts back into the honey well and humming wings that had become her mind.

"A dream," he finished. A collective breath from the group. "It is hard to explain what a gift she is. She has taken so well to this house, even improved on it, and has plans, so many plans to bring it back to what it once was. Why, when you come back again after the summer I imagine you won't recognize the place."

There was chatter then, pleased approval, and she smiled as Alice cooed at her and Patrick patted her hand.

"You speak so highly of me but really, I've only set eyes on the garden. It's such a lovely space, it's a shame it can't be enjoyed more."

"Oh, the garden!" Alice half wailed. "I'm so pleased that you'll be taking up the cause. Was it you who made the little castle with all the plates? Oh, I so loved that, it was delightful! So unique. I do so hope you have time to make more. Our Elias has brought such a beautiful thing to our door." There was a bite to her words, an insult.

The little rooms, all made up. For guests. For the family.

"Yes!" Another voice, another stranger. "Spring is here! The blood refreshed!"

"Orabella, come here, dearest," Elias said, hand out.

She wanted to piece together all the parts they were telling her but they fell into bits as she grabbed for them. There were pieces missing, elements they hadn't said or said in ways she couldn't understand, wasn't meant to understand. She glanced at Claresta, thought she saw her move. *It's an act*, she reminded herself. *I must act too.* There were no answers she could understand, so she stopped trying. She could be a good wife. She went to her husband.

She stood, as he asked, and her eyes swept around the table, her smile plastered on her face.

Once she was at his side, Elias reached up for her arm and pulled her, not gently, forward. She tumbled into his lap and he laughed before pressing a hard, wet kiss on her lips. "Cousin Patrick has had your luck long enough, I'm afraid I'll be taking it back along with all of those tokens."

The room laughed, the tension broken.

Elias whispered to her. "Don't worry for the past. Think only of the future. Our future." It must have seemed he was whispering something sweet. She smiled to give the impression it was. It was what he would want her to do. "Be a good girl for me, now."

She pulled away, smiled brightly at him. *Of course, of course, husband.* Pleased, he kissed her again. The sharp sting of liquor on his tongue, her mouth warmed and numbed with it.

"All right, I'll have my money back now." He pulled away, turned back to the table.

The room roared with laughter and Orabella smiled at them, Elias's grip tight on her thigh, fingers digging slowly into her, holding her down the way he had held down Hastings. Her eyes strayed back to Claresta. She hadn't moved, not really, but on her lap, just under her fingers, her skirts were bunched and wrinkled as if she had gripped them in her fingers. Like Orabella held hers.

Orabella leaned into Elias, watching those hands, and saw one finger twitch. Elias made a pleased sound, his focus on the cards but his free hand stroking her hip. *Does she know? Does she know what her brother has done?*

A cup held to her from a dark-sleeved arm. She didn't look at the face, she plucked the cup from the fingers and sipped from it. The smell hit her before it wet her tongue. The same warming, numbing drink her husband tasted of. "I think this is yours," she said, attempting to set it down.

"Drink," he chuckled, fingers digging, holding. "It's a party." He leaned into her shoulder, back to her ear. "You'll get used to the taste, drink up, love." He nibbled her neck, a shock of teeth.

She did as he asked, fighting a grimace, turning to look at his cards. Diamonds and spades, a king and a queen. She took another drink, moving her eyes back to the window court, back to Claresta. Wondered if he had held her on his lap as he held Orabella now. If she had felt the rise and fall of his chest against her arm. Wondered why that, out of everything, was what she cared about most.

She lifted the cup to her lips, drinking as her husband told her. Tried to drown out all those disgusting and longing thoughts that filled her. Her head swam, the cards blurred. The party carried on.

Someone pulled out a fiddle. Its whine mingled with the laughter. More cards were thrown across the table, more tokens in return. The basket next to Elias ebbed and flowed with each hand and his laughter spilled more and more freely from his throat but he didn't release her.

Her thighs and rear began to ache and she squirmed, trying to find comfort, and he shifted under her, refused to let her go. Smoke bloomed in the room, the sun set slowly, casting long shadows cut with amber light. Her cup emptied and refilled. Elias laid wet kisses on her and the family made lewd jokes around them.

Candles were brought out. The silver of their holders slowly turned yellow with wax. *The candles are made here, why did I never notice?* she thought idly as the cards were swept away and the table was reset. The oily, thick, greasy smell mingled with the bitter smoke that filled the room.

A clatter of dishes. Servants clearing the remains of boar from the table. Dinner would be soon. She looked over at Hastings's still body. His brother sat with him and other, older men she didn't know. All in black save Claresta, who at first glance sat as still as the corpse of her father. But Orabella knew better now, knew her little tells, her little tricks. The corner of her mouth twitched, her fingers scratched and twisted. Teeth and claws aching to be released.

Is he the dinner, this the burial? His body, his blood, and we're all blessed. They'll make candles of him. She ran her fingers, half numb, against her cut palm to keep them from her fine skirts. Remembered the bite, remembered her flush of desire at the chase.

A chair was brought for her, dinner was set.

Chickens roasted until the skin shone like dull suns were placed on the card table. Each time she blinked there was more food.

More bread and shallow bowls of gravy. The fruits were refreshed and her cup was switched for a glass of wine, thick with honey. There were no forks, no knives. Claws and teeth only.

Hungry fingers descended on the feast, ripping the birds to pieces. Someone—she thought Elias but she couldn't be sure, everything spun—placed a plate in front of her, the meat torn to infant-sized pieces with a dainty selection of sugared fruits. No more cubes, no more pretending who they were.

"Eat some bread, dear," Alice called from across the table, laughing. A mouth full of meat. A mouth full of teeth.

A glass of water appeared. She nibbled on the bread and drank the water. The window court had disbanded leaving only Claresta, like an idol poised perfectly in her chair. Next to her sat Mrs. Locke feeding her carefully with her clawed hands, and behind them Hastings. A family portrait. *Oh*, she thought. Another possibility with no answer, no proof. Another game her own imagination had come up with. Orabella blinked, shook her head attempting to throw off the drowsy feeling that threatened to consume her.

"Elias," she tried to call him, pull his attention, but when she turned his eyes were dark, his lips pursed. "I've had too much to drink, I think I should lie down."

He touched her face and smiled. Planted a greasy kiss on her cheek. Laughed at something she couldn't hear but his eyes stayed dark. The air was smoky, heavy with incense like a church, and under that smoke, a bitter chord. It clung to her skin, mixed with her sweat and slid down her back and breasts.

The fiddle whined, cutting through the laughter and the smoke like a bell, and some jaunty song began, out of tune and off rhythm. They sang along with it but Orabella couldn't capture the words; her head felt like lead, her belly grumbled and spun. The smoke choked her and blurred her vision. Hot tears ran down her cheeks.

She hooked her fingers on to Elias's lapel, wrapped them in the fabric. "Elias," she thought she called, but she couldn't be sure her voice made it around the thick worm her tongue had become.

"To dance!" someone shouted. The voice was feminine, familiar. *Claresta?* But no, no, that couldn't be. She shook her head and the room spun in response. She felt her chair tipping, her body falling, caught in hard arms. Saved from the sea of the floor.

"To dance! To dance!" the crowd roared, louder than the room could handle, shaking the walls. She looked across the table. Pale faces, twisted noses, loose cheeks, eyes too far or too close, too bright. Ears that poked out from near white, blond hair all around. Made a chorus of the words. Beautiful, beautiful.

The arms were Elias's and he dragged her, whispering in her ear of treats and gifts until she got her feet under her again.

The fiddle player came before her, smiling wide, showing brown and broken teeth. "So lovely!" he bellowed over his playing. "Elias has brought us such a lovely wife!"

No, I'm only Elias's, she thought even as she stumbled forward, following the player. Elias at her side, his arm around her, holding her up, pushing her forward. The others formed a train behind them, singing and hooting as they went forward. They took up candles, another uncle or cousin or nephew, she couldn't keep them straight, making his way forward to light the hall. *What about Claresta, what about Hastings?* she thought as they spilled from the drawing room, knowing there were no answers. It was no funeral she attended. No mourning.

It was a celebration. A party, her husband had said. But it was a funeral.

The procession surged forward, singing their strange song, the sound echoing in the small hall. The men in front seemed to know the way and everyone else followed, the light spilling from the candles, the rich smell of melting wax. The dark pressing around them, creating pools of flickering orange light.

They spilled from the halls into the foyer, the wide stairs ascending to the upper floors, and a panic flooded her, an animal fear that she couldn't place, stabbed through the haze, red and violent. Elias held tighter, pushed her forward into the main hall, past the stairs.

Towards the ballroom.

"To dance, to dance!" someone sang behind her, clear as a bell.

Orabella tried to hold to the lyrics. They sang nonsense, fairy-tale stories. Unbalanced, her head felt like her stomach, an ocean churning with liquor as she stumbled down the hall.

The fiddler and his candle bearer knew well enough the way and stepped nimbly over abandoned planks of wood, piles of bricks and tiles. Above her the hum of wings. The fluttering, buzzing vibration of them, those small folk from the painting in and out of the corner of her eye. She tried to lift her arm, swat them away, but her body was heavy and useless, dragged by Elias, pulled by the court.

Then they were turning, spilling into the silver ballroom where a ghostly crowd waited. The court of forever endlessly repeated in the mirrored walls. Laughter rang along the wall, the candles were left on the floor, carelessly, madly.

"Oh! Oh! The piano! We must! Thomas! Thomas! Come play!" A shout from the crowd.

"Elias," she tried again, but he swung her in his arms, pulling her close as he moved to the center of the room.

"Is it in tune?" A man's voice.

"Who cares? Play!" Another's. They all knew the song.

The piano struck up, fell in tune with the fiddle and they began to clap. *The silver ballroom*, she thought as Elias moved her hands into position. *Wasn't this my dream?* Elias, her beautiful Elias, who was beast and murderer, looked at her with such care.

"I wanted so much to dance with you that night." His voice was a whisper, heavy with an unnamed feeling, sour and bitter on the air.

She couldn't respond, she knew she should but there was nothing, nothing. All her concentration was on matching his steps as he spun around the room with the other couples. Flashes of blue at the corners of her eyes, a high laugh filled her ears. *Everything is beautiful and nothing like I thought.* Her head fell back and she stared into the dark of the ceiling, the candlelight failing to reach its dizzying heights. The angels and their clouds, those faraway protectors swallowed, leaving her alone with them. Those earthly and terrible beings she had married into. *Foxes and more and worse*, she thought. Her eyes fluttered, the lids heavy, her mind buzzing.

The dancers shifted and changed before her. Grew paws and snouts. Owl eyes and pointed ears through hair made from grass. Between their legs darted the fawn, eyes huge, focused on her. Everything smoky, changing, far away, and all that was asked of her was that she keep dancing.

Elias spun her, caught her, dragged her back. The hand that held hers rougher, hotter than it had been a moment before. The world was fuzzy, dark at the edges, bright in the center, and her body flooded. Thick, honey heat pooled all through her at the touch. *Caught.* The word came to her as her belly flooded with flutters, her mouth opened in a pant. A sweet scent mingled with the mildew of the house and poured from him. He moved with her, carrying her weight, her clumsy feet, but his steps were no longer graceful, they dragged and lurched with the music.

She opened her eyes as much as she could and through the slits she could make out a face, the cruel twist of a smile, a wisp of Claresta's hair caught in their dance.

A breath came from her throat, a cry but not quite, and the room laughed and cheered as her partner spun her in time with the music. He pulled her closer and breathed deeply, the sound wet and hungry. She forced her eyes open again to see Elias spinning with Claresta, who laughed, a barking sound, high and mad, the light catching sharp white teeth.

But that's not right, he's here, he's here. Her thoughts spun and sank, the darkness crushed her, pushed into her eyes as his arms crushed her closer to his body, and she could feel that familiar length of him pressing against her belly. She lost strength, her legs crumbled beneath her, she tried to grab him, to hold herself up or push away, but there was no power in her to do either.

The crowd laughed and he picked her up.

They'll swallow me all up, these halls, like the other, Elizabeth's girl. Her eyes were heavy, all the words around her gibberish.

And then she was tumbling, falling, through the floors and stones into a softness like soil. She screamed but her mouth filled with dirt and dust pressed over her eyes and all through her thoughts until there was nothing at all of her anymore.

Chapter Twenty-Four

The light glimmered through her closed lids and Orabella awoke, dragging herself towards that golden glow, forcing her eyes open to meet it.

She stared at her own ceiling, white, unadorned. Under her, her own bed, the nothing scent of her own sheets, her own space, came with every breath. With a groan she sat up, cradled her head in her hands for a moment before she took a deep breath and faced the day.

And day it was, full and true, streaming through the window, dancing on golden light over her carpet and against the wall. The door stood firmly shut across the room. She drummed her lips and turned to the barely-there square. Had they gone through there? "Why and who?" she murmured. *There's no reason, if Elias had been here he would have locked it on his way out and he's the only person who would be here*, she thought. Doubt poked hot spears in her belly but she ignored them. *Too much drink*, she thought.

There was nothing in her memory after the ballroom. It was as dark as the pool she'd seen Elias drown his father in. Dark as the eye of a fawn never born.

"I'm still dressed," she mumbled to herself, staring down at the garment, the fine fabric wrinkled and dirtied with grease from the dinner as if it proved the point. That she had lost herself and forgotten how she came to bed at all. When she had dropped anything on herself she wasn't sure either. *Did I*, she thought then stopped. She breathed in again and the night came back to her in bits and pieces. The wild court of the family. The meal eaten with fingers, not a utensil in sight, like wild people. The song. The silver ballroom. The dance.

She pulled herself from the bed, stumbled to her mirror, and flopped down on the chair. Her mouth tasted sour. Standing again, she poured water from the pitcher into the basin. She scooped it into her mouth with her hand and swished it over her teeth and tongue as she made her way to the window, pushed it open, and spat it all out. The air held more warmth than it had in weeks. Grass scent filled the air.

She leaned forward, found her little castle made of plates and cups, adorned with glass animals. Was that a few days ago or a century? She couldn't tell anymore. Hadn't been able to tell since she walked through the front doors of the manor. She didn't think she'd ever walk out of them. She paused, leaned farther, watched the dark windows below. The rooms weren't empty, the family had stayed over. She shivered and moved away from the pane. She left the window open, let the air flow into the room, let it pull the charnel scent of the candles from her skin.

A knock at the door. The jangle of keys. Mrs. Locke and the girl, Penny, with fresh water.

"Good morning," Mrs. Locke said. "You've slept late."

"I know. A bad habit of mine."

Penny went about the business of removing her dress. Orabella had grown used to it. It was the way of the manor. Her shift went over her head, fatty candles, bitter incense.

The girl wiped her body down. The water pulled away the sticky remainders of the evening that it could. Black blooms of fresh bruises lined Orabella's arm where someone—*Elias? An uncle? I'm not sure*—had held her too tightly. She felt hot hands on her back, rough fingers at her throat. Teeth against her lips. She shivered, her mouth flooded with spit. Like a starving person at the first thought of food, but her belly felt hollow and small.

Fresh undergarments and Orabella sat for her hair. Penny pulled at it, untrained, clumsy, and she took the comb from her, did it herself. *Where is Sloane? Why hasn't she come today? Is she ill?*

The last of the knots picked out, her hair a soft cloud of curls around her, she went back to dress. At the wardrobe she felt her stomach flip again, overwhelmed with the bright colors, the new patterns. She pulled the most subdued garment she could find from the group, an autumn orange-colored fabric with a ruffled collar and loose sleeves.

Her memories were barking laughs and too-hot hands. Elias through the keyhole. A stack of letters. A fawn. An unstable loop of offenses. *Stop*, she forced herself. She pushed out a stuttering breath. "Mrs. Locke, what day is it?"

"It's Sunday, ma'am," she answered.

"Have the carriage readied. I wish to go to church today. I must offer prayers for Hastings, my dear father."

"There's no one to escort you, it will have to wait."

"Of course, the funeral, the family."

"Yes. Penny will help you today."

Penny and Mrs. Locke led her in the usual way, down the stairs to the first floor, down to the dining room, but there was laughter all in the halls and then terse voices and yelling.

The family. They were still there, hidden away behind closed doors along with the sun meant to guide her way. *It's fine, I don't need it*, she thought as she passed down the hallway, less familiar now, the sunlight spaced farther and farther apart. Muffled voices came through to her, not enough to make out what they were saying. Elias walked across the room in her memory. She walked down the hall.

It felt like night in the long stretches between rooms that had been left open but she knew the way, passing old, previously unused parlors and sitting rooms. *They must have moved things, maybe the servants cleaned up before they came.* She had no idea, the world had changed since the day with Claresta. Had become something more feral and unpredictable.

She broke through the dark halls, swept into the dining room, and stopped.

Elias sat at the head of the table, and all around him were the men of the family.

The uncles, nephews, and cousins were draped over chairs, the remains of a large breakfast spread out on the table before them. The platters still held some eggs and bread, bits of fruit here and there, but it was clear from the mess and jumble of plates that they had enjoyed themselves.

"Elias! Send the wife to the women!" one of them shouted across the room, his voice loud, booming.

"Oh now, don't be like that, let the girl say good morning," one of them pushed back just as loudly, ruddy cheeks and crooked teeth. Boyish features that age had settled around. They were all so old. A teasing lilt played in his tone and the rest of the table laughed. "Come, come, girl. Orabella, isn't it?"

The others joined in, calling her closer. She found Elias among them, his cheek resting against his fist, a frown pressing down the corners of his lips. His clothes were of quality, older and dark but stately in a manner he did not often dress. He looked like Hastings.

"That's enough," he declared, standing, his chair pushed back along the bare floor with a rattle.

"Oh come on, let's get to know her before she's whisked away to bed with a belly full of babes." The man with the crooked teeth laughed, held out his hand, and beckoned with long fingers. "She just woke, she'll be hungry."

"More than enough for her to eat," said another man, and the table roared with laughter.

"Actually, I'm not hungry at all. I'm afraid my stomach is a bit sour, you'll have to excuse me. I only came down to make sure Elias wasn't still waiting but it's clear that he's got along just fine without me." She stepped back. Mrs. Locke was still there. Why had she brought her to that hall, to see her husband like that? Hadn't she already seen enough of what he could be, what he was? The hall she had come from seemed to creep closer, welcoming her back into its dust-and-rot embrace. The men stared at her with bright, hungry eyes. *The house would be better*, she thought, *it'll swallow me whole, won't rip me to pieces.* The heat of tongue and teeth on her throat, she lifted her hand to meet it and someone grasped her elbow.

She sucked in her breath, stilled, and turned to find Elias, his eyes hot, his lips pulled into a tight line.

"Orabella." Her name sounded like a punishment on his lips. No gentleness, no comfort. A Blakersby. "Do you need something?"

She looked past him to those hungry men, his uncles and cousins and nephews. They all smiled at her, some with the decency to show their teeth, others hiding them behind closed lips. All their eyes were wet and focused, the morning light shining in them, playing over golden and white locks of hair.

"No." She smiled. "It's all right. Your family has just suffered a loss and I'm sorry for interrupting."

Something tightened in Elias's face and his eyes moved away, found shadowy hiding places in the tilt of his head. "Are you all right?" he asked, his voice so low, so quick, a little ghost of his care, she wasn't sure if she had heard anything at all.

She smiled again, forced her lips to curve at the edges and held her head still lest they thought her giving him leave. Lest she add to his humiliation. His eyes caught hers again with such care. *I didn't see what I thought. None of it, I was drunk last night, and the night before I was . . .* She stopped because she couldn't lie. The letters. The pond. The pursuer on the upper floors, the beast in the woods, and Elias, her Elias, in that room. Her lips stretched wider, a peace settling over her. She nearly laughed at her own foolishness. *He has never hidden anything, I just chose not to see it and now I am trapped here like . . . Claresta.*

"I'll leave you to your duties, then. Perhaps if you have the time you'll see me this afternoon?"

"I'll see." He looked past her, into the hall, to Penny. Handed her over. He was done with her. He had produced a wife for whatever reason he needed one and his father was dead so he was king in this place and she was the bride.

Smiling, she turned back. Sick, so sick with her own guilt. Claresta was trapped, playing her role, and she had thought her a villain. What could she do but submit? What could either of them do but say yes, give Elias whatever he wanted?

The door to Claresta's room stood open, as it normally did during the day. Claresta waited at the window, her back to the door.

How do I ask? I must ask her, I must speak to her but she will not speak to me at all. She must be afraid, there's always someone but, she looked back at Penny, *they left us here, alone, all the time.*

"Claresta! I'm so sorry about your father." Did she know that he'd drowned in the pool? Did she know that it was Elias? Did it matter?

She stood and smiled. The blue eyes that stared back at Orabella were clear and bright. She seemed to see through her, her gaze still fixed on the picture scene outside the window.

"What are you looking at today?" Orabella asked. A song played along with her words and she pushed it away, by the thrum of wings, so many wings, as she scanned the familiar tree line, searching for deer or the flame red of foxes. She leaned closer to the glass, her eyes tracking for movement.

Something dark lay on the ground under the window, sprawled along what existed of the patio that the forest hadn't taken back.

She sucked her breath in hard, sharp, the image clear but her mind refusing to make sense of it, refusing the reality of what was before her, below her. Her chest hurt from the scream, held back but boiling in it.

"Ma'am, what's wrong?" She turned to the voice: Penny, standing, her hand out.

She couldn't bear to say anything, to let any sound through her throat. To release a single noise would be to unleash it all. That scream would come tumbling, ripping from her and would never stop.

She looked back at Claresta. Not a hair moved on her but her lips had stretched, turned just at their corners into a small, nasty smile. *She knows, she knows, oh god, she knows*, she screeched in her mind.

Her head spun as she stepped away from her, closed her eyes and tried to make it disappear. The girl on the ground, the woman in the chair.

"Ma'am?" Penny called again, her hands closing on Orabella's arm.

"Don't touch me!" she screeched, the scream coming out as

a howl chasing the words. She yanked her arm away so violently Penny's nails caught the fabric, pulled the threads, ruined the sleeve, but Orabella had no mind for it.

Claresta filled her view again, the doll, her lips turned upward into that cruel smile as if they had been painted on, perfect like the rest of her. Orabella heard her laughter, it echoed all around the room. Her guts slithered and twisted and she knew that she had been right about Claresta before, that she should have never pitied her at all. Right about the family. The halls held no mysteries.

"How could you?" she accused, her vision swimming, blurring the room until the shadows became mouse brown hair, a dark work skirt spread out like wings.

"Ma'am, please! What's made you so upset? I'll get help, I'll—" Penny must have looked out the window then, her offers dried up in her mouth. She must have thought her lady was mad but she saw now, maybe didn't understand it but saw it.

Orabella raced out the door, gathering her skirts, her vision all shadows on shadows but her feet knew the way. The same path she had taken for days and days. For weeks and months, and a spill of years, time slippery and wrong. Alone now but the route no different, she moved through honey, her legs slow, the air hard to draw. She barreled past the coat room, ignoring the heaps of rotting fabric and her own cover. She flew through the halls until she burst through the doors that led to the garden, her garden, Elias had come to call it.

She stilled for a moment, her head swinging from side to side as she tried to orient herself, figure out where it was that Claresta's windows looked down onto, where she had once exited the forest. *A fool*, she realized, the words coming through the endless scream of her mind. It didn't matter where, she had only to follow the shadow of the house. She ran along it, through the overgrowth like a deer.

From far away someone called her. A male voice but it didn't say her name. There were others too, all chasing her, like foxes on a rabbit, howling and yipping at her heels, but she couldn't stop. *Maybe there's time, maybe, maybe*, she panted and prayed in every breath, the dark angel greeting her, filling her vision as she finally reached her.

She dropped to the ground, the beautiful gown billowing out, trailing in the sticky mud that formed around the creature on the dirt. She reached her hands forward to the dark, wet form that should have been a head and hauled it up, praying for a miracle, but whatever god walked the halls and forest of that place did not lend itself to miracles, it only demanded sacrifice.

The face, what had been a face, had turned all red and broken but still she knew who it was. She clutched the woman to her chest, her blood dried tacky, she had sat so long, undiscovered save by the single person who did not see fit to move her lips to tell.

Sloane's body, devoid of whatever had made her more than just stiff pulpy meat, rested in Orabella's arms and she wailed over it. The only warmth in her came from the sun that shone down on the world, heating it for a perfect spring day despite it all. Orabella tried to brush the hair away from her face but that only made it worse, only revealed the broken parts that used to be her cheeks, her nose, her eyes. The dark dress, a simple thing, was pulled down, revealed pale breasts, the skin blue-white, body drained, in contrast to the red darkness above it.

Orabella's mouth wouldn't form words. She should call for help; only howls fell from it. She gripped her friend's stiff fingers, found them out of shape and wrong in her hand.

"Miss! Miss! Oh god! Don't look!" Penny was yelling, her hands on her shoulders, pulling her away.

She fought her, howling and spitting, clutching the body to her breasts as if those empty sacks would nourish the broken, thin thing in her arms back to life. Someone screamed, a shrill sound, higher and louder than her own wails.

A man worked his hands between her arms, pried the woman, what had once been her friend, once been Sloane, away from her. Hauled Orabella up from the gory scene. She found the woman screaming, a maid who held her hand in front of her face.

Who is she? The question raced across her mind as her eyes swung across the gathered crowd, pale faces, men and women, clothed in black, like ghosts, like ghouls, and she didn't know them. They had bled from the walls of the house. Beetles, insects, come with the spring. She couldn't force her mouth into the shapes to form words, to turn the sound that poured from it into something understandable by human ears.

The man who held her spun her, turned her away from the scene, and she stopped her fighting, startled. The scent held the muskiness of the house, the dust that covered everything, and mostly, that smell of that place that existed between the walls.

"No!" She fought against it. *It's him, oh god, it's him.* She panicked, kicking and scratching at the man who held her, the man who had danced with her. The beast that hid in her prince.

"Orabella! Orabella! Control yourself! You're safe! Stop!" The man grabbed her hands, wrapped her in his arms, and closer to his skin now she could smell him. Smoke and ginger.

Elias, red faced, panting.

His mouth hung open, hard breaths pouring from it. "Orabella!" Her name came on the wind. Her husband, her beautiful husband. She blinked, the air felt heavy, she couldn't breathe. Her head fell back, saw the tower that held one little bedroom above them. *A beast, a beast.*

Tears tumbled from her eyes and he swept her up from the ground, bundled her in his arms. He was moving with her. She couldn't breathe. The dark rectangle of the open door filled her vision, the gaping mouth of the house.

"No!" she shouted, finding her words, fighting against him. He held her tighter.

"Calm down, love, please!" Pleading and the edge of something else, something she had heard before that lived close to his anger but wasn't.

Fear. The word came to her suddenly, flooded her with the emotion. She stopped fighting his hold, her body shook, and he passed the threshold with her, his bride in a beautiful new dress covered in blood.

Two steps and the hall was crowded with bodies. Faces so close to beautiful, every one of them, but none her husband's. His eyes, his nose, his mouth, the curve of his jaw, all the bits and pieces of his face scattered over a handful of others. His family. The men of his family but none of them him.

"She's hysterical! Poor dear!" A cousin, an uncle, she couldn't tell, the voice could have been any voice but she was sure that it was real, that someone had diagnosed her from that crowd. Proclaimed her mad like her sister-in-law.

A hot drop of liquid hit her face and she turned back, expecting tears from her husband, but instead there was a long cut across his cheek, a line of red bubbled and flowed down his skin. She had scratched him, ripped him open, and his blood dripped on her, mingled with her tears, with the leftovers of Sloane.

"Sloane! Sloane!" She pushed away from him but he held her

tight. Foxes had followed her, drawn by the scent. *They'll turn her to candles, they'll butcher her on the kitchen counter and turn her fat to light.* Heard their glass-falling laughter, saw them from the corners of her eyes. The words spun in her mind like a dance, nonsense chatter for a moment that made no sense, that could make no sense.

"I'll take her to bed," Elias said above her, his voice hard, commanding but not enough against the gathering men. They refused.

The crowd parted. Her head pulsed, a sharp twist in her guts, and she thought she heard that wet sound that came through her door, the dragging steps that followed her in the dark. The scent of the walls filled her nostrils and she expected to see him when she looked up. See the beast.

A line of women who looked like Claresta came for her. Her eyes. Her nose. Her mouth. In a dozen faces but none so perfect as hers. They raised death-white hands to her, helped her out of Elias's arms.

"I'm fine, I just need to go to my room and lie down." Orabella's words came out quickly, blurring together, and were ignored. The women took her arms, pulled her to them.

They cooed and petted her hair as they moved away down the halls, Orabella pulled along in the tide of them. They passed by the wide steps that led to the upper floors and went through the double doors that led to the ballroom. They hushed her and ushered her into a room, one she hadn't been in but that she knew had been changed recently because nothing in that wing was new but this room smelled of paint and the cushions weren't nests.

The space had been dusted and swept. A new carpet on the floor. Freshly upholstered chairs. A pleasant and perfect sitting room that showed her a familiar space. Her courtyard, that secret courtyard. *When?* she wondered but there was no time to ask, no time to think. Her course was being set for her.

"Calm down, dear, we've heard, yes, we've heard." Alice touched her face. Wiped her tears and pushed her hair back into place.

The other women agreed, crowded around her, and her nostrils filled with the scent of powder and, under that, cedar and dust. She wasn't surprised, every piece of news traveled so quickly through the shadows. *Carried by mice through the very walls.* The vision bubbled laughter in her and she bit it back before it could spill from between her lips.

Orabella pulled away from Alice's touch, placed her wrist against her forehead. "I've just had a shock, I just need—"

One of the women, she didn't know her name, younger than Alice but older than Orabella, took her hands. The woman stroked Orabella's knuckles with her thumbs, just like Elias had in her family's garden. Passed her thumb over the sticky mess of Sloane's blood, followed the path of Orabella's bones and skin. The woman whose name she didn't know but whom she must call family held her hand the same way her husband held it and smiled at her like her sister-in-law.

"It's not your fault," the woman said, her voice low, soothing.

"Not at all, dear, they have such small lives." Alice now. She placed her hands on her arm, petted her hair.

"They?" Orabella's head throbbed and spun. She looked at her hands. Her sleeves were stained red, bits of hair stuck to them, hair not her own. Her hands were dark with drying blood. The woman who held them paid the mess no mind. Her thumbs slowly moved back and forth over each knuckle. Gentle, never crushing.

"The others. The ones who aren't family. That girl tried to warn you away, didn't she? I'm sure you were good to her, I'm sure, but her life was so small. But you'll be better here. You're family now."

"I don't understand. She was my friend, she was trying to help me." She closed her eyes. Red fur in her vision, sharp teeth at her throat. Memory, dream. "I think someone hurt her," she whispered, daring the words to live in the world, free from her.

The woman stopped her ministrations to Orabella's hands; the aunt stopped petting and soothing. The room held its breath.

A moment then another. Alice cleared her throat and took Orabella's face between her palms, turned her so their eyes met. Dark brown pools to her bright blue ones. Like Claresta's, and for a moment Orabella could see what the woman must have been once. Who she must have been once. "Don't concern yourself with it, dear. You're fine. This is your home."

The world spun. Turned red and gold. She looked at her hands, soft brown, wrapped in white, and red drying to black between them.

"Things get out of hand, dear, sometimes they do. Sometimes a boy breaks a toy out of anger when he can't have what he wants. But you're fine, you're safe! You don't need to worry about that girl. We'll get you a new one. You're better, you're special to us. A gift, our pet. Elias brought you here and what a wonderful creature you are. Isn't she? Such beautiful eyes, such beautiful hair." Orabella felt a lock lift from her back. "It will be lovely to have this color, won't it?"

She shook her head, the wrongness of their words ringing around her. "Someone hurt her."

The door opened. Maids flowed into the room. Orabella watched as they moved, placing a tea serving on the table and handing cups to the waiting women. A day like any other.

The woman released her hands, took her own cup. The maid returned with another, held it to Orabella with a smile on her face. This woman she did recognize. It was the same blond maid that served dinner to them. The maid smiled, pushed a steaming cup towards her.

Orabella looked down at her fine dress streaked with gore. She felt far from herself. The sun spilled into the room through the windows but everything seemed dark, cloudy. The sound of the women faded around her, her own heartbeat flooded her ears.

"It's prepared the way you like it, ma'am," the maid offered. Friendly, helpful. Didn't they care that Sloane had died? That her face was gone?

The women of the family. Jewel eyed, old as the men. She and Elias were the babies, the new life. The new blood. There, nestled sadly among them, was Elizabeth, dark haired, hollow eyed, staring straight at her.

"Oh," Orabella said. She thought it was Claresta's future she should avoid but she had been wrong all along. Claresta did not need help and Orabella could do nothing for the person who did.

Bloodstained hands held in front of her face. Sloane's blood dried and cracked over them. It had soaked into the sleeves of the fine dress that Elias bought for her. Her eyes moved back to the familiar woman and her stomach twisted. Orabella, quick as a cat, knocked the cup from the woman's hands.

The maid, surprised, stepped back, letting out a small shriek as the cup deposited its contents on Alice before shattering on the floor.

Alice, who had been so kind, stared wide-eyed before her face twisted into a snarl. "You've ruined my gown, you little beast!" she hissed.

Orabella stood and swung in one motion, the palm of her hand meeting the woman's face with a loud crack.

"I am not a child!" she shouted. "I'm not your little dear! I'm not your pet! I'm . . ." Words failed her. Who was she besides Elias's wife and what did that matter in this family? In this place? "I'm," she started again and the room erupted in laughter.

High, mad laughter that hurt her ears and made her head pound.

"Alice, she put you in your place!" said a voice.

"We must watch for the claws on this little pet!" followed another.

"Trust Elias to bring us back someone with such fight! Such life! Imagine the blood!" said a third.

"Such fiery blood!" came from across the room.

"Such strong passions. Such energy. Just what the family needs." Alice rubbed the cheek she had slapped. "But hit me again, girl, and I'll see you buried with that bitch in the garden."

They loved it, that mad family, of course they loved it. They wanted more. They wanted claws and teeth, a beast. They wanted Elias and Claresta but Claresta couldn't have children. Those little white gravestones, that fresh grave, she hadn't noticed, such a small thing. Nothing could live in Claresta.

They wanted Orabella to care for the garden. Her garden. They wanted children.

Orabella gripped her skirts in tight fists. Her chest hurt, her heart beat too quickly, air passed too hard. "You're all mad. It's not just Claresta, it's all of you." She took steps backwards, towards the door.

Alice smiled at her, holding out her hands for an offered cup from the dinner maid, who acted as if nothing at all had happened in the room. Another knelt on the floor picking up the broken shards of porcelain and bundling them in her skirts.

Sloane had been there since she was a child. She knew her place well and even then she had tried to warn Orabella, tried to help her, but there was no help in that place and now she lay cold and dead for it. *Why did she do such a thing?* Orabella wondered, but there was no one to answer the question. Sloane was gone and she was alone.

"No, dear," Alice said softly. An elder to a child. "Claresta is the best of us."

Orabella, overcome, turned and fled to the hall, back towards the double doors that led out of the wing. The yipping, high laughter followed her all the way down.

Chapter Twenty-Five

Orabella huddled in her room, squeezed against the corner created by the wardrobe and the wall. The blood, Sloane's blood, had dried tacky and maroon. It itched, flaking from her hands like a second skin. She gripped her elbows, the fine dress ruined with the violence of her friend's death, and tried not to shake.

She didn't remember the journey to her room, her body knew the halls well enough and she ran, through those dark passages, her breath and the sound of her feet all there was, and then the other sound. Stomping above her where there should be none, the rumbling and tumbling of living things in the walls.

My room, she thought frantically, as she reached the hall, *I'll find the sun and myself back in bed and this horrible thing, this horrible day, will not have happened at all. Sloane will come and wake me and tell me I've overslept, Elias will feed me sweets, and then we'll walk in the garden and this terrible thing will never have happened.* But she burst through the doors and her bed stood empty.

Nothing but blood and crushed bone and meat, she heard in her head, but it was not her voice. It was Claresta's, angelic and lovely as herself.

Those women, those people. She chased the words, attempting to form some thought that would push Claresta from her mind but everything ran and jumped away from her, leaving behind only the barking laugh of her in-laws, her family. Jewel eyes, hair spun of sunlight, and bright, bright teeth that chased her thoughts, chased her, snatching at her mind and leaving bloody handprints where she tried to pull away until they captured and held her, and all around her head their screaming, barking laughter. *I thought them fairies but no, no, they sting, they bite. I've stolen their honey.*

Laughter sprang from her, turned into hot tears all down her face. She couldn't stop either of them, her body was a foreign thing, feral and free from her.

She shivered with a cold that the sun couldn't touch. Sweat broke out over her back and face, stuck her underthings to her skin, caught her loose hair on her cheeks. Everything itched, her head pounded, and the world was uncomfortable and loud, so loud. Her eyes blurred, tears turned her vision dark, and she slipped beneath the honey of the thoughts, sweet but suffocating, that lived in her, strangled by the scream that stuck in her throat and dragged her into darkness.

"Oh love, oh darling, it's all right."

"Elias?" Her voice came out creaky and broken. Aged like her father-in-law's.

"Yes, be still," he murmured. "I shouldn't have let them take you, I should have tended to you myself." He whispered while he smoothed a hand over her hair. Her face.

She came to herself slowly, pulled herself from the twilight she chased from her eyes. The gold of the day had turned to orange in sunset, the light stretched across the floor, and she was no longer alone.

Elias had come. Three raised red lines streaked down his cheek. A long scabbed-over trail from earlier.

"I scratched you, I'm so, so sorry, I didn't mean, I thought . . ." She stopped, unsure of what she had thought, who she had thought he was. *A rowdy son of this family*, but that was Elias too. But she was his wife.

"I shouldn't have left you so long, that was thoughtless of me. I was attending to business," he said softly, pulling more hair from her throat, gently placing the locks behind her shoulders, revealing her skin marked afresh by so many things.

"And now you're here, for the business of being a husband." Tittering, red anger, fear made her bold.

His hands stilled in their care, hovered above her shoulders before pulling away completely. He stood but her eyes did not follow. She kept them on the space where he had been, now filled with his lean legs. His clothing smelled of age, of mildew and dust. *He never wears them near me, he strips naked before he climbs on top of me. Not these fine clothes, for me it's his work trousers and coarse shirts but for them it's tailored jackets. For them, for them.*

She couldn't see him but she imagined his movements, the way he pushed his hair back, tilted his head, and closed his eyes. She had learned them so well. She was a good wife. He sighed, the sound registering as real only when his knees bent and his hands slipped under her arms, lifting her off the ground.

Orabella let herself be pulled up. Her legs felt rubbery and weak but she pulled them under herself. Elias guided her to the chair before her vanity, sat her down gently without a word.

Her own face stared back at her. Puffy, red eyes from her tears, her hair wild and knotted. Her skin pale, washed out in her horror and grief. Behind her Elias was a body, no head, taller than Sloane had been. He moved gently, slowly, undoing her dress, slipping it from her shoulders.

He picked up the comb from the vanity, took a hank of her hair, and began to comb out the knots as he spoke.

"The girl will be buried in the cemetery," he explained, his words as slow and gentle as the comb he moved through her curls. "You don't have to worry. She will be given a proper burial, I will see to that."

But you haven't even buried Hastings. You drowned him and put him on a table and the family came for a feast. The comb caught on a knot, a sudden shock of pain. A punishment for her thoughts. He slowed, picked at it in silence for a long moment before speaking again.

"You mustn't pay them any mind. You are one of us now, you will be cared for by the family, loved by me. Protected. You have nothing to fear." He moved the comb through the knots, his fingers growing adept at the task quickly, learning to groom her as swiftly as he had learned to please her body.

He combed until the tangles were gone and her hair floated around her, the curls pulled near straight but slowly finding their way back, lifting gently from her shoulders. The light tea-colored from the setting sun. He left her, crossed the room, and lit the lamp at her bedside first. Then came back for the one that waited on her vanity. Its mate, returned by Hastings.

"This dress is filthy," he sighed.

"Ruined," Orabella countered, glancing down at the dark patches that bloomed all over the orange fabric, black in the shadow of the room. But it was her own hands she fixated on, the patches of blood that clung to them, dry now, darkening her skin.

Turning her, in the shadows, to a rotten being, a body blooming with decay.

"Ruined," she repeated, turning away from the stains to look at her husband.

"The dress means nothing. I'll buy you another, I'll buy you thirty more and you'll never have to look at this one again. Here, I'll help you from it." He stood her up, slipped the dress down from her, let it pool on the floor. He studied her as she stepped from it, slid her feet from her shoes and was left in nothing but her underclothes, wrinkled and sour-smelling from sweat. Obedient. The smell filled her nose, overpowered the dust from his garments. The smell of her fear, her despair. He sat her back on her chair, took the key from around her neck, and placed it on the vanity before turning to the basin and pitcher that waited there.

He poured day-old water into the basin, emptying what was left from the pitcher that Sloane would have filled while they ate dinner and left waiting. But there was no Sloane anymore. All that remained were the dregs, the last pitiful bit. He wet the cloth anyway, gently dabbed at her face and neck before moving to her hands. Rougher now, he rubbed the cloth over her fingers and knuckles, silently, focused on the task before him. His knuckles were bruised. He wiped at her skin until the traces of blood were nearly gone; only the bits that had been trapped by her nails remained, but she couldn't be sure who they belonged to. Sloane or Elias.

She looked up at him, his head was bent forward, focused on the last of the blood. She slipped her fingers from his, tilted his head up to see him again. The light caught the scratches, the small, thin marks she had left on him. Orabella touched them.

"What's one more scar?" she asked as he leaned into her touch, his breath, a sigh.

"It's nothing, don't worry yourself, my love," he replied.

"Your family said I had claws, they keep calling me pet. Is that what I am? Tell me the truth, Elias. You promised." She moved her hands down to his chest, slid them lower to find her way under his shirt. He liked that, he would be sweet to her if she calmed him, tamed him.

He sighed at her touch, leaned forward, begged for more as her hands spread up his chest, tracing the patterns of his scars. *Did her nails do this? Did she carve pieces of him away with her fox teeth? Did he like it?* She squeezed her eyes closed against the sick, hot images but that only trapped her with them. The press of his mouth against her throat made her gasp.

"Not a pet, love. Ignore them, you're mine, you're mine," he murmured into her skin, his breath wet in the moment before his lips met her throat, fluttering like moths against her.

"Do you mean it? Or is that just another word you've learned to say?" Her voice still cracked, her throat dry, everything wet in her used up in tears and sweat. Grief and fear.

He stopped, rested his head against hers. "Mean what? You are no pet, I brought you for a wife and I mean—"

"That you love me."

He stilled, pulled away so the air could pass between them. His hands shifted, rested awkwardly against her. "Why do you doubt it? Why wouldn't I mean it? Of course, I married you, I told you, I've wanted you for years."

"Wanting is not love, and I saw you with your sister." She sighed, felt lighter for having said it, released the secret, all her pitiful little secrets from herself. She was so tired of being careful.

He pulled back, looked her in the eyes. "What are you talking about?"

"I was worried for her, can you believe that?" A laugh bubbled up in her, floated from her lips. The words came fast, whatever anchored the secret in her loosening. "That I would be concerned that she was in danger. I thought the servants were hurting her but nothing hurts her, am I right? I'm right. I figured that out, at least."

"Orabella, what are you talking about?" Elias gripped her shoulders, locked his eyes on hers. "Stop. Her mind is gone but that's all. Do you hear me? That's all!" *There are no mysteries in Korringhill. She is a Blakersby. You are a Blakersby.*

But she couldn't stop, there was too much, it was all too much. "My nighttime husband! You disappear in the day like some, like some cursed prince! And you leave me here, all alone! But I can't even have that! Nothing for me! Even that little bit you give to her! To this house! I left my room and I saw you! Through the keyhole, I saw you go to her bed with my blanket on your shoulders! So how can you say you love me when you would do something, something so—" She stopped, covered her mouth, her face hot.

The color drained from his face. His peach-white skin turned sickly yellow, his lips hung slack, and his ghost-gray eyes were wide. "No," he said simply, shaking his head. "You did not." He paused, pushed his hair back with a trembling hand, releasing her to stand, to turn away. "Orabella, what you thought you saw, it was not, it is not. I am not." The words trailed, dropped, heavy with shame, and blocked whatever truth he would have said, leaving him only with "You don't understand."

She sucked her breath in, stared at his pleading eyes, his lips turned down, and she laughed. Reckless, insatiable laughter spilled from her in high keening tones and he crumbled under them. His shoulders buckled, he backed farther away.

His shame held open the dam in her and more spilled out. Her fear, her worry, all came tumbling from her. Everything she held back to be a good wife for him, the wife he had married her to be. "That's why you brought me here, isn't it? Because Orabella is dull and childish. Orabella is careful and earnest. Orabella is obedient. You treat me like a child! Everyone treats me like a child! Thoughtless, careless Orabella! I can't even walk down the hall without Sloane—" She stopped suddenly, the mad laughter died in her, left nothing, not even an echo. Her body went numb, she lifted trembling hands to her face, found the maroon of dried blood around her nails. "Sloane, oh god, what did this place do to her? What did you do to her?" She wrapped her hands around herself to hide them, to hide the remnants of the creature that had once been Sloane. Quiet, small as she was small. "What is this place doing to me? You're driving me mad. Like Elizabeth. Like Claresta. So I'll be like the rest of you."

His jaw went hard, his lips tight. "You disobeyed me," he said, his voice low, commanding.

"I did. But you're a liar who I should have never trusted. I should have never come here." She locked her eyes on his, dark to light, and found no comfort in them. No kindness. But he was a beast, a murderer, and she should not have expected it.

He reached for her, wrapped his hand around her bare arm, pressing too hard, his fingers digging into her skin. She could feel the fresh flowers they would leave on her.

"I told you not to leave this room at night. I told you to stay here and you didn't," he growled, low and close to her. The boar. "I trusted you to obey!"

"I trusted you to be good! To be human!" She snatched her arm away, pressed her hand over the space he had held, pressed out the pain of his touch. "I thought you would be . . ." She paused, looked away, down at her arm, the still clean one, but not for long. She could feel the ruin of his fingers on it. "And you lied to me. You never sent any of my letters. And Sloane was my friend! She was good, and you, and you!" The words stalled in her, the stone of grief swelled in her throat, in her belly. She had gone with him because he was charming and she was charmed and now trapped. Trapped in the dark maze of bricks and forest. "I trusted you." Her head pounded. She caught sight of herself in the mirror, all shadows and wet eyes. A small and scared creature. A rabbit surrounded by teeth.

Saw herself, not herself. *What I've become in this dark room, in this dark house, on the edge of these dark, dark woods*, she thought, singsong and childlike. She walked away, wanted to leave the room but the sun had set, the world was night. The halls were full of foxes.

She went to her bed. Pulled herself up against the headboard in the nest of the unmade sheets and blankets, her castaway night-clothes. *I'll bury myself, I'll hide away in dreams.* The world spun around her and she clutched the words to her, held them tightly to hold on to anything at all. She twisted her hands in the sheets, saw them turn red in her mind.

"Orabella." Her name sounded on his tongue like she had never heard it before, and dragged her from her memories. Sharp, angry. His hands slipped over her cheeks, firm but without the violence of his first hold. "Do not ever accuse me of something like that again."

"I saw you," she hissed back, defiant.

"You saw nothing! It was the dark or the flames or your own imagination playing tricks on you! Think whatever you want of them, of Claresta"—her name came out like a curse—"but you will not accuse me of such profane things."

She thought of the dance, of the man who spun her. Smelled him on Elias's clothes, heard him in the close whisper of his words.

Had there ever been anyone else? *No*, acceptance. Her imagination, the dark and the flames just as he said. *He's someone else, like Claresta. I should have listened to Cullen, to Sloane's warning, and they paid for it.* A fawn pranced golden hooves past her, stealing her memories. She tried to snatch them back, mixed them all up to make new ones, better ones.

Blood in the air. The family coming to feast, swallowing her mind and thoughts and leaving that madwoman, that creature closer to Claresta, that beast the house was driving her to. Madness.

"Who am I?" she asked the room, the air, the fawn.

"My wife." He was pressing his lips to hers and she bent to them, let herself be kissed, wanted to be kissed. Let his mouth form hers into an entrance, accepted the invasion of his hot, wine-sweet tongue as hands, cold and trembling, sought their way under her thin clothes. He released his kiss only to pull her shift from her, to expose her body to him. "It's only you who drives me to this. This frenzy. This need." He yanked off the dusty jacket. Tugged the fine shirt from his waistband and over his head, revealing the map of scars all over his torso and arms. A life spent as something else, as someone else.

A fox, she thought as she watched him unbutton his trousers, his movements quick and violent. Then the mark of his manhood, his cock, stood proud and free from the cloth that had been pushed down just enough to expose him. *No, a boar. A different thing but here all the same.*

"No one," he growled, moving over her body, opening her legs with his weight pressing himself to her so their hips met and she could feel him moving against her, "makes me like this. Has ever made me this hungry. How could I even see another woman when you're here in this room?"

He didn't wait for an answer, entering her with the same

fierceness with which he had ripped the shirt from his chest. The same wild violence he had broken Cullen with. Her body, a wild thing too, clasped around him, caught him, held him. The building pressure of pleasure pounded from high between her legs into her gut and all through her. His lovemaking was measured and overwhelming with every thrust, and she wanted this. Her body ached for it, his touch, his violence.

"You think I've done this horrible thing but look! Look how you open for me! How you clutch at me," he hissed into her ear before nipping the lobe with his teeth.

He stole half of each breath with his kiss. She made small sounds, begging doe sounds, which he swallowed before sucking at her skin, making fresh blooms. The world spun, her body pulsed, and he felt like nothing but arms and a thousand hungry mouths, teeth and tongues and lips pulling at her skin, her breasts, her own panting mouth.

"Because you're mine," he growled, his mouth planting dark flowers on her throat, marking her as he had promised before, the bruises he left, a pattern made in the violence of his love, his desire.

And all she could do was wrap herself around him, pull him closer. *You should push him away, slap his face, he's lying, he's lying,* but in all the heat and hunger of him she could only hold him tighter, let herself drown in the pleasure of him. Press her arms and legs into him so hard that the crisscrosses of his scars embedded themselves on her skin. Made her something that could live in that terrible place as he had, as he did.

Because she wanted him. In that mad, swirling, wet hollow of herself she wanted him and nothing else and she was a horrible, mad thing and maybe she had always been so.

"Orabella," he moaned, the sound pleading, begging. His

hips moving faster against her, his arms tighter. His breath came quick against the bruised dark space of her neck. He pushed into her, held her tightly, buried his face into her shoulder as he came, his cock pulsing in her. The feel of his release against her, inside her. Spent, his body relaxing over hers, crushing her with its weight.

Her mind rested with each breath, hers, his, theirs. An invisible tangle of life between them that tied her to something real and solid outside of herself.

"Orabella," he said again, softer, the invisible boundary between them broken. He nuzzled his nose against her skin, laid gentle kisses along her throat. "It's done now," he whispered. He pulled away from her, and where she expected a smile there was only the grim line of his lips.

Silently he moved away, leaving her cold and alone in the bed.

"Elias?" she called, wanting him back, needing him back. It was only in his presence that things felt safe, felt grounded. Where she was safe. If he was holding her, he wouldn't let them have her. She'd be safe until he drowned her.

He swept up her dirty nightgown, no Sloane to leave a fresh one. "Put this on," he commanded.

He dressed while she dressed, silent, thoughtful.

"You make me lose all sense. You do something dangerous to me, I can't think straight when you look at me and the thought of you upset makes me reckless."

"Reckless?" she repeated.

He covered his eyes, breathed deeply. "It's too late now, what's done is done." He dropped his hands, looked at her. His eyes were red.

Her body felt heavy, well used, well pleased. Filthy. "Elias, I don't understand."

"No, you don't, but I will tell you because you're mine and

you're a good wife so you will listen." He pushed his hair back with both hands, leaving it messier than it had been. "This is what will happen." He looked back to the vanity and picked up the key. It glittered in the light.

"When I leave, I will lock this door. You will stay inside this room. Maids will come. They will wash and feed you. You will stay here until the morning. Tomorrow you will sit with the women and you will drink whatever they give you. You will do whatever they ask. You will be still and good."

"Is that all you wanted? My whole life has taught me to do that. You promised me something different but it's all right, it's all right." There was nothing else. Things were as they had always been, always would be.

Elias came back to the bed, took her in his arms. "You will do this, for me. This one thing, you will do it and I will give you every-thing. We must for the family, to appease them, and then it will be just you and I. Drink what they give you and I promise you won't remember any of it in the morning."

And Claresta and the maids and me in my little room and you in yours.

He released her, helped her settle into the bed, and then turned away. She watched his back disappear into the darkness and then the door closed, the lock clicked.

Body heavy, she settled into the bed, dozed until the door clicked again.

Penny and Mrs. Locke. A tray and fresh pitcher between them.

She didn't speak as they stripped and bathed her. They replaced the soiled water in her basin, filled the spent pitcher while she, clean, sat and ate the simple dinner they served. They gave her a fork but she could have used her fingers, like a child, like an ani-mal. No pastries. That game was done between them.

A glass of wine.

What will happen when I fall asleep? she wondered, touching the stem of the glass, her fingertips cold, her gut twisting.

The scent rose to her, thick, familiar now. She knew, maybe she had known from the start. She wasn't sure anymore.

She released the glass and stood. She turned away from the vanity and walked to her bed. "The effects of it come over me so quickly, I'd rather be settled before I take it."

She slid between her sheets and Penny picked up the glass, presented her with it. She crossed the room, the dark liquid nearly still. She stood so close to the bed that Orabella could smell her. *She smells like this place,* she thought, *like everything here must smell, like I must smell by now. How quickly Sloane was replaced, how well planned it all was.* Penny bent, held the glass to Orabella's lips herself, and Orabella drank it down to the last drop, the honey thick and sweet on her tongue. She didn't blame Penny, she, too, had to survive this place.

Orabella closed her eyes and counted her breaths, sure there wouldn't be many more.

Chapter Twenty-Six

Orabella sat at her window staring out into her little garden. Overgrown, left to be wild but trapped behind the walls of Korringhill. It would never be free as she would never be free. Her head pounded, stomach sour. She'd risen before the sun, stared at the ceiling until it became light.

She had dressed herself, a red dress trimmed in white lace. The lace covered her throat and arms while the red, deep, bloody red, covered her chest and flowed down to the full skirts that dusted the floor with every step.

She had taken the time to comb out her hair, none of the care her husband had taken; she yanked the knots from her tresses, pulled it into submission then let it flow around her, light as a cloud, just as her husband liked.

The only jewelry she wore was the ring Elias had placed on her finger. In her hands she held the book of fairy stories she had brought with her. All of those terrible tales for children. She read them again, ripping the pages out as she turned. They fluttered to the floor like leaves, like wallpaper. She had been sitting for some time. The sun moved lazily across the window, morning turning to noon.

She heard the family in her dreams. Screaming, barking laughter. Night things. And she was meant to have been sleeping, like a princess. *Asleep for a thousand years. I'm still sleeping. This is a dream.*

"Good morning, ma'am," Penny said, entering. Had the door not been locked? Did it matter anymore?

Penny busied herself with the bed. A girl, truly. A child with red cheeks and thin blond, nearly white hair. "Do you have any family, Penny?"

She looked shocked, unsure how to answer. "Yes, they're renters."

"Of course. Tell them, tonight when you leave, tell Mrs. Locke that I want another maid tomorrow. An old woman like her. Someone who knits." Someone should make use of her needles and that fine yarn. She would be a statue soon like Claresta.

The girl's faced dropped. "Ma'am! Please! I'll be very good, I'm hardworking! I'll learn the stitches."

Orabella stood, the skirt falling around her. She crossed the room to the girl and cupped her face.

Smiling, she said, "No, dear girl, no, you are lovely, I'm sure. Don't let Mrs. Locke punish you for my whims." She'd made that mistake with Sloane. Made it too much.

Birdsong, but birds should have sung only in the morning. Here they sang all day. The sound lulled her into the soft compliance that was needed for her role, for her to be the lady Elias had wanted of her. *For Elias because there is nothing left of me. I'm a ghost now.* She thought for a moment that she should have worn white. Should have asked for the ill-fitting flower dress she had worn during that first dinner. *Claresta's dress*, she recalled slowly but chased the thought away. *No, you are not Claresta. You are not anyone at all.*

"You are to take me to the dining room, no? Or perhaps the tearoom or a drawing room? You've been told to escort me somewhere, have you not?"

The girl nodded. "The tearoom."

Another mouse for their feast, Orabella thought idly, leading the child with a soft hand on her shoulder.

"You're Elias's wife? I—I heard about you. Well, everyone has." Alone, the girl tried. To save her employment. But she was not Sloane, Orabella would not make that mistake again.

"Who else would I be? Why else would I be here? What do they say?"

"Oh no, nothing. Just that he married. That you're from the city."

"That seems very boring to talk about. I'm sure they say something else."

Quiet now. She had only just started in the house. She hadn't learned that the servants kept their gossip and that the lords didn't care. That foxes did not consult with mice. But she was young and, after all, Orabella was no fox either. "That you were different. That you weren't a Blakersby."

Orabella chuckled. "Oh? Is that all? Well, I suppose that's all in how you see things. Elias is my husband but is Elias a Blakersby?"

The girl nodded. "Of course, ma'am. He comes and takes our rent. He'll inherit the house and lands, everyone knows that."

"Hasn't he already? Didn't you see, Hastings is dead and Elias brought a wife. Doesn't that mean he's won? Or maybe he hasn't always been what he is now."

If the girl heard her falseness she didn't respond to it. "Well, there was some talk, because of his mother, but he's always been in the house. They've always called him their own."

"Is that all it takes, turn here, then are you a Blakersby? You're in the house, and they say they own everything and everyone on this land."

The girl laughed, a nervous sound that made Orabella's spine itch. "Of course not! I don't have the blood. We're just common people."

"Don't you?" she asked, lifting a lock of blond hair. So many blonds. "Is that all that matters? Does it have to be theirs? There's been so much blood." She wondered what stories the girl had heard about Elias's mother. What stories the family let filter down to their people through all that gossip. She would be the next one, they would give her a name.

The girl thought as they walked along. "No," she said finally. "But you must be someone if Mr. Elias married you, and that makes you a Blakersby, I suppose."

She smiled. "Wait, now I think of it, you should leave now. Go home if your people will take you back, go somewhere else if they won't."

"I'm not allowed," Penny said, panicked.

"You are a young and lovely thing. You do not belong here. Go home. Don't ever come back here. Don't follow me. Keep from the dark." Orabella stepped past her. She would go alone. Sloane could not be saved because Orabella was too fearful, too trusting. She could have lived if Orabella had been a better friend, a better Lady. So she would save Penny. Tell her she was a pretty and good girl and to go back to that world outside of Korringhill. It was all Orabella could do, there was nowhere for her to go.

She was a kept thing, had always been a kept thing. A pet. That was what the women had called her, what she, after all was said and done, had been all along. A pet in this house, and before that, a pet to her aunt and uncle to make them seem better than they were. More generous, more upstanding. And for Elias, to make him normal. A lord married to a lady. A show, a farce because all she had ever been was a kept thing and that was all she would be.

She found the room on her own. She knew the halls now.

Laughter leached from the room towards her, high barking laughter. She had been there only once but the map was woven into her bones, she would have found her way back in the dark, in silence.

She crossed the threshold and was back in that same tearoom she had fled from. The late afternoon sun flowed through the window, her little courtyard outside, her little castle of dishes and plates and glass things peeking through the grass. The women of the family sat waiting this time. There was a buffet spread, plates of cakes and muffins. Sausage and fruit. It reminded her of her first breakfast with Elias. Sweet things, the food and him, meant to hide the house, the truth of what he had brought her into.

"Good afternoon. I'm terribly sorry for how I acted yesterday. I was quite shaken."

They smiled, her new family, and opened their arms. "Of course, dear," Alice sang, and the other one who had rubbed her hands came to her, surrounded her, the smell of powder, of wood and rot. The stale scent of their finery, kept for these moments when they crept from their cracks and corners to fill the house.

"It's all right," Alice said sweetly, wrapping an arm around her, leading her to the couch. "We were all a bit off yesterday, weren't we? Oh, that's it, pet, here, sit!"

Orabella did as she was told. *Is there a choice?* she thought, looking out the window into another closed space. *If I ran, I couldn't find my way through the woods. They would just drag me back from the church, say I'm mad like Claresta but I'm not. If I were it would be better but I'm not.*

They petted her hair. "Oh, look at this lovely color! And the curls!" said one.

Another: "You look so plain! Why not wear the jewels? It's just us but these ears would look lovely with some pearls!"

Another: "That color! I could never wear anything like that with my color. It's so rich!"

"Look how well your husband keeps you," one or another purred at her.

They pulled her skirts, ran fingers over her lace. Tucked curls behind ears, inspected the simple ring on her finger. A tart was presented to her. Sugar sweet, the insides of it sticky and as red as her dress. It shimmered in the light with a soft crust. Easy to cut with just a fork, which waited for her.

Alice presented it from her fingers. "Oh no, we wouldn't want you to mess your dress, would we, pet?" She cut the tart, offered her a piece, the berries rich and brilliant.

Orabella opened her mouth and accepted the bite.

The women cooed and took turns feeding her. Small bites of pie, sausage. She ate from the offered hands. She drank from the cups and let them wipe the corner of her mouth when juice dripped from it. Like a pet.

Alice grabbed her hands suddenly and Orabella turned to her. Her too-large eyes, the tiny, pert nose. She smiled, and in the sun looked younger, brighter than she had before. "You're a good girl, a lovely girl. Just like Elias said you were. And you, you look well, so healthy. So lovely. Tell me now, dear, has that boy left anything in you?"

What's done is done, he said in her memory as tiny paws scratched at her belly from the inside. *But isn't that the point? Isn't that what they want?* "No." She smiled. She knew enough not to try to beg them off, to hide behind propriety. That didn't matter around this subject. Had never mattered.

"He's always been so good," Alice said wistfully. "Now, how well do you listen?"

"Very well, dear aunt."

Alice smiled, seemed pleased with the title. "Pull up your skirts, open your legs, and let's make sure you're all in order."

Orabella shut her eyes. There was no point in arguing. Her skirts lifted, her legs spread. There were paws, tipped with hard nails, they pushed and prodded at her softest parts. Opened her, entered her.

It wasn't purity they checked for, they didn't care about that; they knew her husband had been there, had already claimed that for himself weeks ago. No, what they searched for was life, proof that she had been truthful with them. They poked in her and pressed on her belly and above her barked back and forth. The shape of it, the color, so healthy, so welcoming.

A little den, just so, for a bundle of kits.

Finished, they released her, settled her skirts, and a maid brought her a cup of tea. Heavy with sweetness from a flower she couldn't name, honey mixed in to mask the taste of whatever they tried to hide from her.

Was it Elias? She thought of Sloane's death-blue shoulders, bare and soiled under her bloody hands coming to her. *Lovely, lovely, lovely*, the voice in her head sang. The mirror version of her, the garden woman. Sloane was dead and there was nowhere for her to go.

Why is Claresta never here in this room, with these women? Their perfect daughter who can't give them any more sons.

She took the tea and gulped it down in long swallows. Too fast for that strange spice, that heavy sweetness, to touch her tongue, it disappeared down the hall of her throat, nestled in her belly, soaked all the treats they had fed her with its ichor and she floated.

"It's a celebration, then!" the woman who had rubbed her arms and hands sang. Orabella turned to the sound. Alice clapped, the room stopped, the servants looked to her.

"That's enough from you now. Go help in the kitchen, the men went hunting and I'm sure they'll bring back a feast tonight."

They nodded and filed out, a line of dark shadows returning to the house. *I've never seen their quarters. That's strange, isn't it? I can't see anything beyond the garden, it all just fades to nothing. It doesn't matter, it's too late now.*

"Like my wedding night," she said quietly, absently. "My husband shot the deer."

"Yes." Alice patted her hand. "It was quite the beast. Beautiful. A rare one. I doubt they'll bring home something so glorious, but the hunt will be grand all the same."

"There was a fawn," Orabella said. There it was again, standing on golden hooves, trailing a bloody cord now. Eye on her. It opened its mouth and a fox laugh came from it.

Around Orabella the women were laughing, the sound going higher and higher as they unpacked small packages and lit oil lamps. The room filled with bitter smoke, the laughter climbed higher.

"I haven't seen Elias today. Is he hunting too?" She tried to hang on to herself; thick incense, heavy with scent, covered the bitter smell of the first smoke. She snatched at the idea, at his face, it was the only one she could. A beast, her beast.

They laughed. "Oh no." Alice or was it the other? Pale faces, bright eyes, wet teeth. "He's already done his part for the family."

"Oh yes, he's brought you." Another voice and more hands, so many hands. Petting and pulling, they pushed cups into her face, fingers into her mouth. She opened to them, it was all she could do.

It's what I was brought for, to be this. To act the way they expected. And look, husband, look, I am so good, be proud, be proud. Her body felt heavy, numb, but under her skin her blood vibrated from her fingertips to her toes. She couldn't feel anything but that buzzing, like bees inside all of her.

I am the honey, she thought as Alice cradled her head. Petted the lace that covered her collarbone. The sun moved across the floor. She slipped, lost track of things. Blink, the world was orange. Blink again and it became deep blue. Blink. Fluttering flames and shadows.

Had she moved? They had moved her. Released her from their petting holds. Propped her up on the chair. Folded her hands in her lap and fixed her hair. Like a child. Like a doll.

They had made her perfect and now night had fallen.

The high whine of a fiddle floated towards them, carried on shadow, dragged by mice, she didn't know how, but it found them, twisted around her, filled her ears with a sound like a string pulled too tight, about to break.

The women laughed and clapped.

"Come, come! It's time!" Alice shouted, jumping to her feet, laughing that barking laugh that all the women in the house seemed to share.

"But Claresta isn't here, shouldn't she be?" Orabella mumbled, confused as to why she would mention the woman's name but knowing only that she had to, that she couldn't help but to. They ignored her, pulled her to her feet.

They were singing, all those women, their voices high and mad in the dark halls as they dragged her down them. They sang a round of the strange song they had sung before, the night she had danced in the silver ballroom, when she had danced with Elias. Her thoughts swirled with visions through the keyhole of him walking across the room, rutting his sister like an animal in flickering candlelight, drowning his father in the pond, feeding Orabella cake and cookies and asking her for a simple favor, just one thing, for he was her husband and didn't she want to please?

They carried her, tripping and stumbling, down with them. Surrounded by candlelight and oil lamps held high, they laughed and sang, the shadows dancing as they passed and the house breathed. They stepped daintily over the long-left planks and bricks blooming with mushrooms that crept up the wall and spread over the floor. Repairs meant for another time, another life, and she was that time, she was that life. Left for a fairy ring on every floor, the whole dark house a portal to somewhere, and hadn't she found joy with Sloane? Hadn't she found pleasure with Elias? They sang all around her head. Those winged little creatures from Claresta's painting. They climbed up the wall. Claimed her as the bride, claimed her to be the garden they'd waited on for so long.

They met the fiddle player at the door to the main hall, that strange, bright procession. Alice and the other—she tried to pull her mind back by searching for her name, any name, but the woman was as blank as the servants, interchangeable, unimportant. There was no safety there.

I'll be what they want and then I won't be anymore. Just meat and bone and blood even if I'm breathing still. Nothing of importance, like Sloane, like the rabbits in Elias's bag, nothing, nothing at all.

The man smiled, all teeth like all their smiles. Violent in its joy, ready to stain their cheeks and chin with blood, her blood. Her chest heaved with every breath, the world felt cold, her body too light. They held her tight, kept her from floating away, escaping. They wouldn't let her fall, they would choose where they dropped her.

"Oh, you're beautiful! You look even more gorgeous every time I see you," the nameless musician said as he came closer, bent, and took her hand. He left a wet kiss on her knuckles, his tongue cold against her skin. "Give us many daughters." His eyes sparkled and then he bent towards her again, drawing his mouth to her ear. "Give us many wives."

The words should have startled her, she knew in some core part of her that she should be disgusted, but there was no feeling beyond the vibration in her blood, coursing in her bones. "Can you feel that?" she asked instead. "I'm full of honey, I need to let it out."

He laughed with a chorus of women behind him. Laughter like bells, like plates crashing, like glasses breaking. Like foxes in the wood. It hurt her ears and she didn't understand why, couldn't fit her mind around what was so funny. She had made the joke but was not privy to it. Would never be privy to it.

"We've been waiting for you! The hunt went well and dinner is ready!" he sang as he led them through the halls to that familiar dining room.

The smell of blood and meat, the laughter of men. *They had a good hunt today*, she thought or tried to think but the words were quiet in her.

They burst into the room. It was ringed with candles, their greasy smoke, fatty and rotting in the air. Their oily light dancing against the windows, turning the world warm and soft, chasing the shadows to the ceiling, where they danced along with the fiddle player.

The smell was stronger, the meat was on the table, laid out, the skin of the poor creature they had killed red, its head still on, but something was wrong, so wrong. The shape of the animal wasn't what it should be.

A bear, did they bring a bear? No, a boar, and they've left the head, they've left the head, they've—her thoughts came wildly, repeating in a train, impossible to stop as her eyes darted from face to face as they dragged her to the head of the table.

She should be looking there, she knew, that there was something else, but her eyes were locked on the animal. Her vision blurred, the world spun and flared all around her and she couldn't, the meat on the table was not right.

They stopped finally.

"Your bride!" the player announced but she did not look, did not turn because the boar was not a boar.

Cooked to make his skin pucker but not enough to stop the flow of blood from him, trussed up like an animal, his head shattered, but she could tell, could still see, it was Cullen.

Meat and blood and bone, just like your Sloane, just like you, punished for trying to spirit me away. She opened her mouth to scream but warm hands came around her face.

The smell of old wood and dust, of the damp and untended, filled her nose. The smell of the house in its darkest, truest places, and mingled with the bitter smoke smell, no wool, no ginger.

"My Lady." A deep voice. A fox voice.

"Elias," she stuttered out.

"No, that's your husband, but tonight you're a Lady for a Master. You're a Blakersby."

He was beautiful. She had never seen anyone so beautiful. More beautiful than Claresta. His hair was white, cropped short, it fell like Elias's, but he did not have ghost eyes. His were blue, like sapphires, and sparkled in the light. His nose was straight and perfectly set above full lips. His chin squared his face and his pale, plaster-white skin made him look like a statue. Like a god. Like Elias but not. The man in the portrait.

"I am the Master, Orabella," he said.

He pressed his mouth to hers and the family, those near perfect portraits of men and women, howled in joy and celebration, chanting his name, the Master of the house, not her husband but "Lovell!"

Chapter Twenty-Seven

His tongue tasted bitter, the way the smoke smelled bitter and the tea and wine under the honey tasted in Orabella's mouth.

She wanted to bite it off, spit it onto the floor, and smear her face with his blood, but she could not. Her body wouldn't respond, it only bent and opened to his force. Her eyes stayed on the meat. Was it Cullen? Or Hastings ready for the feast? It was all flesh, all wrong.

His kiss, what passed for his kiss, ended and he pulled her close and wrapped her in that horrible house smell that he wore like a coat. He carried her to the head of the table and took his seat.

In the mirror she saw herself, not herself. She saw her husband, not her husband. The family gathered around, howling and barking as they set into their feast, endlessly.

Lovell held her in his lap, like Elias had done before him. He offered her fingers heaping with food, with the flesh carved from what had been a person, still red, still bloody. *A gift from your husband*, the fawn in her arms. The fawn that danced on golden hooves down the table now.

She let her head fall back and away from the offering.

"Don't bother, we fed her well!" Alice, she thought it was Alice, yipped over the music and the plates.

"So you can stick her later!" One of the men, and they roared with laughter, with joy.

The shadows raced and spun across the ceiling. Fairies, insects, wings.

He swept a hand over her breast, following a line to her throat to pull her back. "It's all right, pet. You'll eat in the morning. Wouldn't want you to be sick all over the bed." His breath against her face was sour, rotting, something dead deep within him.

Orabella's body wouldn't respond, wouldn't answer her calls. A whimper, small, an animal call, begging, pleading, came from her throat.

"Don't be frightened," he whispered to her. "I won't hurt you."

Only he would, she'd seen the bruises. Seen the pain he'd left on Claresta that looked like love to them. *I don't want to feel*, she thought, and fear moved her to bend forward, out of the haze of rot and into the miasma of blood and sweat instead. She snatched up his cup and drank deep. Wine, sharp with alcohol, spilled out the corners of her mouth. She dropped the empty cup, fell back, defeated, and the night moved around her.

The family, her family, the foxes laughed and barked as they carved pieces of their hunt away. Bloody, raw, they put slices of it on their plates, biting and chewing as they laughed and made perverse jokes. She floated above her body, somewhere between the dancing darkness and the fox feast below.

She watched as they paired off, kissed and rubbed at each other, blood and grease smearing with each touch. She watched as the man who called himself Master moved her body from arm to arm, like a toy, like a doll. She blinked, and he was kissing her neck, biting at her skin hard enough to bruise, and there was a pie on the table now, set with honor before him.

Servants, she thought, clinging to the word. She hadn't seen them, there was no one but the family. The family and her, even though the servants were everywhere, around every corner. But for that feast, they were gone.

He picked up a knife with his free hand, and she watched as he sliced into the crust, breaking it open, and out swarmed mice and rabbits and little birds. They ran over the table and down to the floor, flew to the ceiling crying, singing, in a panic while the family laughed, hands darting out to grab what they could. The small bodies breaking between sharp teeth and disappearing down dark throats.

The fiddle was playing and she could hear all the small things squeaking and crying in pain and terror, that terrible family chasing and catching them, swallowing them up one by one with glee, and her husband, her true husband, laughing at the sight of it all from his chair.

Head of the family, head of the beast. Elias, Elias, were you ever real? She tried to recall his face, but how quickly he had become this brutal creature, a fox in the skin of a man. *But Elias wasn't, he wasn't . . .*

"I'm sorry, I'm not feeling well. I think I need to lie down. I need to go to bed for a while," she tried, the words coming in mumbles, slurred through a thick tongue. Weak and pitiful and useless.

He turned to her. His eyes were gems set in the marble of his face. A man not birthed but crafted and perfect at a glance. But in those jewels, those perfect eyes, there was nothing else. No soul, no feelings, just mad glee.

Like the eyes of Claresta. Perfectly inhuman.

Orabella's head fell to the side, too heavy for her neck, her lids too heavy to keep open, everything weighed down by some invisible force. *Foxes don't have souls.*

"Do you hear that? The Lady is ready for bed!" he shouted, not to her, but to them. Those beautiful creatures with their imperfect suits. The fae court that she had married into, would become.

"Stuff me full of foxes. Rip me open. Like . . . mother." The words fell away from her, nonsense in a feast of nonsense.

"Yes," he growled next to her ear, licking the cusp of it, and his hot, stinking breath splashed over her face, sour with the rot of him.

He stood up from the table, the chair clattering back while the family barked and howled around her. Her feet touched the floor but she couldn't get them under her and she dipped and tripped in his arms, the only thing keeping her standing at all.

The family jumped up, stopped their wild, gross hunt, and swept up candles from the tables, those melting votives, and formed a procession to see their lord and his bride up and off. They wouldn't leave them alone, not like last time, no. They meant to see the ceremony, to be part of it. Feast on her when he was done as they had feasted upon Sloane, upon Cullen, as they had swallowed up all the mice.

He dragged her, her toes scraping the floor, the sound drowned by their wild yips and barks, their human selves shed for their animal nature.

They sang their strange song but it seemed muted under his voice in her ear. His whispered promises of all he would do, all he would show her. A repeat of the past night, and she couldn't tell if it had just been a day or a thousand since then. Time bled together, her memories, the very halls she passed through breathing and covering her in the musk of their rot. The thick darkness, that space that light never touched becoming liquid with every step they took, swallowing her. She couldn't move, he held her too tightly, dragged her with joy under its viscous surface.

They turned down halls she hadn't gone through before. Places where the house was truly falling to pieces all around them. Or maybe they'd just gone farther into the circle, into the fairy realm where she would be bride forever, no need for changelings because she would birth them endless sons, endless daughters. Endless brides. The walls were falling, the difference between out and in gone. Like the garden. *Are we in the garden?* Animal eyes, larger than mice, staring at her from the darkness they passed before scurrying away.

Run, run, tell them that the king has brought a bride, she sang to herself. A broken sound that mingled with the rest came out of her mouth and she wondered how long she had been humming, how long he had dragged her along, but then they were taking the stairs.

Up to his tower bedroom. *His lonely little bed, his lonely little desk*, she sang to herself.

They took the next flight of stairs, followed it up to the top of the manor, where things had only gotten worse. All the doors were thrown open, the silver of the moon flowing through them, save for one. At the very end of the hall, the orange-red of flame made the shadows dance, beckoning her forward. They passed bedrooms, some with broken windows, others with the entire roof collapsed into them. Each with its own collection of treasures, of ghosts from a time past when the family must have been something else, something better. Intricately carved beds made from hard woods, now only nests for forest creatures and birds, returning to the world they came from. Paintings hung on the wall, the images water- and time-damaged, rotting from their frames, disappearing from the world. Toadstool rings and little white caps shot up everywhere.

In her haze, she could see the lives of what must have been, still laid out on the vanities, sheets half rotted away on beds. Mice-eaten carpets on the floor. The ghosts of splendor that the family held on to even as the remains decayed and fell to nothing all around them. It was beautiful, beautiful.

They reached the door where the dancing shadows greeted them merrily and he, the not-Elias, Lovell, swept her over the threshold, his replacement Lady, sullied and ruined by the house. Made into their perfect ground, fit for breeding.

She tried to focus, so tired, her sight danced and blurred but she could make out another room half left for the forest. The decay that spotted the rest of the house was here too. The bed curtains eaten away at until they were spiderwebs, the walls dark with water stains. Orabella's eyes swung over the room, attempting to grasp something, anything besides that bed, anything other than what it held. *Red*, she thought, *red and wrong and no no no.* She dropped her gaze to the floor, took in the rug that covered it. The thick carpet was filthy with dirt. She focused on it, blinked her eyes clear, and recognized it for what it was.

A larger version of her own salacious footprints made after traveling those dark routes between walls. His routes. She followed the steps back to the wall. A panel built into a bookcase waited, open, familiar in its way. "Watching me," Orabella moaned.

But he didn't answer her. "So you came, dearest," he purred, pleased, to someone else. To the bed. The procession was quiet, a sea of whispers as those standing at the door frame shared the scene with the others. A play put on for their amusement, and finally the missing actors had shown themselves.

"I won't allow this."

Orabella's breath caught and she lifted her heavy head, bleary eyed, and looked on the woman who spoke. Claresta, beautiful Claresta would save her.

"Help me," Orabella gasped as his hold tightened on her.

He laughed, deep and cruel. He tossed her towards the bed; she stumbled and fell at Claresta's feet. Orabella looked up, a Lady to the Lord filling her vision, and she knew how wrong she had been a breath before. Claresta was waiting to eat her, just like everyone else, but she wouldn't, couldn't, not until he was done. Not until the Lord had had his fill, filled her up, and she had done her service, spat out his issue, whole and good, as Elias's mother had done.

Not until she had birthed them many daughters, many wives.

Because Claresta couldn't.

The secret of it all spun in her mind, just at the edge of things, but the tea, the smoke, the blood, and the darkness all held it down and apart from her. A body broken into profane pieces, bloody ends separated leaving wet patterns on the ground as they traveled farther and farther from each other.

Orabella knelt between them, brother and sister, Master and Lady, and beyond them, their mad court fallen silent before this display of opposition.

"Claresta, come here, away from them. You know our ways, you know how it is to be." Reasonable, soothing Alice.

Everything grew dark around her. The smell of fat from the candles, the dirt and dust from the floor, the rot from the walls—an overwhelming miasma that made Orabella's guts twist in her. A breeze, small and cool, rolled over her hand. She looked up at the open panel, the road that waited to take her out. On hands and knees she forced her body to move towards it.

"I was promised! I did everything! You said I would be the Lady and then you said it would only be once! That it would be someone from the land! And now you've had that bastard bring home another!" She jabbed her finger at Orabella. "You promised!"

Lovell swept her up again, tossed her like a doll on the bed. She landed on her elbows. The sour smell that filled his breath rose from the sheets and blanket as her body pressed onto them. Before her next breath he was on her, having brushed his sister from him, his fingers tearing at her skirts, searching.

She closed her eyes, tried to remember what Elias was like when he was tamed and soft. But Lovell was lusty and crushing. *I'm sorry*, Elias said in a dark hall. Orabella's face pressed into that sour mattress, Lovell's hands, rough, wild, searching under her skirts for their prize.

"No!" Claresta shouted.

The glass globe of the lamp shattered on the heavy arms of the canopy. Oil and flame splattered, caught the gauzy curtains, and they disintegrated, dropping like petals to the bedspread, which burst into heat.

Fear flowed through Orabella, a jittery, wild emotion that fueled her limbs and chased out the tea and smoke that held her down. She fought against him but he had no sense of preservation, only his own desire. The flames jumped over the blanket, kissed her hand and took the lace of her sleeve, caught them both, climbing up his body enough to finally break him from her, howling and screaming at its touch.

She yelped, the pain not as sharp as it should have been, everything dull, everything ready to be forgotten by the morning.

The family screamed and surged, attempting to put the fire out. Orabella dropped to the floor and they, in their panic, kicked and tripped over her. She heard their screams as they caught, the room filling with bodies as if they could smother the flames with themselves. At the wall, the fawn hovered, turned its dark eye away, golden hooves disappearing into safety. A forest of legs formed around her and she crawled through them until she reached the cool darkness of the world beyond the hidden panel.

She lifted herself up to her knees and pulled the door open. A staircase, leading down. To safety. She turned to see the fire rolling across the ceiling, bodies that got too close dancing in the flames.

A cracking noise and the ceiling fell, swallowing half the room, separating Orabella from the others.

Claresta stood across the divide, on the wrong side to free herself, her teeth bared, hair wild as it had been that day in the sun. She stood and watched the room turn red without blinking, her rage and pain made physical and real, ready to swallow them all up.

Oh, Orabella breathed, her head swinging back and forth between the two of them. The Master and the Lady. The Lady and the Master. *He doesn't want to hurt me*, she thought. She had been afraid of him, the man who raged at her door, who stalked her and played with her like a cat. She knew that he would hurt her, couldn't help but hurt her, but that he never wanted to, that her pain was a side effect, not the goal, of his amusement.

But Claresta was different. Claresta wanted to hurt her, had always wanted to hurt her. Since before Elias brought her into that dark house, since before, likely when he had been sent to fetch a wife. Wanted to hurt whoever came between her and what she claimed as her own. Orabella pushed the thoughts away, focused on her legs, pulled herself up. She had to run.

"Orabella!" Lovell howled, begging, pleading, drawing her gaze to him, across the barrier of flame.

She turned, slipped inside the door, and slid down the stairs, back into the darkness.

Chapter Twenty-Eight

Her feet wouldn't stay under her. She pressed forward, into the passage, sweat dripping down her body. The smoke filled the small space and she kicked at the walls, looking for a door, a weak spot, anything at all that would free her. All around her, the wood shifted, grabbed at her face and hair, tried to hold her, pull her back.

"No!" she shouted, her foot connecting with the wood, which splintered and gave, releasing a panel. The little light of night shone through and she laughed wildly to keep from crying as she dropped, pressed against it with her weight, and fell through into another room.

She toppled books that no one had read in ages, children's toys left to mold tripped her feet but she didn't stop, couldn't. The door was a dark square. She picked herself up, ran towards it and into the hall.

She tried to place herself, to figure out where she was in relation to where she had been. Directly below, she thought, but there had been twists and turns to get to that room, that wing; they had gone places she hadn't been before. She was lost but she could see the smoke pouring around her, hear their feet like so many mice above her, and she moved to be away from the sound.

Breaking into the hall, she looked wildly back and forth, no direction making sense, but she found the light, an open room.

"There she is!" someone yelled, and she turned back to see him coming for her. Coming to collect his bride.

She ran to the light and he ran behind her, faster, stronger than she thought, grabbing her skirts as she turned in to the doorway. She tripped and covered her face as she fell, hitting the floor with her full weight. The building was in no shape to hold her, it cracked and fell away under her, dragging him along.

The air rushed from Orabella as she landed on the table and he, just behind her at the doorway above, landed at the edge of the table below, placed in the middle of the room, the cards and tokens still upon it.

She dragged herself from it, away from the Master. She stared at his prone body, waiting for it to move. She turned her head up, found ghostly faces staring back down at her. They pulled silently away. She stood on unsure legs. *I'll run to the woods, I'll find one of the Londoners' homes, I'll explain. They'll contact my uncle and he'll tell them who I am*, she thought, the fairy palace of a plan building in her mind. Enough to get her to turn away, to move.

The thought of freedom driving her, she pressed out through the house. The fire hadn't reached far enough yet, the halls remained dark, and she was lost. *I know this place, don't I?* she questioned, turning slowly down another hall, finding more rooms filled with the treasures of a dying family. She heard them, through the walls, all around. Searching, scratching for her.

There were no little portals to crawl through. Only the endless halls with closed doors, too heavy for her to kick and fight against. In the dark she ran like one of the mice cut from the pie, searching for a way to escape the dark throat and white teeth of the house that surrounded her.

She crashed into walls, tripped over bricks and planks. Her hair and dress snagged on hanging nails and she cut her palms on exposed plaster. She felt none of it but could smell the smoke, knew that Claresta's rage was coming for her.

She pushed through it, the pain far away but the fear eating at her insides. *I'm lost, I'm lost*, her mind screamed as she turned into a dark hall, passed closed rooms until finally, like the dawn, came the flickering of light.

She ran, greedy for it after so much darkness; she dashed forward, tripped and spilled into another hall and then down it, towards that golden glow. Squealing, she turned into the room that the light flowed from because she knew it, knew exactly where she was, but the sound turned into a scream.

The silver ballroom, that beautiful fantasy spread out before her, just as she remembered. The mirrored walls that stretched into that dark ceiling, and in the center of it all lay Elias. An oil lamp and an empty bottle by his side.

Cold washed over her, chasing away all the heat and pain, forcing her broken and bruised body forward across the floor to him, her husband, the man who had placed her in this den of foxes, of fairies. She found him staring at the void of shadows above, his eyes half closed and glassy.

"Elias," she breathed, and he moved.

The glass eyes flickered and his body shivered, slow, underwater. He moved onto one elbow, wrapped an arm around her, took her into his embrace. He smelled of sweat and the sour scent of wine but under that of himself, and she broke in his arms.

"Is it done, then? Can I take you now? Did Lovell hurt you?" His words were slurred and childlike.

She tried to say *I should be angry*, wanted to explain to him, but she could only feel relief that it wasn't him after all. That he hadn't done all those terrible things. No words left in her.

He pushed her away, brushed back her hair. "I'm sorry! I'm so sorry! I had to, you understand? I'm nothing."

She stroked his back, like a child. She didn't know what to say, didn't have the words to explain that you can only be what you are, that there is no worth in becoming part of a world that doesn't want you. That Lovell and Claresta were awful but he could be better.

"Give her back!"

Orabella turned, still held tight in Elias's arms. There at the door stood Lovell, come for them, ready to take back his Lady, the only Lady now.

"I'm sorry, I'm sorry." Elias cried into her shoulder, his face buried in her neck.

There was no fight left in her. Orabella's body was broken, tired. She had run as far as she could and it wasn't enough. Would never be enough. The house groaned around them.

"Give her to me, I've waited too long. Waited for the last failure from Claresta, waited to see she was healthy. Waited and waited and I want what's mine."

Above them the house cracked and she looked up. The angels blazed with light before the ceiling ripped open and the entire thing came tumbling down.

Then there were hands on her arms, squeezing hard. Pulling her back. Promise of pain in their pressure. Resistance and Orabella was dragged forward, tossed away. She went limp, her body a doll, as wood and plaster crashed to the floor, burying Lovell and knocking Elias down with him.

Elias was alive, screaming, the house a bonfire of rubble over him. *I should help him*, she thought, *my beautiful husband.* But she didn't know which one she meant then. They were both there. Elias and not-Elias. The Boar and the Prince. She pulled herself up. Threw herself at the glass that separated the ballroom from the garden.

Under her weight it cracked, shattered, birthed her onto damp grass.

She dragged herself away, the fire swelling, bursting behind her. Thorns and branches grabbed at her as she pushed herself up, got her feet under her, and continued forward.

Look how it pulls for me, she thought madly, moving towards the garden, her garden, what was meant to be her garden. *Look how it wants me. If I could only rest*, she thought, the house cracking and tumbling behind her.

She looked at the flames, captivated by how quickly they moved over everything, how quickly they devoured the greatness of the house, the family, all the shadows made into nothing in a moment of one woman's rage.

"Ah, Claresta, you saved me after all," she sang to it.

She kept her eyes to the light and saw foxes dancing in it. She saw visions of lives that could have been. She saw herself crowned their forest queen. She saw her own babies buried in the sad graveyard. She saw horrible things one after another swallowed in the flames, destroyed by the light.

Time fractured around her, she blinked, and the sky was golden with sun.

A rustling, and she looked to see a fawn, a real and true one, leap off into the forest.

Epilogue

Orabella's first full memory was of a room and the sun. Under her were clean, crisp sheets and over her body was a simple quilt, soft and well loved. The air smelled of lavender from the open window and the walls were white and unadorned with any wallpaper. There was a stand that held only a basin and pitcher. A rocking chair where some knitting waited.

No mirrors.

She looked down at herself. Her body was covered in a cotton gown. Simple and soft as the quilt. Made, she could believe, by the same hand. Her arms poked from the sleeves, bruises fading, cuts scabbed over on her right hand. On the left, her hand was bandaged, from finger to elbow. She lifted it to her face. The smell of herbs and medicine wafted from it. Clean and cared for.

She touched her face, her neck, her body, with her free hand, searching for injury, and found tender spots but nothing broken. The burn seemed to be the worst of it.

Her mouth was dry but she ignored the pitcher and slid out of bed.

Her legs, weak and unsteady, tried to get away from her but she grabbed the bedpost and held until they were sure. She stumbled to the open window and looked out into the world.

Spring was fully there, edging into summer. Flowers bloomed in a field she did not recognize.

A door opened and she nearly fell, turning too quickly.

An old woman. Hair in a bun. Orabella stumbled back, crying out.

"You're awake, ma'am," a woman, not Mrs. Locke, said brightly. Orabella nodded.

The woman came to her side, clasped her arm gently, and helped her to the chair, moving her yarn so Orabella could sit. The old woman smoothed her hair back. She turned away, went across the room to the basin.

"Where am I?" Orabella asked, her voice cracking and breaking from disuse. *I've lost so much time, so much of me*, she thought, attempting to piece it all together but there were too many gaps, too many things she didn't want to remember.

"This is the estate of the Taylors, miss," she answered. She handed her a glass.

"Why am I here?" She took the glass. Sniffed it. Just water.

"When news of Korringhill's tragedy reached us, Mrs. Taylor asked us to inquire. It seems she is the relation of some acquaintance of your aunt, who wrote to her about you. The townspeople found you in the garden and said you were Orabella, recently married. You've been sick for the last weeks. It's no surprise, you were outside for hours." Warm and pitying.

Orabella asked no more questions. She fell into silence.

Days or weeks passed, she wasn't sure, time floated around her like dust in the sun, insignificant and sparkling as it went. The old woman tended to her, at the bequest of her employers. When she was well enough she ate dinner with them. They were kind, a little older, a loving husband and wife, their children. She told them fairy tales about a beautiful garden after they ate. They gifted her dresses, simple things from the dressmaker. It was all she had. Everything else had burned.

They told her everyone had died in the fire. That it raged for hours. That she was the only one to make it out. They didn't ask when she would leave but she felt the question just past their tongues.

The lawyers came. Orabella sat in a chair across the table from them in her gifted dress.

They explained things but she couldn't capture their words; they flew around her head like birds until they found their way out, but she understood, when they left, that there had been decisions made for her and that she was not without means.

They did not speak of her husband.

"What will you do?" the Taylors asked.

"I'll go home," she answered. It was all she could think to do.

It was only after she arrived and the smell of the city made her sick and weak that she realized Elias hadn't left her alone after all.

Her uncle stared at her, his face hard, his lips tight in the drawing room where it had all started. Nervous. Everything was the same. The same maids. The same sofa and chairs. The same garden with its little bench.

But everything was different.

"How are you?" her aunt asked, voice bright.

Orabella's hands sat in her lap, crossed over each other. The bandage gone, a silver scar remained, the imprint of the ring burned into her finger, impossible to ever remove. She had purchased a new wardrobe. All black. She couldn't look at the pretty fabrics and colors any longer, the hum in her mind was too loud when she did.

It brought memories she did not want, could not bear, so she wore black. "I'll be staying here, in my old room for a few weeks until I can secure other lodgings."

Her uncle's face paled. "You can't! We've done right by you, done what we could for my brother's wishes, rest his soul, and whatever you got into in that house is none of our concerns and we will not have it here!"

They had read the papers. She had not but she knew. Knew that with the family dead the townspeople talked, everyone talked. Knew what they would say. She had finally been in *The Candle*. "You sold me to pay your gambling debts. I think society may look further down on that than on letting your poor, possibly mad niece stay with you for a season. Think of it as charity."

She visited Jane, in her church, who cried over her, said she missed her and had tried to write. Orabella nodded, told her it wasn't her fault. Wished her well and disappeared back into her own little life.

As promised, she left weeks later, having purchased a home in Nice, far away from all of it. The women she hired to sweep her floors tutted at her growing waist, chatted to each other about her in French, which she didn't understand but sounded like a memory. She ignored them and motioned for them to keep the curtains open at all times.

Time passed, spring into summer, summer into fall. She learned some of the language, enough to get on. The women who made her dresses convinced her to try some other colors. She wore pinks and foam greens, pastels. She chased away the deep colors of fall, threatened to go back to black.

The nightmares lessened, the baby grew, she stayed in the sun.

She hadn't thought of him in weeks, she was sure, but still, some part of her expected him to come back. Had always expected him to come back.

The maids brought him to the garden where she sat, a book, un-read, in her hands, her eyes on the bees buzzing contently around the dying flowers. The bees had taken some time to accept. What had happened wasn't their fault and she knew it wasn't really them she heard in her mind. Still, she kept no honey in her cabinets.

He spoke to the maids in French and they giggled and blushed, flattered. Charmed as she had been charmed.

His clothes were light, new, well made. His cheeks thinner, his jaw harder. His hair had grown. He walked with a cane and stood before her more the gentleman than he had in her uncle's garden. Elias dropped to his knees in front of her, took up her hands.

"You're beautiful," he said, finally breaking the silence between them.

She didn't know what she looked like. She had no mirrors in her home.

"Why have you come here?" she asked. There was no point in replying to the compliment. He meant it, she was sure, could hear in his voice that he meant it, but then, he had said many things and meant them all.

He looked away. Shame? Annoyance? She couldn't tell. It didn't matter. "It was time. I thought to give you space to make your own way." He looked up at her again, catching her eyes, his cheeks pink. "I didn't know about your condition. I wouldn't have left you alone so long if I had." Shame, then.

"And what do you want now?" The maids were just on the other side of the door, which hung open, just a touch. Listening, always listening. But they didn't speak the language.

"My wife." Simple.

She thought of their wedding, their legal wedding before every-thing else, done with such haste. Had he signed Robinson or Blak-ersby? Did it matter?

She wanted that simple man. She wanted the man she met in the garden before she went into the darkness and parts of her never returned.

On his knees he looked up at her, his eyes like glass, the mirrors of the last nightmare room, in the sun. He looked at her hands then, made a small sound at her scar before running fingers over it, kissing the imperfection.

"Orabella, I never meant to hurt you. I thought I would be able to . . . Ah, it doesn't matter. I was wrong. I need to fix this for you, for us. Please, I will spend my life repairing this damage. But I promise I will not let our children know of that place. We will be free of it all."

She smoothed his hair back. Soft, soothing. She would be a good mother.

She looked at him, his mirror eyes wide and wet, full of love and reverence, and she believed every word because he was her husband and in those last moments he had told her he was sorry. The family was gone, all of those foxes died in the fire, their warren burned to nothing, and it was only fists and feet she felt in her womb. All was right, all was well, and yet there was darkness in him. Would always be darkness in him. And her, too, now, after it all. And yet.

She moved her hands to cup his face, the smooth skin. He had shaved and washed, donned his best for this meeting. She smiled. There was only one thing left to ask. One thing to settle between them and then nothing else would matter at all. "Elias, we must be honest with each other. Now and ever after this moment, do you agree?"

Eager to please, eager to move past this moment into something better. "Yes, love. We will be true to each other. Ask, I'll tell you anything."

"Then this is all I will ever ask you about before. Answer me and we'll be done with the past, with the Blakersbys, with it all. We'll be Robinsons and make a new life, a new family with none of that place to hold us."

"Anything. I'll answer anything you want." He turned and kissed her palm, then the smooth curve of her belly. A promise, sealed, meant to be kept.

There were a thousand questions she could have asked. So many things she didn't know. So many secrets that would never see the light because they were buried in ash and ruin. But she only needed to know the answer to one thing to know the truth of it all, of him. Whether he meant to drive her to madness or if he was true in his love. "That day I met you in the forest, at the graveyard. Do you remember? When you broke poor Cullen. When we walked back to Korringhill, afterwards, I saw Claresta in the window and you told me there was nothing there at all. Did you really not see her?"

She watched as his face went slack, his brows pressed together. Eyes wide and wet, he looked like a trapped animal between her hands, sick with nerves, panicked. The silence widened and the darkness began again, sputtering and growing between them.

The End

Acknowledgments

There are so many people without whom this book wouldn't exist, who have cheered me on to becoming a grown-up writer.

Mike for believing in my ability to do this and supporting me in taking a chance on my art. Gertz for laughing at and supporting my first silly little idea that grew into this book (and for loving TSP so much). Kat for reading the first chapters and telling me they were good and that I should keep going.

Alyssa Day and Sarah Winters for both encouraging me to work on this Gothic novel at a time when Gothic wasn't popular. For telling me to send it out into the world. To Alex Hofelich and Jon Padgett, who printed some of my early works and had nice things to say about them which gave me the confidence to even write this at all.

My agent, Lane Heymont, who saw something in my little stories and took a chance on this work.

Kim and Teri, who talked me through the hard times with this manuscript. My cousin Jem, who was always there to support me and keep me going. Brooklyn Ann, who stayed up with me all night while I did edits.

The editorial team at Amistad, who worked to bring this book to life.

My vast and gracious community who helped me stay afloat while I was out here chasing my dream. Thank you all, look, I did it!

About the Author

Donyae Coles is a daydreamer, mostly. Sometimes she writes her daydreams down and they come out as strange little speculative fiction stories. *Midnight Rooms* is her debut novel but she has had a number of short stories published in places that you've maybe heard of. In her free time she paints which is really just another type of dreaming.

You can find more of her work on her website, donyaecoles .com, follow her on Twitter (X, if that ever catches on) @okokno or on Instagram @artbyDonyae.